PILGRIM'S STORM BROODING

Volume I

DAMIEN BLACK

CONTENTS

ISBN:

978-0-9954928-6-8 [paperback]
978-0-9954928-7-5 [ePub]
978-0-9954928-8-2 [Mobi]

To the fans, who weave the fires upon the fringes

MAPS OF THE KNOWN WORLD

For detailed map graphics, please visit facebook.com/
brokenstonemaps or simply Google: @brokenstonemaps

The Great Western Ocean
The Island Realms
West Principalities
Free Kingdoms
The Empire
Pandaria
Mennenos Kingdoms
Steppes of Noth
Steppas of Koth
Vindos River
Zingar
Ravindka
Kallandhar
The Great Inland Sea
Vergon Islands
Sultanate of Neshangha
Horocracy of Sendak
Zhosa Desert
The Arid Kingdoms
600 miles

PART I

A LONG-ANTICIPATED ARRIVAL

The dungeon cell was dank and cold, but Horskram could still feel the heat where the irons had been applied to his chest. He'd used all his elan not to cry out as the sizzling brands charred his flesh, but when Cyprian had instructed the torturer to apply red-hot pincers instead, he'd screamed like a child before fainting from sheer pain.

A splash of cold water had reawakened him to his nightmare. Cyprian still stood before him, cruel face buried in his bushy greying beard. It flowed to his waist, all but covering the black scapular he wore over his white robes of office. Once again, the chief inquisitor of the Temple asked in his methodical, insistent voice: 'Are you in fact a witch, Brother Horskram? In service to Abaddon and the Seven Princes of Perfidy, as His High Holiness Abelard of Montrevellyn has repeatedly asserted? All that is required is your confession, and we can end your suffering.'

Horskram scoffed through gritted teeth. 'If the Arch Perfect... is so sure of my guilt... surely no confession is necessary.' He spat the words at Cyprian, hoping his bloodied spittle would carry far enough to taint the perfect's spotless robes. Sadly, it didn't.

Cyprian's face hardened. 'Would that we could execute you and all your fellow demonolators in the Argolian brotherhood on the just ordinance of His High Holiness. But alas, the Supreme Perfect has bowed to the King's demand, and no executions are to be conducted without a confession, as well you know.'

How typical of the man, Horskram found time to think through his pain. *Like most fanatics, he is completely immune to irony.*

Horskram forced a sneer through blood-caked lips. 'Of course, if you had any evidence or proof, such niceties would be unnecessary,' he said. 'But be of some cheer, Cyprian, at least His Supreme Holiness's injunction gives you the opportunity to indulge in your favourite sport.'

If he couldn't return Cyprian's chastisement in kind, at least he could take some pleasure in tormenting him with words.

Cyprian's face contorted in rage. A fanatic just like Abelard, the chief inquisitor moved to anger far too quickly – but then the Temple had been corrupted by such men for centuries. Now that corruption had culminated in a purge of the Argolian Order, on the insistence of Arch Perfect Abelard, the most dangerous fanatic of them all.

'You dare to cast aspersions on our Holy Mother Temple's inquisition?' Cyprian fulminated, his face blanching almost as white as his robe. 'Think you that I do this for amusement? Poltroon, thou shalt confess! And when you do, your just end awaits you at the stake, along with all your tainted brethren. The Order of St Argo is a weed in Palom's fair garden, as Abelard has preached for years – for centuries, you and your kind have consorted with necromancers and demonologists, increasing the compass of your knowledge in despite of the celestial laws laid down by Reus Almighty Himself!'

This time, Horskram could not even be bothered to torment Cyprian with irony.

'Arrant nonsense,' he sneered again. The chains that held him suspended from the cell wall jangled as he nodded to where the torturer skulked in the shadows by the tools of his horrid trade. 'Have yon rug-rat go about his business, Cyprian – he may get me to scream, but I'll never confess!'

Cyprian's face tightened in an evil smile. 'As you wish,' he said. 'Perhaps it is time for you to die accidentally under torture. Such a thing happens occasionally, no fault can be imputed to the Temple if it does.' He motioned to the torturer, who grinned and tugged deferentially on his leather cap as he reached for the pincers again. Cyprian motioned a second time for him to stop. 'Nay,' he said. 'On second thoughts, I think we've had enough of simple butchery. Our witch is proving most resilient to acute pain, and in truth I've no wish to end his righteous punishment just yet. Time to see if his stamina can hold up over time. Give him the fork.'

The torturer's grin broadened as he plucked the double-headed two-pronged instrument from his toolkit. Horskram knew enough of the inquisition's methods to understand what lay in store. Through bleeding lips he muttered the

Psalm of Fortitude as the torturer fastened a leather strap about his ravaged chest, the prayer broken by an agonised yelp as he passed the rough leather across the bloody gouge where his left nipple had been. The strap he looped through a buckle in the centre of the fork, fixing its two sets of sharp prongs between the underside of Horskram's chin and the middle of his breastbone. Any motion of the head was now unthinkable.

Cyprian's eyes burned blackly as he stared at Horskram. 'Seeing as you are so reluctant to confess, you will not mind being deprived of the ability to talk,' he said. 'But we'll see how you fare with no sleep for a couple of days. I am sure that when I return, you will be of a much more *contrite* disposition.' Without another word, the chief inquisitor turned on his heel, leaving the torturer to pack up his tools and follow in his wake.

'Rest well now,' said the torturer, laughing at his own joke as he slammed the cell door behind him. From a few doors further up the passage, Horskram heard more screams as they began torturing another one of his brethren...

Horskram sat bolt upright, clutching his left breast. Even now, twenty years after the Purge, it throbbed painfully, along with the other injuries Cyprian had inflicted on him during those dark days. Blinking feverishly, the adept looked around. He was below decks aboard the *Jerfalcon*, in the space he'd shared with Adelko since leaving Westerburg.

Of the novice there was no sign – he was probably up on decks, taking in the sights as their ship took them upriver on the final leg of their journey to Rima.

Wincing at the hideous memories his recurring nightmare had brought back, the adept rose from his bedroll, eager to seek fresh air.

Two days Cyprian had left him like that, unable to sleep, eat or drink. He'd barely even been breathing when the reprieve had come, and with it the startling revelation that Abelard himself had been arrested on suspicion of demonolatry, malfeasance in an ecclesiastical office, and conspiracy to pervert the Temple. Senior Argolians who had managed to avoid being incarcerated had petitioned the Supreme Perfect to allow a divination to decide the truth of the matter, after Horskram and the other apprehended brethren had steadfastly refused to confess. His Supreme Holiness had finally relented – the divination had not only revealed the Argolian Order to be innocent, but had incriminated the very man who had led the pogrom against it. Such were the Fallen One's devices, crafty and devious beyond belief. Abelard and a dozen of his dark disciples had received their just deserts, and been burned at the stake on Temple Square in Rima.

And yet, Horskram reflected as he wearily climbed the stairs to the deck, not all endings were just. For Cyprian had been horrified by the revelation of Abelard's crimes, and exonerated of any wrongdoing after being cleared of all charges of witchcraft. Not long after, he had been appointed to Abelard's role as Arch Perfect of Montrevellyn. A few years later, Cyprian had been elevated to Supreme Perfect.

And for all his disavowal of Abelard and his corrupted ilk, his jealous and irrational hatred of the Order had not diminished.

Horskram took in a deep lungful of fresh air as he emerged from the darkness of the hold. He wasn't looking forward to being back in Rima.

Adelko craned his neck for a better view as the *Jerfalcon* passed beneath the looming arches of the Crescent Bridge. High enough to comfortably admit the cog, it was the biggest bridge he had ever seen. Sculpted friezes of nymphs and satyrs leered down at the young novice, each one larger than a man and so queer-looking as to be almost grotesque. In amongst those frivolous decorations, he could make out sculpted angels and demons, whom the Ancient Thalamians had regarded as gods of good and evil. Though not nearly as lifelike, the friezes put him in mind of the eldritch sculptures of the Warlock's Crown, where he and his mentor Horskram had put an end to Andragorix's experiments with demonology and necro-mancy. They had put an end to the mad warlock, too – but not his unknown master's plans to reunite the Headstone of Ma'amun.

Adelko shivered at the reminder of their mission, which had brought him across so many leagues from his home-land in the far north of Urovia. Somewhere, a latter-day warlock was trying to recover the power of the Elder Wizards; to reunite the Headstone and undo the last deed of

Søren, the Northland hero who had broken it after slaying his faithless mistress Morwena seven hundred years ago.

We've learned so much, and yet we're still none the wiser as to who it is we're after, he thought as the bridge's vast shadow swallowed them up. *Two of the four Headstone fragments gone, and who knows how long before the others are stolen as well?*

On either side of the river, clustered around both ends of the bridge, he could make out the stuccoed tile-roofed buildings of two towns, each the size of a small city. But then Pangonia was the richest and most populous of the Free Kingdoms – even its smaller cities would be big compared to those he'd seen up north. The *Jerfalcon* had left behind the roiling waves of the Athan Estuary several days ago, making slower but calmer progress up the Athos river towards the Pangonian capital. Adelko had thanked St Ionus for that on more than one occasion, for his sea legs were not strong, although the bent-backed serfs working the lands through which they sailed was a painful sight. Horskram hadn't been lying about the miserable conditions of the local peasantry.

What's the point in becoming the wealthiest nation in the Free Kingdoms if hardly anyone feels the benefits? Adelko had wondered that aloud on many occasions, but his mentor had merely said it was the way of men, and that the Redeemer's message of equality before the Unseen had long been lost.

Was it ever truly found in the first place? Adelko didn't have the heart to give voice to that question. Instead he chose to ask an easier one, about Pangonia's distant past. Like all the southerly nations of the Free Kingdoms, the realm had once been a province of the mighty Thalamian Empire.

'Why didn't the Thalamians found Rima here, Master Horskram?' he asked as they began to emerge from the bridge's shadow. His mentor had just emerged from below decks, wearing a pained look on a pale face, but Adelko was too preoccupied with his curiosity to give that much thought.

'The land is too flat,' his mentor explained. Adelko sensed he was grateful for the distraction his questions provided. 'When we round the next bend, you will see the hills whence the Athos flows. The Thalamians chose to build their city there, where it would be more easily defended. Rima was just an outpost in those days, when Alcius had but lately made conquest of Upper Vallia. The Crescent Bridge was built much later to facilitate trade.'

Oblong banners bearing the argent and purpure crescent insignia of the Purple Garter, the elite knights who formed the Pangonian King's most trusted advisers and bodyguards, testified to the bridge's name. On a high hill overlooking each of the towns, a tall white castle gleamed in the sunlight. Each was the size of Linden or Staerkvit in Northalde.

'Blanctoire and Blanchemure – the Castellan's Teeth, locals call them,' supplied Horskram. 'Built in the time of King Vasirius, when he consolidated his reign during the Third War of the Royal Succession.' He pointed at the southern castle, on the river's right bank. 'From Blanchemure, the Chivalrous King assembled his last army to sally forth and do battle with the Traitor Prince Ancelet. And though he was victorious, Vasirius perished along with

Ancelet, and thus did the apogee of Pangonia come to an end.'

If only Vaskrian were well, thought the novice glumly. *Such a sight would please him.*

But the squire had seen little of daylight during their voyage. The curse of the draugar lingered on him, as it did on the knights Braxus, Torgun and Wrackwulf and the Harijan warrior-woman Anupe. The undead lieutenants of the Elder Wizards who had cursed them had foretold of a second coming: another reminder of what would happen to the Known World if the Headstone were reunited and its power unlocked. At least the Argolian adepts at Heilag monastery had bought them enough time to get to the Order's head-quarters at Rima, where the superior skills of the brethren would hopefully save them from the Rotting Death.

But for all that he helped us, the abbot of Heilag is a suspect too, Adelko reminded himself. Horskram seemed convinced that prior Johann had had something to do with the freeswords hired to kill them during their journey to West-erburg. That thought made Adelko more fearful than recol-lection of the draug lords – just how far and deep did this conspiracy to return Abaddon to the mortal vale go?

I suppose it won't be my concern for much longer, he reflected philosophically. His eventful year of secondment to Master Horskram, the most celebrated Argolian of Ulfang, their remote chapter in the highlands of Northalde, was drawing to a close. Soon they would dock at Rima, where Adelko would be returned to full-time tutelage at the the Most Reverend Priory of St Argo. As much as the prospect of studying at the heart of the Order excited him, he couldn't deny a sense of disappointment: their quest to expose the mastermind behind the fragment thefts had ended in failure.

Perhaps we're too late to stop whoever it is. It wasn't the first time he'd had that unsettling thought.

Adhelina and Hettie came up to join the monks as the *Jerfalcon* took the next bend in the river, cooing excitedly as they caught sight of the receding bridge. Adelko was too shy to speak to the haughty damsels, but felt glad to see them fully recovered from the draugbreath – Heilag's monks had been able to treat those with no blood on their hands more easily.

But Adelko knew Adhelina had more recovering to do besides: he couldn't imagine how horrible the poor heiress of Dulsinor must feel, watching her father and household being murdered in sight of her ancestral home at the Graufluss Bridge Tourney. Having treacherously disposed of the House of Markward, the rival Lanraks would be laying siege to Graukolos, the seat of power in Dulsinor. The castle's defences were legendary, but even if it held out, the lands about were ripe for despoiling.

Adelko flinched as he recalled riding past razed manors through fields of butchered yeomen. But then he supposed that was what came of living by the sword, as Horskram had tried to tell him all along: the same knights who guarded the peasantry lived for war and plunder, and took lives as often as they protected them.

Perhaps it will be a good thing to get back inside the cloisters, mix with my own sort again. I've seen more than enough of the world, perhaps more than anyone should. Their welcome at Heilag hadn't been a warm one, but surely at the heart of the Order he would find new friends.

The sun reached its zenith as they rounded the bend. Adelko found cause to gawp again as they caught another splendid sight. Two vast statues hewn from marble, the height of the Castellan's Teeth, stretched up on either side of the river, which now snaked up into verdant hills. One was fashioned to depict a muscular man dressed in carapace armour clutching a wedge-shaped sword and an ovoid shield. A high plume crested his helm, frozen forever in time by the hand that had mocked the ancient warlord so well in stone. The other was a woman outfitted similarly, but instead of a sword she clutched a long spear.

'Behold the Athos Colossi, erected in honour of Alcius and his concubine, the Harijan Queen Antipole,' declaimed Horskram with characteristic dramatic flourish. 'Together they led a conquering force across the River Burinoc and began the expansion of the Thalamian Empire.'

'What a pity Anupe isn't well enough to look upon this sight,' said Adhelina, echoing Adelko's sentiments about Vaskrian.

'It would bring her little joy to see it,' replied Horskram. 'After the conquest of Upper Vallia, Alcius had Antipole murdered – the new emperor didn't feel comfortable sharing power, especially not with a woman.'

Adhelina's face fell. 'Men have ever ruled women with an iron hand,' she said. 'The sooner we're in the Empire, the better I shall like it.'

'Don't be too sure the Imperials will treat you any better,' said Horskram. 'I've travelled amongst them, they aren't as progressive as you like to think. Don't forget the Urovian New Empire was forged from the ruins of the one the Thalamians built.' The adept gestured meaningfully at the towering statue of Antipole. Gazing on its grim countenance, Adelko wondered if the warrior-queen had had an inkling as to her fate when she posed for the sculptors. As they glid past the statues, he could see they were pitted in many places, crumbling away in others. The lesson was clear: all empires receded before time's onslaught. Adelko suddenly recalled the vision bequeathed him by the Earth Witch in the Argael Forest, when the Angel of Death had stared him in the face.

All shall meet me in the end.

Despite the summer warmth, the young monk felt an all-too familiar shiver creep down his spine.

They caught their first glimpse of Rima from the forecastle later that afternoon. It was there, just as Horskram had said it would be, swathing the high hills that reached up towards a dark line of forest on the horizon. Adelko could tell at a glance it was several times the size of Strongholm; his mentor had told him it was home to a hundred thousand souls. He hoped its ordinary citizens would at least be better off than the peasants who tilled the lands. Ruined villas that had belonged to patrician families of Old Thalamy were dotted about the hills; though their majesty was long faded, the spacious courtyards, elegant obelisks and square colonnades put the manor houses of the King's vassals to shame. But then this was a lesser epoch to the Golden Age, itself but an echo of the Platinum Era when the Elder Wizards had ruled the Known World.

Question everything, the Earth Witch had told him. A dark thought came upon Adelko as her words floated back to him. What if reuniting the Headstone was a *good* thing? If the *Codices of Zhorrah* told it true, the Elder Wizards had crafted a world empire that knew nothing of sickness or war or famine. Horskram had said so himself, back in the cave overlooking the Brenning Wold, when they had just left Ulfang and their adventure had barely begun. Things hadn't gone wrong until Ma'amun had overstretched his hand and been tempted into ruin by Abaddon... But what if such power could be controlled, more wisely used? The world Adelko had seen was far from peaceful or just – was their quest to prevent the Headstone's power being unleashed really in mortalkind's best interests?

That thought troubled him more than any other, so much so that he wished it hadn't occurred to him.

'Rima ahoy! We'll be done with hard tack before nightfall, so make sure to get yourselves a bellyful of Armandy wine and a roasted joint down you when we dock!'

It was Captain Abrehan, yelling at his men. Adelko got the impression he was trying to sound encouraging. A cheer from the crew indicated his success. Abrehan turned from the rail overlooking the main deck and sidled over to join the novice. He certainly seemed in jolly spirits – Adelko supposed he must be pleased to have arrived in Rima without any supernatural calamities befalling his precious ship. It had taken all of Adhelina's guile and authority to persuade the superstitious captain to take Argolian friars aboard. Though the Order had survived the Purge, it was distrusted as much as it was revered.

'Well now, young friar, it's been a pleasant enough trip, wouldn't you say?' beamed Abrehan. 'You must be looking forward to returning to your cloisters!'

They had spoken little during their week aboard the *Jerfalcon*, and mealtimes at the captain's table had been strained affairs. Not that there had been much in the way of hard tack – to Adelko's relief the ship's biscuit had been saved for the ordinary seamen. Though portions had been small, he'd appreciated the salted boiled pheasant and seasoned parsnips served up by the galley cook. But then Pangonians were noted for their fine food.

'I'm actually from Ulfang chapter, in Northalde,' he replied, unsure whether to tell the captain too much. 'This is my first time in Rima – but I'm looking forward to seeing the headquarters of my Order.'

Abrehan grinned and took a sip from his silver hip flask. 'No need to look forward, Master Adelko,' he said, clapping the novice on the back and pointing ahead with the flask. 'Looking will suffice.'

Turning, Adelko saw it perched on a higher belt of crags overlooking Rima: the Reverend Priory of St Argo, Grand High Monastery of the Order. It looked like a squat fortress in its own right. Taking in its circular crenelated walls, glowing richly as their sandstone blocks caught the sunlight, he felt his excitement and foreboding twist up a notch. Atop the inner sanctum a great standard bearing the silver lectern motif of the Order fluttered in the breeze; a flash of light caught the sun just below it. Squinting, he could just make it out: the sheen of glass that told of the monastery's famed observatory. From there, Grand Master Hannequin and the archmasters could gaze up at the night skies, observing the stars in their myriad constellations. He supposed that was the closest he would come to viewing the legendary fixture: he had no intention of trespassing on forbidden ground again. Doing that at Ulfang six months ago had got him embroiled in the biggest adventure of his life. One he'd barely survived.

For all that, Adelko couldn't help but wonder how long it would be before his next adventure came calling.

I'm not even a journeyman yet, and already I've seen more than I'd have liked.

They weren't far from Rima when the stink of the city made itself known. Swaddled by five hills in a basin of land, the metropolis didn't benefit from Strongholm's location, and the smells of the warren of winding streets that threaded between its sweeping boulevards had nowhere to escape. The stench belied the city's magnificent appearance, grand whitewashed buildings where the nobles and merchants lived surmounting the meaner structures that clustered next to its filthy alleys. Unlike the Northlending capital, there was no citadel: the rich lived cheek by jowl with the poor, although the areas surrounding the Palace of

White Towers and the Supreme Temple were noticeably richer.

'Finest city in the Free Kingdoms!' declaimed Abrehan proudly. If he noticed the encroaching reek he gave no sign of it. 'No curfew on our taverns or brothels either – come nightfall I'll be drunk as a lord and up to my nuts in-'

'Yes, captain, thank you,' said Horskram sharply, appearing on the forecastle. 'My novice requires no instruction in the blandishments of the city.'

Abrehan started at the monk's sudden appearance and cleared his throat, looking somewhat abashed. 'Pray forgive me, master monk, just had a few drops and I'm right pleased to be home safe is all.'

Horskram smiled brittlely. 'Yes, captain, and the absence of any supernatural calamities as promised must only sharpen your joy. Adelko – come along! I shall need your help to get our charges ready to disembark.'

Reluctantly Adelko followed Horskram below decks. They had said prayers with the Redeemer's blood and holy water night and day for their companions. The five warriors hadn't seemed to worsen significantly, which was something to be thankful for. None of them seemed to have been affected by seasickness either – but then Adelko supposed they were too busy being ravaged by the draugbreath to worry about getting their sea legs. For his part, he hoped he wouldn't have to brave the waves again any time soon.

Link boys were scurrying to and fro, lighting streets leading off from the harbour by the time they pulled in amongst the forest of masts. Rima's port was busy and almost the size of Westerburg's; the sounds of yelling sailors and catcalling doxies – keen to ply a lusty trade with the new arrivals – greeted his ears as the ship pulled in, mingling with the noise of accordions and fiddles and raucous singing from the waterfront taverns.

Gazing at the brightly painted whores lifting up their skirts enticingly, Adelko felt a mixture of embarrassment and desire. Girls. He was beginning to see what the fuss was about, after all.

'Keep your eyes on our stricken companions,' Horskram whispered pointedly in his ear. 'I'll need your help to get them in the saddle – and you can rest assured that's the only mounting you'll be doing here tonight! Remember what I told you about the iniquities of the city!'

'Yes, Master Horskram... I couldn't help but notice them, sorry. They're so, well, forward.'

'We're in the Southerly Kingdoms now, lad – they lack our restraint, so you'd best get used to it! Look on it as a challenge from the Redeemer, to test your chastity!'

It was impossible to tell from his stoical expression whether Horskram was joking or not. Some of the sailors on board the *Jerfalcon* had begun enthusiastically yelling back at the harlots as they berthed the ship. They were speaking in Panglian too quickly for him to follow, but he gathered their speech was fairly coarse.

Suppressing a sigh, Adelko went below decks to where their horses were being kept.

'Milady, are you sure this is wise?' Hettie's face looked anxious in the lantern light. Adhelina struggled to concentrate amidst the noise and bustle of the port. The only thing of value she had was the jewellery she'd been wearing on the day of the tournament melee, when the murderous Lanraks had struck without warning: she had to hope it would fetch enough to get them started. She'd used her time – and Horskram's coin – in Westerburg to visit an apothecary, so she was fully replenished with herbs. If worst came to worst, she could sell her services as a healer.

'We're of noble blood,' she reminded Hettie firmly. 'That means any respectable innkeeper will take us in at our word. That should give us time to hock my jewels to pay for our bed and board.'

'Yes, we're of noble blood,' said Hettie pointedly. 'That means the King himself would receive us at court, if you'd only announce who you are!'

'Oh Hettie, how many times must we go through this?' replied Adhelina peevishly. 'As soon as His Majesty realises who I am and why I'm here, he'll never let me leave! I'll be doomed to remain at his pleasure, another pawn in his great games. Why, he might even turn me over to the Lanraks – Carolus has a reputation as a scheming monarch. No, I won't have it – I haven't come through everything we've faced simply to end up under another man's control!'

Hettie screwed up her face, but knew better than to argue. The sailors lowered the gangplank and Horskram began leading their erstwhile bodyguards down to the harbour. The five of them looked a pitiful sight. Adhelina felt a stab of pity for her two amours: after all the heroics they had been through on her behalf, Sir Torgun and Sir Braxus deserved a better fate. Loading ramps were being opened from the side of the hull, allowing animals and other cargo to be taken off the ship.

'Adelko is below with the horses,' said Adhelina, before Hettie could argue again. 'Let's go down to the wharf and meet him.' To her disgust, a couple of the more enterprising harlots were coming up the gangplank to engage with the sailors. Adhelina pushed past them, ignoring their indignant remarks. 'Blasted southerners,' she muttered under her breath, trying to ignore the smell of their cheap perfume.

Presently they were all gathered on the dock. The last she saw of the captain was the sight of him standing at the head of the gangplank, taking a swig from his hip flask, his other arm snaked around the waist of a slender doxy with raven hair and gap teeth.

'And now good friars, I must bid you to Reus!' Abrehan called out cheerily. 'You won't mind if I venture below decks to enjoy the reward of my labours while the men unload! It was most pleasant doing business with you!' Grabbing the shrieking harlot by her scrawny backside, he turned and disappeared.

'Insufferable man,' said Adhelina. 'The Pangonian chivalry might be the finest in the Free Kingdoms, but the manners of their commoners are disgusting.'

'Sailors aren't the most refined of characters anywhere you go,' put in Horskram dryly. His face grew serious. 'You mean to go ahead with your plan then?'

The heiress nodded. 'We'll send word to you as soon as we've found somewhere suitable to stay. I intend to visit our brave champions as often as your Grand Master will permit. We won't leave until Anupe is well enough to travel with us.'

Though she was speaking of the Harijan, Adhelina found her eyes lingering on Braxus and Torgun.

Horskram nodded. 'Very well,' he said. 'It is not for me to counsel you in this matter. I shall inform Hannequin of your interest in their wellbeing. He does not normally welcome women at the monastery, but I'm sure something can be arranged in light of the circumstances. Good e'en to you, and may the Prophet watch over you both.'

With a curt nod the adept turned on his heel, beckoning to Adelko, who had just helped the last of their companions into the saddle. Adhelina watched the two monks mount their own horses and ride away from the harbour, jostling past the link boys and night hawkers towards the crowded city streets. Turning to survey the ramshackle row of run-down hostelries that catered to the city's maritime visitors, she shook her head.

'Well I don't know Rima, but I do know that this part of it is no place for a lady,' she told Hettie. 'Time we were in the saddle ourselves – I think we've some exploring to do.'

Hettie waved away an importunate hawker with a flick of the hand. 'Indeed, milady,' she agreed, 'the sooner we're away from this wretched dock the better.'

Adhelina felt a curious mixture of elation and nervousness as they picked a street at random and nudged their horses into the throng. They were alone and unguarded in a foreign city, but for now they were free.

CHAPTER 2

A MISSION DEBRIEFED

The seven monks remained staring at Horskram as he finished his report. The flagstones felt hard beneath his knees, but protocol demanded that he kneel before the High Circle of Seven. Consisting of the Grand Master and six archmasters in reflection of the Seven Seraphim, it had been founded early on in the Order of St Argo's five hundred-year history, to provide wisdom and guidance. In theory that meant it was drawn from the most learned savants of the Argolian Order. Horskram knew that was still true to some extent, though he personally would not have approved every man that sat before him. But then even a holy order had its politics, he reflected dryly as the monks continued to scrutinise him.

The wan candlelight made their faces resemble those of the carved stone saints that lined the circular walls of the auditorium; high overhead through its oculus, he could see the faint glimmer of distant stars. The chamber was unheated, and despite the summer night it was chilly. Hannequin had convened an immediate meeting of the High Circle as soon as Horskram had arrived; if the archmasters had looked disgruntled at being disturbed from their evening devotions, at least they looked engaged now.

The Grand Master was the first to speak, in accordance with custom.

'Thanks to the King of Northalde, most of the details of your mission were already known to me,' he said. 'Though the Order is overjoyed to learn of your triumph over Andragorix. The Prophet Himself smiles upon thee, Horskram, adept and hierophant of St Argo.'

The archmasters followed suit in making the sign, some more reluctantly than others. Not all the Seven were kindly disposed towards Horskram.

But there was something more than that. Horskram's sixth sense had been doing strange things since he entered the monastery. Normally so placid in the sacred headquarters of the Order he had served for two score years, it was jangling.

No, that wasn't quite right. It was jangling, yes, but *muffled* somehow as well.

He didn't have time to reflect on that as Hannequin continued, his voice hardening: 'But Brother Horskram, you yourself must allow that you have been perilous reckless on your latest adventures. Straying into Tintagael, and then the Draugmoors – and dragging ordinary mortals into your business! What in the Known World were you thinking?'

Horskram sighed inwardly. He had been expecting this.

Hannequin was as wise as any in the Order and slow to anger, but did not shy away from levelling criticism wherever he thought it warranted.

'I regret that some of my actions brought others in the way of harm,' he replied, running through his carefully prepared speech. 'And you have my thanks for your assurances that the brethren shall take the warriors protecting us into their care. But surely you will see that under such duress I had no choice but to make decisions–'

He was interrupted by a short bark of laughter from Wolaf. Sat at the farthest end of the semi-circle of sieges, he was a portly balding man. His fifty winters had done little to abate his gluttony, or apparently his rumoured nocturnal forays into the stewes of Rima whenever he could get away with it. The Vorstlending was weak in his adherence to pleasures of the flesh – it was a wonder he could muster any kind of elan any more. But then that was the way of things, Horskram reflected sadly: in its latter years, the Order had developed an unfortunate tendency for promoting timeservers to high office.

He glared contemptuously at Wolaf as the archmaster said: 'Why, already he offers excuses for his misconduct! And for all his misadventures he hasn't even found this secret mastermind. We still don't know who is trying to reunite the Headstone!'

'Brother Horskram can hardly be blamed for that,' sighed Hannequin. 'However, I am seriously wondering if it was necessary to take a drop of the Redeemer's blood for your protection – the Strongholm Temple's possession of such has been an open secret for years. Bad enough we've given the Supreme Perfect ammunition against us in allowing the Headstone fragment to be stolen from our chapter at Ulfang, now we've further provoked him by taking a relic he believes is rightfully his. Horskram, you of all people should know that we can't afford to make an enemy of the Temple again!'

Horskram felt his old torture scars throbbing again. He certainly did know. 'With all due respect, Grand Master, but have you not just heard my story in full?' he protested nonetheless. 'Without the Redeemer's blood we could not have triumphed over Andragorix, or survived the journey here!'

'And yet for all that, we still do not know who ordered Andragorix to send demonkind to kill you,' put in Gabrien. A native of Pangonia, the short archmaster was less flawed in his appetites than Wolaf, but just as cavilling – another placeman, forever chastising those who braved the wilderness and did the Redeemer's hard work, while he politicked and intrigued behind safe walls.

'Don't stare at me like that,' scowled Gabrien, divining his thoughts. 'I know all too well how lost in your own self-regard you are, Horskram of Vilno! Your precious mission has done little to advance the Order.'

'The same could be said of you for the sum of your entire life, Gabrien of Leon,' Horskram shot back.

'Enough!' cried Hannequin, waving a hand to silence Gabrien's spluttering protestations. Cathbad and Edelmir stifled sniggers as they reacted to Horskram's acid retort. At least he had a couple of allies in the High Circle: men he respected and was friendly with. They were welcome to speak in his defence any time soon.

But instead it was Adamantus who spoke. Tall and lean, the Thalamian towered over the others – not only in stature, but in birth too. His family traced its roots back to the imperial bloodline of Ancient Thalamy, though he had been marked out for a career in the Order from an early age. An able exorcist and scholar, at least he had earned his position by merit. Along with Hannequin, whose father had been castellan of Blanchemure, he was the most aristocratic member of the High Circle.

'Brother Horskram, no one seeks to apportion blame,' – the moustachioed monk shot a warning glance at Gabrien and Wolaf – 'but in order to confront the danger presented to us we must endeavour to learn from whatever mistakes have been made already.'

Horskram sighed exasperatedly. Adamantus was fair, but a stickler for form like Hannequin.

'At least acknowledge that we've done the world some good by ridding it of Andragorix,' said the adept, struggling to conceal his irritation. 'His grimoires, scrolls and potions we destroyed. Had the fool Harijan not slain him, we might have learned more.'

'The same Harijan we now shelter within our walls!' barked Wolaf. 'One given over to the sapphic lust, a pagan idolator from savage lands!'

Hannequin raised a slender hand again, his aristocratic features looking visibly pained. 'Please, Brother Wolaf, we do not require a sermon on the ungodly provenance of

Horskram's... unorthodox companions. I have already given my word that they shall be treated. And who knows,' – the Grand Master allowed a smile to play across his lips – 'she might even be moved to embrace the Creed once she experiences its restorative powers.'

I wouldn't wager on it, thought Horskram, but he kept his sentiments to himself. For all her impetuosity, Anupe had helped them overcome Andragorix: he felt he owed her a chance of survival for that much at least.

'Rather than rake over what might have been done differently, why don't we focus on what needs to be done next?' The speaker was Edelmir. At forty winters, he was the youngest of the Seven. With his blond hair and handsome features he might have been a trouper, not a monk. In fact a fisherman is what he would have been – only Horskram had plucked him out of his seaside village thirty years ago after spotting talent in the lad. Edelmir had gone on to become his first understudy, seconded to him for a year as a novice. That had been in happier times – before the Purge had seen them both questioned under fire and iron.

Horskram suppressed the memory of his nightmare as Edelmir went on: 'Our last divination revealed naught but Andragorix and another witch in the north – presumably this Abrexta you have spoken of. I say we convene another divination this Rest-day – with a hierophant joined to our efforts, surely we might learn more?'

There were a few mutterings at that. Gabrien and Wolaf plainly looked resentful at the acknowledgement of Horskram's superior divining skills, although in theory the

Seven together should be mightier than he. Possessed of unusually potent elan, hierophanti were extremely rare, even among adepts of the Order. That Adelko was one had occurred to Horskram some time ago during their adventures together – that only made him more concerned for the lad's future. Besides himself and Hannequin, the only other known hierophant their generation had produced was Malthus of Montrevellyn. But that old worthy had gone his way long ago, vanishing from the haunts of civilised men to who knew where.

'Clearly whoever was controlling Andragorix has mustered some potent Counter-Scrying,' ventured Horskram. 'and is using it to confound the Order's attempts to find them.'

Hannequin looked thoughtful. 'Nonetheless, with your elan joined to ours we might glean a little more... It's worth a try at least.'

'Is it?' barked Wolaf. 'What concern is this relic to us anyway? The third fragment is guarded night and day by druids on the Westerling Islands, the fourth could be anywhere in Sassania or beyond, in the clutches of the revenant boy Cael... assuming this legendary pagan islander ever took it there in the first place! Whoever this warlock is, they must be mad even to think of reuniting the Headstone and uncovering the lore needed to wield it! I say we have more pressing matters to worry about – Cyprian will use this unwelcome news to mount another Purge against us, you see if he doesn't!'

Gabrien was nodding vigorously, while Edelmir shook

his head. Hannequin and Adamantus didn't look so sure. Cathbad, sat on the other end of the semi-circle, looked decidedly nervous and held his peace. But then that was hardly surprising given his background. Horskram felt pity for the Thraxian: he had initially opposed the admission of a former Right-Hand magician to the Order, but over the years he had come to be convinced of Cathbad's loyalty. He had even consented to be shackled with iron for his first couple of years at the monastery. And he could hardly be blamed for being raised by a hedge witch who had taught him the rudiments of sorcery.

Only Bartho seemed unmoved. The eldest of the High Circle, he had seen more than eighty winters. His only contribution to the debate was the wracking cough that plagued him. It had got worse since Horskram had last seen him. The liver-spotted Mercadian had a blotchy bald head and shrivelled skin, but his dark eyes gleamed intently. He was the longest-serving member of the Order on the High Circle, and Horskram wanted to know what he thought.

'Brother Bartho, what say you?' he asked.

Bartho favoured him with another wracking cough before replying in his hoarse whispery voice: 'I say Brother Horskram has shared information with us, now it is time we repaid him in kind.'

The other archmasters exchanged nervous glances, but the leathery old monk was looking pointedly at Hannequin.

The Grand Master nodded curtly and said: 'Yes, Bartho, I was coming to that. A couple of weeks ago, we detected strong sorceries being used on the hills near the Arbevere.

As you know, there are remains of the Elder Wizards' civilisation there.' The Grand Master paused to make the sign. He looked pained as he added: 'I sent Adamantus and several adepts to investigate.'

Horskram raised an eyebrow. 'You sent an archmaster to do front-line work? Meaning no disrespect to Brother Adamantus, but when was the last time that happened?'

Hannequin fixed him with his grey eyes, his gentle features hardening again. 'When was the last time we had a manifestation so close to the heart of the Order? For such it was... Adamantus, you may conclude.'

The Thalamian tugged at his moustachios and complied: 'We couldn't find anything when we arrived at the scene, no remains, no blood, nothing. But a demon had undoubtedly been summoned. *Summoned* Horskram, right here under our noses. What's worse, it was powerful – deadly powerful. Third tier, possibly even second – if it's the latter then it must have been temporarily bound to a victim, for until the Headstone is reunited no demonologist has the power to cause such entities to manifest in their true form, thanks be to Reus. And yet for all its potency, we only caught wind of its spoor after the fact. Cattle in the area blinded or driven mad overnight, peasants awakening in the night screaming at nightmares they could scarce describe. All the telltale signs... but we didn't sense a thing until the manifestation had already happened.'

'So yes, our sorcerous mastermind is clearly a *very* good counter-scryer,' Hannequin added dryly.

It took Horskram a moment to digest the information.

'But... you mean to say he or she could be *here*, in Rima?'

Hannequin shrugged, though Horskram could sense he was troubled. 'Or somewhere in its environs, who knows? Whoever they are, they must be passing powerful if they can cover their tracks like that.'

'Then we must conduct another divination as you say,' said the adept, though already his heart was sinking. If the entire adepthood of the Order's most powerful monastery couldn't pinpoint the warlock's whereabouts, he didn't see what difference he could make. Even if he was a hierophant.

'Then I doubt very much that the result will be any different,' sighed Horskram. 'However much you may think I regard myself, Gabrien, I am not so vain as to think otherwise.'

'Nevertheless we must still try,' said Hannequin. 'Frankly, I see little else that we can do for now.'

'And if that fails, as it surely must,' asked Wolaf. 'Then what do we do?'

Hannequin glanced at him sharply. Horskram didn't need his sixth sense to tell him that the fat archmaster was seriously trying the Grand Master's patience.

'Then, Brother Wolaf, we shall decide what to do about the other fragments.'

Wolaf folded his arms. 'I believe I have made my sentiments clear on this matter.'

'I say Wolaf is right,' put in Gabrien. 'We don't have time to waste on a wild-goose chase. We need to decide how to prepare ourselves for when His Supreme Holiness moves against us. Need I remind you all, Cyprian has the ear of the King now.'

'A king who cares far less for matters spiritual than his father ever did,' Hannequin pointed out. 'I seriously doubt Carolus the Younger will be hoodwinked into supporting another pogrom against the Order.'

'No, but he could be leveraged into doing so,' persisted Gabrien. 'You know Carolus needs Cyprian to sanction the new pilgrim war he yearns for. That way he can get the barons who hate him out of the way when they go off on crusade. That'll leave him free to mount that invasion of Vorstlund I've been hearing all about lately.'

'I think you pay far too much attention to the affairs of lords temporal,' suggested Hannequin crisply. 'Enough of this prattle about the wars of mortalkind – they are no concern of ours. Now, it is late and we all have prayers and studies to attend to before bed. Right now the chapel is given over to treating Brother Horskram's companions. We cannot use it to conduct a divination with such a tainted presence there, so it'll have to wait until they are well.'

Wolaf and Gabrien tutted disapprovingly, and even stoical Adamantus frowned.

'The extra time can be well spent in prayer, fasting and meditation to gather our elan,' went on Hannequin, pointedly ignoring them. 'Then we convene with the adepthood to try our chances at another divination. Until then keep your tongues from wagging, all of you.' The Grand Master shot a glance at Wolaf, who snorted indignantly but did not demur.

'You may rise now, Brother Horskram,' added Hannequin, sounding more cordial. 'After all you've been through, you must be famished. I'll have a cold supper brought up to my rooms – I would speak with you in private.'

Horskram rose gratefully, wincing inwardly as his old knees cracked. He wasn't surprised at the Grand Master's request, and had one or two things he wanted to discuss without the others prying.

His eyes fell on Cathbad as the archmasters rose to leave. He was the only one who had not spoken at all. Horskram hardly suspected him despite his chequered background – Cathbad had been a hedge witch at best before joining the Order at fifteen. The adept tried to catch his eye to offer him some comfort, but the archmaster left hurriedly. As much as he had distinguished himself, he would never truly remove the taint of guilt that hung over him because of his past. He had been among the first to be tortured during the Purge: even now he limped because of it.

As Hannequin ushered him from the receiving chamber, Horskram noticed his sixth sense was still there: tolling away at the penumbra of his psyche, like a distant alarm bell behind a locked door in a vast keep.

'So Horskram, are you going to tell me why you think those freeswords came after you on the road from Heilag?'

Horskram turned from the inner sanctum window overlooking the monastery grounds. He had to smile: nothing escaped Hannequin. The adept had deliberately glossed over his theories as to the mercenaries' motives, knowing full well his Grand Master would pick up on the omission:

he hadn't wanted to voice his suspicions about Prior Johann in front of the fractious High Circle.

'I suspect the freeswords were commissioned by the Knights Bethler to come at us,' he said. 'And given that the Bethel couldn't know what we looked like, that leaves... Johann.'

Even now he felt anxious about voicing any accusations against the abbot of Heilag. Accusing members of the Order of treachery was not a thing done lightly. In fact it was almost unheard of within their own ranks – for all their internecine bickering, Argolians were usually loyal to a fault.

Hannequin was clearly thinking much the same thing. 'Are you sure you realise what you are saying?' he asked. 'I must say I'm surprised... If you were suspicious of anyone in the Order, I would have thought it would be Sacristen. After all, he let the fragment vanish from right under his nose.'

Horskram had to laugh again. The fat abbot of Ulfang suddenly seemed very far away, which he supposed he was. 'Sacristen? Nay, the only crime he's guilty of is incompetence.'

'Indeed,' said Hannequin, his voice hardening again. 'I've a good mind to dismiss him from his post.' The Grand Master let out a sigh. Horskram knew him well enough to know he would never make good on that threat. 'No, he can't be blamed for having such a dreadful heirloom in his keeping,' Hannequin went on. 'The blame is mine, Horskram – I should never have allowed it to be kept so remotely, on the fringes of the Order's reach.'

'It was precisely that remoteness that made it seem wise to keep it there,' Horskram reminded him.

'I suppose you're right,' replied Hannequin, gazing distractedly into the embers of the fire. He was sat at a walnut table in the centre of his private study. One of several chambers given over to the Grand Master's quarters, the spacious room was lined with creaking shelves crammed with tomes and scrolls on a myriad of subjects: Hannequin's personal library was nearly as vast as the main one at Ulfang. Rumour had it the Grand Master had read every single volume in his personal collection at least twice. Horskram believed the rumours – in all his years, he had never encountered an intellect as formidable as Hannequin's.

That was why it was so disconcerting to sense how troubled he was. Jammed as his sixth sense was, Horskram could tell that much.

'So, out with it – why Johann?' demanded Hannequin. 'I agree that in theory he could have told the local Bethler preceptory of your whereabouts and clandestinely arranged to have you killed... but why on earth would he do such a thing? I know there is no love lost between the two of you – but this is something else you are suggesting, Horskram.'

The adept nearly winced beneath the Grand Master's penetrating scrutiny. 'I know it doesn't sound very convincing,' said Horskram. 'But who else could have told those freeswords about us in such detail?'

'Motive, Horskram, we need motive,' persisted Hannequin. 'And as for the Bethlers being involved... should I be worried? After all, I have contacts with them in the Pilgrim Kingdoms. We've always been neutral on the crusades, but our Order has relied on the Knights Bethler for protection and guidance whenever we've sent members of our Order to consult with sages of the Faith. Why, even I've enjoyed that protection before – you'll recall I was in the Blessed Realm myself a few years ago, to consult the Kishan Scrolls after they were uncovered by the Sufieli Sect in Nazharya.'

Horskram shrugged, genuinely at a loss as to how to pursue his line of deduction further. 'All I can offer is circumstantial evidence... Who else could have given our descriptions to a bunch of Vorstlending freeswords? The Lanrak knights who were sent after us would surely have turned away once we vanished into the Draugmoors.'

'You don't know that for sure, Horskram,' countered Hannequin. 'Sir Hangrit Foolhardy might have sent one or two knights further south, just in case. Posing as errants they wouldn't be stopped, especially during tournament season. And then you mentioned there were other knights at the first inn, where you had your spectacular three-way showdown and managed to get half the town of Volfburg involved.' The Grand Master pursed his lips. 'You've left quite a trail behind you, Horskram.'

The adept sat down on the other side of the table. Hannequin was a teetotaller and drank only milk and water, but had been thoughtful enough to provide Horskram with a cup of Aquitanian red with his meal. He sipped at the wine as Hannequin sat pondering, lost in thought.

'We shall have to tread carefully in the absence of evidence,' he said presently. 'I'll relieve Johann from his post, have him recalled here. That way I can keep an eye on him. As for the Bethlers, I can make discreet inquiries, see what can be learned. I really hope this shadowy conspiracy doesn't involve them, because they are a far more powerful an Order than we are!'

'You said you had something you wanted to tell me in private?' asked Horskram, keen to change the gloomy subject.

'Yes, it's about your messenger,' said Hannequin, frowning. 'The knight who brought me news of this frightful business in the first place.'

'Sir Wolmar?' Horskram had scarcely spared a thought for the arrogant princeling.

'Yes, that's the one,' said Hannequin. 'I'm afraid he's disappeared – vanished into thin air.'

That caught the adept off-guard.

'Really? When?'

'Around the same time as we detected trace elements of sorcery in the foothills of the Arbevere – we don't know if the two are connected or not. It could just be a coincidence.'

'But you're not sure?'

'No... the Northlending knight was spending a lot of time with Ivon de Vichy, a prominent noble at court. I've heard enough about him to know the man's a schemer – rumour has it he's involved with this absurd plan to invade Vorstlund.'

'It doesn't sound so absurd now,' said Horskram grimly. 'The northern barons of Vorstlund are at each other's throats and half the freeswords in the south are heading in that direction to sell their services. I'd say King Carolus couldn't have picked a better time to attack.'

'You know what I mean, Horskram,' said Hannequin, somewhat irritably. 'All wars are absurd, when you boil it down. Hardly in anyone's interest but the nobility's and the freeswords' – and the moneylenders and merchants who fund and supply them.'

'You'll get no disagreement from me there, Grand Master.' Unlike Hannequin, the adept had experienced the horrors of war first hand. They weren't any better for being holy either.

'Anyway, I don't like it,' said Hannequin. 'A prince of royal blood who's privy to a secret plot we're trying to expose takes up with a man notorious for intriguing, and the next thing we hear he's gone – quite possibly on the same night as a summoning took place.'

'You don't think he was–'

'I don't know, I'm just speculating,' said Hannequin. 'But like you and Johann, all I have are circumstances. No motive. Ivon by all accounts is a worldly man, given to fornication and wine and other bestial pursuits.' Hannequin's lip curled in disgust. 'Typical of the Pangonian nobility.'

'That same Pangonian nobility you come from,' Horskram dared to remind him.

'Yes well, my father was cut from a different cloth than most,' said Hannequin. 'A loyal servant of the crown. In any case Reus saw fit to favour me, and my life has been the Order's ever since.'

Horskram sensed some deep conflict within him. 'You don't sound so overjoyed with your fate, Grand Master.'

Hannequin met his eye, and for the first time he appeared to show some vulnerability. 'Horskram, what is to be done? You and I, we are the finest minds our Order has seen in a generation – and yet here we are, guessing! Andragorix was our most likely suspect – he was the most powerful known warlock in the Free Kingdoms. Now you tell me he served another, apparently against his will... Who does that leave? Abrexta the Prescient is known to me, but I don't believe she would have been powerful enough to enthral Andragorix. That leaves the Earth Witch, who has proved herself an ally, the druids of the Westerling Isles, and maybe a couple of master warlocks in the Sassanian Sultanates.'

'Well, it's better than nothing,' ventured Horskram. 'The Earth Witch said her sorcery detected a presence here at Rima, and a power stirring in the Far South, so at least we've something to go on.'

Hannequin shook his head. 'Abdel Sha'arza is a recluse – a demonolator and a blackguard to be sure, but as you said yourself he has never craved world domination. Holed up in the Watchtower of Leviathan, he could have had access to an original grimoire of the Elder Wizards for decades – why start coveting the Headstone's power now, all of a sudden? That just leaves the Sultan of Halepo, an accomplished sorcerer by all accounts, and a former under-study of Abdel's...' Hannequin tapped his lips thoughtfully. 'I suppose he could have stolen the Grimoire from his old tutor, but I doubt Sha'arza would let him get away with that. Besides those leads, what do we have to go on?' Something else occurred to the Grand Master as he continued to tap his lips. 'A power stirring in the Far South, the Earth Witch said. That could mean the hierocracy of Sendhé, beyond the Sultanates – they're said to be descended from lesser Varyans of antiquity, any one of their accursed priest caste might be mad enough to covet a reunited Headstone. But, fie on it Horskram, even if it were any of the above, that still doesn't answer the riddle of who's practising black magic right here on our doorstep!

'So what are you suggesting? Do we just give up?'

'I'm suggesting we stop trying to work out who is behind it all, and focus more on what to do about the third frag-ment. Do we send someone to the Westerling Isles to warn the druids? And what of the fourth piece – do we hope our mastermind never finds it, or do we try to take the initiative there?'

Horskram considered his Grand Master's words. 'You mean try to find it ourselves?'

Hannequin shrugged. 'A few months ago I would have said such a plan was sheer folly. Now, I'm prepared to consider all possibilities.'

'I remain at your service,' said Horskram dutifully. 'Whatever you decide must be done, I shall of course defer to your judgement.'

'Yes well, let's see what the divination turns up, if anything,' said Hannequin. 'With two hierophanti mustering their elan, perhaps we can glean something new. In the meantime, Brothers Wolaf and Gabrien have a point – I'm afraid His Supreme Holiness is going to come at us any way he can. He hasn't ever forgiven us for turning the tables on the Temple twenty years ago.'

Horskram felt his scars throb again. It was a pain Hannequin could not know. Like Adamantus, his high status had meant he was spared torture during the Purge.

'Cyprian is a vain and tyrannical man,' said Horskram, nearly shuddering at the recollection of his sadistic tormentor. 'I need no reminder of his character.'

Hannequin looked pained. 'I can never claim to know what you and so many of our brethren suffered during that time,' he said sympathetically. 'But I can take action to prevent it ever happening again.'

'What can Cyprian do, realistically?' asked Horskram. 'We exposed the Temple for what it was – Abelard the Arch Perfect of Montrevellyn and his conspirators were found to be demonolators, learning at the feet of Sha'amiel, Prince of Perfidy. We located all the sorcerous tomes that Abelard had garnered and burned them on a pyre before the monastery grounds,' Horskram went on. 'Grand Master Hannequin, you put them on the fire in sight of the entire Pangonian nobility and perfecthood, the ones like Cyprian who had been duped! Our Order was exonerated in full – even His Supreme Holiness had no choice but to pardon us after the evidence we amassed.'

'And yet the taint of our accusation lingers,' sighed Hannequin. 'You have experienced this first hand many times on your travels.'

'I have,' Horskram acknowledged. 'But our Order has ever attracted suspicion and envy from the wider Temple – and people are all too easily led. What does Cyprian have to bring against us? So a drop of the Redeemer's blood has been entrusted to my keeping – the remainder lies in

Strongholm Temple. If anything, that reflects badly on the perfecthood, not us! And as for the fragment at Ulfang being stolen, well... Unless Cyprian can prove we had something to do with it...'

'And yet you yourself have just suggested we might have a traitor within our ranks,' Hannequin said. 'If that turns out to be the case and Cyprian gets hold of it...'

'All right, dammit, I see your point. So what do you suggest?'

'Tell no one besides me of your suspicions about Prior Johann,' said Hannequin. 'Your novice I presume is sensible enough to keep quiet.'

'Adelko can be trusted,' Horskram assured him. 'Though young, he has been exposed to far more than most his age in the past year. And as my account of his contribution should make clear, there is ample reason to believe he is a hierophant himself.'

'I had suspected as much from what you said of him,' said Hannequin, nodding. 'He will remain here at Rima. I'll take time to instruct him personally if I can.'

Horskram felt a welcome sense of relief. He had been hoping the Grand Master would agree with him about his erstwhile second. Clearly Adelko was a rare talent, one that needed nurturing.

'As for Cyprian,' continued the Grand Master. 'We must be seen to be doing everything we can to root out this evil. We can't afford to give the Supreme Perfect anything he can use against us, Horskram – I won't put the Order in jeopardy under my watch! After the divination, we'll need to decide about the remaining fragments if we can't locate our mystery warlock.'

'Understood.' Suddenly Horskram felt very tired. It was late. 'Well, if that's everything for now, Grand Master, I think I'll retire.'

Hannequin nodded, rising to show him out. 'Your usual chamber in the adepts' quarters has been prepared,' he said. 'I shall see you for dawn prayers.'

'We'll need them,' replied Horskram glumly.

CHAPTER 3
ON HALLOWED GROUND

Vaskrian awoke to darkness and the sound of chanting. Hadn't he heard something similar before? Only now it was much stronger; it resonated off the walls of the large circular chamber he was in. Sitting up he looked around him, struggling to focus in the gloom. The narrow windows lining the wall only allowed slivers of light to peep through, between columns that supported a domed ceiling of rough stone. The only ornamentation was a vast statue in the middle of the room, the height of three men, depicting an elderly bearded man dressed in sandals and flowing robes: one hand clutched a circifix and the other was raised palm outward, as if to ward off evil.

A chapel, then. A score of grey-robed monks paced its flagstoned floor, chanting prayers in Decorlangue as they sprinkled him and four others with holy water. Who were they?

Of course – his companions, Sir Wrackwulf and Sir Torgun and his guvnor Sir Braxus, and the strange foreign swordswoman Anupe. Hadn't they been through a mighty adventure together? Vaskrian shivered and screwed his eyes shut again, as inchoate forms returned to tell him of his ordeal, whispering of horrors that came by night to steal his soul.

Forcing himself to open his eyes again, he tried to focus on the prayers of the monks. His knowledge of the High Speech used by nobles was patchy at best, but he managed to grasp some of the words. They seemed to pertain to holiness and comfort: Vaskrian had never been one for the Temple, but right now he felt such words could only do him good.

The squire relaxed slightly and examined himself. He had been arranged on a pallet along with the others in a semi-circle facing the statue. He was wrapped in a winding sheet of white linen. With a shock he realised his arm had healed from the burns inflicted on it by Andragorix; flexing it he found that the scars did not impair his movement. That was a relief and no mistake.

Reus' wounds, but how long had he been unconscious?

No, he hadn't been unconscious. He dimly recalled a night-shrouded journey through moorlands, open country-side, cities and... even the sea. None of those memories felt quite right, though: the images that flicked through his mind lacked coherent form, as though made of shadow.

Probably best not to dwell on it, he decided. *I'm here now, wherever here is.*

One of the monks broke off his chanting and approached Vaskrian with a wooden platter. On it was some coarse unleavened bread and – to his delight – a pewter bowl of wine.

'You are the first to awake from the half-death,' said the monk softly. He spoke in Decorlangue, so Vaskrian struggled to make him out. 'Your soul is less tainted by blood than the others. Drink the blood of our Redeemer. Eat his flesh. This sanctified repast shall help you regain your strength.'

The squire didn't have the slightest idea what the strange monk was talking about, but bread and wine seemed like a very good idea. Without a moment's hesitation, he plunged a crust into the wide-brimmed bowl and made himself a sop to feast on.

Several sops later and he was feeling well enough to stand. The linen bindings sloughed off him as he did, revealing a body naked but for a loincloth – where in Reus' name were his clothes? He got another shock as he examined himself further. He'd lost a fair bit of weight. That wouldn't do: a warrior needed his strength.

The monk who had brought him the food and drink approached him again.

'You should go outside,' he said in the same hushed voice. 'The dawn light will help your soul to recover. I will send someone to bring you back inside, after the Order has said morning prayers. Don't stray beyond the inner courtyard.'

'Outside... right,' faltered Vaskrian. Mastering Decorlangue had been last on his list of knightly skills to learn, along with courtly love. Why bother talking to foreigners if you were only going to kill them anyway?

The monk was pointing towards an archway exiting the

chapel. Vaskrian kept his ungodly thoughts about violence to himself and left.

The archway took him into a small vestibule lined with statues depicting more saintly figures. At the far end was a single large door of oak studded with iron tacks. Approaching it and lifting the bar, he emerged into a wide courtyard, also circular in shape. Blinking in the sun, Vaskrian looked around him. It was deserted of people, but lined with buildings of all descriptions. Most striking was a venerable edifice of sandstone two storeys high, hugging the edge of the courtyard, and a tower at its centre, to which the chapel was adjoined. Covered walkways connected this central building from its upper floor to the top of the crenelated walls surrounding the courtyard.

Barring the Warlock's Crown, this was without a doubt the strangest building Vaskrian had ever been in. A shudder jolted his spine at the recollection of that fearful place. He'd travelled far from his homeland in Northalde and seen many fell things... perhaps his hazy memory was there to protect his sanity.

The squire was distracted by tolling from the belfry directly above one of the courtyard's four exits. This was closely followed by the sound of many trudging feet. From each exit emerged a party of monks, their hoods pulled up despite the mild morning. At the same time another group emerged from the central tower. There were hundreds of them altogether. Vaskrian watched them all file in orderly fashion into the chapel. They paid him not the slightest bit of notice and not a word was spoken. The monks were dressed in grey and brown, just like Horskram and Adelko. Argolians then. He supposed his companions must be in amongst that throng somewhere. Last to enter the chapel were seven monks dressed in black.

Had he and his stricken friends lain there all along, while the monks said their prayers morning and night? Just how long had they been here? His stomach was already rumbling again, his nostrils filled with baking smells from the nearby refectory. He wondered if they'd fed him much before now. The Argolians must have put them in a trance of some sort.

The sound of hundreds of monks chanting filtered out of the windows of the chapel. It felt soothing. Sitting down against the wall, Vaskrian shut his eyes and drank it in, feeling the sun harden pleasantly on his face.

He awoke with a start to find someone nudging him. He made to grab the monk instinctively... then realised who it was.

'Adelko! Where in the Known World have you been?' It was a stupid question really, but he didn't know what else to say.

The novice smiled at him, his pudgy face creasing as he fixed him with his goggle eyes. 'Dawn prayers,' he answered. 'Brother Elias – he's the adept in charge of your recovery – told me you should go back inside now. Don't worry, the Order will take care of you – they've got so many adepts here to pray for your souls you should all be fine, Reus willing.

Redeemers' wounds, but it's good to see you back to normal again!'

Vaskrian frowned. Normal wasn't quite how he would have put it.

'How long have we been here?' he asked, feeling this a less stupid question to ask.

'Five days now,' supplied Adelko. 'I've been released from Horskram's service and reassigned to the cloisters – I have to go to classes now, but I'll have some free time after supper. We'll catch up then – if Elias says it's all right.'

Without another word, Adelko turned and hurried over to catch up with a group of novices walking towards one of the exits. Vaskrian was digesting his words when the monk who had given him the bread and wine emerged from the chapel.

'It is time for you to come back inside,' he said. 'You must partake of the Redeemer's flesh and blood again, then it is time for you to rest some more. Your soul has yet to fully recover from its ordeal.'

Vaskrian still wasn't entirely sure what all that meant, but he wasn't about to say no to more food and wine. Picking himself up, he followed the monk back inside.

That was his routine for the next fortnight. Brother Elias didn't permit him to seek out Adelko, but a few days later Sir Torgun emerged from his trance. A few days after that it was Anupe, followed by his guvnor and the errant knight Wrackwulf. They said little to one another during their daily strolls about the courtyard. It was as if they were spirits from the Other Side, but lately arrived to the mortal vale; bewildered and slow to accustom themselves to their alien surroundings. Vaskrian itched for his sword of Staerkvit steel: now his arm was good again, he was dying to make use of it. What's more, his strength was slowly returning to him. The shadowy half memories of their frightful journey through the Draugmoors gradually receded. His companions had initially looked gaunt and half-starved too; but by the end of the two weeks something like normal colour had returned to their cheeks, and their bodies were fuller. Not a bad improvement, considering the Argolians were feeding them on naught but bread and wine. Perhaps the blessing did do something to them after all.

To pass the time spent in the courtyard during mornings and afternoons, Braxus began teaching him Decorlangue, muttering something about Vaskrian needing to speak it properly if he ever wanted to become a true knight. Vaskrian hadn't forgotten the Earth Witch's prophecy, and was sceptical as to how useful any language would be to him now. He didn't care to remember the prophecy in its entirety, but there had been a lot of stuff about fighting at the side of a chosen one, dealing death to their enemies... and getting no credit for it.

That was the part that rankled. *He shall be low born but rise high, yet no man shall honour him with title for his deeds.* He remembered that part all right, along with the bit about the sweet taste of victory souring in his mouth. Gloomy stuff for anyone of ambition to chew on. Adelko had counselled him not to take a witch at her word, but Vaskrian couldn't shake the nagging feeling that her prophecy would prove true.

The damsels came to visit them, too. To Vaskrian's dismay, Sir Braxus and Sir Torgun both resumed their courtly love suit, vying for Adhelina's attention. Didn't they ever learn? The disinherited heiress looked pretty sorrowful much of the time and seemed only too glad of the distraction, but Vaskrian was sure no good would come of it. On more than one occasion he caught Hettie looking at him. He couldn't deny it pleased him: he could use an amorous distraction of his own and besides, when was the last time he'd had a woman? But his hopes were soon dashed there as well. On the couple of occasions he tried to talk to her, she merely faulted him on his Decorlangue and told him he needed to eat more.

And a glance in the well water told Vaskrian all else he needed to know: though his facial burns had healed too, he would be disfigured for life. Well, what else could go wrong? At least he was alive and not turned into some shade, screaming beneath a full moon. Truth to tell, his scarred face didn't bother him all that much: he'd never been much of one for the ladies. Yet he felt a nagging disappointment when the damsels didn't visit for a few days.

Those days were noticeably getting shorter when Brother Elias called them all into the chapel. Down south the summers were longer, but even so the approach of autumn was undeniably in the air. There was a slight chill in the wind, one that followed them into the vestibule as they re-entered the sacred precinct.

'Your time here is at an end,' said Brother Elias. 'By the

grace of the Redeemer, your souls have been shriven and preserved from the half-death. To what end I cannot say, for the Draugbreath is a fierce ailment and all of you have blood on your hands. As such, you should return here the Rest-day after next – we'll need to check your psychic condition, just to be sure. In the meantime, you may be on your way. I shall have a novice show you to where your belongings are being kept.'

Well that's a blessed relief, thought Vaskrian. The squire couldn't wait to get back into some proper clothes and get some decent food down his gullet. A pity he hadn't had a chance to see Adelko again: monks weren't supposed to mix with sworders, but the thought of never seeing his friend again brought a stab of pain to his heart. They'd shared so much together.

The monks intoned a final blessing, and Elias summoned a novice to show them on their way. Torgun made to proffer his thanks, but the adept simply shook his head and smiled. The novice led them out of the courtyard and via its southern gate. This led into a colonnaded walkway that passed into an even bigger courtyard. The size of the place was dizzying. The young monk led them to a building abutting the monastery's outer wall. Their belongings were all there. They dressed and rearmed before heading over to the stables, where they found their horses had been well kept.

They were just about to saddle up when a familiar figure approached them from the inner courtyard. It was Horskram.

'So you're all fully recovered then?' he asked, unsmiling. 'That is well. Do you have lodgings in the city?'

Vaskrian had a sinking feeling he knew what the answer would be.

'Adhelina and her lady-in-waiting have been visiting us regularly,' said Braxus. His tone implied an unspoken *which is more than you've done*. 'We know where they're staying and will be attending their pleasure there.'

Horskram's face betrayed no emotion as he replied: 'Fine. Don't stray too far, though. Now that you've vacated the chapel, we need to use it for some pressing business. Depending on what we find... There may be further need for all your services.'

Torgun and Wrackwulf exchanged uncertain glances, while Anupe stroked her bulging money pouch meaningfully, but Braxus snorted. 'I think I'm done with sharing in your misadventures, Horskram of Vilno! It's high time I went back to Thraxia – my father has long been expecting me.'

A pained look crossed Horskram's face. 'I regret to inform you that your father is dead. News arrived in Rima while you were indisposed. Northern Thraxia has been overrun, though the southern wards have formed a resistance movement. I would that you stayed a while before returning home. It is possible that our missions may dovetail.'

Braxus said nothing, but just stood and stared. He suddenly looked as pale as he had done a tenday ago.

'I am sorry for your loss,' added Horskram, before turning on his heel and walking back towards the inner courtyard. 'Don't go anywhere, any of you,' he barked over his shoulder. 'Like it or not, you're all caught up in events larger than you now.'

Vaskrian felt a slight chill, despite the last of the summer sun. Hadn't the Earth Witch said as much?

'Wait!' Torgun called after the adept. 'What news from Northalde?' But Horskram ignored him. It took all of the perfect knight's generosity of spirit to bite down on the curse that escaped his lips.

Turning to his guvnor, Vaskrian put a hand gingerly on his shoulder. 'I'm sorry, Sir Braxus,' he said tentatively. 'I had no idea.' Normally he would have said something about heading back up north to avenge his father, but in light of what Horskram had just told them... The other three stood dumbfounded. To his credit, Sir Torgun was the first of them to offer his condolences, despite their love rivalry.

Sir Braxus said nothing. He just stared blankly across the courtyard, as though the Draugbreath had returned to curse him. Then he shook his head, blinking back incipient tears.

'Let's be gone from this place,' he said in a hoarse voice. 'I need a drink.'

Without another word, the five of them mounted up and rode towards the buttressed gatehouse. A drink seemed like a very good idea to Vaskrian right then – and this time he wasn't too fussed about any blessings.

CHAPTER 4

DIVINING THE DEVIL

Hannequin's crisp voice echoed through the chapel as he invoked the Redeemer and intoned the opening words of the divination.

Horskram felt rather than heard the syllables as they reverberated about the colonnaded chamber. St Argo had first spoken them five hundred years ago, when the avatar had called upon Palomedes to reveal the whereabouts of Avarek the Half-handed, the Thalamian master warlock who brought calamity upon his homeland. Argolians had been using the litany for centuries since then to uncover witches of all kinds, tapping into their psychic spoors so they could track them down and bring them to justice.

But since then, sorcerers had learned to adapt their craft; apprehended witches had revealed under inquisition that the arts of counter-scrying could now be used to abjure divinations.

Horskram had little doubt such would prove to be the case now, with or without his contribution. Candles guttered as chilly air swept through the chapel; the Wytching Hour on Rest-day was the best chance of divining a Left-Hand practitioner. The air between the eight monks seemed to crackle as their elan pooled between them, brought together by the sacred words:

Seven swords for seraphim who fought the King of Liars,
Seven hells for demon princes dwelling in blood and fire,
Seven circles for the saints who learned of Palom's preachings,
Seven schools for sorcerers who studied Abaddon's teachings.
Two prophets for the wise to lead us to salvation,
Two paths a warlock chooses when he courts damnation.
One god to rule us all, and judge us at the ending,
One god who seeth all, whersoe'er we're wending.
No eyes or ears the savant needs to find where spells are spoken,
No senses mortal bring him to the place where they are broken.

Horskram kept his eyes shut as he slowly raised his arms until they were stretched out, just as the Redeemer's would have been when he was broken on the Wheel. Had they been open, he would have seen seven other men doing just the same, arranged in a circle around the statue of St Argo. He would have seen blood stream from the statue's eyes, as the avatar's spirit stirred from the Heavenly Halls in answer to their call.

But he saw none of these things, though he knew they

were happening. Instead he sensed the entire Known World stretched before his mind's eye: a silvery sheen that might have been best described as a blanket of light. Here and there were dark patches: areas where the Rent Between Worlds was pronounced, or a wizard might be practising. Normally, with a successful divination these patches would be starkly noticeable; the stronger the warlock, or the greater the supernatural entity, the darker and bigger the patch would appear.

And therein lay the problem.

The patches that appeared before Horskram's psychic perception were uneven and unstill; they shimmered in intensity, growing now bigger, now smaller, constantly changing size and shape and shade. Whoever was counter-scrying was doing an excellent job of it: it was nearly impossible to pinpoint anything. At one point the cursed forest of Tintagael seemed to cover half of Northalde; the next it was no bigger than Strongholm.

As if from down a deep, deep well he heard Hannequin repeat the invocation. Screwing up his eyes and trying to regulate his breathing, Horskram forced himself to concentrate. The stuttering energy field was trying to distract him, to exasperate him away from focusing more intently. Summoning all his elan, he tried his best to reach out, while willing the others to do likewise.

Horskram felt his fingertips tingle. Slowly, agonisingly, the blanket began to settle down a little, enough to get the lie of the land.

There was a strong presence up in Thraxia and on the borders of Northalde and Vorstlund: that was clearly

Abrexta and the Earth Witch. Farther south were two other potent indications of sorcery, probably Abdel Sha'arza and his princeling apprentice in Halepo. Sendhé was a cluster of dark points, but then that was to be expected in that blasphemous realm, where the descendants of the Elder Wizards practised sorcery openly. None of the most powerful individual warlocks appeared to be there: Horskram had read that the priest caste of Sendhé had strict rules about what could and could not be practised, forbidding any single left-hand warlock from becoming too powerful.

No one appears to have broken with that custom yet, he found space to reflect. *Perhaps the mad priests of Sendhé aren't mad enough to seek the Headstone, after all.*

The reading was the same up in the far north-west, where the Island Realms operated similar laws for the Right Hand Path of gramarye. Likewise to the east, in the Urovian New Empire, which blasphemously permitted Palomedians to practice so-called white magic, subject to severely enforced restrictions. Across the Sea of Valhalla, at the northern fringes of the world, he sensed another spoor; this one was familiar, like that of the Earth Witch. Horskram guessed the Sea Wizard had been busy since fleeing Northalde after failing to usurp its throne using his puppet Krulheim. There were weaker points in the Frozen Wastes, too: probably the best of the hedge wizards there.

But it was right here in Pangonia, closest to home, that the field was at its most distorted: some potent wizardry was indeed being practised on their doorstep.

But where *exactly?*

The blanket shimmered, growing large and incoherent again. Horskram forced himself to refocus, concentrating on the part that represented Pangonia. The other seven monks reached out towards the same spot, he could feel their elans intersecting with his...

Something jolted him. He withdrew, refocused, and reached out again... an invisible, intangible force field was blocking him. No, more than that – it was *repelling* him. Beads of sweat started to form on his forehead, but Horskram paid them no mind as he refocused yet again. He felt the most powerful elan in the room beside his own, questing out towards the same spot. It was Hannequin.

Furrowing his brow he tried to communicate directly. Sixth sense could be used between hierophanti to communicate directly during a divination, but only by the most supreme of efforts. Sweat trickled down Horskram's brow as he sent the message out.

Are you meeting the same obstacle?

He waited. The air crackled and hummed between them, the keening wind a forgotten force.

After a while, a response.

Hard to be sure... Something blocking us, yes... it's close...

Horskram gasped as his concentration was abruptly broken: his eyes flicked open to see the others were standing in their spots, blinking and looking around the room. All of them looked as drained as he felt.

'It was no different from last time,' said Wolaf, his fat face flushed and sweaty. 'Whoever is jamming the signal, they haven't been put off by your contribution, Brother Horskram.' The archmaster's words carried a tinge of scorn.

'Nor yours it would seem,' replied Horskram, not taking the bait. 'They are somewhere in the region, but Reus only knows where.'

'We got close though, you and I,' said Hannequin. He tapped fingers against lips thoughtfully. 'Whoever it is, I think he or she is in the vicinity of the capital.'

'It's hard to be sure of that,' said Horskram. 'Our conjoined sense was virtually opaque at times – our counter-scryer has done his work well.'

'Perhaps we should have the temporal authorities conduct a sweep of the city,' suggested Adamantus, as he lifted a long horn spoon from the fount by the sacristy and began moving among the brothers. After expending such effort, it was advisable to take a sip of holy water to replenish one's elan.

'And that would make us even more popular,' said Gabrien sarcastically. 'Our Order is already on thin ice with the nobles. The King would never sanction it.'

Adamantus sighed as he administered a sip to Gabrien. 'I suppose you are right.'

'No, it would cause far too much of a stir in any case,' said Hannequin. 'The last thing we need is a general panic.'

'So what do we do?' asked Edelmir, taking the spoon from Adamantus. 'We've got warlocks stirring up trouble in the four corners of the Known World, aye and at its very epicentre too – we can't stand by and do nothing!'

Horskram had to suppress a wry smile. He liked and respected his former understudy, but Edelmir's ethnocentricity was typical of Pangonians.

'No, we can't,' agreed Hannequin, taking a sip and

passing the spoon on. 'We must decide on a course of action.'

Horskram was the last to drink of the water. He felt instantly replenished, invigorated by the sanctified water. And just as he did, his sixth sense returned to him with a jolt. Something was amiss, though he couldn't say what.

'I say we sit on what we know and leave it at that,' persisted Wolaf. 'The island druids have ever kept their fragment under close watch, and as for the fourth... Do we even know if this boy Cael ever existed?'

'If he did, he must long have succumbed to the half-death,' said Adamantus. 'For all we know, his shade still wanders the deserts of southern Nazharya.'

'Deserts that lie not so very far from Abdel Sha'arza's watchtower and the Sultanate of Halepo, a realm currently ruled by his former apprentice,' pointed out Bartho, his words punctuated by his wracking cough.

'But what of the power to wield it?' Horskram reminded them. 'The Earth Witch suggested that any warlock would need to have uncovered one of the original tomes written by the Elder Wizards, and not just a diluted copy.'

'I can think of few better positioned to discover such than Sha'arza,' spluttered Bartho, reaching for a rag to cough into. Horskram wouldn't be surprised to see blood on that cloth. He wondered privately how much longer the ancient monk had left in the mortal vale.

'And yet Sha'arza has lived in the Watchtower of Leviathan for decades,' said Hannequin. 'Leading the life of a recluse. He has never showed any indication of wanting such power as the Headstone would bring, though a Left-Hand warlock could easily succumb to such temptation.'

'Well if it is him, he's hundreds of miles away from the fragment on the Westerling Isles!' barked Wolaf. 'Whoever's behind the first two thefts, they're clearly mad – I say we keep vigilant and say no more about the matter to anyone!'

'And what of the divination we have just conducted?' demanded Horskram sharply. 'It's fairly evident someone is operating here in Pangonia – it could well be them behind it all.' His sixth sense had not left off. Glancing sidelong he caught Cathbad fidgeting nervously. Horskram couldn't help but notice he had kept his silence once again. In fact he had barely spoken a word to Horskram since his arrival at the monastery.

'And how do you suggest we find them?' asked Gabrien acidly. 'Our mystery warlock is proving elusive to say the least!'

'We need to try and draw him or her out,' suggested Horskram. 'Between Ulfang and Strongholm, we were pursued by a demon sent by Andragorix to eliminate us. Now I carry the blood of the Redeemer that threat has been neutralised – for now. But if we were to split up – half of us journey to the Pilgrim Kingdoms to try to locate the fourth fragment, and the other half head north to warn the druids on the Island Realms...'

'And what good would that do?' sneered Wolaf. 'Our mystery magician obviously knows he can't send any more demons to attack you.'

'Wait,' said Hannequin, raising a hand. 'I think Horskram may be onto something. Pray continue, brother.'

Horskram nodded in acknowledgement. 'Our master-mind can't send anything to attack me while I have the Redeemer's blood – but a second party heading north...'

Edelmir gawped. 'You'd sacrifice your own companions, just to draw this wizard out?'

'Let me finish,' replied Horskram testily. 'I didn't say I'd send them without any protection – in any case, I want them to reach the Westerling Isles. No, we have a relic here in our possession that might protect them. It isn't as potent as the Redeemer's blood but...'

This time it was Adamantus who spoke. 'You are referring to the Circifix of St Argo – our most sacred relic! Brother Horskram, what foolishness are you speaking of!? You would give up such an artefact to a party of – of questing knights!?'

'Hardly the first time such a thing has been done,' countered Horskram. 'Twas granted to Sir Lancelyn of the Pale Mountain, when he went to do battle against the necromancer Azavolus the Blue Fingered. He returned it safe and sound once he had slain the warlock.'

'Sir Lancelyn was the greatest knight who ever lived!' protested Gabrien, not losing the opportunity to praise a compatriot.

'Sir Torgun of Vandheim, whom I have in mind for this task, is one of the greatest of our era,' said Horskram. 'He is devoted to the Code of Chivalry, and his puissance is unsurpassed by any knight living today I can think of, save perhaps Sir Azelin of Valacia.'

'If only Sir Azelin were here,' mused Edelmir. 'As pious

and brave a knight as any that ever lived. He'd be right useful to us in this thing.'

'Let's not get sidetracked,' said Hannequin, raising a slender hand again. 'No, I think I can see where Horskram is going with this idea. St Argo's fingerbone is a powerful relic, but not as potent as a drop of the Redeemer's blood... That might just encourage our warlock to try his luck. And in so doing, he may weaken his counter-scrying enough for us to divine his exact location.'

'Or hers,' put in Edelmir.

'Or hers,' repeated Hannequin. He looked sharply at Horskram. 'I take it this is what you have in mind?'

The adept nodded. 'If our mystery mage decides not to send a demon to attack Sir Torgun and his expedition party, then they can get to the Island Realms and warn the druids. If he – or she – does send one, it gives us a chance to expose them. Either way, we win.'

'You'd still be putting your brave knight in a lot of danger,' Bartho pointed out. His coughing had subsided to wheezing.

'I would,' acknowledged Horskram, trying not to think of his dislike for Sir Torgun. 'But the Circifix of St Argo will certainly give him some protection. And he has fought demonspawn before.'

Bartho puckered up his papery face, his eyes crinkling to gimlets as he considered Horskram's idea. 'It might just work,' he said.

Horskram looked around at the others. Gabrien and Wolaf looked stubbornly unconvinced, but he could tell

Adamantus and Edelmir were coming around to Bartho's way of thinking. His gaze fell on Cathbad last.

'What say you, brother?' asked Horskram pointedly. 'You've said nary a word so far.'

Cathbad looked nervously back at the adept. 'Just been pondering the matter, is all,' he muttered. 'There is much to consider.'

Horskram's sixth sense had settled down to a persistent throbbing. Something wasn't right. He caught Cathbad flick a sidelong glance in Wolaf's direction.

'Well I don't know why you're looking at me, brother,' said the fat Vorstlending. 'I've already made my opinion on the matter quite clear. I say this business is foolish, giving up our most sacred relic, so a man of the sword can head to the world's end on a fool's errand! Let the Five and the Seven and the One stay where they belong – in demon's prophecy!'

Horskram's sixth sense screamed up a notch. Turning to face Wolaf, he stared hard at the archmaster. His left eye was twitching, as though consumed by a nervous tic, and his hands were shaking slightly.

The Five and the Seven and the One... I bid thee a fond farewell, until we meet again...

No. Impossible.

Wolaf was sweating now. Cathbad was staring at him too, his mouth half open.

It couldn't be. They were on sacred ground, at the heart of their Order. He'd just taken a sip of holy water, for Reus' sake...

Wolaf stared back at Horskram. The twitching had subsided and his hands were no longer trembling. The others seemed oblivious, except for Cathbad. Horskram's sixth sense was now focused directly on the Vorstlending monk.

'Well?' demanded Wolaf. 'What is it now, brother Horskram? Cat got your tongue?'

'I think our psychic travails have taxed you over much,' said Horskram, sounding suddenly affable. 'Pray take another sip of holy water, that you may consider my counsel with a sounder mind.'

'What nonsense are you speaking of?' demanded Wolaf in a shrill voice. 'I just took a sip!'

'Why, but no,' pressed Horskram, still sounding affable. 'I think in your haste you spilled it. Many a slip twixt cup and lip, as the saying goes... Brother Adamantus, you are standing right next to him. I think he spilled it, no?'

He had to hope his guesswork would pay off. Adamantus glanced cursorily at the flagstones around Wolaf.

'Why yes,' he said. 'Hard to be sure with such a small amount of water, but it does look as though you spilled some, brother.' The tall monk returned to the fount and pulled out the spoon. 'Better to be safe than sorry,' he added, returning to Wolaf with the full spoon. 'Here we are...'

Wolaf shrieked as Adamantus proffered the spoon, instinctively recoiling. Cathbad gasped as Hannequin rounded on the Vorstlending suspiciously.

'Brother Wolaf? How now?' he asked in a stern voice. ''Tis only a drop of consecrated water, what is the meaning of this?'

But Horskram knew the meaning of it all too well.

Stepping forwards, he reached into his habit and produced his circifix. The twitch returned to Wolaf's face as he caught the silver rood flashing in the candlelight. He suppressed it instantly, but by now Horskram was thoroughly attuned to his spoor: he wouldn't be needing the Redeemer's blood for this if he was right. Brandishing the circifix, he intoned the same words as he had done on the windswept highlands in Northalde months ago.

'Belaach, denizen of the Third Tier of the City of Burning Brass, by the power of the Seven Seraphim, the Redeemer and the spirit-father Reus Almighty, I compel thee to return to thy tower!'

Wolaf emitted a horrid screech that no human throat could have uttered.

'Belaach, let the hellfires there engulf thee, let darkness enshroud thee! Return now to languish in the prison to which thy black betrayal condemned thee aeons ago!'

The monk's body quivered from head to toe, the flesh rippling with a hideous life of its own as it began to suppurate before their very eyes, oozing pus from a thousand sores that suddenly bubbled up from beneath the skin. The other archmasters were staring astonished, but Hannequin was already reaching for his own rood.

'Belaach, pollute this mortal vale no more!' cried Horskram. 'The Third Tier awaits thee! Go now and seek thy infernal master, crawl to his feet like the serpent thou art, and trouble mortalkind no longer! It is the heavenly powers that compel thee!'

'IT IS THE HEAVENLY POWERS THAT COMPEL THEE!' cried Hannequin, joining his voice to Horskram's.

Even with the element of surprise, a Third Tier demon once named could not hope to compete with the combined powers of two hierophants. Wolaf's form grew suddenly bloated and amorphous, his habit tearing as it burst out of his garments. The screech turned into a hiss; the body collapsed in on itself as an ethereal column of flame roared free of it. The monks gagged and wretched at the noisome odour that suddenly permeated the chapel, as the thing that had been Wolaf fell to the floor with a wet plopping sound. Looking down in horror on his remains, Horskram realised the entrails had exited Wolaf's corpse via his rectum, his body horribly misshapen and broken in a hundred places. The eyes stared up at the domed ceiling sightlessly, the whites plainly visible against their shrunken irises.

Bartho made the sign. 'Reus' teeth,' he gasped. 'This was no ordinary possession! This was a *binding!*'

Horskram looked at the old monk aghast. 'But how...? To one of our very own, here in the heart of the Order!'

Adamantus pointed at the bloated torso, partly exposed beneath the torn black folds of Wolaf's habit. 'Brother Bartho has the right of it,' he said grimly. 'Look at yon markings on his chest.'

The hieratic symbols that seemed to dance and glow across Wolaf's mangled body were unmistakeable.

'Somebody bound a demon to Wolaf using the Sorcerer's Script,' said Hannequin. 'Only that way could he have escaped our detection for so long.'

Amidst the writhing symbols was a flash of silver. 'But he was wearing his circifix,' said Horskram. 'How could he have kept the holy rood next to his flesh and tolerated it?'

The Grand Master shook his head. 'It takes exceptional craft, but a skilled demonologist can use magic to secure a host body against the symbols of the Creed. Not enough to protect against ingesting holy water, but enough to protect it externally...'

'... and prevent us from detecting it,' finished Adamantus.

'But Horskram sensed it,' said Gabrien, looking at the hierophant askance.

'Because I was attuned to Belaach's psychic spoor,' said Horskram. 'Were it not for that, I would have been deceived as you were. In fact I was anyway, right up until he mentioned the Five and the Seven and the One.'

'Sometimes a demon cannot resist giving itself away,' said Adamantus. 'Even when its binder desires otherwise. It longs to escape its new master's thrall, so it can wreak havoc on the mortal plane.'

'You mean to say this warlock we're hunting bound a demon to an archmaster?!' cried Gabrien. 'This madman must be sought out and destroyed!'

'Only a moment ago you were suggesting we follow Wolaf's counsel and do nothing,' Edelmir pointed out.

'That was before!' protested Gabrien. 'If we've got a warlock intent on killing us off right under our noses...' His voice trailed off as something occurred to him. 'But wait...'

He turned to look at Cathbad, who was standing stock still, a stunned expression on his face.

Gabrien's eyes narrowed. '*You!* I always said we could never trust a former witch in our most sacred order!'

Cathbad stammered but finally found his speech. 'I had

nothing to do with this!' he said. 'It's years since I practised the art, and I was but a hedge witch of the Right Hand Path... I could never do such a thing, even if I wanted to!'

'And who's to say you haven't been working at it in secret?' demanded Gabrien. 'As Horskram himself pointed out, you've barely said a word about this whole business! And the look on your face before he uncovered Belaach – you *knew* something, didn't you?'

'I – no!' stammered Cathbad. Horskram's sixth sense was still reporting, but he was too drained to get a lock on where it was directing him.

'I say we hold him securely, pending further questioning,' spat Gabrien. 'We can't afford to trust anyone now, least of all a former witch!'

Horskram didn't like the malice he saw in Gabrien's eyes. The haughty Pangonian had never liked the unassuming Thraxian. But all the same, he had to admit the archmaster had a point. Under the circumstances, Cathbad was a suspect, though an unlikely one.

Hannequin was clearly thinking much the same thing. 'Brother Cathbad,' he said. 'No one here is saying you are guilty of anything but... in light of what has just happened, we will need to take you into custody. Just until we get this infernal business cleared up.' He eyed the soggy pile of flesh that had been Wolaf with mingled horror and distaste.

Cathbad looked pleadingly at Horskram.

'I think it might be best to do as the Grand Master suggests,' the adept said gently. 'The Order is wiser in these matters than the mainstream Temple – no unjust harm shall befall you.'

Cathbad looked at the monks, a helpless expression on his face. 'All right then,' he said at last. 'If it's a scapegoat you're after, let it be me. And may Reus prove my innocence for all to see!' He made the sign dramatically.

'I've no doubt that He shall,' said Hannequin, though his voice was etched with sorrow. 'Adamantus and Gabrien, take our brother to the smithy and have him bound with links of cold iron. Escort him to the interrogation chamber afterwards, then convene the adepts – we'll need to tell them what has happened right away.'

'We'd best get this mess cleaned up,' added Edelmir, shaking his head sadly as he looked at Wolaf's remains. 'Was he a willing sacrifice, do you think?'

'There is no way we can be sure of that until we have conducted further investigations,' sighed Hannequin.

Edelmir nodded and left the chapel, followed by Gabrien and Adamantus with the hapless Cathbad walking between them.

'I hardly think it likely he did it,' said Bartho when it was just the three of them left.

'Nor do I,' replied Hannequin. 'But if we're to recruit the adepthood to help us in this dark hour, we need to be seen within the Order to be doing something. And needless to say, no one is to breathe a word of this to anyone but the adepts that dwell within these walls. I don't want the novices or journeymen knowing anything, or any visiting adepts from other chapters.'

'There is sound sense in your words,' said Horskram. 'Though I warn you, my former understudy Adelko of

Narvik is notoriously good at ferreting out secrets that don't belong to him.'

Bartho fell into another fit of coughing, pressing his face into his filthy rag again. The preternatural stink had not left the chamber.

'We'll need to try another divination when we've recovered our strength,' said Hannequin. 'See if it was Wolaf – or rather Belaach – countermanding it.'

'But we could all sense each other,' said Bartho, spitting more bloody phlegm into his rag. 'How could we not have noticed?

'It's possible the binding could have allowed the demon to control the host's powers and manipulate them for itself,' suggested Hannequin.

'But that is unheard of!' exclaimed the old monk. 'Argolian powers are sacred – we channel the power of a saint and the Redeemer himself! How could a demon or black magician controlling it do such a thing?'

'That is what we must try to find out,' said Hannequin grimly.

The three monks lapsed into silence. Another gust of keening wind fanned across the chapel, snuffing out the candles and leaving them alone in the dark with Wolaf's reeking corpse.

CHAPTER 5
THE SAD KNIGHT MOURNS

Braxus sat in the courtyard of the inn, listlessly running fingers across his Thraxian harp. The plangent notes echoed the sorrow he felt, though he didn't have the heart to strike up a proper tune. Out of the corner of his eye, he caught Adhelina looking at him anxiously. She had encouraged him to come and sit outdoors, telling him the Ripanmonath sun – still warm this far south – would do some good for his melancholy spirits. But the dying rays of late afternoon did little to comfort him. Likewise the bitter herbal concoction his amour had prepared him earlier had done naught to assuage his grief, though her presence did something.

His father was dead. Butchered by highland savages hundreds of miles away, while he had been off questing with Horskram and his merry band of intrepid idiots. His homeland laid waste, conquered by those same savage tribes that had stuck the old man's head on a spike and sent it down to Ongist as a war trophy. Not only that, but the ensorcelled king who ruled in that city had pardoned his father's killers – and given them his ancestral birthright.

Braxus could not decide which of the two losses pained him more. He had never seen eye to eye with Lord Braun, but in his deepest heart had always believed he would make the old man proud of him one day. Likewise he had seldom relished the prospect of rule, but secretly believed that when the time was right he would mature and grow into his title.

All gone. Snatched away from him, by Azazel's bloody hand. How the archdemon of war and rapine must be laughing at him now. Or was it Sha'amiel, avatar of deceit, who was laughing? For surely the young knight had been utterly deceived, to think that going errant would bring his father the aid he'd so desperately needed.

Reaching for his cup, Sir Braxus slugged back another mouthful of Aquitanian red. At least he could get drunk down here, in lordly fashion, until his purse ran empty and he had to beg credit just to get more drink. Or perhaps he'd sell himself as a freesword, and fight for the highest bidder. Or better yet, why not a troubadour?

Adhelina reached over and grasped his hand. Once, the touch would have thrilled him, but now he registered it as a faint glow, a light glimpsed far across stormy seas by a stricken mariner.

'Sir Braxus, I don't think you should drink any more,' she said. 'It doesn't mix well with the St Elenya's Root I gave you earlier.'

'Doesn't it?' snorted Braxus. 'Why my sweet angel, I think

you should drink with me. That would please me more than all the herbs in the hanging gardens of Shamaria.'

Her beautiful heart-shaped face grew earnest, her green eyes flashing. 'Sir Braxus, I know the pain you feel,' she said imploringly. 'I too have lost my father and lands – but you cannot succumb to melancholia! We still have life in us, and must go on with it!'

'Ah yes,' replied the knight, gently pulling his hand free and refilling his cup. 'We must look to the future.' The inn they were staying at catered to upmarket visitors, wealthy merchants and travelling nobles, and it did a fine drop. 'As I've said for the past many days, I would happily seek a future with you. We have passionate feelings for one another, and now know a bond of sorrow that few others can know...' He gestured melodramatically with his cup. 'But wait! My lady also loves another! And she cannot choose betwixt us... What a fine dilemma, one befitting the *Lay of Olwen and Her Twin Paramours!*' With a flourish he downed another cup.

'Sir Braxus, stop it,' she said, rising to her feet. Hettie spared a glance from the embroidery she had been pretending to concentrate on, and frowned disapprovingly.

'Forgive me, my lady,' said the knight, putting down the cup and taking a knee unsteadily. 'I live only to oblige you – just name me a task, any task, and I shall endeavour to perform it.'

He was sincere despite his drunkenness, but the damsel only shook her head. 'Oh, Sir Braxus, we've been through this already! Now is hardly the time to be playing games of courtly love – you and Sir Torgun are still recovering from your ordeal, and if everything we've heard lately is true, we're in a country that's about to go to war with my own!'

The damsels exchanged anxious glances, and not for the first time. Freeswords had been flocking into Rima in the past week, as rumours of the planned invasion circulated.

Braxus sighed and got to his feet. He was about to refill his cup when the door to the courtyard burst open. In strode Torgun.

Speaking of the devil, thought Braxus resentfully.

The Northlending knight was still dressed in his mail hauberk, though with his plain black surcoat and cloak he might have passed for a freesword himself. But then he'd forsaken the heraldic insignia and chequered cloak of the White Valravyn the minute he'd left his native Northalde to join them as an errant.

Nodding curtly at Braxus, he took a knee before Adhelina, far less unsteadily than the Thraxian had. But then Torgun didn't drink to excess. Torgun didn't wallow in misery or self-pity. Torgun did everything a knight should do, perfectly. Braxus hated him for it.

'My lady, I have been at the waterfront,' said Torgun, pausing only to kiss the damsel's proffered hand. 'Circulating amongst the riffraff and ne'er-do-wells. I regret to inform you that the rumours we have been hearing are most likely true. I spoke to a party of knights but lately arrived from Vichy – they say their liege supports this war, and is currying favour with other margraves further west.'

The knight rose, sparing a glance for Braxus who had slumped back into his seat. If he felt contempt for his rival he did not show it. He had only done that once, when

Braxus had tried to attack him from behind at the tournament at Graukolos after losing a duel to him. The memory of that shameful incident still burned.

'So what do we do?' asked Adhelina. 'Anupe isn't ready to travel with us to the Empire yet... and nor are any of you. The monks said you need more time to complete your recovery.'

'That is true,' said Torgun. 'And I feel honour-bound to wait on the monk Horskram, and see what he will ask of us – though I must confess I find the man's manners deplorable.'

The blond knight frowned. Braxus felt a viper of jealousy bite his heart as Adhelina reached up to caress his rugged cheek.

'Good Sir Torgun, sit with us a while,' she said. 'Take some wine – you have more than earned it.' The viper bit again as Braxus reflected on his recent slovenliness. Torgun, being perfect, hadn't given up his afternoon to morbid self-contemplation. But then his arch-rival hadn't just lost his father and been disinherited. Yes, what did the sanctimonious Northlending know of real loss? He was justified in his sorrow, Reus dammit!

Torgun joined them and the Thraxian shifted uncomfortably to accommodate him.

'Well, Sir Torgun, you have surpassed yourself down at the docks, I see,' said Braxus sarcastically. 'Pray tell us, what salty brigands did you have to vanquish to bring us this priceless information?' Adhelina rolled her eyes. Braxus knew he shouldn't pick a quarrel, but he couldn't help it.

'I have done only as any good knight would under the

circumstances,' replied Torgun, his voice calm as ever. 'And pray tell how fares my compatriot, young Vaskrian? A squire is a responsibility – a knightly master should use his free time to instruct his charge in the ways of chivalry and knighthood.'

'I left young Vaskrian in the company of Sir Wrackwulf and the Harijan,' replied Braxus, refusing to take the bait. 'That's plenty enough instruction for him – he needs some levity after all he's been through.'

The Vorstlending knight had collected his pay from Horskram and joined Anupe in a week-long bout of carousing. Braxus hadn't felt like joining them – he wanted to stay close to Adhelina – but had suggested Vaskrian accompany them in their tour of Rima's wineshops and brothels.

'Well, I'm sure his knightly master knows best,' replied Torgun courteously, though Braxus could tell it cost him some effort.

'Besides, I thought to stay here and protect our lady love, whilst you were off gallivanting about town,' added the Thraxian, patting his scabbarded sword where he'd left it propped up against the table. 'If it's going to be dangerous for Vorstlendings in Rima, I thought it best if one of us at least keeps an eye on Lady Adhelina.'

Torgun met his eye, fixing him with a cold stare.

Finally Adhelina lost her composure. 'Oh stop it, both of you!' she exclaimed. 'I can't stand to see two good knights sniping at each other like this.'

'Then do what needs to be done,' said Braxus. 'You know the rules of courtly love as well as any damsel. Give your knights a task, and let us begin the business of wooing you in earnest!'

Torgun nodded his head in acknowledgement. 'For once Sir Braxus and I are in complete agreement,' he said. 'We have both declared our love, and you have taken our favours at tourney. We humbly await your commands.'

Adhelina shook her head in exasperation. 'This is absurd! We've just barely survived the most horrible adventure imaginable, *and* we're in the middle of an encroaching war, and now you want to play games of chivalry...!' She sighed and took a sip of wine. 'Well, I suppose this is what I wished for all those years stuck in that castle, so I shouldn't be ungrateful when Ushira finally smiles on me.'

She sat back and thought a bit, running a pale hand through her strawberry tresses. They looked like spun red gold in the waning sunlight. How lovely she was...

'All right,' she said presently, 'if it'll get you out of your melancholia, Sir Braxus, and stop the pair of you arguing like page boys, then here is my first task...' She sat up, suddenly looking imperious and regal. 'Take your horses and ride from the city. Do not stop until you have reached two great statues that flank the river Athos. Sir Torgun, you are to climb to the summit of the statue of Alcius. Sir Braxus, you are to climb to the summit of the statue of Antipole. Each of you must bring me back a handful of rock dust from the head of your statue. Then I shall know the sincerity of your love suit.'

The knights exchanged surprised glances as Adhelina took another sip of wine. For someone put on the spot, the former heiress had a lively imagination. But their mission was clear enough.

As one, the knights rose and bowed.

'Thy will be done, my lady,' they chorused. Braxus felt his head swimming as he headed off towards the stables with Torgun. He was sobering up, fast.

'Milady, are you mad?' asked Hettie when the knights had left. 'That'll take them days! If they don't break their necks, or get arrested by the authorities that is.'

'If they ride swiftly, they should be back in time for the Argolians this Rest-day,' Adhelina told her crisply. 'And I know full well they've faced graver dangers ere now.' She finished her wine. 'Besides, I had to do something to get them out of here for a few days – I can barely think straight with that pair moping around!'

'Well, as you yourself said, this is the situation you longed for your whole life,' said Hettie, returning to her embroidery. 'Not one, but *two* brave knights seeking your favour! Lucky you!'

There seemed to be a tinge of bitterness to Hettie's sarcastic humour, but Adhelina was too preoccupied to take much notice.

'No, Hettie,' she said sadly. 'This isn't the situation I longed for. I wanted to be courted while safe at home, with my father and his trusted retainers alive and well, in time of peace... War is upon us, and I've a nasty feeling it's all connected somehow to the theft in the Werecrypt.'

Hettie looked up from her embroidery. 'You mean that fragment thingy you mentioned, the one that was taken from beneath Graukolos? Why, our homeland is being put to the sword, and you concern yourself with old legends!'

'Well it makes more sense than concerning myself with a piece of stitched cloth, Hettie!' Adhelina felt her temper boiling over. Her mood swings had become more erratic of late.

'I'm doing embroidery precisely because our homeland is at war,' sighed her lady-in-waiting. 'What with that and everything we've been through, it's the only the thing that's keeping me sane.'

'Better that than quaffing, I suppose,' sighed Adhelina, though she poured herself another cup of wine. She hadn't succumbed to the Melancholy Sickness, but there was a tight pain in her gut that never went away. That, and a deep hole in her heart. Even now she couldn't bring herself to think of her father, or poor Berthal the seneschal. Had Graukolos fallen, she wondered? No, surely not so swiftly. The treacherous Lanraks had taken them by surprise, but she had to trust that Brigmore, the captain of the guards, would have acted quickly to secure the castle. Who knows, with an invading army from Pangonia marching into Vorstlund, the Lanraks and Markwards might be obliged to call a truce, to unite against a common foe... Perhaps it was for the best. Truly the Unseen worked in mysterious ways.

Her reverie was disturbed by the sound of crashing and yelling from the common room. Adhelina sighed. What now, she wondered?

The Pangonian freesword fell to the ground, blood spurting from his nose.

'That's *Sir* Wrackwulf to you,' said the Vorstlending knight, still holding the pewter flagon he had just used to break the freesword's nose. 'And to answer your question – no, I don't think I should be leaving Rima any time soon.'

The bloodied mercenary grovelled on the floorboards as his friend helped him up. A third freesword glared at Wrackwulf with hatred in his eyes. Reaching for his blade, he took a step forwards.

In an instant the flagon was on the floor and a dagger in Wrackwulf's hand instead. Vaskrian stepped up next to him and pulled his own dirk free. Anupe had already drawn her knife. The *Gilded Seagull* was a well-to-do hostelry, so full harness wasn't allowed in the common room. If it was going to kick off, it would be close work all the way. That suited Vaskrian just fine, of course.

'As you can see, it'll be three on three,' said Wrackwulf calmly, favouring the freeswords with a snaggle-toothed grin. 'As you're naught but churls with blades, I'm content to leave matters as they stand, having chastised your friend like the commoner he is. Take another step forward, and I shall consider the matter a duel of honour.' The freelancer glanced at his dagger meaningfully.

The freeswords exchanged uncertain glances before sizing up their opponents. The squire almost laughed. A motley band of foreign fighters but lately torn out of the wilderness, with blood on their hands and a haunted look in their eyes: not the usual types you'd pick a fight with in the taverns of Rima, if he had to guess.

The Pangonians looked at one another again, then turned abruptly and left. The other patrons, mostly master craftsmen and wealthy merchants with their bodyguards, turned back to their drinks and resumed conversations and dice games. No spectacle for them.

'And the foreigners have it!' cried Wrackwulf, banging the pommel of his dagger on the counter and calling loudly for more ale. Pangonian wine didn't sit well with him. Nor Vaskrian – getting drunk on the rich red liquid gave him horrendous bouts of the Drinking Sickness. Best to stick with what you knew.

Anupe muttered something to Wrackwulf as the two men got stuck into the frothing tankards of golden ale placed before them, then clicked her fingers for another stoup of wine. Clearly the Pangonian stuff didn't disagree with the Harijan.

'What's she saying?' asked Vaskrian, leaning in.

'That I should tread carefully and not talk so loudly,' said Wrackwulf. 'Seems like Vorstlendings aren't going to be welcome around here for a while.'

'Maybe she's right,' put in Vaskrian. 'And doesn't it bother you? I mean, it's your country about to be invaded.'

Wrackwulf shook his head. 'We Vorstlendings don't really view ourselves as a single country... more like a people, loosely bound by language and custom. And you forget, I'm a freelancer. That means I fight for the biggest purse. Our friend just now wasn't smart enough to see it, but any Pangonian lord would pay handsomely to have a seasoned fighter who knows the language and territory on his side.'

Vaskrian's eyes widened. 'You can't mean to betray your country?'

Wrackwulf laughed. 'When the Eorl of Ostveld went to war against the Eorl of Aslund eight years ago, I fought on the Ostvelding side – even though I've got blood ties to the Aslunders. Why? Because Eorl Ugrim paid better. That's the reality for a landless, lordless knight, Vaskrian – you follow the coin, always.'

'Then you really are just a freesword with a title,' spluttered the squire.

Wrackwulf considered that. 'Yes, I suppose so, if you want to look at it like that. Probably why I had no qualms about smiting that idiot just now. The likes of Torgun or Braxus wouldn't have even deigned to strike him, unless he was really threatening them. Then they would have been obliged to gut him like a pig where he stood.'

That made sense. Brawling was beneath a knight's dignity. Death duels on the other hand were perfectly acceptable.

'But you're a belted knight,' Vaskrian persisted. 'The Eorl of Aslund gave you spurs just like your father, even if he couldn't afford to keep you as a bachelor!'

Wrackwulf sighed. 'Perhaps I've spent over long rubbing shoulders with the dregs of society,' the burly knight conceded. Then he laughed and took another swig.

Vaskrian shrugged and took a deep draught himself. He couldn't understand how any knight could hold their title so lightly. Some folks didn't know they were born.

But at least the freelancer was cheerful. That was a lot more than could be said for his guvnor Sir Braxus. Vaskrian was beginning to grow weary of the Thraxian's bleak moods. So he'd lost his father and lands... That was hard, but warrior-lords were supposed to die in battle, and at least he'd had a title to lose in the first place. They hadn't trained at all since leaving the monastery. He'd had to practise on his own, in the hostelry courtyard. Still at least Sir Braxus didn't give him bollockings, like his old guvnor Sir Branas had. In fact, his master didn't seem to care much at all what he did nowadays, he'd just left Vaskrian to spend the past couple of nights drinking and whoring with Wrackwulf. By Reus, but Pangonian women were pretty fine, even if they were foreigners! Their harlots were just as haughty as the rest of them though. The one he'd lain with had made him feel like she was doing him a favour, before taking him between her legs. It had been worth it though. And what with Wrackwulf paying, he couldn't complain. Couldn't complain at all.

For no apparent reason, he suddenly thought of Hettie. She wasn't as pretty as the tavern doxy he'd bedded, but something in her soulful eyes had caught his own. Without quite knowing why, Vaskrian suddenly felt ashamed of what he'd been up to. He felt sure the prim Vorstlending lady-in-waiting wouldn't approve.

Wrackwulf nudged him in the elbow. 'Come on, let's finish these up and be going. Anupe wants to have a look at some of those whores we were telling her about.'

That surprised the squire. 'What? I thought her kind disapproved of women selling themselves for men.'

'They do,' clarified Wrackwulf, wiping froth from his beard. 'In her land, it's the other way around. But she's mourning a loved one... I think her desires lean in another direction.' The rotund knight winked. Anupe for her part leaned against the counter, calmly finishing her wine and looking around the common room, as if daring anyone to meet her eye. Vaskrian hadn't talked to her much – they were both still learning Decorlangue, making communication difficult, and in any case, he wasn't sure what to say to a woman who smelled of steel and leather.

Anupe turned to look at him and raised her empty cup meaningfully. Vaskrian had to admit, he almost felt afraid of the Harijan. Almost.

'Right,' he nodded, downing his stoup. 'Tavern wenches it is then.'

They were just on the point of leaving when the door was flung open. Vaskrian's heart sank as a group of mail-clad watchmen strode in. Behind them came the freesword with the bloody nose, his broken face breaking further into a scowl as he pointed them out. The serjeant-at-arms stepped up and said something in Panglian. Anupe and Vaskrian exchanged confused glances, but Wrackwulf looked cool enough as he answered in their tongue.

Whatever he was saying, it had better be good. There were half a dozen of them, plus the three freeswords. The watchmen's hauberks were of the best quality, and each one carried a stout sword at his belt. The richest city in the Free Kingdoms could afford to equip its common soldiers well, and Vaskrian did not doubt their training.

After a few words had been spoken, Wrackwulf translated. 'They are putting me under arrest,' he sighed. 'They want to assess whether I'll be a help or a hindrance in the coming war. They say I'll be taken to the palace and quartered according to my status as a knight. Can't see them lying – Pangonians are a haughty bunch, but honourable after their own fashion. So, this is farewell... for now anyway. Reus be with ye, lad, it was fun carousing and adventuring with thee!' The knight took Vaskrian in a bear-like hug. 'They say I can bring my things,' he said, walking towards the stairs to his room with a couple of guards in tow. 'Give my regards to Sir Braxus and Sir Torgun when you see them!'

He had just disappeared when Adhelina appeared from the courtyard. 'What on earth is going on?' she asked Vaskrian.

'Wrackwulf's been arrested,' he told her. 'Because he's from Vorstlund and there's going to be a war. They say he won't be treated–' The squire stopped in his tracks as he remembered who he was talking to.

The serjeant was eyeing them suspiciously. Stepping forward, he addressed Adhelina. The common guardsman clearly only spoke his native Panglian. The damsel kept her demeanour cool and collected as a noblewoman should, but even so Vaskrian could tell it wasn't going well.

He had to protect her. It's what his guvnor would want him to do. He was reaching for his dirk when he felt a light touch on his arm. Turning he saw Anupe, who shook her head. She had surreptitiously pulled the hood of her cloak up.

The watch captain was barking orders at his men. Two more now stepped over.

'He's realised I'm from Vorstlund too,' said Adhelina. 'He's decided to take us all into custody, says he doesn't like the look of any of us.'

Hettie had just entered the taproom. Adhelina turned to her and said something in Vorstlending. Hettie blinked, a look of dismay crumpling her pretty features. Vaskrian felt a hot flush course through him. All thoughts of wenching had gone.

She muttered something to her mistress in Vorstlending, but Adhelina shook her head firmly. Resignedly, Hettie went upstairs, presumably to pack their things.

Anupe found time to whisper something to him in stilted Decorlangue.

'We go with them,' she said. 'Say nothing. Our friends find us.'

The squire nodded reluctantly. 'Tell the guards I need to get my things too,' he told Adhelina. She complied and the captain nodded, gesturing curtly upstairs as he sent another watchman to escort him.

Climbing the rickety wooden steps, Vaskrian couldn't help but feel excited. Maybe it was the beer addling his wits, but the Palace of White Towers seemed for all the world like a distinct improvement on a hostelry. He just hoped they didn't end up quartered in the dungeons.

CHAPTER 6
ANOTHER REUNION WITH OLD FRIENDS

The past few weeks had felt surreal. At times, Adelko almost convinced himself that his mighty adventure had never happened: the North Wind had simply taken him in its cold embrace, and swept him from Ulfang to Rima. The regime at the Most Reverend Priory of St Argo was much the same as that of Ulfang: prayers, more prayers, study and classes. He even had a bunk in a dormitory just like before, this time in South House. Some of the other novices there claimed South House was special, because it abutted on to the main entrance and faced in the direction of the Redeemer's birthplace in Ushalayim. The rivalries between houses were no different here either.

The main difference, besides the climate, was the size of the place. A single quarter of the monastery's outer enclosure was bigger than the whole of Ulfang. It made Adelko dizzy. Graukolos and the Warlock's Crown were comparable, but he'd been passing through those places; they were just milestones on his great journey. This was a place he would call home, for the foreseeable future. There were five hundred novices, from all over the Free Kingdoms, high-born and low. Some of them were as young as six or seven summers, but then the Order wasn't strict about what age one joined at – latent psychic talent was still talent. A few were adults, mostly crusading knights who had returned from the Pilgrim Kingdoms and forsaken lance for lectern. Just like his erstwhile mentor.

He had barely seen Horskram since their arrival at the monastery. Only at mealtimes had he caught so much as a glimpse of him, when he ate with Hannequin, the archmasters and six score other adepts on the raised dais in the middle of the refectory. At such times Adelko was generally too busy trying to follow the banter of other novices, or studying the statues lining the wall to pay his mentor much attention. They weren't set into alcoves like the ones at Ulfang, but friezes flush to the walls, painted to seem more lifelike. Adelko's roving eye had soon found St Ionus. The avatar of travellers was next to Gaspian, the stern-faced patrician saint of Rima who had defected to Palom's side during his rebellious wars against the Thalamians. The former general had earned his martyrdom when he was executed by the legion he had deserted. St Gaspian didn't look too happy about that, dressed in his intricate plate armour, with stylised entrails spilling from a gaping wound in his side. As at Ulfang, St Ionus was the only statue with a smile on his lips.

Only now the smile seemed to be mocking Adelko, as if to say *I gave you more than you bargained for, didn't I?*

Besides the refectory, the only other important building

in the inner enclosure Adelko had been inside was the library.

The library! Set on three storeys, one of them underground, it was by far his favourite part of the monastery. Ulfang's had been impressive for having hundreds of tomes; St Argo's had *thousands*. When the master librarian Bertram had shown him and another clutch of fresh novices around, he had gaped his way through the tour. Each level was lined with carrels for studying and shelves crammed with books, scrolls of vellum and parchment, and even some papyri from Sendhé. Many of them dated back to the Golden Age, treatises written in Decorlangue by the great loremasters and sages of the Thalamian Empire. Journeymen and adepts could be seen climbing great wheeled wooden contraptions to reach the books on the upper levels of each floor, and the basement was given over to the scriptorium, where monks sat illuminating manuscripts sometimes long into the night. The first and second floors were broad galleries overlooking it, and at the summit of the building was a stained-glass window depicting life scenes of the Redeemer. The giant circular pane of multicoloured glass refracted the sunlight in a myriad hues, giving the place an otherworldly feel. Adelko knew the holy houses of the Orthodox Temple in the Empire were famed for their stained glasswork, and could only wonder at the staggering price such an expensive import must have fetched.

But if Adelko had hoped to delve into the library's secrets, he was soon disabused of that notion. For Brother Bertram told the new arrivals sternly that they were not to be admitted except during study periods, and only then with permission. If he was to complete his tutelage here, he had time for patience he supposed. In a year or so, he would begin studying for his initiation as a journeyman of the Order. Then he could explore the library to his heart's content.

The other novices treated him with a mixture of curiosity and awe. Word of his adventures with the legendary Horskram soon spread, though Adelko remained tight-lipped. His experiences had changed him: no longer did he seek to regale with tales of his wanderings through the world. He had looked across the mortal vale at the Other Side, and something truly dark had touched his soul.

If that had sobered his temperament, it had also strengthened him. Always among the best students, now he excelled beyond all his age and most older novices, too. His new tutors were visibly impressed by his prowess at counter-demonology and exorcism, and his knowledge of lore advanced with a swiftness that left his cohort astonished. Within a few short weeks at the monastery, his knowledge of Decorlangue and Panglian went from proficient to fluent. Adelko was always cordial and polite, but couldn't deny his growing powers kept him aloof from the others. He mostly kept to himself, seeking the solace of the library whenever he could get it.

Truth to tell, he didn't feel at all comfortable with his newfound superiority, and the one exception didn't bring him much comfort either. After all his experiences with demonkind, draugar, gaunts, fays, elementi and wadwos, Adelko was still a near hopeless fighter.

Quarterstaff classes were taught by Brother Edemus, a

taciturn Thalamian in early middling years. One morning, early in his fourth week at St Argo's, Adelko was lying flat on his back after yet another drubbing when the journeyman walked over to him. The early autumn sun was shining high in a clear blue sky, providing ample opportunity for the other novices to view his ritual humiliation.

'Adelko, sit out the remainder of the class and observe the others,' said Edemus. 'I will speak with you afterwards.' The Thalamian's expression never changed: whether giving praise or criticism or simply instructing, his tanned face always looked the same.

Gloomily Adelko did as he was told. He already sensed that other novices liked to be paired with him: the one opportunity they got to show up the strange newcomer. Frankly he didn't care what they thought. It was more the knowledge that his quarterstaff technique wasn't getting any better that bothered him.

When class was dismissed Edemus walked over to him.

'The problem lies with your footwork,' explained the journeyman. 'A fighter unsteady on his feet is like a castle built on poor foundations – no matter how high you build the walls, it will always come crashing down. Get up.'

Adelko made to reach for his quarterstaff, but Edemus shook his head. 'No more staves. Not until you master your footwork. Assume basic stance.'

Adelko did as ordered. The monk stepped in close and adjusted his feet with his own before straightening his shoulders. 'There, that's better,' he said. 'Now, I'm going to call out commands and you will obey them to the letter. Do you understand?'

'Yes,' said Adelko, though his guts were churning. Strange how fighting class could still horrify him after everything he had been through.

'Good,' said Edemus. 'Now – forwards! That's it! Forwards! Backwards-backwards! Crouch! Step left...'

They went on like that for almost an hour, until Adelko's legs were stiff and sore. He felt as though he were on the road again. But Edemus still wasn't done.

'Over to yon stables,' he said, motioning towards the buildings abutting the outer wall. Adelko trudged over achingly, the monk saying nothing as he accompanied him.

Edemus reached up and tapped the lintel of the stable doors with his quarterstaff. 'I want you to jump up and grab this – then hang there. Don't try to pull yourself up, just hold the position until I tell you to release.'

Adelko groaned inwardly as he complied. By the time Edemus told him to let go, he was groaning outwardly, too.

'For all your travels, you're still physically weak,' said Edemus, in the same neutral voice. 'We need to build up your coordination and stamina. From now on, we will train every morning after dawn prayers, save for Rest-days. I'll have Brother Gustaff keep breakfast for you in the scullery, but from now on you'll have to earn it! Palom's wounds, but I'll make a fighter out of you yet. Dismissed.'

Adelko trudged back towards where his quarterstaff lay on the clay, feeling even gloomier than he had done at the beginning of class.

He was just returning his staff to the rack when the sound of horses alerted him to new arrivals at the monastery. Turning he saw four monks ride in under the gatehouse, before nudging their steeds towards the stables where he had just been exercising. They were too far away to make out in detail, but the brown and grey habits told of two novices accompanied by a pair of adepts or journeymen.

His sixth sense told him there was something familiar about the younger monks.

The extra training with Edemus had eaten into most of his study period; he still had ten minutes or so before the noonday meal. Walking back over to the stables, Adelko saw the four monks dismount and hand their horses over to the novice on stabling duty.

The two novices turned to look at him as he approached. It took Adelko a few seconds to register that it was really them.

'Hargus and Arik!' he gaped. 'I can't believe it! What in the Known World are you doing here?!'

His old friends from Ulfang looked much the same for being half a year older. Hargus still had the round pale face and big yellow teeth that made him look so comical. Dark-haired Arik was slightly taller at sixteen summers, but had the same quietly confident demeanour.

Both monks grinned broadly as they recognised him.

'Adelko!' exclaimed Arik. 'We could ask the same of you! Seven seraphs, but how long have you been here?'

'Just a few weeks,' replied Adelko, still scarcely able to

believe his eyes. 'I arrived here with Master Horskram at the end of last month.'

'And how is the crabby old friar?' beamed Hargus, before dropping into one of his impressions. "I trust, young Adelko, that your adventures have been a *sobering* affair."

That had the three of them laughing, though Adelko felt slightly queasy at the mention of his adventures. There was so much he wouldn't be able to tell his friends.

One of the journeymen came over and nodded curtly at Adelko. He recognised Brother Alrich from Ulfang.

'Adelko, good to see you well and whole,' said the journeyman, before glancing at the other two. 'Five minutes and no more – we're just in time for the noonday meal.'

'Yes, Master Alrich,' the two novices chorused as the journeyman stalked off to unpack his saddlebags.

'We both got seconded,' explained Arik. 'We've spent the past three months on the road. Terrible business about the civil war back home.'

'We passed through the Argael to get here,' added Hargus. 'Prior Aedric at Ørthang said you'd gone that way and something about a war of witches, though it was quiet enough by the time we travelled through.'

If only you knew, Adelko thought ruefully. 'What about Dulsinor?' he asked. 'There was a war starting there too, when we passed through it.'

Arik nodded. 'The Stornelendings have Graukolos invested,' he confirmed. 'They hadn't taken it when we passed by, but they've ravaged the lands about. Remnants of the Markward knights have been fighting hit-and-run skirmishes with the Lanraks. We saw some horrendous sights, Adelko.' He made the sign dutifully.

'I know,' said Adelko sadly. 'War is horrible. I saw our King defeat the Young Pretender, too. It isn't at all glorious like they make it out to be in the lays.'

His friends stared at him. 'You've seen an awful lot haven't you, Adelko?' asked Arik. Adelko could feel him probing him with his sixth sense. He had forgotten how competitive his friend could be.

'But anyway, you've both arrived here in one piece,' Adelko said, quickly changing the subject. 'That's the main thing!'

'Well, we had a few close shaves, what with all the robber knights and freeswords knocking about, and we've had a lot of work besides,' said Arik. 'The Rent Between Worlds has been widening, but then I'm sure you know that. Our mentors had to look in on quite a few villages. We've taken part in exorcisms – we even fought off a gale-force invasion of Aethi in Westenlund!'

Adelko could sense his friend's pride waxing. If only he knew how much his own adventures would put theirs to shame, but right now drawing comparisons with Arik was the last thing he wanted to do. Besides, he was too overjoyed to see his friends really to care about who had done what.

'How long will you be staying?' he asked enthusiastically.

'A few weeks at least, possibly longer,' said Arik. 'Our mentors need to report to the Grand Master, so we'll probably be reassigned here for tutelage in the interim.'

'That's great news!' said Adelko. Then a sudden thought struck him. 'What happened to Yalba?' It seemed peculiar for the three of them to be reunited without their loud-mouthed fellow novice from Ulfang.

Arik and Hargus exchanged rueful glances.

'He failed his entrance test to become a journeyman,' said Hargus. 'After that he got caught pinching more of Sholto's scrumpy. They expelled him from the Order. Last I heard, he was seeking to be ordained in the mainstream Temple.'

'Probably the best thing for him,' said Arik, with a hint of contempt. 'He always did lack discipline.'

'And if the Temple won't have him, I'm sure he could get a job as a freesword,' said Hargus brightly.

The three of them laughed again. Adelko was sorry for his friend – but not that sorry. Yalba had always been a lout and a bully, truth be told. He wasn't cut out for the Order, Adelko's travels had taught him that much.

He felt so happy to see his old friends again, it took him a while to realise they were hiding something.

'What is it?' he asked tentatively as his sixth sense needled him. 'Why so glum? We'll be cohorts again – maybe they'll put you in South House, too!'

Hargus and Arik exchanged nervous glances.

'What is it?' he pressed. 'Surely you don't have more bad news? What is it, has old Sholto choked on his scrumpy?'

Arik bit his lip. 'No... actually, he died. And so did a lot of people.'

'What?'

Hargus reluctantly took up the thread. 'About a month before we left, there was an outbreak of the Wasting Sickness. Spread across the Highlands, you know how bad these epidemics can be, and we hadn't had one in years...'

'A lot of the older monks didn't survive,' Arik went on. 'Calistrum, Silas, even Lordqvist the apothecary...'

Adelko's heart sank. He had spent so long fighting warlocks and elementi and evil spirits, he had almost forgotten about the diseases Ma'alfecnu'ur inflicted on mortalkind.

'What about Sacristen?' he asked. Surely the old prior couldn't be dead too...

'No, he survived,' said Arik. 'The Almighty must have been keeping an eye on him.' He made the sign again.

'It didn't even spoil his appetite,' quipped Hargus. 'He's so fat now he can barely stand.'

They laughed again, but it was hollow, sad laughter now.

His friends still looked downcast. Brother Alrich was ordering them to hurry up and help him carry some bags.

'What is it?' asked Adelko. His sixth sense was still needling him uncomfortably.

'We had news from villages in the area, not long before we left,' faltered Hargus. 'Adelko, your father... he didn't survive the sickness.'

The words felt like lead weights dragging him down. His aching limbs were forgotten as he felt a hole open up in his heart.

'Adelko, we... we have to go,' said Arik uneasily. 'Sorry to leave you in the lurch like this but...'

'We thought you should know right away,' said Hargus. He laid a kindly hand on Adelko's arm. 'He must have seen near fifty winters, Adelko. That's not a bad tally for one of our folk.'

That was true enough: highland life was harsh. But it didn't stop the hole from growing wider, a great pit of numbness that beckoned Adelko downwards.

His two friends bade him an awkward farewell. He watched them follow their mentors towards the inner enclosure. Hot tears suddenly limned his eyes, stinging them and contrasting oddly with the inner numbness he felt. He thought of Adhelina and Braxus. They had recently lost their fathers; now he had, too. Adelko had not seen his for five years, and never would again – not in this world at any rate.

As the bell tolled for the noonday meal, Adelko shut his eyes tightly, and prayed for his lost father's soul.

CHAPTER 7
A QUEST RENEWED

'Whoever was countermanding our divination, it wasn't Wolaf – or Cathbad.' Hannequin frowned as he tapped his fingers thoughtfully against his lips. He was staring out of the window of his chamber at the deepening grey skies. Another Rest-day had been and gone; another divination had revealed nothing more. Horskram stared across the inner enclosure, its warm sandstone at odds with the leaden clouds that permeated the skies. Ripanmonath was drawing to a close, and the long southern summer was over. The adept fancied the autumnal gloom presaged darker times.

'Have you spoken with him – Cathbad I mean?' Horskram could not bring himself to believe the mild-mannered Thraxian guilty of anything. Initially he hadn't trusted him any more than Gabrien, but over the years he had become convinced of the sincerity of his repentance.

Hannequin turned and sighed. 'Only but briefly. I've been busy trying to fend off His Supreme Holiness. Cyprian is calling for another investigation against our Order, following the revelation of the fragment theft from Ulfang chapter. When he isn't busy preparing for the next Pilgrim War, that is. I've had to visit the palace in person, to persuade the King not to listen to him.'

'What is His Majesty's view on the matter?'

'You were right about Carolus being less pious than his father was. He has agreed to intervene on our behalf and put pressure on Cyprian not to sanction another Purge – for now. In return, he expects us to be silent on the matter of the new crusade.'

'We have ever stood neutral on such matters,' said Horskram, trying to ignore the dark memories mention of crusading brought up. 'That shouldn't be a problem.'

'It isn't,' said Hannequin. 'Just as long as no one learns a demon was bound to one of our most senior members. If that gets out, the King will have no choice but to let Cyprian have his way.'

Horskram's old torture wounds throbbed as he asked: 'What did Cathbad say when you interrogated him?'

'I didn't interrogate him,' replied the Grand Master sharply. 'Because as you well know, an interrogation of any suspect witch cannot be conducted alone. But to answer your question, he reiterated his innocence, though he confessed that his former knowledge of sorcery might have helped him sense something was amiss when Wolaf began acting strangely.'

Horskram had been wondering about that. A binding worked differently to a possession. It made the demon harder to detect and less susceptible to holy powers – had he not already been attuned to Belaach's spoor and known his name, casting him out would have been the work of days, even for the best of the Order.

'And Wolaf's remains?'

'Adamantus and Edelmir inspected them thoroughly before disposing of them,' said Hannequin, his aristocratic features curling. 'The markings on his corpse were certainly in the Sorcerer's Script, though it's impossible to tell when they were tattooed. He could have been infiltrating us for months, perhaps even years.'

Horskram's sixth sense picked up on the tension in the Grand Master. Though outwardly calm as ever, he was deeply perturbed.

'Then we must act on the knowledge we have,' said the adept. 'Wolaf, or Belaach, was trying to persuade us to do nothing. So it would make sense to do just the opposite.'

Hannequin nodded thoughtfully. 'I think your suggestion to send a party north with the protection of St Argo is a good one,' he said. 'I suppose you will head south, to the Pilgrim Kingdoms?'

'I don't see who else would do it, by your leave of course, Grand Master.' Hannequin's elan was perhaps more powerful than his own, and his lore surpassed all in the Order. It wouldn't surprise Horskram entirely if he undertook to make the voyage himself, especially given his familiarity with the Pilgrim Kingdoms.

'No, my place is here,' sighed Hannequin, reading his thoughts. 'Playing politics with kings and perfects while the real battle for the world falls to others. My days of representing the Order in person abroad came to an end as soon as this calamity revealed itself, but that I'm afraid is the responsibility I assumed with the position. Brother Horskram, you have served us well enough so far – though at times your recklessness borders on sheer folly!'

Horskram allowed himself a slight smile. Behind the Grand Master's sternness was a genuine kindness and trust. Hannequin had vouched for him a long time ago, when he had first asked to join the Order. Not all approved of admitting former knights and soldiers with blood on their hands. But Hannequin had recognised Horskram's sincerity and psychic talent, counselling forgiveness and nurturing. The adept was eternally grateful to him for that. That was why it pained him to sense how troubled his old friend and mentor was.

'I shall endeavour to learn from my past mistakes,' the adept said humbly. 'Though the mission will be reckless in itself – seeking out Abdel Sha'arza in his sorcerous lair and asking him to help me locate the final fragment is sheer folly as it is.'

Hannequin returned the wry smile as he got up to light a hanging lantern against the twilight. They had already decided that any fact-finding mission to Sassania concerning the whereabouts of the fragment borne there by the boy Cael would have to include a consultation with its most powerful known warlock. 'It is a dangerous gambit,' Hannequin allowed, 'but we have to hope we've guessed rightly that Sha'arza isn't mad enough to covet the Headstone's power.'

'Even though he is mad enough to live in a Watchtower and practise Left-Handed magic,' said Horskram, shaking his head. 'And I thought seeking an alliance with the Earth Witch was unpleasant enough.'

'Reus sees all and notes your sacrifice,' said Hannequin piously. 'The Redeemer shall guide you in flesh and spirit, and the prayers of the Order you shall have daily.'

'I thank you,' said Horskram, and meant it. If his next madcap mission was to succeed, he would need all the prayers he could get.

'At least we have solved one riddle,' Hannequin went on. 'The Five that Belaach referred to when you first exorcised him are not the five tiers of Gehenna, but the four fragments of the Headstone and the Grimoire needed to activate them.'

'Yes, but we've still no idea who "Hell's Prophet" is,' replied Horskram, following the thread of the demon's obscure prophecy. 'I hope for my sake it isn't Abdel Sha'arza!'

'As do I,' said Hannequin. 'Thanks to my contacts in the Pilgrim Kingdoms, I can at least ensure that your mission gets off to a good start in Ushalayim. But we can talk about that later. In the meantime, I sense you have something to say about the other expedition.'

Nothing escaped Hannequin. Or not until recently anyway. His sixth sense was sharper than anyone else's in the Order. Whoever had snuck in a bound demon right under the Grand Master's nose had to be an astonishingly accomplished warlock. A warlock with a grimoire written by the Elder Wizards at his disposal.

'Yes, I wanted to talk about it,' confirmed Horskram. 'As discussed, we should send Sir Torgun on an expeditionary force to the Westerling Isles. Perhaps the other knight Sir

Braxus can be persuaded to accompany him – his way lies home now in any case, and that lies on the way. The freelancer whose help I enlisted might also be persuaded to go with them, for more coin.'

Hannequin raised an eyebrow as he sat back down. He hadn't approved of dipping into monastery funds to pay Sir Wrackwulf.

'We may have further need of his services,' pressed Horskram. 'And he already has some inkling of what's at stake, after his experiences on the Draugmoors.'

'If those experiences don't prompt him to flee for the hills clutching his full money purse,' countered Hannequin wryly.

'He's enjoying the fleshpots of Rima, last I heard,' said Horskram. 'So his money purse will run empty soon enough, don't you worry. But that isn't the only thing I wanted to suggest.'

Hannequin didn't seem entirely surprised. 'Go on,' he said.

'Wolaf wanted us to stay here and do nothing – presumably our sorcerous mastermind put him up to saying such a thing. Ask yourself why. We already know Abrexta is planning an invasion of the Island Realms, and that she was connected to Andragorix.'

'The Earth Witch said as much,' Hannequin recalled. 'Go on.'

'So evidently our master mage wants to catch the druids and marcher lords unawares, to maximise his or her chances of attaining the third fragment.'

'Indeed – and why are you pointing out the obvious?'

'Because... we should try to do just the opposite. Something our mystery warlock would never expect us to do...'

Hannequin's eyes gleamed in the glow of the lantern light. Horskram had his attention.

'What if we were to send Sir Torgun with an expeditionary force, not only to warn the island druids of the pending invasion and plot to reunite the Headstone – but also to persuade them to part with it?'

Hannequin gaped. 'Have you taken leave of your senses? The druidic synod would never consent to that in a thousand years – and even if they did, where would you have it brought?'

Horskram shrugged his shoulders. 'Here. Where the Order can keep it under watchful eye.'

'Are you mad? Here, where we've just been infiltrated by a demonologist whose identity we still don't know... What makes you think it would be any safer than the first fragment was at Ulfang?'

'We were caught unawares at Ulfang,' said Horskram. 'After so many centuries, we had grown complacent. Who is to say it is not the same with the druids? And if our original plan works, we may well have drawn our warlock out of the shadows by the time Sir Torgun reaches the islands. We could kill two birds with one stone – eliminate the warlock and have the fragment in our safekeeping. Put it under guard with the Circifix of St Argo, aye and the Redeemer's blood if need be, and make sure we never grow complacent again!'

'And what if our mystery warlock doesn't fall for our trick, and still remains at large?' argued Hannequin. 'We would be bringing the fragment back to a very viper's nest!'

'So what did you have in mind for the fourth fragment, should I succeed in finding it? Just leave it with an undead boy in the middle of the desert? Wolaf's binding has us all on the back foot, but we can't just abdicate our responsibility! Both remaining fragments should be brought back here, if possible. Then you will have something to take to the Supreme Perfect, next time he accuses the Order of dereliction of its duties.'

Hannequin sat back, deep in thought. Horskram sensed something within him... some elation perhaps. Had he struck at the heart of the matter? The Grand Master was a great disciple of St Argo, but he was also a wily politician. If the Order was seen to recover one or two fragments it would claw back a lot of lost reputation.

'I still think it's a huge gamble to take,' he said presently.

'Only the brave shall reap the rewards of courage, as the prophet sayeth,' returned Horskram.

Hannequin nodded slowly. 'All right,' he said. 'It's worth a try at least. Your brave knights will be passing through Thraxia – I will give them a letter of introduction, to Brother Joram of Kilucan. No doubt you will have heard of him – one of our stronger adepts, if somewhat impassioned at times. He's our chief witchfinder in that country, and has long studied the ways of the Westerlings – perhaps he can be of some help in this mission. But mark this, Brother Horskram, even if I do send your men to the Island Realms with a relic and Brother Joram in tow, I seriously doubt the druids will consent to let them take the fragment.'

'Probably not,' Horskram allowed with a sigh. 'But we have to try. And if they say no, at least they will be forewarned against any theft attempts, assuming they haven't already been robbed by the time our expedition force gets there.'

'We'll just have to trust the druids to keep their eyes peeled a while longer,' said Hannequin, reaching towards a pewter decanter and pouring Horskram a cup of wine. 'Brother Elias says your companions are recovering, but will need further prayers on Rest-days for a while yet. By the time they are fit to travel, winter will have come to the Sea of Tanagorm. So the journey to the Westerling Isles will have to wait until spring in any case.'

'Sir Braxus may want to leave for Thraxia before then though,' put in Horskram. 'That's a sea journey that can be made in autumn.'

Hannequin nodded as he pushed the cup over to Horskram, before helping himself to some cow's milk. 'That is of course his prerogative. Perhaps your champion can be persuaded to accompany him. If Sir Torgun helps him with the war on the mainland, there's a chance the Thraxian will repay him in kind when the seas thaw come spring.'

Horskram shifted uneasily. The two knights had been at loggerheads over that blasted damsel for weeks. Courtly love – even when a knight, he'd scarcely understood it.

'I shall see what I can do to convince them both to help one another,' he said diplomatically, 'and the Vorstlending knight as well. In the meantime, I had better be making plans to journey to the Pilgrim Kingdoms–'

Hannequin cut him off. 'Yes well, I'd been meaning to

talk to you about that part of the plan,' he said. 'I think you should delay your journey, too.'

Horskram blinked. 'Why? Time is of the essence surely?'

'I do not like the idea of you going alone,' said Hannequin. 'This is too dangerous a venture.'

Horskram frowned. 'You want to assign another brother... I understand, but why the need for a delay?'

'Because the monk I have in mind will be perfect for the job – when he's ready.'

Horskram puzzled that over. Then his eyes widened as he realised. 'You can't mean–'

'I have found some time to observe him since he joined the monastery,' said the Grand Master. 'Your faith in the youth is not misplaced. His elan is strong, more powerful than any I have felt in a lad his age. And his knowledge of your mission is intimate – it would save having to risk telling anyone else the full story. And this business with Wolaf underscores just how little we can afford to trust anyone right now.'

'But Adelko is far too tender in years for such a mission,' protested Horskram. 'In fact he should never have been embroiled in it to start with, it was only by accident–'

'No Horskram,' said Hannequin, interrupting again. 'The boy is a hierophant, there is no doubting it. He may even be as potent as Malthus of Montrevellyn.'

'Malthus' powers drove him mad because he used them too soon,' said Horskram. 'He sought the Fays in Tintagael at the Redeemer's behest, or so he believed!'

'Those same Fays Adelko – and you – survived,' pressed Hannequin. 'Those same Fays who pronounced him the greatest of his kind – you said yourself this is what the Faerie Kings meant when they spoke to you in prophecy.'

'Aye, that's true,' Horskram allowed. 'But he isn't ready yet! Hannequin, for Reus' sake, he's but a novice!'

'Right now, yes,' said Hannequin. 'But in time, and no great time at that... I've already instructed Brother Edemus to bring him up to speed on combat training.'

'Why did you not tell me of this?'

'Because as Grand Master it's my business what I do with novices under my charge, and you are no longer his mentor, remember?' A rare hint of steel had entered Hannequin's voice.

'I am sorry, Grand Master, pray forgive me for speaking out of turn. But still I must insist–'

Hannequin shook his head. 'Already his powers by far surpass the best novices we have here, at the largest chapter in our Order. He even puts some of our journeymen to shame. No, I'll have Edemus knock him into shape physically, as he continues to hone the rest of his talents. Come springtime, he'll be ready to accompany you.'

'But he's only just seen fifteen summers!'

'Greatness comes even unto the young, as the prophet sayeth. Horskram, by the time we're finished with him, Adelko will be a journeyman, ready to undertake his first official mission at his mentor's side. I haven't been Grand Master all these years to ignore a gift from Reus when it's placed right in front of me! Adelko is a tool, sent to forge us a path through dark times to come. In the meantime you can wait out the winter here, and try to help me get to the bottom of this mess with Wolaf. If we haven't apprehended our master warlock by then, we proceed with the plan as discussed.' Hannequin drained his cup. 'I consider this the end of the matter. I have listened to your counsel and like it well, now it behoves you to do me the same courtesy.'

The wine tasted bitter on Horskram's tongue as he took a sip. He could not deny the Grand Master's logic, but even so he felt unhappy. Adelko had already been through far too much for one of his years. He would for all the world have given the lad time to mature more fully into his powers.

But the world rarely gave one enough time.

'So be it,' he said resignedly, before draining his own cup.

Just as he did, a small bell tolled in the corner of the chamber. It was connected to the ground floor of the sanctum by an ancient mechanism; it allowed the Grand Master to be alerted to visitors without having the sanctity of his quarters disturbed.

Hannequin raised an eyebrow. 'A messenger on the eve of sunset prayers,' he muttered. 'It must be a matter of some urgency.'

The two monks exited the Grand Master's private suite. Descending winding flights of stairs, they emerged into a mosaicked antechamber on the ground floor. There they found Brother Elias, standing by a series of ropes, each one ending in a plaque inscribed with the names of the Grand Master and six archmasters.

'What ails thee, brother?' asked Hannequin. 'Can't it wait till after prayers?'

'It concerns the patients we treated but lately,' replied Elias. 'The ones travelling with Brother Horskram.'

'What of them?' asked Horskram, his sixth sense tingling uncomfortably.

Elias frowned. 'They didn't turn up for treatment yesterday, so I thought it best to send a journeyman into town to inquire. He only just returned. The innkeeper told him one of them, the Vorstlending knight Sir Wrackwulf, was involved in a tavern brawl. This caught the attention of the watch, and they arrested him.'

Horskram cursed. 'I should have known that rakehell sot couldn't be trusted to behave himself!'

Hannequin glanced at him sidelong. 'This is the knight who you were suggesting might help us out?' he asked pointedly.

'I'm afraid this isn't the only bad news I bring,' Elias went on. 'When the watch captain realised the damsels were from Vorstlund too, he arrested them as well. I believe he took the squire Vaskrian and the warrior-woman Anupe with them for good measure.'

'That'll be the King's blasted new war against Vorstlund,' said Horskram. 'He'll want to hold them for information, or even to use for ransom money. What about the other two? Sir Torgun and Sir Braxus?'

'The innkeeper said they left in a hurry shortly before the fight broke out. But a few days later servants and guards from the palace came by with instructions to pick up their things. Apparently they've been arrested, too.'

'But why?' quizzed Horskram. 'They aren't from Vorstlund and they weren't there when the brawl took place.'

'According to the rumours, they were apprehended out

of town.' Brother Elias licked his lips delicately. 'They were caught climbing the Athos Colossi... Something about a courtly love challenge.'

Horskram had to resist the urge to slap his own forehead. Hannequin stared at him, half amused and half amazed.

'These are the men you would pick for our task?'

'Do you know where they are now?' he asked, ignoring the Grand Master.

'As far as we can tell, they are all being held at the Palace of White Towers, detained at the King's pleasure. I should send a party of adepts to continue their treatment, by your leave Grand Master. The Draugbreath is a powerful curse, and the after-blessings should not be neglected.'

'Yes, yes,' said Hannequin impatiently. 'Have it done right away. Thank you for informing us.'

Elias nodded and left the antechamber.

'Well, Brother Horskram, it seems we may need to reconsider our northern expedition party,' said Hannequin.

Horskram stood and thought a while. 'No,' he said. 'They might be reckless and unruly, but they've proven their mettle ere now. Like as not, the King will hold onto the damsels but can be persuaded to let the knights go. I shall visit him in person, by your leave.'

Hannequin sighed. 'You have it, though as you know His Majesty is a notoriously stubborn and self-seeking monarch. He knows of our business, but cares little for things that do not concern his own worldly affairs.'

'The quest for the Headstone fragments concerns all worldly affairs,' Horskram pointed out.

'Oh, I know that,' said Hannequin, 'but it is the King you will have to convince.'

Horskram let out a sigh of his own as the bell in the yard began tolling for sunset prayers. Thoughts buzzed around his head as the two of them exited the inner sanctum and trudged over to the chapel. The silhouetted monastery walls loomed above and around them, doing little to lift his flagging spirits.

Truly it was said an Argolian's work was never done.

CHAPTER 8
WHEN WARLOCKS SCRY

Abrexta's face looked anxious in the shimmering silver plate. Ragnar could understand why. He did not envy the sorceress her position.

'The swords of the south are flocking to the resistance banners,' she said. 'They could put as many as a thousand knights in the field – there must be something you can do!'

Ragnar remained unmoved. 'If the Master cannot help you then I certainly can't,' he said. 'We have but lately consolidated the Principalities under my sister's rule, and just begun to construct our war fleet. You have the northern wards of Thraxia and the highlanders in your thrall – that should be sufficient. Crush this rebellion, and see your battle-hardened veterans take to the waves on the ships you have built come spring.'

'If only it were that easy,' Abrexta frowned. 'The lords of Tul Aeren, Garro and Penllyn have invaded Garth. They've taken Port Craek and set up a regional government there.

We've sent an army to halt them in their tracks, but they are proving... remarkably resilient.'

'Perhaps it would help if you hadn't killed all the King's marshals,' suggested Ragnar helpfully. 'I'm sure you could use some good generals right now.'

The witch's beautiful face looked ugly in its sudden rage. 'Did you expect me to enthral everyone?'

'No, in fact I was hoping you'd have the sense to rely less upon your powers of Enchantment and resort to old-fashioned diplomacy and intrigue. Valuable men that could have been won over have been lost to your petulant whims – now you will have to manage without them.'

Abrexta struggled to master her emotions. 'Very well, White Eye, I'll just have to manage without any help from you either.'

'Indeed,' confirmed Ragnar. 'Remember that we both report directly to the Master now. And he does not tolerate failure.'

Ragnar mouthed the closing words of the spell, and Abrexta's face disappeared into running quicksilver. Rising from the table holding the mirror, he took up his trident and exited the chamber. It was cold in the palace at Landarök, but that did not bother him. His trident echoed through the corridor as it tapped against the rude stones of the floor. His people were not renowned for their stonemasonry, but all that would change once the Master succeeded in reuniting the Headstone. Then the power of the Elder Wizards would be reborn, and Logi would return to Middangeard once more. All of His servants would share in His glory then.

Ragnar was not surprised to have replaced his erstwhile

superior. Though his elan had been more powerful, Andragorix had ever been an unwieldy instrument, volatile and unpredictable. The Thraxian witch was cut from a similar cloth: she let her emotions rule far too often. Ragnar had been content to bide his time, suffering the warlock's scorn silently. Now Andragorix was dead, while Ragnar lived on to see the Master's plans come to fruition.

The great fire pit was burning in the centre of the hall. His sister was sat upon the Stone of Thoros. It had been hewn from the Fenris Mountains by the Lord of Skies, in the Age of Gods and Heroes, when deities had walked an earth made anew after the Ragnarök brought down upon it by the Elder Wizards. Thoros had brought the stone here to Landarök, thousands of years ago, and set it down in the earth.

His sister looked slight enough perching on the giant chunk of ebon stone. The pine throne that rested upon it likewise looked a poor successor to the age-old might of the gods. Magnhilda had been approved Magna of the Frozen Wastes after her husband's tragic death, in accordance with custom. Some of Guldebrand's followers had muttered darkly after he had fallen to his doom from a high palace window on their wedding night, but none had dared try their luck. They could never prove the foul play they suspected, and who could possibly know his half-sister had learned basic Enchantment at his feet? Ensorcelling Guldebrand and ordering him to take his own life in a drunken stupor had been all too easy for Magnhilda. All too easy... thanks to Ragnar's teachings.

A party of thegns knelt between the firepit and stone

throne. So the Skjel islanders had arrived to pay fealty at last. That was well. Ragnar surreptitiously took up his position by the throne, as his sister bade the men rise.

'Welcome, lords of Skjel,' she intoned, her high clear voice reverberating around the hall. 'And what is your verdict? Shall there be more war amongst our people, or shall we unite and carve an empire from the flanks of the mainland?'

'We have held an All-thing to decide the matter,' replied the lead islander, Ravek Hrorson. He was the tallest and oldest of the party. His braided hair and beard were as white as the snows that even now swathed the Fenris Mountains far to the north. 'Our allegiance you shall have! A hundred longships will sail with you on the spring tides.'

The warriors lining the hall let out a triumphant yell. The decision had been expected, but the islanders could be unpredictable at the best of times. It was something of a relief to know the Frozen Principalities were truly united under one liege.

'Excellent!' cried Magnhilda, looking resplendent in her robes of brocade, lined with otter and beaver furs. Upon her brow rested a crown fashioned of twisted silver and gold, its centrepiece wrought to resembled the prow of a longship.

'Now hear this,' she declaimed. 'Another fleet of longships we are building, and our *leidangs* are mustering even as we speak. Through long winter shall we gather weather of weapons, and sea horses to bring the blood ember across the sail road to our effeminate cousins the Northlendings! A new empire shall rise, one not seen since Olav Ironhand drew his sword upon the site of Strongholm!'

The queen drew her own blade for emphasis; it caught the light streaming through one of the high windows. The warriors roared out her name, just as they had once roared Guldebrand's. The rule of mortal kings came and went, like the light that flashed upon his sister's sword: it was here one instant and gone the next. But the master Ragnar served would put a fleshless king on this earth, one who would rule it forever. In the shadow of that prospect, the ambitions of his sister and all her worldly ilk seemed but as a game of boys with toys.

But Magnhilda and her kind undoubtedly served a purpose.

'And what of the Elder Wizards' Cauldron?' Ragnar asked suddenly. His cold voice silenced the hall. All eyes turned to peer at him furtively. Such mice they seemed to him. 'Will I be granted access by the priesthood of Skjel, as promised?'

The island thegns exchanged uneasy glances. Magnhilda favoured her brother with a slight smile before addressing the visiting lords.

'He asks a fair question,' she said. 'Granting Ragnar ingress to our most sacred site was part of the proposed agreement.'

The thegns conferred quietly among themselves. Eventually Ravek addressed the hall again. 'It shall be as Ragnar wishes,' he said. 'Though many in the synod were against it.'

Ragnar allowed himself an icy smile. He could well imagine his erstwhile brethren had strongly opposed his return to the fold. But the thegns' ambition and greed had won out in the end, and they had applied some leverage as he had hoped.

His half-sister clapped her hands and called for music and mead to celebrate the occasion. From his place in the shadow of her throne, Ragnar smiled as he watched the mortals he would one day rule make sport beneath the high hall.

CHAPTER 9
A PLAN ON THE HOOF

Leaning back in her chair, Abrexta stared resentfully at the mirror's darkened surface. With an exasperated sigh, she stood up and began pacing the chamber fretfully. Much as she hated to admit it, Ragnar had been right. She had acted too carelessly, relying over much on Enchantment to ensorcell her way to the top and remain there. Now the resistance movement was gathered on the plains north of Craek, awaiting reinforcements. The Crimson League they called themselves, something to do with the colours of the Clan McCullogh that led them.

She needed to know more about her new enemy. And how the muster of the King's forces was going.

Time to kill two ravens with one arrow, she thought as she called for her page boy.

Presently her new Royal High Constable arrived. The title was a mockery on him. At nineteen summers, Lord Gann scarcely cut an imposing sight. Lean and pimply, his drooping nether lip gave him a look of stupidity. But he was the highest-ranking noble left in Umbria that she had not imprisoned or had killed, and she needed men of birth to lead Cadwy's forces in the King's absence.

At least she had not had to enthral young Gann; seducing him had been enough.

Oh Ragnar you see, I am learning, she thought with some bitterness as she beckoned the feckless marshal closer.

'Lord Gann, how speeds the muster?' She regarded him under her painted eyelashes. She could practically feel the lad trembling with desire and fear.

'We have made all the necessary preparations,' the lordling stammered. 'The bannermen of South Umbria will be here in a few days. All told, that should give us seven hundred knights and two thousand footsoldiers to send to Garth. Plus we'll have the same amount of levies.' His eyes rolled up as if he were making a complex calculation. 'Oh, and we'll have about a thousand archers, too.'

Abrexta resisted the temptation to roll her own eyes. She would never understand the feudal system. Why did men insist on following those of birth and not merit? Perhaps she shouldn't have had his older brother executed: Bannon had been a capable general by all accounts. But he had also been loyal to the realm, leading the first uprising against her more than a year ago. And therein lay her problem – all the best knights and lords tended to be difficult to enthral, not kindly disposed to pagan sorceresses bewitching their king. Ragnar could poke holes in her strategy all he liked, but the Northland priest didn't have a complex kingdom to worry about.

Lord Gann was staring at her inanely. He'd spent some

time down south, with his cousins in Penllyn. Time to make proper use of her latest pawn.

'Lord Gann, my sweet darling,' she said, honey dripping from every word. 'I would have further news from you. Tell me more about your relatives in Penllyn. What do we know of Clan Pellyw that might be useful to us in the coming conflict?'

The pained look on Gann's ingenuous face told of the youth's inner conflict. She almost started to visualise the symbols of enthralment... Then remembered she had a much simpler way to control him. Slipping a perfectly formed foot out of her slipper, she rubbed her instep against his groin, squeezing playfully with her lacquered toes. The lordling let out a stifled gasp and she felt him stiffen.

'Lord Gann,' she said with a playful grin. 'You enjoy the favour of the King's mistress. Tell me everything I need to know about the Pellyws, and you may enjoy those favours again.' She glanced meaningfully towards the door leading to the bedchamber, where she'd had him before. She found it convenient nowadays to send King Cadwy off on as many hunting trips as possible.

Gann's inner turmoil lasted another few seconds, and then he began to tell her what she needed to know. It was always a fair bet that there would be rivalry between lords; she had spent enough years among clan chieftains before coming to Ongist to know that much.

'Clan Pellyw have ever resented McCullogh its richer lands,' stammered the lordling. 'They tried to broker an alliance several years ago when they married the Lady Rowena off to a cousin of Lord Penric's.'

Rowena. She'd heard that name too often already. The First Lady of Clan McCullogh had thus far proven a wily general, despite having no formal training in the arts of war. Her army had invested Craek by dead of night, bringing in a fleet of ships to assail it with fire arrows. That had been a mere distraction, allowing her land forces to take the city unawares. Had Abrexta not been so busy keeping half a realm together, her Scrying might have told her of the resistance leader's plans. She would not make the same mistake again: from now on, she would watch this Rowena like a hawk.

'Tell me more,' she purred, still massaging the lordling's crotch with her foot.

Lord Gann gulped and went on. 'The idea was for Penric's cousin, Liam, to inherit the ward of Tul Aeren from Rowena's father Rowan, once he passed. The marriage of Rowena to Liam was supposed to bind the two lordships together, you see...'

The lordling hesitated again. Putting her foot down, Abrexta sat upright and pulled Gann towards her, slowly unfastening his baldric.

'Go on,' she said.

'When... when I was visiting there, Liam died in a hunting accident. That was last year. It was seen as nothing more than a tragic accident at first, but then something strange happened...'

'Indeed?' She paused from unfastening the lordling's belt and caught his gaze in her lustrous eyes. Yes, she could bewitch a man easily enough without her magick. Bring him to the brink of desire... and then hold out on him. She had often used her sexuality and sorcery together to devastating effect, but the two need not always be used in conjunction to ensure success.

'Do go on,' she smiled up at him.

'... her father Rowan died months later, in another hunting accident. That's when rumours of foul play began to swirl about court. It seems the Pellyws couldn't get over the fact that a woman would rule over Tul Aeren, instead of one of their own. But the law is quite specific on this matter, if a-'

'Yes, yes,' the sorceress cut him off. 'I'm well aware of how limited the power of women is in our country.'

'Twas not always thus, she might have added. *Nor will be, once I am done.*

'So if the Pellyws hate the Lady Rowena so much, why appoint her head of the Crimson League?'

'From what I can gather, there was some sort of vote,' Gann went on. 'Tradition dies hard in the southern wards, and Tul Aeren has ever been foremost among them. It was there that Anarlion, the capital of Tul Aerant, was founded in the days of the Four Old Kingdoms, before it was burned to the ground by the Westerling invaders during the Forty Years Kin Strife-'

'Yes, Lord Gann, I am well acquainted with the history of the Middle Time, it's the present I'm more concerned with,' snapped the sorceress. But she finished unfastening his sword belt as she spoke, letting his scabbarded blade fall to the ground. Lord Gann would soon have his reward.

Perhaps sensing this, the lordling flushed a deeper red and began talking more quickly.

'Lord Penric was angry when half his bannermen voted against him. Those of Tul Aeren voted for Rowena of course, and Garro, well, they backed her once they saw which way the wind was blowing. But my friends in the south tell me the lord of Penllyn grows more resentful by the day. It wasn't supposed to turn out like this, you see. Penric expected Rowena's marshal, Cathsach, to take control on her behalf. No one thought she'd be such an inspired leader. But now she's winning victories she cements her power by the day. Penric would fain find a way to slander her, so he can take control. I haven't had a message from the south since they took Craek though, so that's all I know.'

'That for now is all I need to know,' said Abrexta, favouring him with another silken smile. The halfwit certainly made a better spy than a general. Or a lover, come to that. But still, if she was to keep the lordling on side without magic, she would need to give him what he wanted. And she would need what little spare elan she had left for her next trick...

Standing up, she pushed Gann back towards the bedchamber. At least there would be some perverse thrill to be had cuckolding the King again in the Royal Cot.

'You have performed very well,' she breathed in the lordling's ear. 'Now come and take your reward.'

Happily Lord Gann was swift in the act. The green gemstones on Abrexta's ankle bracelet glowed faintly in the half dark as she wrapped her lissome legs around the grunting lordling. Likewise when he was done, the sigil tattooed on her inner thigh glimmered with a faint light. As long as they guaranteed her immortality, Abrexta would not need to worry about disease or some fool's seed taking root in her belly.

'I hope we can do this again,' Lord Gann managed to stutter as he pulled his hose back on.

'Continue to serve me well, and perhaps we shall,' replied the sorceress, pulling her red smock down and rising from the four-poster bed. The walls of the chamber were lined with tapestries depicting King Brendan the Blood-Drenched defeating her highland ancestors at the Battle of High Fells, nearly two centuries ago. Her lip curled involuntarily as she caught the woven massacre, embroidered knights butchering highland footsoldiers in a threaded tangle of limbs. Her mentor Yathaga had survived that conflict and gone into hiding, only to be caught and executed by the Argolians decades later. She could have ordered Cadwy to have the thing burned, but she had decided to let it linger as an incentive – until the conquest of Thraxia was complete. By Kaia's beams, but she'd avenge her ancestors fully! Even if it meant serving a Left-Hand warlock.

She showed the lordling out, sending him on his way with a long, lingering kiss. It hurt her to have to whore herself out to such inept mortals, but not even tapping her Fay ancestry would grant her enough power to succeed without making such sacrifices. Not yet anyway. But once the Master succeeded in his grand designs, all would share in his reward. Compared to that prospect, the thought of opening her legs once in a while for an idiot stripling was scarcely worth repenting.

Shutting the door behind Gann, she walked over to her cherrywood table and sat down before the polished silver mirror. Leaning back in her cedar chair, she took a deep breath and began intoning the words for her next spell, visualising a bird, an eye and a divining rod in quick succession. She repeated the litany several times and the mirror began to shimmer. Locating a spot she had never visited would be more difficult, but she was a past master in the arts of Scrying and it didn't take her long.

A grey windswept evening coalesced before her. She saw tassels of cloud being beaten into hasty retreat across an austere sky. The city of Craek, half its walls in ruins, clutched the north bank of the River Fern, a flotilla of rebel warships clustered greedily at its harbour. Past it she moved, following the river upstream like a bird in flight, until she reached the confluence of the Fern and Gurn, where the ruins of Anarlion lay bathed in an eldritch light. Beyond that the shadowy eaves of the Fernwood beckoned, and for a moment Abrexta felt her heart clench as she looked upon her old home, where she had lived after Andragorix usurped her place at Roarkil and banished her.

By rights Morcant should still be in that forest, holed up in the bizarre cottage they had shared for ten years, though she had not heard from him in weeks. Perhaps that was for the best, she reflected; her erstwhile understudy had been resistant to her powers of Enchantment and an uncertain ally at best.

Dismissing the mage from her mind, Abrexta focused on the army camp, pitched within sight of Anarlion. Shades of dead warriors were beginning to stir within the ruined city, summoned to their eternal haunt by the coming of night. On the plains just north of it, living ones scurried to and fro amongst pavilions, as cooking fires winked into life against the descending dark. In the fading gloaming, the enchantress spotted the standards of the clans coming to unseat her. Three mighty banners writhed on the fierce winds, as if daring her to draw closer. She could just make made out the heraldic sigils depicted on them: a ship, a mountain, and a wheel.

Touching a white stone talisman around her neck, Abrexta murmured another word and pictured a looking glass, drawing ever closer to the central banner: this was the one with the wheel motif, a spiked affair picked out in black against a green background. Atop it perched a crimson eagle, its wings folded and its head reared proudly. Clan McCullogh, the house leading the charge against her.

Maintaining the looking-glass symbol in her mindset, Abrexta zoned in on the pavilion next to the standard. She needed to get inside. Shutting her eyes tightly, she pictured a hand passing through a wall and the eye symbol in quick succession... Opening her eyes again, she saw she was inside the tent.

She could not hear aught, but she could see plenty. Trestle tables had been set up in the middle of the pavilion, and around this knights and nobles stood, engaged in a heated debate. Lady Rowena needed no introduction, for she was the only woman in the room.

Hardly a great beauty, thought Abrexta scornfully as she zoomed in for a closer look. The First Woman of Clan McCullogh had ginger braids and pale freckled skin, with buck teeth for good measure.

She won't be charming anyone in a hurry, magick or no magick.

But a minute's observation gave the lie to that notion. For what Rowena lacked in comeliness, she more than made up for with presence. Even bereft of sound, Abrexta could see in her mien that this was a young woman who expected to be obeyed. And was.

The enchantress felt her gut tighten. By the looks of things this Rowena would be a formidable foe. But where was her rival?

She soon located him by his family crest: the silver mountain on a diagonal green-and-purple background emblazoned on his surcoat, worn over gilded mail, gave Lord Penric away. That and the fact that he clearly appeared to be doing most of the talking. Otherwise, she might have missed him easily enough: his weaselly demeanour was accentuated by his broken face, and one eye was bigger than the other.

They're no great lookers these southerners, and I thought Lord Gann was ugly.

She forced herself to concentrate. This next part would be difficult, and she'd have to let a few thralls go temporarily: mixing Enchantment with Scrying was always going to be a challenge at the best of times. At this range she wouldn't be able to do anything more than give a faint suggestion, just enough to nudge the First Man of Clan Pellyw where she wanted him to go. Taking another deep breath she murmured more words, picturing an open book and a puppeteer as she scrutinised Lord Penric, feeling for his resentment.

She found it soon enough. It was there, bubbling just under the surface.

Ah, prideful men! Perhaps this won't be so difficult, after all.

'We should strike now and follow up on our victory,' said Lord Penric, shaking his fist for emphasis. 'The lords of Garth are on the back foot – we wiped out a third of their forces when we took Craek.'

Nods and murmurs of assent showed that at least half the nobles agreed with the First Man of Clan Pellyw. Suppressing the urge to sigh, Rowena reiterated her argument.

'Outriders tell us the King's forces are mustering south of Ongist,' she said. 'We're still waiting on Clan Ingall to bring the rest of its land forces up here from Garro.' She fixed the rivalrous lord with a pointed stare. 'Not to mention half your forces from the southern wards of Penllyn.'

Lord Penric scowled at that but she paid him no heed. 'Our lightning strike won us Craek and half of Rathlain,' she went on. 'The price of that speed was to launch our campaign without a full muster. I would not see speed converted into haste – we must give our comrades a chance to join us before we press further into enemy territory! Surely you can see it would be courting disaster to march north as we are?'

The nods and murmurs shifted back in her favour. Rowena wondered wryly how such vacillating nincompoops would ever manage a campaign without her. A good job father had encouraged her to explore the library at Liathnoc, even if he had forbidden his only daughter from taking up arms. It hadn't boasted more than a few dozen tomes, truth be told, but Alcius' *The Subtle Arts Of Making War* had told Rowena all she needed to know: the Thalamian master general and empire-builder knew more about fighting battles than all her bannermen put together. What a shame so few of them could read, they might have benefited from his wisdom.

A cunning enemy will always appear weak when he is strong. So Alcius had written, more than a thousand years ago. 'Lord Fael's troops got a hiding from us all right, but the lord of Rathlain won't brook that a second time,' she pressed.

'Fael is but a boy,' scoffed Penric, getting a few laughs from his bannermen.

'Aye, but his uncle who rules Rathlain as regent is anything but,' put in Sir Cathsach. It was good to have the marshal of Liathnoc by her side. He had known Rowena since she was a babe, and proved loyal thus far. 'Lady Rowena has the right of this – Lord Ongus will be preparing a counter move, mark that.'

'He knows we're only in a position of relative strength, and that's why he seeks to draw us out,' persisted Rowena.

'Once we're deep into Rathlain, he'll bring archers and levymen and all his knights to bear. We only decimated the footsoldiers guarding Craek and the castles about – Ongus has plenty more troops in reserve, not to mention the lords of Irisfallen and Colherin right behind him. They would seek to bait us in our victory!'

'And how would Ongus know our own tally?' Penric shot back. 'For all he knows, we might have twice the numbers of all the lords of Garth!'

'You forget who we go to war against,' replied Rowena. 'A sorceress sits on the Seat of High Kings. She could have used her pagan witcheries to scry out our position and numbers weeks ago, and relayed the information back to Ongus and the other lords of Garth. That's how he knows, Lord Penric! If we march north as we are, we're marching straight into a trap! Falling back and giving us lower Rathlain is obviously a stratagem!'

Lord Penric scowled again, his lop-sided eyes black pinpricks in the brazier light. Something seemed to change in his demeanour then... was it a trick of the flames, or did he suddenly tremble?

He paused a moment more. All eyes were turned on the wiry lord, expecting another vociferous counter-argument.

What they got surprised them a whole lot more.

'Well,' he said, his voice dropping to a sibilant whisper. 'I'm sure the Lady Rowena knows all about stratagems, after the manner in which she came to power.'

Another silence. Rowena did not grasp his meaning at first. Then her eyes widened in shock as she did.

'You would dare...?!' she managed to utter, before the nobles around the table fell to bickering.

'A husband and a father both dead of hunting accidents within a few months!' roared Penric. 'And you tell me that isn't suspicious?'

'You have no grounds for making such an assertion!' cried Cathsach. 'Retract your words immediately!'

The angry voices flared, a rising tempest of pent-up ire. The shadows curling about the fringes of the tent suddenly seemed darker, the autumn evening chiller. As she watched the notables arguing, flustered and powerless, Rowena found herself remembering another quote. But it wasn't the warlord Alcius, but their national troubadour Maegellin whose words came floating back to her.

When rumour speaks with unbridled tongue, her words amount to poison.

Leaning back in her chair, Abrexta smirked as she watched the spectacle unfold. Even without being able to hear, it was obvious that her plan had gone as intended. Lord Penric was gesticulating and pointing accusingly at Lady Rowena, who was shaking her head furiously and yelling back at him. Nobles from both parties were interceding: some trying to mediate, others perhaps seeking satisfaction in the lists.

With a sigh she broke the spell, letting the mirror grow dark. Her body was drenched in sweat and she felt exhausted; she could not be bothered to re-enthral the handful of knights she had released from bondage. Let them struggle with their loyalties a while longer; once ensorcelled a man was easy enough to bind again at a distance. Enthralling someone for the first time at long range was another matter, hence her sense of triumph now: she hadn't been at all sure her plan would work.

But work it had. For the first time in weeks, Abrexta felt firmly back in control.

Let's see how long this Crimson League stays together now.

The Captain of the Garter watched suspiciously as the double doors were flung open to admit the monk. From his place at the King's right hand, Sir Hugon had a good view of the Argolian as he swept purposefully across the marble floor of the Oval Chamber. The monk stopped a few paces away from the Crescent Table, as protocol dictated, and took a knee.

'Horskram of Vilno salutes thee, thy Majesty, and all the most noble knights of the Purple Garter,' the greybeard intoned.

Sir Hugon's lip curled slightly. The Argolians were ever ready with the niceties when they wanted something. And what did the monk want today, he wondered.

The knight tapped gauntleted fingers impatiently against the curving table's polished rosewood surface as the King bade Horskram rise. For a few seconds, he let his gaze rove about the ovoid hall. The kingdom's history fairly screamed from its walls: pale autumnal light from the slitted windows caught painted friezes that depicted King Vasirius and the original knights of the Purple Garter, locked for eternity in age-old deeds of derring-do.

That about sums up the country, he thought glumly. *Frozen in stone, living off our former glories.*

'Master Horskram of Vilno,' said Carolus, his voice as neutral as his face. 'What brings you here, on mission of such urgency that you seek to disturb a council of state?' The King's tone hardened as he pronounced the last three words; Hugon supposed that would intimidate lesser men, but he wasn't impressed.

Nor, apparently, was the old monk.

'I would fain ask this of you in private, Your Majesty,' he said, switching from the High Speech of Old Thalamy to Panglian. The change was pointed: formalities were over, and now the Argolian presumed to address the King on more level terms. But that was typical of the friars of St Argo: they seldom had respect for anything outside their own hermetic rites.

'I see,' replied the King, still speaking in Decorlangue. 'And just what is it you would ask of me?' His liege sounded colder now; evidently Horskram's bravado was not going down well. Other knights at the table exchanged uncertain glances: Sir Odo the seneschal growled next to him, while young Sir Aremis wore a perplexed look on his uncomely features.

'You have certain allies of mine in detention,' said Horskram. 'Three knights you brought here a week ago, together with some of their associates. The Order has need of their services, and I have come to petition for their release.'

The King sat back in his ornately carved high chair, scrutinising Horskram. He had his game face on now, like a master Jedrez player contemplating his next series of moves across the board, but then Carolus rarely gave much away. Clean-shorn and slender, with thinning sandy hair and wearing close-fitting clothes of nondescript black, he didn't even look like a true monarch.

He plots and schemes like a freebooter, thought Hugon disparagingly. *How different to our kings of old.*

'I see,' replied the King. 'Sir Odo, remind me as to who these visitors are.'

Hugon had to suppress a wry smirk. *Oh, you know full well who they are.*

'Three knights, from Thraxia, Northalde and Vorstlund,' replied the barrel-chested steward. 'The first two are from high-born families. The latter is a minor noble, little better than a titled freesword.'

Several of the thirty knights sat at the table sniggered at that, but Sir Hugon wasn't sure he found the joke funny. He was a scion of one of the highest houses in the land himself, and fiercely proud of it, but then many of the original knights of the Crescent Table had been minor nobles. In Vasirius' day, a man had distinguished himself by feats of arms and courtly prowess, not just title and rank.

How far away those days seemed now.

'With them came a single low-born squire and an outland savage,' continued Odo, 'a warrior woman from some far-flung tribe beyond the Great Inland Sea, and two damsels from Vorstlund. They are refusing to disclose their true identities, but judging by their speech and manners both are high-born.'

'Well, Master Horskram,' said the King. 'A motley group of wayfarers indeed. Trust that I have lodged them well enough, as befits their station. But I am not minded to release them just yet, as their behaviour in the kingdom has been... somewhat unruly.'

Horskram bowed his head in acknowledgement. 'I cannot deny that,' he said. 'But rest assured, I intend to take these knights out of the country as soon as possible. I'm sure it would be in your interest to see such *unruly visitors* on their way.'

For the first time the King cracked a smile, if thin creasing of lips could be called a smile.

'Indeed, I'm sure one might think so,' he replied. 'But you seem to forget that the realm is on a war footing now – I cannot be releasing outlanders so liberally, until I have verified their intentions. Especially not when three of them hail from the very land we plan to invade next year.'

'I can assure you they are of no consequence in this coming war of yours,' said Horskram. Was it Hugon's imagination, or was there a hint of contempt in the monk's voice now? The pending invasion of Vorstlund was the first good bit of news he'd heard in an age, but then the Argolians were pacifists. 'Sir Braxus and Sir Torgun will take no part in it, and as for Sir Wrackwulf – well, he is indeed little more than a freesword who will take service for coin. I'd see him take service for the Order, and it please you.'

The King shot a sidelong glance at Hugon. 'Well, Sir

Hugon, what say you to this? As Royal Marshal, I would value your counsel in this matter.'

Sir Hugon cleared his throat before replying. 'I cannot see how releasing the knights into Horskram's custody would do any harm, if he makes good on his pledge to see them out of the country with all due speed. But as for the damsels, they could be valuable pawns in the coming war – it's obvious enough they are notables of Vorstlund. Ransoms will doubtless be exchanged when hostilities commence, they could be worth a lot to the enemy.'

The squire and the outlander didn't concern him in the slightest, but then they weren't of noble blood. In any case, he assumed they would go with their respective masters. The Harijan had apparently been in the employ of the mysterious Lady Helene, though Reus knew why. Some peculiar story there, no doubt.

The King nodded perfunctorily. 'There you have it, master monk, the knights you shall have for an appropriate ransom – as long as you take them with you before they can cause any more trouble. I trust this pleases you.'

Horskram winced. He almost seemed obsequious as he said imploringly: 'Your Majesty, would that I could agree with you, but unfortunately two of the knights in question are pursuing a courtly love suit for the Lady... Helene. I doubt I'll be able to convince them to join me on my next mission if it means being separated from her.'

'Such insolence!' barked Odo, his nostrils flaring. The irascible old seneschal was well known for his temper. 'How dare you spurn the King's generosity, I ought to have you-'

'Peace, Sir Odo,' interjected Carolus, laying a hand on

the knight's arm. 'I might have expected as much. It's courtly love that got them into this mess in the first place – that ridiculous business with the Athos Colossi.'

This time Sir Hugon couldn't resist a smile. The two knights had still been arguing over who had been first to reach the top when they'd arrested them. He could not help but admire their reckless courage, it smacked of the halcyon days of Vasirius.

We wrote the book on courtly love, yet nowadays it falls to crude northerners to set us an example, he sighed inwardly. The smile faded at that thought. His eye caught the frieze again. It was the part that showed Sir Danton the Knave of Hearts, clambering up the tower of the White Blood Witch to save the youth Alcest, son of his lady love Yveline le Coeur Vivant.

Perhaps we should put those two foreign knights in a relief, he thought bitterly as Sir Danton's petrified face leered down at him. The Knave of Hearts had ever been a jester, or so the troubadours told: he might well be laughing at them now from the Heavenly Halls.

The country needed a war. Badly. What Sir Hugon doubted was whether it needed another crusade as well.

Crusading, the thought of it made his gut lurch. Thanks to his elder brother Sir Azelin, his entire homeland lay in escrow to the Knights Bethler. He would have Valacia back one day – in his name. At least his brother had gone missing in the Blessed Realm; served him right for deserting his family and country for a fool's war in the name of the Almighty. That wouldn't have happened in King Vasirius' time – knights back then went to war with their own kind, for glory and spoil, not to butcher heathens and their women and children. Sassanians were weak and effeminate, unworthy opponents for good Urovian men of arms.

'Sir Hugon! Your King asked you a question!' Sir Odo was glowering at him.

Caught in his reverie again. He'd spent one late-night tryst too many with the King's wife. Hugon suppressed that thought instantly – Argolians were said to be able to read men's minds, and the old monk was staring at him keenly.

'Forgive me, Your Majesty,' Sir Hugon dissembled. 'I was distracted by thoughts of the war preparations. Pray repeat your question.'

'I said, what sum would you recommend for ransoming the three knights and their fair damsels?' said the King, his voice tinged with scorn. 'The Argolian Order is offering to compensate the crown for its loss.'

Sir Hugon drew himself up and did his best to look alert. 'Sir Torgun is a younger son and therefore a bachelor, but hails from a high house and lately served an elite knightly order. That should make him worth a typical vassal, say a hundred doublons. The errant from Vorstlund will be worth about half that. But Sir Braxus of Gaellen is now a lord in his own right – though he has lost his lands to a highland incursion, if the news we are hearing is correct.'

'Nonetheless,' replied the King with a sly smirk, 'he is technically still a lord apparent.'

'... indeed, Your Majesty. That should make him worth a thousand doublons, in theory.'

Horskram's eyes bulged. 'This is daylight brigandage! Sir

Braxus has not even been anointed to his title, and perhaps never will.'

'Oh really?' put in Sir Odo. 'And you are telling me this mission of yours will have nothing to do with Lord Braxus returning to Thraxia to reclaim his birthright?'

The old monk scowled. He'd been caught out by the wily seneschal. Hugon and Odo seldom agreed on anything, but the thick-set knight was undeniably a useful man to have around.

'As for the damsels,' continued Hugon implacably, 'until they divulge their true provenance it will be impossible to say for sure how much they are worth.'

'... but given they are so reticent about said provenance, it is reasonable to suppose the lady in charge is both wealthy and influential,' said the King. 'I cannot afford to let her go for a trifling sum – we've a war to fund, after all. So let's set their ransoms at two hundred doublons for the high lady and another fifty for her lady-in-waiting... Odo, the tally if you will.'

'Fourteen hundred gold pieces, Master Horskram, and it please you,' sneered the steward.

'Outrageous!' spluttered Horskram. 'And I'm supposed to take this travesty of an offer back to the Grand Master?'

'I've already told Hannequin I have little interest in this recondite mission of his,' replied the King. 'I'm not in the humour for your sorcerous games, we've a real war to fight. Oh, and you may of course take the squire and the savage free of charge. The King is feeling generous today.'

All thirty knights erupted into laughter at this. Even sincere Aremis could not help but smile, his hare lip looking even more grotesque. But then Pangonians loved to make fools of foreigners.

The monk wasn't quite done though. 'You know full well that ransoms can take years to be redeemed, especially in times of war,' he said, a note of defiance entering his voice. 'I understand you plan to invade Vorstlund next spring, in which case you'll be wanting ready money now. And whilst I'm no Bethler, as I understand it, convenience costs money... The Order will pay you half what you ask.'

Horskram met the King's gaze.

Carolus sighed languidly. 'Such tedious calculations are beneath a king's dignity,' he said. 'But you've made your point, Master Horskram. Let's call it a thousand gold doublons for the seven outlanders then, and *not a groat less*.'

The monk seemed about to protest, then thought better of it.

'Agreed, assuming the Grand Master gives his assent,' he said stiffly. 'Before I relay your offer to Hannequin, might I be permitted to see your expensive guests?'

Carolus smiled again, looking almost affable now. 'By all means. Sir Odo, see it done.'

With a curt nod, the bulky seneschal rose from his siege and walked around the sickle-shaped table, impatiently motioning for Horskram to follow. Horskram favoured them with a half-hearted bow and left, a black mood trailing in his wake.

'Ever a slippery lot, the Argolians,' said the King. 'Best to remind them of their place now and again.'

'Indeed, Your Majesty,' replied Sir Hugon. He still didn't think much of his liege, a man who'd never showed any real prowess at arms, but Carolus did know how to raise coin for a war. Speaking of which... the monk had rudely interrupted his latest report. All eyes turned to the Royal Marshal as he resumed.

'The Occidental margraves have agreed to join the invasion, since our tax arrangements were finalised by Sir Uthor.' Hugon indicated the grizzled crescent knight serving as Lord Treasurer, who nodded self-importantly.

We used to be the heroes of the realm, thought Hugon. *Its thirty best knights. Now we're just used as pawns against the margraves, to check baronial power.* Sir Uthor was the younger brother of the Margrave of Toulon, only too glad to leverage himself above his sibling in the echelons of power.

'That means come spring we should be able to field two thousand knights, assuming the Occidentals keep their word,' Hugon went on carefully.

'What of light cavalry?' put in Sir Alaric. Hugon splashed a cold glare across him. Tall and sleek and every bit as smug-looking as he was refined, the Sea Marshal was forever overstepping the boundaries of duty. The invasion of Vorstlund would be mostly a land affair. Twenty war galleys would be used to blockade Westerburg, but the rest of the navy would be despatched to the Pilgrim Kingdoms to attack ports held by the sultanate of Kallandhar.

'We should have four thousand mounted serjeants,' replied Hugon patiently. 'Together with seven thousand foot, all freshly equipped with the latest cut of mail hauberks and-'

'Yes, yes,' said Carolus with an impatient flick of the

hand. 'Spare me the details and give me the sum, Sir Hugon.'

The marshal cleared his throat again and finished his summary. 'Together with two thousand crossbowmen that should make us an invasion force of fifteen thousand trained fighters, plus the usual peasant conscripts to use as arrow fodder.'

'Superb,' simpered the King. 'The Prince of Westenlund won't know what's hit him.'

If you think Prince Leopold won't have heard about plans to march a vast army across the Orne ranges into his territory by next Mercus, you know even less of war than I thought.

'And what of the crusade?' queried Sir Alaric. 'Must we really give up the southern margraves to another pilgrim war?'

At least the uppity Sea Marshal shared Hugon's distaste for crusading.

'It can't be helped, I'm afraid,' sighed the King. 'Aquitania and her brethren are far too troublesome to be taking with us. Their zeal is best channelled overseas, against the heathens they so despise.'

You mean they despise you for murdering a pious king they revered, and that's why they'll never support you in anything. That said, Hugon couldn't say he was altogether sad to see Carolus the Elder gone; a zealot was the last thing Pangonia needed on the throne. Unfortunately the schemer who had killed him seemed to be just as in thrall to the Temple, albeit for different reasons.

'We don't need the Lower Vallians in any case,' said Sir Hugon brusquely. 'We've enough of an army to crush the

Vorstlendings, and thanks to Her Majesty the Queen we should have the Thalamians to count on, too.'

Thought of Isolte made Hugon's loins flare. She would be wanting to see him after this council. 'Thalamy hasn't shown any aptitude in matters martial since Wulfric of Gothia sacked Tyrannos,' sneered Sir Uthor, getting a general chorus of approval.

'No, but they'll provide us with enough fodder to keep Aslund and Ostveld from coming to Prince Leopold's aid,' Hugon reminded them. 'Westenlund is the most powerful of the Vorstlending baronies. Once it falls into our hands, we'll have the rest of the country on the back foot.'

'And yet we'll still have the northerners to contend with,' put in Sir Aremis. 'I have heard much said of the prowess of Dulsinor and Stornelund.'

The ugly knight rarely spoke, but was usually gentle of tone when he did, not unlike the Northlending hero Horskram had come to bargain for. Sir Hugon admired him for it – Aremis was a true exemplar of the Code, dedicated to his country.

If only half the knights sat here could have that said of them.

'And I've heard it said Dulsinor and Stornelund are busy killing each other after some marriage alliance was foiled by a sorceress,' said Sir Uthor archly. The Lord Treasurer twirled elegant moustachios as he once again presumed to hold court. That only made Hugon despise him the more.

'A sorceress was it?' Hugon shot back. 'I heard it was a party of errant knights who caused trouble at a tournament held to celebrate the wedding. That led to harsh words being exchanged between the two lords and provoked a conflict.'

'And I heard there never was a marriage alliance to begin with,' put in Sir Alaric. 'They went to war after talks of such came to naught.'

'Whatever the true cause,' interjected the King, 'I think we can at least trust silver-tongued rumour on the central point – our two mighty baronies are at war, making this a propitious time to invade.'

'Doubtless they'll call a truce once word of our attack reaches them though,' frowned Hugon.

'By which time they will be weakened by a season of fierce fighting,' replied the King archly. 'As for the middle baronies, they should be no match for Pangonian mettle in the field.'

And what would you know of that, pray tell?

Come to think on it, there were other reasons why Hugon tupped the King's wife, for all that she was seductive and beautiful. Why, it was divine justice that she should lie with a true warrior!

'Excellent good, in faith,' said the King, oblivious to the thoughts of his cuckolding general. 'One last matter – has that Northlending princeling turned up yet?'

Uneasy glances flicked to and fro across the Crescent Table. It was Sir Aremis who spoke up. 'I did order a search of all the winesinks, brothels, and manor houses in the city and its environs,' he said. 'Lord Ivon de Vichy says the North-lending emissary took off one evening, saying he had something pressing to attend to. Wouldn't tell him anything more, and refused to be stayed on the matter. They'd just been hunting up in the Arbevere, but instead of returning with Ivon and his cronies, Sir Wolmar rode off east on the same courser he'd been using on the trip. He didn't even return here to collect his warhorse, and its one of those fine northern breeds the Northlendings guard so fiercely. In his absence we've requisitioned it for the war effort, but I'm afraid we're none the wiser as to Sir Wolmar's whereabouts, sire.'

Carolus sighed. 'Well, explaining that away to King Freidheim will be entertaining, to say the least. Still, if young knights will go gallivanting off on their own... and Sir Wolmar was by all accounts more hotheaded than most.' The King brushed his hands together, as though wiping them clean of an irritating speck of dirt. 'Sir Odo, you will dictate a message to the King of the Northlendings, informing him. Do try to put us in a favourable light – I don't want our northern cousins thinking we can't look after royal guests properly.'

A royal emissary and proven warrior goes missing, and you show about as much concern as if he were a runaway bondsman, thought Hugon bitterly. *I won't pretend to like Northlendings, but Sir Wolmar deserves more respect than that.*

'And that brings us to an end of table business for today,' said Carolus, rising lightly from his siege. 'The King has other matters to attend to.'

Yes, you attend to your mistress – I'll attend to mine, thought Hugon eagerly as they all rose in his wake.

As they filed out of the Oval Chamber, the marshal flicked his gaze to the ceiling. A sweeping velvet curtain of purple stared back at him, its silver crescent moon and thirty stars seeming to mock him in the greying light.

Be worthy of the Crescent.

That standard had meant something once: pray Stygnos and it would again, right soon.

She was waiting for him in an upper chamber of the garret, in one of the outlying towers of the palace. It was their usual trysting spot; the Palace of White Towers had been conceived by Vasirius, a sprawling complex designed to commemorate the glory of his reign after the truculent barons of Lower Vallia had finally been brought to heel. The Knights of the Crescent Table had led the charge against Lord Fulk of Aquitania and the Chivalrous King had slain him single-handedly in the Battle of Pellan Fields, ending the Third War of the Royal Succession. An era of peace and prosperity had spread gentle fingers across the realm, until the White Blood Witch and the Traitor Prince Ancelet arose to make trouble in the land once more.

Or so the troubadours and loremasters told it. Stepping into the circular chamber at the tower's summit, Sir Hugon wondered if such halcyon times had ever really existed. Perhaps future bards and sages would speak of the grandilo-quent era they lived in now, when King Carolus III of Pangonia had crushed the Vorstlendings and carved out a mainland empire for his heirs. Would they also leave in the parts about skulduggery, treachery, and intriguing that inevitably shadowed glorious deeds done in the field?

Hugon suspected such things did not make for good songs in castle halls.

'You're late,' said the Queen, not deigning to remove the shawl from her head, or turn from the window she gazed out of languidly. 'I take it that means you have interesting news.'

'Interesting, after its own fashion,' hedged the knight, acknowledging her two handmaids with a curt nod. They barely returned his salutation. Brought across the Burinoc River from Thalamy with their mistress, the two noble-women hailed from high houses in that ancient kingdom. At least they could be counted on to be discreet.

Pangonians were a haughty bunch, justly proud of their heritage (for all that the apple had fallen from the tree). But Thalamians had an altogether different air about them. Pangonia's glory days were a century behind it; Thalamy's a millennium. That had given its nobility an aura of lingering melancholy unsurpassed in the Free Kingdoms.

'I shall be the judge of its fashion,' replied Isolte, turning at last and slowly removing her shawl. Even now, after lying with her countless times, Hugon struggled to find his breath every time he was exposed to her beauty. He tried not to think about his own blunt, heavy-set features next to hers.

The light radiating through the window's blue glass panes struck an odd contrast with her lustrous olive skin; the darkness of her silky tresses matched her eyes as she transfixed him. Pride and sadness were mingled therein, as though the Queen carried a thousand victories and losses in her gaze alone. A single barely perceptible nod of her head, and the ladies-in-waiting vanished with curtseys. Isolte was dressed in a multicoloured patterned beluque that well concealed her lithe figure; likewise the gold-embroidered barbette gave nothing of her ample bosom away. That only fanned the flames of his desire: Hugon knew all too well what lay beneath her garish yet modest mantle.

'Tell me everything that transpired in the Oval Chamber today,' she said, without taking her eyes off him.

Obediently, Sir Hugon did as his queen and mistress bade him.

'It is well,' she nodded. 'The muster continues apace. Though I am less pleased to hear of this monk and his mysterious quest.'

Hugon blinked. Though he had left nothing out, that part of his report hardly seemed of importance.

'What business is it of ours if a clutch of foreign knights are released? So long as we have good ransom money for them.'

The Queen did not answer, but reaching towards the gold-filigreed ebony table beside her long chair, she held a tiny splint to a low-burning lamp and took up a carved ivory bowl with a long wooden stem. The pungent scent of intoxicating fumes filled the air as she lit the strange object, which Hugon had learned was called a pipe. The knight did his best to hide his revulsion. *Shisham*, an import from the Pilgrim Kingdoms his lady was fond of; he did not share her passion for the tarry resin, though he could not deny it added spice to their lovemaking.

'Anything the Argolians are up to is likely to be bad for the realms of mortalkind,' said the Queen after a few puffs. 'But you leave me to worry about that.'

Her tone gave nothing of her true thoughts away, but then it seldom did. Isolte was the kind of woman who could seem utterly present, yet thoroughly disengaged at the same time.

Turning to stare back out of the window, she sat in silence smoking for a while. Sir Hugon shifted uncomfortably, trying to ignore the cloying stench and suddenly feeling the weight of his armour. When would they tryst, in Luviah's name? That was all he wanted to do right now, he was sick of talking politics.

'Things are changing,' the Queen said presently. 'And to the good... for those on the right side.'

'This invasion will certainly be good for the realm,' replied Hugon. 'About time we had a proper war after Carolus the Elder's peaceable ways.'

'That is not quite what I meant,' she said, glancing at him sidelong through a wreath of smoke. It caught motes of dust and for a minute Hugon thought himself entranced by their silvery play in the blue beams of light... that blasted *shisham* was going to his head.

'Then what do you mean?' What else could she be referring to, not that bloody crusade he hoped.

'Oh, the conquest of Vorstlund will undoubtedly be a good thing,' she assured him. 'And you can count on my cousin the King of Thalamy to take part. However, I believe it is time – and high time at that – we thought bigger.' She stopped to relight her pipe, her eyes twinkling as she caught his gaze once more. 'Wouldn't you agree?'

'You know my feelings about the kingdom all too well,' said Sir Hugon. 'Pangonia is the most powerful of the Free

Kingdoms. We should take advantage of that strength and write a new chapter in our glorious history, in the blood of our neighbours!'

The Queen smiled wryly. 'I take it you do not mean Thalamy,' she said quietly. Without waiting for a reply she continued: 'Sir Hugon, this realm could sit at the heart of an empire, with the right kind of leadership. Right now it is not getting that leadership.'

'The King is a schemer and a vacillator, ever has been,' replied Hugon, feeling suddenly guilty. 'But at least with this war he has found some mettle.'

'My husband has ever been a cautious man,' said Isolte. 'He does not think big enough, as is the wont of cautious men.'

Hugon's lip curled again and he approached the Queen, making so bold as to seize her hand. Lustrous diamonds on them caught the smoky light; imported from the Sultanates beyond the Pilgrim Kingdoms, they shone with an ethereal beauty even few nobles could afford. 'My lady love, Your Majesty,' he said, taking a knee. 'You know full well what I think of Carolus. He is a poor successor to the Chivalrous King, but he is King for all that! The best we can do is to encourage him to bolder ways. Surely this invasion is a good start.'

Isolte put the pipe aside and reached down to caress his dark brown hair. Grown long after the fashion at court, his locks rivalled her own. 'My dearest sweet,' she said, cupping his square jaw with her other hand and addressing him kindly for the first time. 'Not for nothing are you Captain of the Garter, and my lover to boot. Have you forgotten the tasks you performed for me when we were courting?'

'Nay, my love! 'Tis the Crescent Bridge Tourney victory I treasure the most!'

That recollection brought back bittersweet memories. Hugon had finally triumphed at the prestigious joust, but only after his older brother had taken the Wheel and gone off to fight in the Blessed Realm. Still, it had been a memorable victory: the original thirty Garter knights had been picked from that heralded tournament. Since his victory he'd never won it again – Sir Aremis had made his stunning debut, and Sir Hugon had had to make do with being a serial finalist once again.

That is the story of my life: to be second best, always.

'Don't succumb to self-pity,' said Isolte, measuring her words and leaning down to kiss his brow. 'I see such pain in you, Sir Hugon, and I would fain relieve it.'

He felt a rush of desire at the touch of her full lips. Lunging forwards, he made to straddle her on the long chair. He would take her now, they would tryst the afternoon away-

She pushed him back with hands that were gentle but firm. 'Why my darling amour, you are straying wide of the piste I fear, for trysting is not what I had in mind this afternoon.'

Hugon felt cold disappointment dilute his hot desire, robbing it of flavour and heat. Why in the Known World did she want to keep talking so? He silently cursed the rules of courtly love, which accorded a woman far more power than the laws of marriage. But he was determined to keep to the

Code of Chivalry. Someone had to, now that his wretch of a brother had forsaken country for god.

'I have something far more important to tell you,' she said, reaching for the pipe again. 'Do you think it any coincidence that I allowed one of the realm's greatest and most influential knights to court me?'

Sir Hugon puffed up at that, his pride eagerly clutching at the scraps his mistress now tossed it. 'I would expect the Queen of Pangonia to have nothing less than impeccable taste in lovers,' he declared, feeding on his own arrogance as a drunkard quaffs wine.

'Yes, I am sure you would,' replied Isolte. That old sadness had re-entered her voice; she gave the air of having seen and said all things before. In fact, wreathed in blue smoke, she seemed altogether more than human. Which she was, in his eyes. Never had he courted a lady of her like, and nor would he ever again.

'Sir Hugon, what if I told you that you could be Royal Marshal over an army that would conquer not just the Vorstlendings, but all of the northerly Free Kingdoms?'

The knight blinked. This he had not expected. It had taken an age just to get one war going – now the Queen was talking about conquering half of Western Urovia.

'You mean Thraxia and Northalde as well? I quail before no challenge, but is that not a little... premature?'

The Queen pressed the pipe into his hands. 'Take a puff my darling, the *shisham* will invigorate thy fancy, that you may imagine greater deeds than you have ere now.'

With the greatest reluctance Sir Hugon did as she bade him. And they wouldn't even get to enjoy the resin's aphrodisiacal properties, by the looks of things. His head started to make giddy turns as he hacked on the pipe. Isolte continued talking in her soft voice.

'Nothing is ever premature to those who plan well enough. There are forces already in motion that will turn the world order upside down, once they reach their final destination.' Something in the way she said this sent a shiver winnowing down his spine. The blasted *shisham* wasn't helping, the stuff always made him agitated unless he was making love. 'This war will be but the beginning, not the end in itself. The coming crusade is nothing more than a distraction, a ploy to get less malleable knights and barons out of the way. They'll be taken care of in the Pilgrim Kingdoms.'

That last remark caught his attention. He'd known well enough that sending the Lower Vallians off on crusade amounted to a stratagem. But the Queen seemed to know something about this ploy that he didn't.

He handed her back the pipe, feeling relieved when she did not demur, though his head was still swimming. The cobalt beams strafing the room seemed even more hypnotic now, intensifying as the sun lowered in the sky. Blasted Imperials and their fancy glasswork, give him plain shutters any day-

'My love,' said Isolte, snapping her fingers in his face. 'Pray concentrate! I am telling you things you need to know.'

'Yes of course, my lady...' Sir Hugon stared at her, feeling lost and anxious. She looked on him as a noble might look upon a sick horse, a mixture of love and regret in her dark eyes. Did she really love him as an equal? Or was he merely loved because of his usefulness? He had never dared ask himself that question directly until now, though it had bubbled away unpleasantly at the back of his mind.

'My people once ruled an empire that straddled the Sundering Sea,' she went on, putting the pipe aside and taking his hands. 'The Imperial Hawk standard of the Iron Legions was seen from here to Sassania. Our heroes carved tranches from the land with their intrepid swords, provinces that men today would call kingdoms.' For all that her words took a histrionic turn, her tone remained even, the touch of her hands light.

'We had our heroes too,' faltered Hugon, though he knew enough of bard's song to realise there was no comparison.

'The deeds of Sir Lancelyn and Sir Guillemin and the other knights of the Crescent Table are justly renowned,' the Queen allowed. 'But you cannot deny that where your forebears rescued damsels and fought robber barons, the heroes of Old Thalamy built civilisations and conquered whole peoples.'

It was true. Vasirius had seen off invasions from Thalamy and Vorstlund, but had never done more than consolidate his own kingdom's borders. Though the exploits of the Crescent Knights had indeed been heroic, they had left no legacy besides tales of yore to mark their passing.

'Whereas Thalamus and Tycius and Alcius were truly heroes of the Golden Age,' pressed Isolte. 'They weren't just warriors and generals – they founded an empire that lasted beyond their lifetimes, and many more thereafter.'

Hugon's eyes found his mistress' bejewelled fingers. So

matter-of-fact and sure of herself, she was right as usual. The peace of the realm had not even outlived Vasirius, and his death at the Battle of Avalongne had been followed by the Fourth War of the Royal Succession. His ancestors' legacy was but one kingdom, albeit a powerful one.

'Some would say the Pilgrim Kingdoms are a sort of empire,' he muttered.

The Queen laughed softly at that. 'Try telling that to the Princes of Palom in their royal seats across the sea. Or the Bethlers, who rule a third of the Kingdom of Ushalayim and much besides that. They might trace their origins back here, but you cannot deny there is no real unity, my love.'

Hugon's heart hardened at mention of the warrior-monks. 'They should never have been allowed to flourish,' he snarled. 'The Crescent has for too long been overshadowed by the Bethel.'

'Ah, but that is where you and I differ,' breathed Isolte. 'For still you think too small. What if I told you that Pango-nia, the Pilgrim Kingdoms, the Bethlers, the Garter – aye and all the rest! – were but pieces in a great game of Jedrez, each with its own potency but all serving the same player?'

Hugon met her eyes again. Deep inky pools, they seemed to spurn the sylvan light that bathed them as the sun descended to its nocturnal grave.

'What player?'

The Queen leaned in closer. 'My sweet knight, do you trust me as you love me?'

'Absolutely.' He could scarcely say otherwise.

'Then I think it is time you were better acquainted with

someone at court, somebody whom you already know to be very influential.'

Picking up a small silver bell from the table, she tinkled it. One of her handmaidens reappeared.

'Charmaine, if you would be so kind as to show our guest in now.'

The lady-in-waiting nodded and vanished again.

'Guest?' burbled Hugon. 'You said nothing of another visitor.'

Isolte smiled seductively. 'I am saying something of him now, my sweet. It is long past time the two of you had a proper chat.'

A few moments later, a handsome noble entered. Sir Hugon recognised him instantly.

'My Lord Ivon,' said the Queen. 'How lovely to see you. Do join us.'

The margrave stepped into the chamber, favouring both of them with a florid bow. He hadn't been present at court for a while. His face looked drained and pale, perhaps his debaucherous lifestyle was overtaking him. It could have been his altered perception, but Hugon thought the dark circles ringed eyes that told of some loss, one the flam-boyant courtier struggled to conceal.

'Most noble Sir Hugon, Captain of the Garter,' said Ivon, smiling nonetheless. 'How delightful to find you here.'

Sir Hugon had risen to receive the new arrival. He felt no inclination to return the bow, but said stiffly: 'My Lord Ivon, I trust I find you in good health.'

The pointed remark was intentional. Sir Hugon knew the King used Ivon as his eyes and ears about court; that was exactly the sort of behaviour he despised in the latter-day nobility. What on earth was his beloved playing at?

A pained look crossed Ivon's aristocratic features. 'Would that I could report such, but I have been taken rather ill of late.' The sadness deepened in his eyes.

'Then pray sit and rest yourself,' said Isolte, motioning towards a chair. Drawing herself up she nodded to her lover. 'Sir Hugon, pray sit beside me.'

Thrilled though he was by the tacit show of intimacy, it worried Hugon. Just how much did Ivon know about their relationship? Probably far too much, if he lived up to his reputation.

Small talk followed, but Hugon had no appetite for such.

'Just what is your reason for bringing us here together?' he asked bluntly. 'My la-Your Majesty, you know how little I care for subterfuge.'

Ivon and Isolte exchanged knowing smirks at that.

'Indeed, your probity and valour well bespeak you,' simpered Ivon. 'So much so, in fact, that your lover the Queen and I have brought you here for a specific purpose.'

'I... how dare you?' Hugon made to rise, but the Queen restrained him with a light touch.

'Oh, do calm down, Sir Hugon,' beamed the margrave. 'Your secret is quite safe with me, I assure you – in fact it has been these past six months.'

The knight turned angrily on his paramour, forgetting himself in his choler. 'You told him of our affair? I thought we agreed-'

'I shall be the judge of the parameters of our agreement,'

said Isolte. Her tone remained soft, but there was a hardness to her words now. 'For am I not your Queen as well as your lover?'

'I... suppose so.' Hugon hardly knew what else to say. The *shisham* still clouded his thinking. Oh, for a cup of wine!

'Then listen to what His Lordship has to say,' she said. 'I think you will find his proposal to your liking.'

The Captain of the Garter turned back hesitantly to Ivon, whose pallid features made him look demoniacal as he grinned in the tinted light, now deepening to purple.

'Sir Hugon, I have a very simple question for you,' said the margrave. 'How would you like to enjoy the favours of your royal mistress with impunity *and* inherit the margravate of Valacia?'

Hugon felt a thrill course through him at the thought. Both of them were staring at him intently now. He felt something drawing on his willpower, as blood is drawn by a knife that bites deeply.

'I... should like that very much,' he said in a subdued voice.

Ivon leaned forwards and pressed his fingers together, steepling them under his aquiline chin. The dying light turned a shade darker, giving the margrave a preternatural aspect. Sir Hugon felt suddenly hot and cold all at once: excitement and fear coursed through him, intertwining in his veins and quickening his heart.

'My dear Sir Hugon,' said Ivon, his flashing teeth corpse-coloured in the eerie light. 'I have a feeling we're going to get on *famously*.'

The two knights dashed towards their steeds, gathering speed for the final sprint before launching themselves into the saddle. Anupe watched impassively as Torgun's feet found the stirrups; Braxus was not so lucky, slipping off the cantle and landing with a curse in the dirt of the palace courtyard.

Mingled laughter and applause rippled through the air, now cooling in the waning sun. Most of the Pangonian knights had stopped drilling to watch the contest; she didn't speak Panglian, but guessed that not all their remarks were courteous. They had been 'guests' at the Palace of White Towers for a couple of weeks, and their hosts had lost no opportunity in justifying their reputation for excessive pride. Not that Anupe cared; the opinions of men were of no importance to her.

'That levels up your brave knights in tasks,' she said dryly to Adhelina. 'Perhaps you can take them both to your bed when this absurd ritual is finished.'

Wrackwulf barely suppressed a guffaw at that remark, while Adhelina blushed furiously, shooting the Harijan a glance that might have transfixed a beast of the chase. 'I'll thank you to keep your brutish pagan sentiments to yourself,' said the damsel tartly. 'It's your professional opinion I'm after, not your personal observations.'

'You won't be needing the outlander for a professional opinion while I'm around,' put in Wrackwulf, draining his cup and beckoning a page for more. 'And it's clear enough who the winner is, in any case. That should make up for Sir Torgun's dismal efforts in the poesy task you set last week.'

Anupe had to laugh at that. Though she didn't speak much Decorlangue either, it had been clear from the expressions on everyone's faces that the Northlending's poetry left a lot to be desired. About as refined as a warhammer and twice as hard to bear, had been Wrackwulf's verdict. Apparently the Pangonians had been even less complimentary, though none had dared voice their opinions within earshot of the towering blond knight. On the other hand, Braxus' beautiful ballad, as he accompanied himself on his Thraxian harp, had needed no translation; even the stoical Harijan had felt herself nearly moved to tears by his lilting song. Adhelina had shed hers freely as she pronounced him the victor. Torgun had taken his loss with characteristic good grace.

Not that Sir Braxus was minded to repay his love rival in kind. Calling loudly for Vaskrian to take his horse, he stomped off towards the barracks, tugging irritably at the straps of his armour; to make the task more difficult both knights had been required to wear full harness. The squire turned from the quintain he had been jousting against and reluctantly dismounted.

'Did you see?' he asked Wrackwulf as he hustled past them in his master's wake. 'Ten times I charged the thing, and ten times I hit it! Didn't get caught once on the counter-punch either!'

The squire seemed oblivious to the fact that no one but him cared to see his progress at stick fighting. It was a stupid way to make war anyway; only a man would come up with something so idiotic. The sooner this king of fools Carolus let them go on their way, the better.

Sir Torgun strode over and took a knee as the palace knights went back to their training duties.

'My lady love, another task completed in your honour,' he declaimed seriously, his eyes never leaving the ground.

Adhelina smiled awkwardly and exchanged a wry glance with Hettie. Anupe looked at Wrackwulf and resisted the urge to roll her eyes. She had been in the Free Kingdoms long enough to be familiar with their ridiculous ways, but even by Urovian standards this contest was a farce; everyone but Braxus and Torgun could see that.

But then love was a passion, and passion was the mind-killer. Anupe knew that all too well: a contest over a woman had caused her exile. Only in her case it had been a lethal one, a knife-fight to the death, in true Harijan fashion. What a shame her rival had been such an influential chieftain. That hadn't stopped Anupe from putting her blade through Yula's heart seven years ago, but it had assured her banishment. The ways of her people were strict and unyielding.

The swordswoman let her gaze drift towards the palace

as Adhelina exchanged courtesies with her knightly swain. Roughly twice the size of Graukolos, it was impressive enough, with its hotch-potch of conical towers, their stuccoed brickwork mirroring the white clouds in the sky. But the Harijan had seen more impressive still: anyone who had looked upon the blood-red walls of Illyrium could hardly expect to be transported by much else that men had built.

Pangonia, richest of the Free Kingdoms! Yet still your splendour pales next to that of the Empire whence I came. There was no denying it: this corner of Urovia was a backwater, whatever its haughty inhabitants might think of it.

In any case, she'd had enough of men and their wretched stonemasonry. Even now her heart ached for the wooden walkways of Hamazos, the city of conjoined trees that had been capital of the Harijan Isles for millennia. She had yearned for it all the more since looking upon the benighted ruins of the Warlock's Crown. That awful spectacle had put her in mind of the Songs of Foreboding the priestesses of Hamazos would sing on winter nights, when ghostly shapes sloughed in off the Great Inland Sea, distorting the waves horribly as they reached towards the isles with spectral fingers... Somehow, she had been caught up in a strange quest that had its origins in the city of the Great Elder Ones, at the epicentre of those defiled waters. Only fervid prayers to the Moon Goddess succoured her people during the harsh cold months, when the very seas rose up to curse them, and even then they always lost a few dozen every year. Their farseers had oft spoken of a day when the city would rise again from its grave, putting all who dared oppose its masters into theirs.

But never had Anupe dreamed, during those fearful childhood tales, that she would live to see that day – much less have a hand in its shaping. And if the monk Horskram told it true, she had not done much to shape it for the better: yet another example of how love for a woman could turn one's head. Not that she regretted killing Andragorix. He had been a putrid example of the worst of his sex, and most men were bad enough. He had killed Kyra, the first woman Anupe had cared for since Uviah, for whose love she had willingly embraced exile. He had deserved to die.

And now who should come upon them, but Horskram himself? Anupe stiffened as she saw the adept approaching them, accompanied by the portly knight who served as seneschal to the King. She had come to learn that Horskram rarely arrived bringing good news.

Sir Odo motioned curtly and announced their visitor before stalking off. The royal steward always looked as though he had better things to attend to – but then men in high office were usually pompous like that. She'd met a female apothecary in the Empire who had told her that men and women were composed of different humours, the cruder sex having an excess of something called *choler*. This made them irrational and tempestuous. Anupe could well believe it, although she did not doubt she had her share of choler too.

She banished such thoughts as the seven of them gathered around the crotchety old monk, Vaskrian and Braxus joining them from the armoury. Horskram began to address them in Decorlangue. The tongue was similar to the Nacian and Garac dialects of the southern Empire, but Anupe still struggled with it. At least the monk was speaking slowly and deliberately; she could make out the gist of what he was saying.

'The good tidings are that you are all to be freed shortly,' the adept said. 'Another week to conclude business and you should have the King's leave.'

'And the bad tidings?' asked Braxus pointedly. The Thraxian knew their erstwhile leader all too well.

'Are that your freedom has been bought by the Order, which means you belong to me.'

A hue and cry ensued, both knights protesting as Horskram shouted them down, levelling on each in turn with stern words that Anupe could not follow.

'What's this about?' she whispered to Hettie.

'It's another of Master Horskram's secret missions,' sighed Hettie. 'It looks as though he has plans to send the knights back up north. He's saying Sir Braxus has a duty to avenge his father and reclaim his lands, and that Sir Torgun was made for more important things than wooing damsels.' She caught her mistress a sidelong glance as she said this, but Adhelina was too caught up in the bickering to notice.

'He's saying we're to wait out the winter here,' Hettie continued. 'We can't sail the Sundering Sea in the easterly winds, they'll be too rough at this time of year. But come spring we'll take a pilgrim ship for Ushalayim. He has business there and we'll go with him.'

'That is good news,' put in Anupe. 'A pilgrim ship is likely to stop at Panya in Mercadia to take on more passengers. From there we should be able to take ship to Khronos, it is the southernmost cityport of the Empire.'

'I don't think Braxus and Torgun think it good news,' muttered Hettie. Both knights were raging at Horskram now, Braxus shaking his fist in the monk's face while Torgun shook his head stubbornly. Anupe caught Vaskrian looking downcast, his burn scars making him a pitiful sight. He had been spending a lot of time talking to Hettie, when he wasn't busy training and attending his master. She had been teaching him Decorlangue – perhaps he had been teaching the damsel one or two things in return. The Harijan suppressed a sly smirk as she saw the two of them exchange a bashful look.

Love. It strikes without distinction or remorse, laying low beggar and king alike.

The argument finished with Horskram stomping off, flinging his cloak over his shoulder in that disgusted manner of his, and barking a few more curt words as he left. The two knights looked at each other, temporarily united in mutual rage.

'Well that's given us all something to ponder,' said Hettie sagely.

Anupe shrugged noncommittally. As far as she was concerned, there wasn't over much to ponder. The absurd love suit would soon be at an end, and the wide broad seas beckoned them all once more. The Harijan felt her heart soar at the prospect.

CHAPTER 12
A PARTING OF THE WAYS

They held each other in the moonlit courtyard, keeping the chill at bay with the warmth of their bodies. There was no one else around, beyond the odd bored guard walking the parapets of the palace walls; Hettie and Vaskrian had snuck out together after the latest feast, leaving the high-born nobles to carouse beneath the echoing halls.

Hettie ran her small hands up and down the squire's back, appreciating his toned muscles. He worked hard, there was no denying that. Even though he would probably never attain his cherished goal of knighthood. She had to admire him for that, even if he was a hothead and a fool sometimes.

He leaned in and kissed her again. She felt the rough wetness of his tongue and it thrilled her; she had of course never intended for things to go this far, but one drunken night in the dancing hall nature had taken its course. Small wonder, given the licentiousness of the Riman court; their trysting had been tame, compared to that of others she had glimpsed frolicking in the palace gardens.

She pulled away, those thoughts bringing a touch of the cold night air to her passion.

'We... mustn't go too far,' she faltered. Her body was telling her a very different story. Screaming it in fact.

Vaskrian tried to hide his disappointment, failing spectacularly. Three days had passed since Horskram had arrived with his mixed tidings; word had been sent from the Grand High Monastery that the Order had agreed to the King's ransom terms. The damsels were to winter in the palace; their brave knights would be packed off to Thraxia within the week.

And where a knight went, his squire must follow.

'We maybe don't see each other again,' he said in his halting Decorlangue. Even now, he was trying to impress her. She felt her heart clench as a keen wind strafed the courtyard, mocking her cooling desire with its shivering gust.

'Just speak to me in Northlending, it's easier,' she said, reaching up to caress his burned face. She had even come to love that part of him over the past three weeks. Perhaps something in her was drawn to flawed men, inside and out.

He drew her in with his hazel eyes. Hettie's pulse quickened again. She prided herself on being sensible, but he was her second amour and it was difficult to keep her head. Plus after everything they had been through... Part of her was relieved they would be staying behind at the palace. The more normalcy they had in their lives, the better she liked it.

Not that she liked it at this price.

'I know we've only courted a short while, and you're a high-born lady and all,' he stuttered. 'But I really like you. I think you're pretty and...'

Hettie sighed inwardly. One of the knightly virtues Vaskrian clearly hadn't practised was lovemaking. Not in the courtly sense anyway.

'Don't talk,' she said, smiling sweetly. 'Just kiss me again.'

But Vaskrian hesitated. He seemed to make his mind up about something, then said: 'Braxus will be getting drunk as usual. I don't think he's taking this well, about being separated from your mistress. I'm lodged with him in the guest wing of the palace. We could...' He faltered again, staring at her meaningfully.

Hettie felt her heart petrify, her returning passion freezing over. Why did men always do this? Try and rush things, for the sake of... what? Another conquest? A precious notch on their lances?

'I thought I made it clear, I'm not that type of girl,' she said, stiffly pushing him away. 'And I'm high-born. I must marry before I...'

The squire's eyes blazed over at that. 'But you said yourself, none of that matters any more! After everything we've been through, all we've seen! Why shouldn't we lie together, Hettie? Chances are I'll be dead come spring!'

'Don't talk so!' she exclaimed, reaching up to stifle him with her fingers. 'You're no farseer, Vaskrian. And you said yourself that woods witch thinks you're marked out for great things.'

'Great things no man will ever ennoble me for,' the

squire replied bitterly. 'I suppose that's why you won't have me – I'll always just be a commoner to you, hey?'

'That isn't fair!' she cried. Unbidden, tears pushed at the corners of her eyes, their salty sting an unwelcome sensation. Men always had to spoil things with their horrid talk – and all because they couldn't get what they wanted, right away. An all-too-familiar feeling of disgust began to curdle inside her. What a fool she had been, to let him get this close. Their misadventures had turned her head, all right.

'I thought you could be patient,' she said. 'And wait. But no, you're just like any knight, you think you're entitled to any woman you want.'

'I'm no knight,' the squire retorted. 'And that means you're no lady, for courting me in the first place! Anyway, maidens from Vorstlund don't ride side-saddle – you've long since been broken in by a damned horse, so why not let me have what I want?'

Hettie's jaw dropped. Vaskrian had a fierce temper and said stupid things, but even for him this was coarse and cruel.

'I don't know what I ever saw in you,' she spat at him, tears crawling down her cheeks. 'I hope I never you see you again! You can die in battle, for all I care!'

She turned and stormed off, her tears mercifully blotting out the pock-marked moon that leered down at them. Perhaps Kaia was displeased with her, for behaving like a silly girl. Vaskrian called after her, his voice tortured with regret, but she had no ears for his pleas.

~

Sir Braxus stepped out from the beneath the shadow of a statue of Luviah, where he had been observing the two hapless lovers.

'Well done, squire of mine, bravo!' he said, clapping his hands sarcastically. The whitestone face of the avatar of love beamed, oblivious as to how little she had bestowed her favours on either of them. 'Impeccably done, as always! Thank Reus you wield a better sword than you court a lady's hand – I'd be very worried about taking you home to fight otherwise!'

'How long have you been here?' gawped Vaskrian, shock momentarily displacing his dolour.

'Long enough to see I haven't taught you anything about how to woo a maiden,' quipped Braxus. He was drunk, mean drunk – and loving it. He'd left shortly after the feast to find his squire and order him to prepare harness for a long journey. They weren't leaving for a few days yet, but he was damned if the lad would have all the fun while he stayed in his cups, alone and forlorn.

'You haven't taught me much of anything since you started courting Adhelina,' Vaskrian shot back. 'I've practically had to train myself! Why, even Sir Torgun took time to show me some swordplay, and he's been after her just as much as you have! Not that I'm complaining – he's a better swordsman than you'll ever be!'

That hurt. Memories of the Graufluss Bridge Tourney still clung stubbornly to the back of his mind. Braxus had hoped the Draugbreath would erase the past, or at least put it into perspective, but it hadn't. If anything it only made his sorrows keener – funny how one pain piled on top of another, a towering dung heap that choked a man's heart.

'You insolent Northlending dog!' he snarled, bearing down on Vaskrian with a raised hand. 'I ought to have you flogged for talking so!'

'Go on then!' yelled Vaskrian. 'I'm sick of you and all the rest of your kind, moping around and feeling sorry for yourselves! Try walking in my boots for a day, and learn what real pain feels like!'

Something in the way the squire said that brought Braxus up short. He took in the youth's ravaged face, the suffering that gave his eyes a keenness he'd never really noticed until now. And felt his heart moved to pity.

'Vaskrian, I...' he stumbled, feeling suddenly clumsy of speech. Lowering his hand, he gently rested it on his squire's shoulder. 'Lad, I'm sorry... I've had too much wine. You're right – it's not fair of me to make you bear the burden of my troubles.'

'I suppose we've all had plenty of those lately,' said Vaskrian, looking downcast and sullen.

'Aye, we have,' sighed Braxus. 'Come on, squire of mine, let's go find some ale. A pox on this Pangonian wine, it's too bloody strong.'

'So you've said your farewells, I suppose?' muttered Vaskrian as they made their way over to the royal kitchens.

The knight felt a sting of longing that no wine could abate. 'Aye, squire of mine,' he managed. 'I kept it brief, for all farewells should be sudden.' And at that, keeping his arm around Vaskrian, he broke into song:

·   ·   ·

My mistress she's from Faenlon town,
She wears my soul for a beauty crown,
Now she's gone to the barrow downs,
Across the darkling seas

She taught me how to love and groan
She taught me how to curse and moan
She raised me up and cast me down
To the depths of the darkling seas

Now parted, ne'er to meet again,
Through stormy gales and driving rains,
I'm bound for yonder shores of pain
Across the darkling seas

Oh I will strum and I will pluck,
A ditty of my wretched luck,
I'll sing of how I came unstuck,
Across the darkling seas

A shadow of her face I see,
Whene'er I glance at landward lee,
Her lingering shade will come for me,
When I sink through the darkling seas

.   .   .

The lilting words echoed through the silent courtyard as they crossed it, seeming to loosen the dark shroud of night briefly as they reached the welcoming glow of the kitchen torches. Braxus sang in Thrax, and Vaskrian could have no way of comprehending the stanzas, yet the squire wept silently as they went to drown their sorrows together.

The courtiers formed an elegant circle as they danced the carola, moving in undulating reels in the direction of the sundial. Torgun felt uncomfortable in his court clothes; he missed his hauberk and gambeson, the tang of steel and leather in his nostrils. At least this was a formal dance event, held in the dancing hall in sight of the King, and more restrained than the other debauches he had witnessed here.

The decadence of the Riman court disgusted him. Had this land truly spawned the paladins that birthed the Code of Chivalry? The only evidence of Sir Lancelyn and his ilk to be found here was in the tapestries that lined the walls; the perfumed and bibulous nobles that cavorted in sight of those great heroes seemed an outrageous mockery of their kingdom's rich history. Small wonder Lancelyn looked so sad, as he stooped to receive the Garland of Aquitania, his prize for winning the joust in the legendary Tourney of the Triple Arches.

What was he doing in this dissolute country? Part of the answer to that question glided painfully into view, as they entered the bridge movement. Adhelina looked as ravishing as the day he had first set eyes on her; dressed in an embroidered mantle of pale lemon and bejewelled in sapphires that caught the candlelight with lustrous flashes, perhaps even more so. She spared him a fleeting glance as they passed one another and the minstrels changed tack, their vielles humming frenetically as they skilfully moved the dancers towards the estampie. Her gaze was agonisingly reserved. But then what more was there to be said on the matter? His love suit was at an end, killed in its tracks by Horskram, a man who had probably never known desire. Perhaps Torgun should have left with Braxus; he'd been surprised to see the normally graceful Thraxian stalk out of the feasting hall after bidding a curt farewell to Adhelina.

As they split into pairs and dropped into the sliding steps of the estampie, Sir Torgun found himself relieved that his love rival wasn't here; he was a middling dancer at best, far more comfortable on the battlefield or horseback. He hated himself for feeling that way too, even about such a bitter rival. Was this what love did to a man's heart? Made him pettish and mean-spirited, thinking thoughts no chivalrous knight should think.

He felt his sense of melancholy deepen as he caught Adhelina dancing with Sir Aremis, she taking the swallow position while he assumed the falcon. The crescent knight was the one Pangonian courtier Torgun truly respected; strong yet humble and unassuming, perhaps the only real successor to Sir Lancelyn among all the haughty southern knights. He moved well enough too, despite his uncomely features, his lean muscled torso inching past Adhelina's ample bosom with a closeness that sent hot daggers of jealousy through Torgun's breast. The rebecs twanged cogently, their cadence intertwining with the haut tones of the pipes as they took up the tune from the dying vielles; laughter filled the air as courtiers glid like swans about the shadowed hall, before each pair separated with a twirl and found their next partner. Torgun's heart rate increased as he found himself face to face with Adhelina. He'd scarcely had eyes for the southern beauty he'd been dancing with, the cousin of some margrave who tried to catch him in her hot-eyed stare.

Torgun leaned in and spoke in a low voice, the heady scent of Adhelina's perfume raking invisible fingers through his senses, stirring up his passions to greater heights.

'My lady love, this shall be our last dance together.' He wanted to say more, but the words died in his throat.

'Don't be sad, sweet Sir Torgun,' she breathed as she glid past him, her hip grazing his tantalisingly. Adhelina was scarcely better than a middling dancer herself, but to Torgun that was only another reason to love the honest maiden. 'If Luviah is kind we shall meet again, once your strange business is at an end.'

Aye, strange indeed, he thought as he turned half a dial, his feet sliding awkwardly across the polished whitestone floor. *But not so strange that you don't already know far more about it than a damsel ought.* He found Adhelina's reading habits less endearing than her other traits.

'I shall bear your token wherever I go,' he said, taking a full turn about Adhelina, as he strove awkwardly to mimic the falcon's wings with his mighty arms. 'Your memory shall be a light to guide me, through whatever darkness Horskram leads us into.'

He cursed inwardly. Poesy and fine speech had never been a strong point of his either.

Adhelina said nothing further, but smiled sweetly as she fluttered around him one last time, her sad kohl-limned eyes belying the upwards curve of her full painted lips.

The music shifted again, and Adhelina moved on out of his sight, to be replaced by another faceless lady of the Riman court.

Sir Wrackwulf watched the two lovers parting in the middle of the hall, and frowned ruefully into his winecup. As much as he enjoyed being detained at the richest court in the Free Kingdoms, it was high time they took to the road again. Seeing two great knights like Torgun and Braxus lose their heads over the disinherited heiress had been a pitiful enough sight; now, to make it worse, the squire Vaskrian was at it too, chasing after her lady-in-waiting. A pretty pass and no mistake!

Yes, the sooner we're off questing again the better. This new mission of Horskram's sounded interesting, and it would be well paid. Errantry was appealing to Wrackwulf more and more: it was less tedious than playing the tourney circuit, and just as lucrative. Plenty of glory to be had too, once he talked the monk out of his obsessive secrecy.

What's the point of doing bold deeds, if you can't spin a yarn or two in the taverns and fleshpots afterwards? A man has to enjoy life, after all.

The freelancer glanced sidelong at Anupe, slouching

against a whorled pillar next to him. He'd had to sneak her in after the feast, with a few stern words for the haughty under-seneschal who tried to bar her way. All most irregular, but then the lovelorn knights had left him with the pagan savage for drinking company. Not that he minded over much – he'd sooner drink with a Harijan outlander he'd shared adventure with than an effete Pangonian court knight any day – but carousing with a wench he had no intention of bedding felt passing strange.

Still, there'd be plenty of comely serving girls to have once the King and Queen departed. Then the fun would really begin. Pangonians stinted on food – their fare was far too dainty for the Vorstlending's liking – but they more than made up for it with other appetites.

'Another refill?' he asked Anupe, holding up his empty winecup. He'd had to get used to drinking the lethal ruby liquid, ale was out of the question at the Pangonian King's court.

'Why not?' replied the Harijan languidly. 'Yon foreigners dance so badly, I need another drink just to bear the sight of them. Your music is awful, too – it has no rhythm, no...' Anupe made a pushing motion as if to make clear her meaning.

Wrackwulf chuckled at that. He wasn't one for southern court dancing himself, the merry jigs of the northerly kingdoms were more his style. He grabbed a passing serving wench, taking the opportunity to run a brawny hand across her backside while she poured them drinks. These southern girls were a bit skinny for his liking, but they knew how to use their mouths if you paid them enough.

And one thing the freelancer wasn't short of these days was coin.

Leaning closer to the wench, he whispered a proposition in Panglian that was both saucy and remunerative. What had he told Vaskrian when they had first met? Learning foreign tongues was always useful. He caught Anupe grinning as he propositioned the wench, who favoured him with a coy smile.

'She is fine enough,' said the Harijan in Vorstlending. 'Perhaps she could lie with us both?'

Wrackwulf wrinkled his nose distastefully. The idea of seeing the gnarled Harijan naked didn't appeal. The dark-eyed girl looked at Anupe curiously, blissfully ignorant of her words.

'Find your own bloody whore,' laughed Wrackwulf, stroking the wench's bare back appreciatively as he slurped on his wine.

'That I shall,' breezed Anupe. 'This I think will be our last revel at the palace.'

Wrackwulf nodded. 'Now we're well, Master Horskram has work for us. About time, I say.'

Anupe did not take her lusty eyes off the winsome girl as she replied. 'Yes, though something tells me not all of us will meet again.'

The freelancer raised a bushy eyebrow.

'What makes you say that?' he asked, suddenly aware of the relative silence. The jongleurs had ceased with a drawn out passage of play, and the courtiers were retiring to the edges of the colonnaded hall to refresh themselves and indulge their other passions. The King and Queen rose to leave, the knights and ladies bowing sycophantically as they exited the rectangular chamber with their preening entourage in tow.

Anupe shrugged in that insouciant manner of hers.

'Call it an instinct if you will,' she said. 'The holy man's business is rarely straightforward, I have found. This will be a week of farewells.'

Wrackwulf pursed bearded lips across the rim of his cup as he mulled over the Harijan's words. The troubadours struck up another ditty in the wake of the King's passing, as the courtiers mingled and flirted over wine and sweetmeats. Valour was second nature to him, but he felt a faint chill blow softly through his hackles, as smudged memories of looming kings with dark crowns and terrible black swords ghosted across his memory.

Just what was he getting himself into?

CHAPTER 13
AT THE FEET OF GREAT SAGES

A distant rumble of thunder harassed the skies, as the rain pattered against the library's stained glass ceiling. Leaning back from the lectern in his carrel, Adelko stretched painfully. By Palom, but his muscles *ached*. Brother Edemus had made him hold two pails of cow's milk at arm's length first thing that morning, to build up his strength. Devil's juice, Horskram had ironically called goatsmilk, after revealing that Abaddon had created the irascible creatures. Adelko didn't think the same applied to cows, but now he had other reasons for calling their milk such. His shoulders and back were on fire; surely the City of Burning Brass could furnish no worse torments.

He quelled the blasphemous thought. It was unbefitting a monk of the Order, here at its very heart. Brother Bertram had given him the run of the library, for one hour every morning after his training with Edemus. That had meant getting up even earlier, but to Adelko it was worth it.

Knowledge. It was all he had ever truly thirsted for. Far

more thrilling to him than learning to split a man's clavicle with a quarterstaff, though he was learning that too. He'd been so excited, it had scarcely occurred to him that once again he was being prepared for something big. He wondered if Horskram had been pulling strings for him again, though Bertram had said the order came directly from Hannequin – a new mentor he had yet to meet personally, after being at the monastery for more than a month.

Clearing his mind of distractions, Adelko hunched over the illuminated parchment scroll and re-read its opening passage:

Even now, after nigh on five hundred years of conflict, there is still far too much we do not know about magi and their ilk; perhaps this lack of communication is fortunate, for it can also be said that warlocks do not yet know all of our ways. However, it is an irrefutable truth that we share similarities that it might shock many to learn of.

The clue lies in the very word used both by our sacred Order and students of the arcane arts to describe the sum of our psychic abilities. The word 'elan', derived from the Decorlangue word for 'soul' or 'spirit', can be traced back to an earlier word in an older language, roughly translated as 'soul-disturbance' or 'soul chan-nelling'. Indeed, the very act of channelling supernatural powers constitutes a disruption of the soul, as it brings about an altering of the natural state of things decreed by Reus Almighty at the Dawn of Time.

We Argolians draw upon our elan when we incant the sacred words of the Redeemer – as written down in the High Speech in our Holy Book by the First Acolyte, Hispus – so we can muster the necessary conviction to make them effective; whereas wizards use their elan in conjunction with the Sorcerer's Tongue, a hieratic script that must be simultaneously visualised and incanted. We claim that our power is harnessed directly from Reus, through Palom; they claim theirs is derived from the Unseen, archangels and archdemons who were of course themselves created by the Almighty.

Adelko frowned as he mulled that over, the elegant script seeming to dance across his vision in the flickering flame of his candle. Made of wax not tallow – another expensive import from the Empire – its light was cleaner and brighter, but all the same his reading gave him a headache.

Question everything. The treatise had been written by Arnulf of Balzac, fifty-third Grand Master of the Order, in the year 1053 After Redemption. The Purge had come seven years later, resulting in many of Arnulf's brethren being persecuted by the Temple; some said that the Grand Master's sacrilegious teachings had provoked suspicion of the Order, allowing the clandestine demonolator Abelard of Montrevellyn to militate against it for his own diabolic purposes. Asking questions hadn't done Arnulf – or the wider Order – much good, it seemed.

And yet here I am, following the words of a woods witch and asking them anyway.

Were Argolians so different from the warlocks they hunted after all? Certainly he could see no kinship with the likes of Andragorix, but the Earth Witch had used her magick to create a blessed realm for beast and bird, and helped them defeat the monstrous mage. Were Argolians really kindred spirits with Right Hand magicians? Just as the archangels created by the Almighty were worshipped as gods in their own right in pagan lands, perhaps ultimately all mortals came to Him by differing paths... But where was He in all of this? Why make the road to godhead such a crooked one – did testing mortals like that really make them better, or did it just furnish more excuses for war and conflict?

Adelko rubbed his temples, which were by now beginning to rival his burning shoulders in their expression of pain.

Glancing up at the ceiling, his eye fell on the stained-glass pane depicting the Redeemer turning wine into water on the eve of battle, so his armies would fight better come morning. His soldiers had been so impressed by the miracle they had renounced strong drink for the rest of the campaign, allowing them to outmanoeuvre and outlast the feted Iron Legions. Or so the scriptures told. Adelko had seen enough of fighting men by now to doubt that the absence of liquors would do anything but make them more irritable. How much truth had Hispus and the rest of the Seven Acolytes put into the *Holy Book*, and how much of it was mere bard's song?

Six months ago, Adelko would have been shocked at himself for thinking such thoughts, but now they seemed almost commonplace to him.

Heaving a sigh, he bent towards the parchment once more:

. . .

Many would argue that we Argolians are indeed different, for we know nothing of the arts of Thaumaturgy, that can change the laws of nature by binding Elementi, nor the arts of Scrying that allow one to peer beyond the curtain of time. And yet... our sixth sense enables us to perceive things other men cannot – is this so very different from Scrying? And the hierophanti among us are able to speed up their perception of time, moving with a speed and vigour that defies the natural compass of our mortal frames, when their elan runs quick – is this so very different from using Thaumaturgy to bring down a tree or take to the air and fly? And just as magi sometimes use artefacts to amplify their their spell-casting – wands, staves, rings and other items invested with power – so do we turn to relics and the symbol of our faith, the circifix, to augment ours. Again, where is the fundamental differ-ence between the two, but what our perception – ever flawed, as the Redeemer himself sayeth – leads us to believe or choose to believe?

Looking back upon our struggles with witches of all kinds, it has often struck me how finely balanced we are: a journeyman can, with the right tools and preparation, neutralise the magicks of a hedge witch, but is overmatched by a more powerful warlock; an adept can counter a more accomplished sorcerer using the Psalm of Gramarye's Quenching, if Reus smiles on him and his will is strong; but only the few hierophanti in any generation of Argolians could hope to contend with a master warlock or grand witch. And just as warlocks can sometimes blend disciplines across the different schools of magick, for instance using artifice, the sub-discipline of Alchemy, to bind to an artefact Elementi conjured using a sub-discipline of Thaumaturgy, so on occasion do we use the Psalms of Abjuration and Fortitude in conjunction, the one prayer bolstering another.

There seems altogether too much harmony in this arrangement for me to doubt that we are but two halves of a whole, Argolians and witches acting against one another, yet part of some celestial pattern, which we cannot yet begin to divine for ourselves. Look to the parallel orders in Sassania, established to counter sorcery there, and you will discern a similarly graded balance of powers.

Arnulf had couched his words carefully, for fear of bringing down too much wrath on his Order. Not that he had succeeded in averting that calamity: only when Hannequin and other adepts had divined Abelard's true nature had the undercover demonologist's scheme been exposed and the Order exonerated. Adelko had learned all this and more in the library's treatises on history: so far no tomes had been off-limits to him, Brother Avrik the under-librarian having complied with all his requests. That pleased him, but he wondered what Horskram was preparing him for this time.

It was only then that Adelko realised he'd spent more time thinking about the old monk than his late father. His grief had settled down into a dull ache in his breast: he hadn't seen Arun in years, and truth to tell his family were a distant memory. All except his brother Arik, of course, whom he'd met unexpectedly on the march to war in Northalde. Adelko wondered how he was doing, with his shrewish wife and demanding job as clan armourer back up north in the highlands. Their father's death must have hit him hard. As for his own sorrow, Adelko felt he had little time to spare for it, what with the Known World headed towards disaster.

His reverie was interrupted by Bertram coming over to inform him that his hour was up. For once Adelko didn't mind. He had quarterstaff class next – but even fighting in the rain would be a welcome respite from his troubling thoughts.

The rain had not abated by the time Adelko trudged out to join his cohort in the outer courtyard. At least the packed clay wouldn't be too affected, though Edemus liked to make them fight in any weather. It made sense: Adelko knew all too well you couldn't always choose when to fight your battles.

At least Arik and Hargus were there. His two old friends from Ulfang had stayed on while their mentors conferred with the High Circle on important matters. Did those have anything to do with his recent quest, Adelko wondered? He smiled in greeting at the pair of them as he joined them from the barracks.

'Looks like Adelko's been burning the dawn tallow again,' grinned Hargus. 'Nice to know some things don't change – they'll bury you in a tome not a tomb!'

If only you knew how much things have changed, thought Adelko ruefully. His sixth sense quickened momentarily and he caught Arik sidelong, a dark look on his dark face.

He didn't need it to tell him his friend was growing ever more envious of him. A year older than Adelko, he would soon begin training for his initiation as journeyman. Adelko doubted his privileged access to the Order's most venerable library had gone over too well with his old rival.

His worst fears were confirmed when Edemus paired them for sparring.

'Right then, novices,' said Edemus in his even voice. 'Remember everything we looked at so far this week. I don't want to see any sloppy footwork or stupid overhead strikes that leave your torso exposed. Just because you've read about them in the lays, doesn't mean they're a good idea in real life.'

Adelko had to bite his tongue. He'd seen enough real-life fights to know that.

'Spar!' Edemus did not raise his voice as he gave the order to begin.

The venomous look on Arik's face as he came at Adelko was telling. He'd never been a great one for quarterstaff technique either, but his time on the road had obviously toughened him up. Likewise the intervening year had seen him grow from a gangly youth into a lean, trim young man. But it was the intensity in his black eyes that really shocked Adelko.

He'd never believed Arik could hate him. But it felt – and looked – that way now.

The ferocity of his attack pushed Adelko's improved defensive skills to the limit. Pain seared his thighs as he moved back and circled around his opponent; every morning Edemus made him hold a crouching position for what seemed like ages, sweating it out through rising agony until he told him to release.

'There's more to building muscle than hefting heavy weights, Adelko,' the Thalamian had told him more than once. 'Let the body be its own conditioner. The natural forces that Reus dictated can be bent to our will and made to serve us.'

At least the past few weeks of pain were starting to pay off. Already Adelko moved with a fluency that Udo had been unable to instil in him; the moves he had learned sluggishly over the years were starting to come more naturally. Besides, the pain was quickly drowned out by battle choler, which Adelko strove to refine into deadly force as Edemus had taught him.

Arik feinted towards the right side of his head, before sweeping around with the other end of his staff towards Adelko's midriff. It was a clever move, skilfully executed; but Adelko was quick enough to read it and anticipate. Turning a half circle on feet that always stayed the same distance apart, he parried the treacherous blow with a clang of iron on iron before riposting with a half-overhead strike at the older monk's head. Arik narrowly avoided being struck, scuttling back and interposing his own staff just in time. Sweat began to bead on his forehead, mingling with the rain as he moved back out of range.

Adelko followed him up, trying to keep calm. He was determined to give his rival no respite, but couldn't afford to let his anger get the better of him.

They exchanged another flurry of blows. The rain eased slightly, facilitating their speed, and the next couple of minutes were a blur to Adelko. At last they pulled back again, both breathing heavily. Out of the corner of his eye, Adelko realised the other novices had stopped to watch them. Edemus wasn't barking at them to get back to it; he stood impassively, watching to see how his protégé would fare.

Adelko let such thoughts slip away as he returned focus to his antagonist. Arik seemed to be doing likewise, frozen still in combat stance and sizing him up. Their eyes met, and for a moment he felt a current of energy pass between them, as their sixth senses probed at one another.

His reading in the library flashed back to him.

The hierophanti are able to speed up their perception of time, moving with a speed and vigour that defies the natural compass of our mortal frames. Just as Horskram had done, in his fight against Andragorix at the Warlock's Crown. But Adelko was no hierophant, just a novice learning at the feet of his betters. And yet there *was* something there, an offshoot of his sixth sense, wanting to take control.

No, not to take control: to *guide* him...

Without warning Arik lunged, aiming two crosswise strikes from left to right in quick succession. Adelko blocked them both and retaliated in kind. The pair circled each other, their boots squealing on the soaked clay as they probed one another's defences yet again. Again they clashed, and again they parted, circling one another like birds of prey. Some of the novices including Hargus began to yell encouragement, ignoring Edemus as he sternly told them to pipe down. Adelko let the distraction wash through him...

And then, just like that, the something he'd been feeling clicked into place. Movements that were his own, yet not his own, came without thinking. He barely registered what happened in the next few moments: more clanging of iron staves, Arik stepping backwards on faltering feet, eyes wide open as his breath came in raggedy gasps...

With an elasticity he never knew he had, Adelko slid forwards to Arik's right, his left leg extended at full stretch as he pivoted on his right foot and swept his quarterstaff into the backs of Arik's knees. The force of the blow astonished Adelko as much as it did his opponent, who turned a half cartwheel in the air before landing on the clay with a painful thud. Without thinking about it, Adelko launched himself back up on legs that were coiled springs, planting his feet on either side of Arik's prone torso and placing his quarterstaff at his throat.

Thoughts of Horskram's duel with Andragorix flashed through his mind again.

Gazing down at Arik's rain-spattered face, contorted with a look of bewilderment and fear, Adelko felt renewed anger churning upwards from the pit of his stomach. An ugly demon no warlock could summon clawed its way up into his mind, and he felt a rage he had never known fighting to subsume his gentler nature.

Slowly, ever so slowly, he began to apply pressure to Arik's throat...

'ADELKO!' Edemus' voice was all the more frightening for its unaccustomed loudness. 'You've beaten him! That's enough!'

Adelko held his staff pressed to Arik's throat for a couple

more moments, letting the rage flow through him. Abruptly he pulled it up and stepped aside. He felt the battle choler mercifully ebbing out of him, and looking around he blinked dazedly as he registered the astounded expressions on his cohort's faces.

'All right, that's enough combat practice for today,' said Edemus. Did the cool journeyman actually sound shaken? 'Return your staves to barracks and go about your duties. Dismissed.'

'He improves daily,' commented Hannequin laconically, from where they stood on a parapet overlooking the outer courtyard. 'Perhaps now you see my faith in the lad was not misplaced.'

Horskram frowned. 'I never said it was, Grand Master,' he replied. 'Merely that too much can come too soon. He almost crushed his friend's larynx just now.'

'His elan is quickening at a rate not often seen,' said Hannequin. 'He's bound to have a few displays of anger now and then. But you saw how well he recovered – clearly his mind is strong. It's early Novis now – come spring he will be more than ready.'

'Four months? To become a journeyman of the Order?'

'I've had Bertram give him special access to the library every morning. His knowledge should be more than sufficient by the time the Sundering Sea is safe to sail.'

Horskram's frown deepened. He didn't like to argue with

his superior, but his sixth sense told him he was mistaken in this matter.

'It might help if you at least told him of your intentions,' Horskram contented himself with saying.

'Adelko is humble as befits an Argolian, and I'd sooner do nothing to change that,' said Hannequin. 'He'll have enough of the Seven Princes to contend with as he masters his anger. Let him proceed as is – he shall need no formal examination, his adventures with you this past year have been test of his faculties enough.'

Horskram nodded reluctantly. He had little choice but to accept the Grand Master's decision.

'And what of Sir Torgun and the others?' asked the adept, keen to change the subject. 'Are they ready to set sail?'

'The ransom has been paid in full,' replied Hannequin, his voice tightening. He had been scarcely overjoyed to hear of the princely sum Carolus was demanding. 'All that remains is to give them a final after-blessing for the Draug-breath, and entrust the Circifix of St Argo to your brave knight's keeping. They should be arriving here tonight, you can brief them in full tomorrow.'

At least that was one thing going the way Horskram wanted. Not that his brave knights had been overjoyed at having their freedom bought for them conditionally. 'Very good,' said the adept. 'Though it may take them a while to become enthused by their new mission.'

'Well, you vouched for them,' said the Grand Master. 'Do what you always do – convince them it is in their own best interests.'

'I shall,' replied Horskram, knowing full well it wouldn't

be easy. That blasted damsel and her ravishing good looks – he'd have to keep an eye on her while they were gone, doubtless both knights would insist upon it. *One more thing to worry about.*

'I'll give them a letter of introduction,' Hannequin continued. 'Once they've made contact with the resistance movement in Thraxia, they can present it to Brother Joram. The foremost witch hunter of Kilucan monastery should be of help to their quest.'

'I've been hearing that Kilucan was burnt to the ground on Abrexta's orders a couple of months ago,' said Horskram grimly. 'We don't even know for sure if he survived her persecution of our Order.'

'These are dark times for the Argolians, to be sure,' said Hannequin, making the sign. Horskram could sense the pain in him. 'But Joram is as able a monk as any I've ever trained – and we've heard no word of his demise.'

Horskram resisted the urge to speak his thoughts. Brother Joram had a reputation for zealotry and hot-headedness unbecoming a friar of the Order. Though his elan was undeniably strong, his temper was less so. *Another uncertain ally.*

'Have you spoken with Cathbad?' he asked, changing the subject again. His friend had been on his mind for the past fortnight, but he hadn't seen him since they'd taken him into custody.

'Several times,' replied Hannequin. 'I still don't believe he was behind Wolaf's binding any more than you do, but I'll have to keep him sequestered for his own safety. The adepthood have their knives out.' Six score seasoned Argolians had been unable to add anything to their latest divination. That hadn't stopped them voicing opinions aplenty on what should be done with the apostate in their midst.

'The adepthood covet Cathbad's place on the High Circle,' said Horskram bluntly. 'Our Order has become tainted by Riman ways, it waxes far too proud and ambitious.'

Hannequin favoured him with a keen stare. 'Yes, well, I'd spend more time worrying about who bound a demon to Wolaf, and how they managed to seduce him in the first place. This was no ordinary possession or manifestation. Testimonies from demonologists suggest that only a willing host may be used for a binding of such duration and sophistication.'

Horskram pursed his lips. The novices had filed away, Edemus keeping Adelko behind for a few choice words before letting him go too. The adept's sixth sense flared every time he thought about his former understudy.

'As ever, there is still far too much we do not know,' sighed Horskram. 'Have your enquiries with the Bethlers yielded any fruit?'

'None as yet,' replied Hannequin. 'I've sent word to Brother Sir Godfrey of the Riman Preceptory, asking for a meeting in person, but he hasn't replied. I imagine he's busy with preparations for this damnable new crusade.'

Horskram had to smile at that. Temple bureaucracy seldom proceeded with any swiftness.

Just then a lone figure came riding in through the gatehouse. He wore the dark grey habit of an adept, and though his cowl was pulled up to avert the rain Horskram sensed who he was.

'So you recalled Prior Johann from Heilag,' grunted the adept.

'On the pretext of needing his counsel in the wake of this crisis,' said Hannequin. 'He's to help me pick replacements for Wolaf and Cathbad.'

'Yes, I imagine his overweening pride would leave him susceptible to such a ruse,' sneered Horskram. Then he raised an eyebrow, as a sudden thought occurred to him. 'You're not actually thinking-'

'Of appointing him?' Hannequin chuckled. 'Oh no, don't you worry. But it doesn't harm to have Johann believe that is a possibility.'

Horskram allowed himself a rare grin as he watched Johann dismount and bark orders at the hapless novice on stable duty. 'Pride is a chink in any man's armour, as the Redeemer sayeth.'

'It is indeed,' replied Hannequin.

The Grand Master didn't take his eyes off Johann as he spoke, but Horskram had the uneasy feeling his last words were aimed at him.

CHAPTER 14
A STORM-TOSSED HOMECOMING

Rain lashed the mainsail of the hulk as it crawled up the coastline, the choppy seas rocking the ship from side to side as the crew strove to bring her to port. Up ahead the lights of Craek could be seen, glimmering eerily through the fog. Not for the first time, Vaskrian clutched the taffrail and struggled to master his churning guts. Seafaring was bad enough during summertime; in Kaldemonath it was horrendous. Folk seldom took to the road at this time of year, never mind the waves.

Braxus joined him at the prow, his pallid features doing a good job of mirroring his own, he imagined. Less the burn scars, that was.

'At least it's nearly over, lad,' he said, trying to sound cheerful. 'We'll have a stoup of Thraxian mead and some roasted boar in our bellies come nightfall, mark my words!'

The squire grimaced. Right now food and drink were the last things he wanted to think about. At least he was back on friendly terms with the guvnor again. During their past fortnight at sea – hugging the coastline in such bad weather was painfully slow work – they had bonded again. Braxus had been quick to break out the lyre, belting out tunes in the cramped space below decks as they berthed at night. They were always jolly ones – but all the fast numbers in the world couldn't hide the knight's sorrow at being parted from Adhelina. For his part, Torgun hadn't bothered trying to hide his melancholy, but kept to himself, brooding and absent-mindedly stroking the relic Horskram had given him.

It was a feeling Vaskrian knew all too well. But then at least the two knights had parted with their lady love on civil terms, both vowing to do her honour in their latest quest. Small consolation to be had for a humble squire, who had alienated his amour by saying possibly the most stupid and crass thing a man could say to a woman.

The recollection of it sickened him more than any swaying ship. He doubted he would ever see Hettie again, though that didn't stop him pining for her anyway. How had he let a woman get under his skin like that?

Another knightly experience to cherish, he thought bitterly. *Maybe that earth bitch's prophecy isn't such a bad thing after all.*

He found his fingers reaching for the strange amulet the Earth Witch had compelled him to take, as he thought on her weasel words back in the forest when she had predicted his fate – one of greatness with no recognition. Was it his imagination, or did his seasickness abate ever so slightly whenever he touched the talisman?

'Lad, you're miles away!' Braxus was staring at him intently, a concerned look on his face. 'Surely you've got your sea legs by now?'

Vaskrian shook his head, more to clear it than anything else. 'I've a lot of things on my mind is all,' he cried above the pelting rain, as it mingled with the salty foam that rushed and crashed against the keel of their ship.

A lot of things all right, and not all of them mortal, he added mentally. In the past year he'd been bewitched by a hag, gifted by fays, singled out by a sorceress and burned by a warlock – with more high events to come by the sounds of it. He'd never been one for the temple, but it seemed clear that something from the Other Side was taking a very close interest in him. The thought of that appalled him.

'I'll go below decks and prepare our things,' he said, pulling his oilcloak more tightly about him. 'Any luck, and we should be there in a couple of hours.'

Without waiting for his master to respond, he lurched across the deck, his mind swirling in time to its heaving boards.

Braxus watched his squire go below decks. The lad had changed, and not just physically. But then so had they all... The lingering memories of the draugar's curse stretched tenebrous fingers across his psyche, but the prayers of the monks seemed to have averted the worst. He forced himself to concentrate on the tang of salt spray in his mouth, as he fixed his eyes on Craek and contemplated the immediate future.

Perhaps the irritating monk had been right. He did have a blood-feud to settle, and a ward and a kingdom to fight for. He hadn't loved his father the way he loved the beautiful Vorstlending damsel, but Braun had been his sire for all that. Now his head, if the sailors' tales told it true, decorated the walls of the Palace of Bending Branches in Ongist.

The knight who would be lord clenched the rail in his hands. He would carve out a tale of vengeance in blood on Abrexta's body, or die trying. His love suit with Adhelina would just have to wait. Perhaps she would be more likely to favour him over Torgun once he got his lands back. He could offer her the freedom she so craved, a life in Gaellentir where she would be mistress of her own destiny. Noblewomen had always commanded more respect in Thraxia than elsewhere in the Free Kingdoms, since the days of Morgaena ap Morgaen, Queen of Targets; that fiery monarch had led her elite Ironhiders against the Northland reavers that had ravaged their coasts four hundred years ago, repulsing them once and for all at the Battle of the Rundle. Even now, they sailed towards a rendezvous with another powerful woman - Rowena, First Lady of Tul Aeren, already said to be a distinguished general.

Wrackwulf emerged from below decks and made his way across the lurching deck towards him. He moved nimbly for a man of his girth, and the Thraxian was glad to have him along: the freelancer's jocular humour was a welcome antidote to his own brooding feelings.

'How goes it, Sir Braxus?' he boomed above the lashing surf. 'Fine weather you have up north. The prospect of trying some of your famous Thraxian mead almost pales by comparison!'

Braxus grinned at that, taking his proffered hand in a warrior's grip.

'Almost as joyful a prospect as more of your baritone!' he laughed.

'Aye, be careful what you say there, my friend,' cautioned Wrackwulf. 'Remember the last fellow to criticise my singing lost half his face!'

Memories of the Graufluss Bridge Tourney were mixed ones, and Braxus chose not to dwell on them. 'We've to seek out Brother Joram of Kilucan as soon as we're berthed,' he said. 'He's our first point of contact – the Grand Master has presented me with a letter of introduction.' He tapped his jerkin. 'He should be able to help us against Abrexta, when the time comes.'

Wrackwulf's face grew serious. 'When the time comes, aye – we've half a kingdom to conquer before we get anywhere near her, by the sounds of it.'

Braxus nodded grimly. 'Joram will take us to the Crimson League, they'll be camped not far out of town. We'll see what battle plans they've drawn up, and make our own from there.'

Wrackwulf nodded towards the hatch leading below decks. 'I do hope our glorious leader is ready to rejoin the Known World by then,' he said, only half smiling. 'Yon Northlending has been in a right foul mood this past fortnight.'

'He's no leader of mine,' said Braxus, anger flaring across his breast. 'Horskram may have put him in charge of the mission to the Westerling Isles, but right now we're in my kingdom fighting for my lands.'

'Aye, Sir Braxus, I meant nothing by it,' said Wrackwulf, a look of sympathy opening up a few more valleys in his craggy face. 'But, begging your pardon, it's the mission to said islands that's on my mind! For what makes Horskram so sure these druids will part with an anti-relic they've guarded for seven hundred years?'

The freelancer looked anxious now. Clearly he did not relish the supernatural part of their mission.

'Be of some ease,' said Braxus. 'We're to assess the situation on the ground once we get there, and decide whether it's best simply to warn them or try to obtain the fragment. This Joram should be able to help decide in the matter – it's his field after all.'

Wrackwulf nodded reluctantly. 'Do you know much about him?'

Braxus shook his head. 'Only that he is the most renowned Argolian in my country. That, and he'll have a burning desire to be avenged on the witch who burned his monastery to the ground and slaughtered his brethren.'

Wrackwulf raised a soggy eyebrow. 'I thought Argolians weren't supposed to be vengeful?'

'Men aren't supposed to be a lot of things that they are,' replied Braxus. 'But let's wait until we meet him to get the measure of the man. Come! Let's away below, I've had more than enough fresh air and salt water to last a lifetime.'

As they made their way over to the hatch, Braxus spared

a last glance at the fog-limned lights of Craek, glowing ever more sharply against the encroaching night. He knew full well his homecoming would not be a joyful one.

'State your business or stand by to be boarded!'

The captain of the rebel war galley motioned for crossbowmen to mark them, as their hulk creaked in among the flotilla protecting the harbour. There were no enemy ships in sight, but the tension was palpable, made all the more acute by the thick blanket of fog.

Braxus frowned as he squinted at the rude outlines of hunched buildings thronging the harbourside behind the clustered ships. The war galleys were a handsomer sight than the mean cityport they protected, but then latter-day Thraxians did not excel in architecture. How different to the fabled Middle Time, when the city of Anarlion had crowned a glorious era and looked upon a maritime trading empire.

But then he wasn't here for sightseeing.

He stepped up to the gunwale and declaimed: 'Sir Braxus of Gaellen, son of the late Lord Braun, returns to join the rebellion and claim back his rightful inheritance! We're here on Argolian business as well, and bear a letter of introduction from Grand Master Hannequin in Rima. We would have words with Brother Joram of Kilucan before we seek the First Lady of Clan McCullogh.'

'Oh aye?' the rebel captain's voice was tinged with suspicion, though he could only be seen as a faint outline against the fog-shrouded silhouette of the ship he commanded. 'And what would a disinherited northern lord be doing on Argolian business, arrived from the south on a foreign ship?'

'That's not for you to know,' replied Braxus. He had to hope his well-educated tone would be enough to cow the captain. 'I've my squire and two other companions on board with me. You're to let the four of us aboard and escort us to Brother Joram – this ship is here to trade supplies at a fair price, which we'll all be needing with war coming.'

The captain barked a laugh. 'Pangonians trading at a fair price? That'll be the day.' But his softening tone told Braxus he had succeeded. 'All right then,' he added. 'The four of you may come aboard, but try anything funny and we'll strafe you with a broadside that'll see you straight to the Seakindred's Locker.'

'Understood, captain,' replied Braxus, before translating for his companions. 'We're to go aboard their ship. Our horses and harness will be safely deposited on the harbour along with the goods for trading.'

Torgun frowned in the lantern light. 'I'd fain see Hilmir to the docks myself. He and I were already parted once.'

The Thraxian caught his flinty eyes. Clearly his love rival hadn't forgotten the Graufluss Bridge Tourney either, when Braxus had refused to sell him back the prized Farovian destrier after winning him from him in the joust.

'Oh for heaven's sake, Sir Torgun,' he said. 'I thought we'd agreed to put our differences aside until our mission is done.'

'I agreed to that for my part,' replied the knight coldly.

'But I don't see why I should take the word of a man who strikes like a coward when he has been bested fairly in the lists.'

That cut Braxus deeper than an oiled knife. He had tried to drink that shameful memory from his mind too many times, without success.

He was about to reply something uncouth when Wrackwulf intervened. 'Come now, sirrahs! We've had a hard couple of weeks at sea, and we're almost back on dry land. Sir Torgun, I'm sure that Sir Braxus can insist his countrymen give your trusty steed the care it deserves.'

Something in the way the freelancer said this had a placatory effect. *I can see why Horskram sent him with us, and not just because of his thews*, thought Braxus.

He turned back to address the captain in Thrax again. 'Captain! One of my companions is a sturdy knight, from Northalde. He's agreed to help us with his mighty sword arm as best he can, but has a Farovian destrier that he is passing precious about. Would you be so kind as to give assurances this fine steed will receive extra special care?' Braxus hoped Torgun picked up on his sarcasm, even though he was ignorant of their tongue.

'A Northlending come to help us make war?' barked the captain. 'Now I've heard it all – we'll be detaining you all until Brother Joram arrives, and that's for sure! We'll see what he makes of your fanciful tale.'

Braxus rolled his eyes. Sea captains. They had to be the haughtiest commoners he knew. 'So now we aren't going anywhere in a hurry,' he said, translating again for his companions. 'I trust this development pleases you, Sir Torgun.' He underscored his last words with contempt, but the Northlending was clearly having none of it.

'I for one am more than happy to wait on the Argolian,' he said. 'If his heart is true, he'll soon fathom our veracity. If not, then...' He laid a hand meaningfully on his sword hilt.

Braxus shook his head. *Pompous fool*, he snarled inwardly. But he knew well enough to keep his thoughts to himself: not lightly did you pick a fight with Sir Torgun.

'All right,' he called back to the captain. 'We agree to your terms, so prepare to receive visitors!'

Sir Torgun surveyed the dishevelled buildings of the waterfront, an ugly collection of unsavoury looking taverns and brothels. The rain had eased off enough to allow link boys to light the harbour, but he scarcely felt grateful for that. He was hundreds of miles from his homeland and lady love, in a mean little town. Thought of that made his heart feel heavier than the relic he wore around his neck. He'd never been one for the temple; king and country had been enough to sway his heart. That, and a beautiful damsel he would probably never have.

He suppressed his gloomy thoughts as the ship's crew brought out their horses. Going over to Hilmir, he whispered a few comforting words to him, before grooming him and checking his caparison. Vaskrian was busy doing likewise with his master's horse, the fine stallion he'd won at

Graufluss, while Wrackwulf took care of his own, a tough-looking roan charger with a fierce glint in its eye.

We're well equipped, he thought. *But what will worldly weapons avail us against another magic user?* He knew from hard experience the power their kind commanded. The burn scars Andragorix had left him with still tingled on his chest at nights. He could have sworn no ordinary fire would have left such an after-effect.

But by the looks of it, they had a war to fight before they even got to Abrexta. The thought of that stirred the young knight's spirit. Even if it meant fighting for foreigners, he yearned for the coming clash of arms. Something he knew how to do, and another chance to take his mind off his troubles. He'd dedicate every man he smote in the field to Adhelina. Thought of that put invisible wings to his leaden heart as he finished preparing Hilmir.

Sir Braxus came over from where he had been talking with the captain and some of his crew.

'He's sending for Joram now,' said the Thraxian.

'Where is he?' asked Torgun.

'Interrogating a warlock he's been holding in Craek temple.'

Torgun frowned. 'He's captured a warlock?'

'Aye, an associate of Abrexta's by the sounds of it.'

'That's a good start,' put in Wrackwulf. 'See what yon wretch tells us under iron and fire.'

'From what I know that isn't the Argolian way,' replied Braxus. 'But we'll soon find out what Joram has wheedled out of him.'

As things transpired, wheedling wasn't quite Joram's way either. Half an hour passed before an Argolian journeyman arrived at the docks. The adept was about his work at the local temple and he would take them there to see him, so as not to interrupt the interrogation.

The temple was just a couple of crooked streets away from the harbour. They could hear sounds of yelling as they ascended its cracked steps.

'The captive has proved most elusive,' said the young Argolian as he ushered them in through the temple's weather-worn entrance. In the torchlight his face looked abashed and apologetic. 'Brother Joram has had to resort to more... extreme measures.' To either side of the entrance, pitted life-size statues of St Crispus and St Alysius looked on serenely, oblivious to the violence being committed in their name.

Stepping inside the chilly temple precinct, they saw a tall heavy-set monk standing before a strange-looking outlander suspended from the vaulted ceiling by two thick chains of iron. Behind his bloodied and battered form loomed a statue of the Redeemer, several men high, symbolically laying aside his sword as he renounced violence.

I hope he appreciates the irony, wherever he is, thought Braxus, with more than a touch of it himself.

'TELL US WHAT YOU KNOW, POLTROON!' yelled the monk, treating his captive to another blow with a ham-like fist. The chains rattled fiendishly as the mage spluttered blood and saliva onto the rough stone floor. 'And be thankful my vows prevent me from taking a blade to you!'

'I thought Argolians didn't resort to torture?' whispered Wrackwulf as Braxus cleared his throat.

'Brother Joram of Kilucan,' said the knight, ignoring him, 'Sir Braxus of Gaellen comes bearing letters of emissary from the Grand Master of your Order.'

The hulking adept turned fierce eyes on him. Hatred and violence were in his black stare, only partly dimmed upon recognising a potential ally.

Is this man really our finest witch hunter? Our finest bruiser more like.

'So, the prodigal son returns,' scoffed Joram, washing the blood off his hands in the holy water font before striding over to greet the new arrivals. Behind him the chained warlock groaned pitifully. 'And not with a Northlending army at his back, as was rumoured months ago.'

A spasm of pain lanced through Braxus, as memory of his father's mission brought back thoughts of the old man. 'I regret to say that said rumours proved untrue,' he said, banishing his emotions. 'But nonetheless we are here to help in any way we can – and on a mission of even greater import that also concerns you directly.' He proffered the letter.

Joram snatched it from him and tore open the seal in a single brusque movement. With his rough pock-marked face and close-cropped ginger hair, he looked more like a town prizefighter than a monk of the Order.

His face darkened as he read the contents.

'The Island Realms?' he queried, glancing up sharply from the parchment. 'You're to head there after we overthrow Abrexta... Well, I won't speak further of your mission here.'

Braxus saw the bloodied warlock look up sharply at mention of the Westerling Isles.

'And what of yon sorcerer?' Braxus asked, his curiosity growing. 'Your associate said he was an understudy of the very witch we seek to kill.' He spoke in Decorlangue so the others could understand.

'He was,' said Joram, favouring his captive with a sour sneer. 'I apprehended him in the Fernwood a week ago. I'd been on his trail since we learned that Abrexta used to lair there, before she came to Ongist and bewitched the King. Says he knows the secret of her immortality - as soon as I beat that out of him, the wretch shall go to the stake.'

'This is most unbefitting behaviour in an Argolian,' protested Torgun. 'Your kind are supposed to renounce violence, not embrace it.'

Joram laughed hollowly. 'Fine words coming from a man of the sword! We're at *war*, sir knight – these bastards burned my home to the ground and wiped out half my Order. Just be thankful I didn't give him over to a torturer – then he'd really know pain.'

Not that you'd want anyone outside your precious Order being privy to secrets, thought Braxus. Beyond that, he had the feeling this Joram took pleasure in brutalising the hapless mage. *A vengeful spirit indeed – I wonder what dear Master Horskram would make of him?*

'What have you learned from him so far?' he pressed. It was worth a try at least.

'Only that Abrexta has tapped her Fay ancestry using pagan sorcery, to grant her unnatural long life,' said Joram, his lip curling in disgust. 'He's holding out because he knows his fate is sealed once he tells me the secret, but don't worry I'll soon have it out of him! My elan was strong enough to neutralise his magic, my right arm shall be strong enough to-'

'I know the druids you seek.' The words came from the shackled mage. They were all the more surprising for being spoken in Decorlangue.

Joram rounded on him. 'You speak the High Tongue?'

The sorcerer forced a wry smile from split lips. 'If you hadn't been so busy beating me for information, I might have told you sooner.'

Sir Braxus stepped forwards to get a closer look at him. He was an unprepossessing sight at the best of times, fish-faced and pudgy. Though in his thirties, his hair was early greying. It was tied in many braids, each one fastened at the end with a silver tassel.

'You hail from the Westerling Isles?' he asked.

The mage nodded weakly. 'Aye, so I do. Though not for years have I seen my homeland.'

'I could have told you as much,' said Joram. 'He's been on the mainland for nearly a decade. Worked magick with Abrexta, but they had a parting of the ways before she left for Ongist.'

'Why?' asked Braxus, directing the question at the warlock.

'Too dark a master would she serve,' said the mage. 'Too dark for Morcant, indeed! The Right Hand Path in Druidsbourne we cleave to, not for us the accursed ways of the Left!'

'Silence, you dastard!' bellowed Joram. 'Your warped morality interests me not. Tell us how to kill your mistress, and perhaps I shall have you garrotted, instead of sending thee to the fire as you deserve.'

'I've told you already, I'm on your side,' said Morcant, his breath heaving in painful gasps. Clearly he had long given up on persuading the fanatical monk of that, but Braxus saw a glimmer of hope in his grey eyes as he looked at him.

'What do you mean?' asked Braxus. 'Since when is a pagan witch on anyone's side but his own?' Memories of the Earth Witch and her help put the lie to those words, and he knew it. But best to keep up appearances to forestall any rash behaviour from Joram, whose fists were clenching again.

The adept glowered as Morcant spilled his story gratefully.

'Near a tenyear ago, the Druid Council began to sense something, a deep disturbance in the magic field. The Other Side seemed closer than ever, and believe it or not' – he cast a sidelong glance at Joram – 'that is not something our people have ever desired. Someone or something was counter-scrying, so we couldn't divine exactly where the disturbance was coming from, only that it was somewhere on the mainland. Sent me as an agent they did, to learn more. Came upon Abrexta I did in the Fernwood, after I learned she had been driven out of her old haunt in Roarkil by Andragorix.'

'Wait,' interjected Braxus, 'we slew Andragorix several months ago. What do you know of him?'

Morcant raised eyes to whatever strange heavens he believed in. 'Ah, right glad to hear that I am! For known to us Andragorix was. Came to our islands years ago he did, posing as a student of the Right Hand Path. But he stole forbidden secrets, things no honest sorcerer should delve into. Executed he would have been, but he managed to elude us and flee back across the sea. When I came to Abrexta, I posed as a wandering wizard myself, offering to trade secrets with her. Accepted she did, and much I learned from her – Andragorix had come to her years before, to study under her, and she it was that sent him to us, to learn darker magicks she feared to tap herself. But outstrip her he did, oh yes, the pupil became the master...! When returned to Thraxia he did, Andragorix overmatched Abrexta and drove her from Roarkil.'

'That would have been shortly before Horskram and Sir Belinos sought him out,' said Torgun, joining the conversation. It was good to know his rival had shrugged off his melancholy at last, Braxus was growing weary of doing all the work himself. 'We believe Abrexta was working for Andragorix,' pressed the Northlending.

Morcant nodded. 'For some years after her banishment, Abrexta had little to do with the accursed demonologist,' he said, genuine revulsion entering his voice. 'But one day he contacted her, said she was part of his wider plans. Try to resist him in this she did, but could not – for by this time his power had long outstripped her own. Perhaps in truth she felt the tug of larger destiny, for Abrexta trained decades ago under Yathaga, another witch from my lands. Ah, see I can from your faces that you know her not – a necromancer Yathaga was, who believed that Morwena of old had been doing the Moon Goddess's will, and desired to follow in her footsteps.'

'Morwena?' queried Torgun. 'But she's the witch responsible for...' His voice trailed off as he looked at Joram uncertainly.

'Hannequin has explained the details of your mission in full,' the monk said, waving the parchment impatiently. 'You may speak freely, for I know all about the Headstone fragments.'

Braxus glanced nervously behind him, but the journeyman who had shown them inside had gone.

'Yes, yes!' said Morcant, his eyes catching fire. 'Morwena it was who sought to reunite the Headstone! For she believed that Kaia's will must be done by tapping the power of He Who Must Not Be Named... only thus could the Old Time be brought about again.'

Braxus frowned as he struggled to piece the puzzle together. 'So you're saying Abrexta was trained by a witch from the Island Realms called Yathaga, who was herself inspired by Morwena?'

'Indeed,' said the wizard, his chains rattling as he nodded vigorously. 'Yathaga the Three-Eyed they called her, after the mark made by the Wheel of St Meath upon her forehead, when confront her that savant did during the Battle of High Fells two centuries ago.'

'Mention not that pious Argolian's name!' snarled Joram, looming menacingly over the warlock. 'It sounds foul in your cankered mouth.'

'Peace,' said Braxus, laying a hand on the monk's broad shoulder. 'So what happened after Abrexta left to do Andragorix's dirty work for him?'

'Stayed behind I did, under pretext of keeping our lair secure, in case her mission should fail. All the while I studied and scryed, trying to build on what I had learned and fathom Abrexta's weakness. An accomplished necromancer was Yathaga, but the side effects of using such magic to prolong lifespan are horrendous, and no wish had Abrexta to embrace such. A schemer she is, but not wholly given up to the Left Hand Path.'

'Arrant nonsense,' snarled Joram. 'She is a wicked witch, and will die by the fire.'

'Go on,' said Braxus, ignoring him. 'Tell us what you learned.'

Morcant glanced fearfully at the monk. 'And have this oaf execute me as reward? Withstand I will his buffets a little longer, I think.'

Joram raised a fist to comply, but Torgun intercepted him. The monk was a big man, but Torgun was a shade bigger.

'No more beatings,' said the knight. 'I don't like warlocks any more than you do, Master Joram, but clearly this one may be of more use to us alive than dead.'

'Especially if we're heading to the Island Realms,' put in Wrackwulf. 'Everything I've heard about the Marcher Lords and Druidkind tells me that they guard their shores jealously. One of their own could be an invaluable guide.'

Joram looked at the three knights in turn, sizing up the situation.

'I've no idea what it says in that parchment,' said Braxus, 'but when Horskram and Hannequin briefed us, they said you would aid us in any way possible. We need this warlock's help – both to defeat Abrexta and get to the Island Realms.'

Joram scowled as he considered that.

'Very well,' he said at length. 'On two conditions. I'm coming with you to the Westerling Isles, and I'll be taking this recreant back with me after our business there is done.' He shook his fist at Morcant. 'You shall not escape justice for your crimes!'

Morcant quailed at that, but Braxus could see the gleam of hope had not left his eyes.

'A stay of execution is better than none at all,' said Braxus. 'Do you agree to help us if we let you go?'

Morcant nodded enthusiastically. 'You have my word, as a disciple of Kell,' he intoned sincerely. 'I want to see Abrexta finished as badly as you do, for instruct me the Druiding Council did to stop anyone seeking to disrupt the cosmic balance between worlds. That includes an attempt to reunite the Headstone, assure you I can!'

'What do you know of that?' asked Braxus , suddenly suspicious again.

'I managed to beat that out of him, too,' interrupted Joram. 'Abrexta let slip that Andragorix was involved in trying to reunite a powerful artefact, but he doesn't know much else besides.'

Best to keep it that way, thought Braxus. *I don't trust this Morcant any more than I trust the Earth Witch.* 'All right, wizard,' he said, 'Master Joram will free you now, but he'll be keeping you shackled until such time as we need your sorcery – so don't even think of trying anything!'

'You have my word, so you do,' repeated Morcant, grinning slyly to reveal bloodied teeth.

Joram called for the journeyman to come and release the warlock, a grudging look etched on his blunt features as the lesser monk set about unfastening the chains.

'Better get him cleaned up before you take us to the Crimson League,' said Braxus. 'A chirurgeon can look over his wounds when we get to their camp.'

'Yes, well, there'll be more to contend with there than this wretch's wounds,' said Joram.

'What do you mean?'

'The rebellion is in disarray,' sighed the adept, looking tired for the first time. 'Some bloody nobles' quarrel about a disputed inheritance, the lords of Penllyn are contesting Lady Rowena's right to lead the coalition.'

'On the eve of a civil war, are they mad?' cried Braxus, aghast.

'Quite possibly,' replied the monk. 'We've had word that the King's army is but ten leagues north of the castles we took on the borders of Rathlain, so they'd best patch up their differences quickly – or else it'll be our blood soaking the fields, not theirs! We could use an influential third party to intercede and talk some sense into them – I hope you're in the mood for diplomacy, Sir Braxus.'

Braxus exchanged pained looks with Torgun and Wrackwulf. He suddenly felt very tired himself. A feud to patch up, a civil war to fight, and a sorceress to slay, followed by a journey to the edge of the world – life wasn't about to get any easier.

CHAPTER 15

THE MOUTH OF THE SERPENT

Ragnar was not a man ordinarily given to excitement, but he felt his pulse quicken as sixteen pairs of oars drew him ever closer to his destination. The ship's clinker-built hull was well able to manage the short sea voyage to the Skjel Islands at this time of year, though another week or two and the Valhalla would freeze over, locking the creatures of the deep in their watery kingdom.

It was a kingdom whose powers he intended to harness.

A stiff breeze raked across the ship's bows as it slid amongst the clustered islands, some of them little more than green-spattered crusts of upwards-thrusting rock. But then the cold never bothered Ragnar, not since Sjórkunan had taken his eye years ago and bequeathed him the powers he desired.

It was time to repay that debt in full: and this time the Lord of Oceans would receive far more than a mortal man's eye.

As the ship rounded another islet, he caught his first

view of it: a complex of log cabins connected by planked walkways, a veritable floating city. Narborg, men called it; the heart of Skjel's thriving prosperity.

But it wasn't really floating, and it wasn't the mundane cabins and walkways and market stalls that interested Ragnar. As they drew closer, he could discern the eldritch foundations of the strange outpost, and his icy heart almost felt warm for a second. The pillars supporting the platform were hewn of an alien stone that seemed dark and translucent at the same time; only the constant litany of spell-prayers intoned by the cityport's priesthood kept its citizens from losing their minds.

But that same priesthood guarded something of yet more interest to Ragnar.

The sculpted friezes of krakens, water spirits, seakindred and tritons that writhed around the circumference of the great pillars were painfully lifelike, even at this range. Ragnar, used as he was to high sorcery, muttered a brief prayer to the Lord of Oceans as their ichthyoid forms slithered into his consciousness.

Half a lifetime have I waited for this moment, he thought reverentially.

He felt the crew's mood sink towards the Seakindred's Locker as they approached the row of wooden jetties, jutting out towards them like the fangs of one of the great sea beasts carved upon the pillars. On the wharf stood a row of priests, intoning their litany to keep the new arrivals from panicking at the close proximity of the Elder Ones' awful wizardry. Even with their protection, traders had to move off the platform every few moons or lose their minds to its magicks; the cityport had no permanent residents besides its priesthood, despite its position in the midst of the Sea of Valhalla making it a wealthy entrepot.

His lone travelling companion joined him at the prow. Ratko looked timorous, as befitted his status as hedge witch, but once again Ragnar found himself in need of such thralls.

'The Mouth of the Serpent is a glorious sight is it not, apprentice?' said Ragnar, enjoying Ratko's discomfort.

'We haven't seen it yet,' stammered Ratko. 'Not truly.'

Ragnar gave him an icy smile. It was good to see the craven had kept his wits about him, despite his fear. 'No indeed, for the Cauldron lies at the heart of Narborg. But we soon shall, apprentice, we soon shall.'

Ratko shivered at that prospect as they glid slowly in to dock at one of the jetties. There were a few other ships berthed there, mostly dromons from the Empire making one last trade before the winter ice set in, but the atmosphere was subdued despite the busy crowds of sailors and merchants. Their faces were as wan as the pallid skies above, and they moved with the alacrity of men keen to conduct their business and leave. Some joked that it was such an atmosphere that caused business in Narborg to be so brisk. This close to the Cauldron, even the sea had a dull sheen to it; waves of tar might have sparkled more. To make matters seem more ominous, a ghostly mist was snaking in from the north-east, carried by a sere, cold wind; but something gave it pause, causing it to ring the cityport in a wreathy halo.

To Ragnar, it felt like coming home after a long and arduous journey.

The head priest met him on the wharf, the others continuing to chant behind him. He did not look pleased to see Ragnar, but then why should he be pleased to see the man he had branded apostate a score of years ago?

'Ragnar of the White Eye,' he said, distaste etched into weather-beaten features that were almost completely concealed by a straggly sleet-coloured beard at odds with his bald pate. 'I shall not say you are well met.'

'Hrolf Olafsson,' replied Ragnar, not bothering to incline his head. 'I for one am overjoyed to see you again. You had news of my coming from Ravek Hrorson, I take it?'

Hrolf's face darkened. 'Alas, I may not refuse the foremost thegn of Skjel this request. Would that I could, for yours is a dark heart, Ragnar – not for nothing are you named after the Breaking of the World.'

'It shall be remade anew under my ken, not broken again,' Ragnar assured him.

'Your words are Logi's,' said Hrolf. 'Only a fool would trust them.'

Ragnar was in no mood to continue sparring with his old mentor. Curious indeed that Hrolf should still live at close on ninety winters. Perhaps the Lord of Oceans had blessed him, in his own way. Or perhaps kept him alive so he could witness this moment: Ragnar's final triumph over the pompous old sacredot.

'I would gaze upon the Cauldron, and it please you.' Ragnar motioned towards the main walkway leading into the platform city's heart.

'It pleases me not, as well you know,' said Hrolf, nevertheless turning to hobble up the walkway. 'But I am bound in this. Follow me.'

The walkway took them through a series of interconnecting canals and enclosed docks, lined with warehouses and dwellings, built atop the eight vast pillars that had supported the original structure. Those mighty columns stretched all the way down to the Seakindred's Locker, sages told: meeting their end only at the bottom of the sea, where the Merfolk and Tritons made eternal war beneath the waves. The Vedict texts spoke of an ancient shrine that had been built by the Elder Wizards at the platform city's epicentre, whose ruins Hrolf now led him towards.

It was the creature that shrine was dedicated to which fixated Ragnar. Tap its primordial power, and the armies of the deeps would rise at his beck and call.

Ragnar felt a gnawing presence in his psyche as they tramped towards the centre. His body tingled all over; it was pleasant and profane at the same time. Each of the pillars was crowned with an eldritch ruin of its own, all that now remained of the outer wings of the shrine. Their multi-coloured stones hurt his good eye, though with his other he saw their trapezoid patterns differently. And a beauteous sight they were.

Not anywhere near as beautiful as the centrepiece, though. The shrine's inner sanctum was its best-preserved section. Wrought by immortal hands more than five millennia ago, the gigantic maw stretched ravenously towards the skies, as though threatening to devour the very heavens. Seasoned as he was, Ragnar gaped as he looked upon the Mouth of the Serpent for the first time in decades. The metal was a black silvery sheen, the scaly likeness of the Great World Serpent fashioned from a mixture of ebonite and quicksliver; it seemed to undulate and writhe, presaging the next turning in the endless cycle of ragnarök and rebirth. Its maw curled inwards unnaturally, the serried rows of fangs almost doubling back on themselves.

Ragnar fancied the leviathan resembled one of Logi's deformed brethren more than any natural serpent. But then the Great World Serpent was beyond natural; it wasn't of nature, it was more a precursor to nature itself. If Aurgelmir the Father of Giants was the flesh of the earth, the Serpent he had fought before the Dawn of Time was its beating heart.

The priest paused at another walkway, this one leading across the moat-like structure separating them from the Mouth of the Serpent. This was no Northland construction, wrought of wood and nail, but another vestige of the ancient civilisation of the Priest-Kings: a covered stone walkway that had probably been a corridor in the original complex, its walls erupting with friezes of demonic sea creatures clutching human sacrifices in tentacular orifices that gaped hideously.

The archpriest looked sourly at Ratko, trembling at Ragnar's side.

'I shall not take your cantrip whisperer, for Hrorson's ordinance said nothing of hedge wizards.'

Ragnar nodded. 'Ratko, you shall remain outside.'

The apprentice nodded keenly. He hardly seemed desirous of entering, but that was only to be expected of the thrall. Hrolf intoned a final incantation to shield their psyches, before stepping onto the walkway. Little did he know that Ragnar no longer had need of such protection. Andragorix had taught him that much at least.

The inner precinct was deathly cold. The walls of the tubular structure sprouted spines that clustered everywhere, their metallic barbs tapering inwards menacingly. The atmosphere was oppressive; feeling as though one was entombed in a slab of ice did not bother Ragnar, but he could well believe few ordinary mortals would choose to venture here. The serpent's gullet allowed daylight to enter, though it seemed paler somehow. The floor was etched with spiral patterns that might have been distended waves. At its centre was the thing he had waited so long to look upon.

The Cauldron was almost mundane by comparison with the rest of the shrine. It resembled a giant well carved from the same stone as the pillars, but bereft of friezes. A simple whorled pattern was graven around its circumference instead, but Ragnar spotted the inference: a spiral staircase leading down into the deeps, through the blue blood of the world towards its murmuring heart.

'Well, here we are,' said Hrolf in a tight voice, interrupting his reverie. 'At long last you have attained your goal, Ragnar – the gateway to the bowels of the earth awaits you.'

Ragnar had the distinct impression the priest was half hoping he would throw himself into the Cauldron. He had no intention of obliging his old rival, though. Stepping up to the eerie well, he peered into its stygian depths. The black hole seemed to suck the light streaming in directly above it, feeding on it as a vampire battens on blood.

'You know full well what lies at the bottom of yon shaft,' said Hrolf, coming up beside him. 'He Who Should Not Be Disturbed lies at the centre of the world, far beneath the seabed.'

'To disturb the Great World Serpent means to bring about another ragnarök, such as when the Elder Ones angered the gods in their contumely,' answered Ragnar, his voice dropping to a whisper. 'Let its coils shift but a fraction, and all the continents shall be unmade.'

'What could you possibly want with such a power, Ragnar? For even could you stir the Serpent, it would avail you nothing but ruin.'

Ragnar smiled into the Cauldron's lightless depths. 'I have no intention of stirring the Serpent,' he replied. 'I would simply tap its power, to enthral those who worship it... in the deeps below.'

'Are you mad?' Hrolf's voice was agitated now, it reverberated off the temple's spiny walls with a metallic ring. 'What infernal purpose would that serve?'

Ragnar turned to face him. 'Hadn't you heard, priest? There is a war of worlds coming, by land and sea. For too long the Tritons have spurned the Lord of Oceans, making war on his loyal subjects the Seakindred. I shall honour Sjórkunan by enslaving the idolators and raising them up to fight in the wars of mortalkind! Let the Merfolk have the blue domains – their age-old enemies shall be put to better use, serving in our armies.'

Hrolf's eyes bulged out of wrinkled eye sockets. 'You really are mad! Such a thing is blasphemy – the Lord of Oceans would never will it!'

Ragnar towered over him threateningly. 'Oh but he will, for Logi is returning, as the Farseers of Norn foretold. He shall rule the kingdom of the earth, while his brother holds the vasty deeps. Thus was it prophesied in the Dawn of Time, and so it shall be – in this, our time!'

The withered archpriest took a step backwards, then found his resolve. 'Nay, Ragnar, such a thing will never be. I know not what sorceries you have studied since I banished thee, but not even you could hope to channel the Great World Serpent's power unaided.'

'I shall not be unaided,' said Ragnar. 'Ratko! Come here – thy master summons thee!'

He pictured a fish on a hook and a beating heart, as he intoned the words of a spell. Best to give the rat some courage to overcome his superstitious fear.

A few moments later Ratko appeared, a glazed look in his eyes.

'How now, Ragnar?' said Hrolf, backing away. 'You swore upon the stone of Thoros not to do me or my brethren any harm!'

'And the God of Storms shall not find me a troth-breacher,' said Ragnar. 'For I shall not lay a finger on you. But he too knows that Logi must have his due – the rightful King of all the earth will be restored to his birthright, and no tepid priest shall deny him!'

Muttering a few more words, Ragnar pictured a hand clutching a knife in a downwards thrust. Ratko advanced on the old priest.

Hrolf tried to stammer a counter-spell but his elan was weak, taxed by continually protecting the city traders from the Cauldron's malefic influence. Not that the tired old priest could have contended with him anyway: Ragnar's powers had waxed too great in their long time apart.

With movements that were strangely jerky, Ratko bore down on the archpriest, trapping him in his arms. The hedge wizard was not a strong man, but he wasn't carrying ninety winters either. Hrolf began to wail as he dragged him back over to the Cauldron.

'O Great World Serpent,' Ragnar intoned, 'that dwelleth in cthonian slumber beneath the vaults of the earth, clothed by the flesh of Aurgelmir! Accept now this humble offering, the first of many! Feast on the body of mortal man, son of thy accursed enemy the Father of Giants!'

Hrolf screamed as Ratko hauled him over the lip of the well. The metallic walls seemed to scream back at him, hooked barbs stretching out towards the sacrifice with a hideous hunger. The archpriest struggled, desperation momentarily gifting him with a strength beyond his years. Ragnar intensified the spell, picturing a clenched fist breaking a rod of iron as he galvanised his thrall. With a cry of his own, Ratko hurled the priest into the Cauldron.

Hrolf's lingering scream died by inches as he disappeared forever from the world of mortal men.

'It is well,' sighed Ragnar as the reverberating shrine pulsed back into silence. 'Come, Ratko, for we have a synod to address.'

Stepping out of the temple, they crossed back over the walkway. On the adjoining platform the rest of the priesthood was waiting for them.

'It is done,' said Ragnar, addressing Hrolf's second. Svinn was a dark-haired man, full of dark ambitions.

Svinn nodded. 'His sacrifice will but be the first of many, if this is to succeed,' he said.

'That is inevitable,' replied Ragnar. 'For this is the will of Godshome. Not even Thoros, who sees all from his celestial palace, can deny the destiny the Farseers predicted. Earth, Water and Air must be ruled equally by the three brothers. Only then can the balance of the world be restored. We must pave the way for Logi's return, and serve his servants.'

Svinn nodded, though Ragnar could tell not all the brethren were convinced. But dissenters could be won around in time – or fed to the Serpent, if they did not relent.

They turned to retrace their steps, Ratko following with a dazed expression on his face. 'Have my things brought from the ship,' said Ragnar. 'We will spend the winter in preparation, and come the thaw we shall be ready. When my sister's fleet begins ravaging the mainland, we shall not want for slaves to feed the Serpent.'

A silence that Ragnar did not find at all uncomfortable descended on the company, as they made their way back to the harbour.

CHAPTER 16
A SOJOURN IN WINTER

'... And then he said, 'Vorstlending women get broken in by their horses anyway'. Can you believe it? Absolutely outrageous!'

Hettie's cheeks were burning as she finished her story. It had taken Adhelina weeks of cajoling to finally get it out of her. At least now that Vaskrian was abroad questing, she felt slightly less mortified recalling his churlish behaviour. Slightly.

There was a time when Adhelina would have been outraged, too. Now she just looked sad and weary.

'Yes well, King Aethelric the Younger has a lot to answer for,' she sighed. 'It was he who decreed maidens could ride full-saddle – to cover up for his daughter's scandalous affair, so he could marry her off to the King of Mercadia.'

Hettie rolled her eyes. Not another blasted history lesson. Did Adhelina never tire of lore?

'If you're going to give me advice, I was hoping you might stay within the past few hundred years,' she frowned.

'I'm just saying that's why maidens don't ride side-saddle in Vorstlund,' replied Adhelina irately. 'In any case, I don't know what you want me to say. Vaskrian is a Northlending – and a common squire on top of it. What did you expect? Frankly, I'm not sure getting involved in the first place was a good idea.'

'That's it?' exclaimed Hettie. 'You spend nearly a month wheedling this out of me, and that's all you have to say to it?' Adhelina was in one of her difficult moods again, but Hettie found she lost her own temper more easily these days. The clear wintry sunlight pouring in through the window of their chamber in the palace did nothing to raise her spirits. At least it wasn't too cold this far south; the open shutters allowed a breeze that offset the heat of the fire pleasantly.

'I'm sorry,' said Adhelina. 'But to be honest, I've enough love issues of my own to worry about. And at least you got to kiss your paramour before you parted company.'

Hettie was startled by her mistress's frankness. Adhelina had always been touchy on the subject of her inexperience with men – respectable noblewomen were supposed to start bearing children in their teens.

'But you just said letting him go that far wasn't a good idea,' she said exasperatedly. 'And now you're acting as if you're jealous!'

'I'm not jealous!' snapped Adhelina, though clearly she was, on some level. 'I was just saying, is all...'

Hettie sighed. 'No, you're probably right – I shouldn't have let it go that far. Give men a horse, and they want the whole bloody stable!'

'They probably would quite literally, if it weren't for the doxies and the wenches,' smirked Adhelina.

Hettie had to return her smile at that. Always there was time for their old humour. When they weren't busy being cursed by draugar or chased by murderous robber knights, that was.

'It's so unfair,' said Adhelina, her face falling again. 'A man can take as many lovers as he cares to before he marries, but for us...'

Hettie frowned. This again. It *was* monstrously unfair, but then it always had been as far as she knew.

'I don't think that's about to change, milady,' she said. 'Unless you fancy going to those Harran Isles, where Anupe's from.'

'Harijan,' corrected Adhelina. Her pedanticism was also beginning to annoy Hettie no end.

'I'm worried about her,' confided Adhelina, oblivious to her friend's ire. 'I don't think the fleshpots of Rima can be doing her much good.'

'That's not what she says whenever she comes to visit,' said Hettie. Anupe had been sent packing once the ransom had been paid off; pagan savages were scarcely welcome at court. The outlander had agreed to winter in the city before sailing with them to Panya come spring. At least she had plenty of coin to spend on wine and women, though her sapphic lusts were really quite inappropriate.

'Yes, well, I'd rather not dwell on Anupe's habits,' said Adhelina.

Hettie had to agree. Only pagans like Anupe would ever consider such depraved behaviour normal. It wasn't Anupe's proclivities she was dwelling on in any case, it was Vaskrian. For all her outrage, she still couldn't help thinking about him.

'Hettie, you're blushing again,' said Adhelina, with far too much exasperation for Hettie's liking. 'Not still thinking of that kiss, are you?'

'I'm sorry,' said Hettie glumly. 'I can't help it, even if he is a swine. It's not just the bloody kissing either! I keep wondering if he's all right, that kind of thing.' She huffed irritably. It made her sick, all this pathetic moping about – how on earth had she let a man get under her skin like that? 'I wish I'd never met him,' she added spitefully.

'Yes well, I've thought that about Torgun and Braxus often enough,' said Adhelina. Something in her dismissive tone irked Hettie even more. As if her mistress' sorrows were always more acute than her own.

'Oh, but you've got your new paramour to play games with now,' taunted Hettie. 'Sir Aremis the Hair-lip that keeps courting you, when he isn't busy planning to invade our country. Why don't you kiss him instead? Assuming you know where to start, on that ugly face of his.'

'Hettie, don't be so cruel!' Adhelina looked genuinely shocked. 'It isn't his fault if he looks...'

'... like a rabbit in armour?' Hettie finished for her. She *was* feeling cruel. 'And you should know better than to encourage a knight from an enemy nation to make love to you.'

Adhelina rose angrily. 'What's got into you? One disappointing tryst and you're acting like a spurned harlot!'

'If I am, it's because I'm sick of you being so damned

miserable all the time!' Hettie yelled back. 'After all we've been through, can't you just... enjoy a bit of normalcy for a change? We go to dances, we attend feasts, we go on pleasure trips. Thanks to Master Horskram we'll be free to leave once the winter thaws. Then we can get to the blasted Empire and finally start this new life you keep talking about! But no, you're so restless you couldn't even let me have my private grief!'

'Grief!? You have the temerity to talk to me about grief?' Adhelina was incandescent with rage now, and Hettie almost quailed before her. 'I lost my father and my lands!' She'd scarcely talked about Wilhelm's death or Hengist's betrayal since they got to Rima, but Hettie wasn't in the mood to indulge her now.

'Father and lands you were hell bent on leaving behind forever, need I remind you?' Hettie shouted, rising angrily herself. 'At least you had Wilhelm until you were one and twenty – do you think I enjoyed losing my father when I was just a girl? Oh, and I too lost my home – when I decided to follow you on your madcap quest for freedom! Even though I tried to talk you out of it I don't know how many times!'

They stood like that for a few moments, glaring at one another like foxes. Hettie was aware of her heart thumping painfully. She could not recall a time when they had been this angry with one another.

There came a knocking at the door. 'Enter!' cried Adhelina. She could hardly expect Hettie to get it under the circumstances.

The door opened and in came Sir Aremis. Dressed in his gilded mail and sporting his usual crescent and stars tabard, at least he looked as though he had bothered to comb his lank hair.

'My lady,' he said, bowing. 'I hope I am not interrupting.'

Must have heard us yelling through the door, thought Hettie. *At least we were arguing in Vorstlending.*

'No,' said Adhelina, her face pale and stiff. 'You're not interrupting anything at all. In fact, I was just getting ready to take a stroll about the gardens. Pray accompany me.'

Aremis inclined his head courteously, what passed for a smile transfixing his crooked face. Hettie picked up her embroidery, feigning indifference as her mistress dressed quickly by herself. If the Pangonian thought that irregular, he said nothing of it.

She kept her eyes fixed on her needlework as Adhelina left without a word. Only when her mistress was gone did she realise that the knight on horseback she had been stitching into a shawl had flowing chestnut hair...

Casting the shawl aside with a frustrated cry, Hettie began to weep.

CHAPTER 17
ONE LAST HOPE

Agravine's face was streaked with dirt and blood, but he wore a triumphant look as his company emerged from the woods into the clearing.

'How did you speed?' asked Sir Urist.

'We came upon them unawares at first light,' said the young knight. 'Another seven Lanraks seek the Judgment of Azrael.'

The ageing marshal allowed himself a smile. For months they had painstakingly made guerrilla war on Hengist's invading forces. As long as Captain Brigmore held Graukolos they could harry the besieging army, defending villages where possible and avenging their dead compatriots where not.

Urist turned to Ruttgur, his second-in-command. The stalwart knight had repaid his faith in him in full; ever since he had watched him spar with Agravine in the castle, he'd known him for a man of mettle. Twenty-three Lanraks had fallen to his sword alone, many of them knights.

'Sir Ruttgur, how many does that make in total?'

'Since we took to the hills that's one hundred and seventy Lanraks we've killed,' replied the knight. 'Forty-three of them knights, the rest mounted serjeants and soldiers.'

Sir Urist felt a flush of pride. It was a noble effort, given that there were but forty-seven knights assembled in the clearing. Only a third of the hundred taking part in the Graufluss Bridge Tourney melee had survived the treacherous attack four months ago; the rest had come from surviving vassals who had not been present. They hadn't had any fresh recruits for many a tenday though, and their numbers where being whittled down by the week: not all sorties were as successful as Agravine's.

It was only a matter of time before they succumbed to sheer weight of numbers, Urist knew. Hengist had commissioned a party of freeswords out of Meerborg to counter the insurgent threat: a hundred hardened mercenaries from the Frozen Wastes now sought them. It was a dangerous game of cat and mouse, one that would most likely end in their slaughter.

But they would make an end of it worthy of bard's song. Urist had never been a vain man, but even he had to admit the *Lay of the Forty-Seven Errants* had a certain ring to it.

'Alright.' he raised his hand to get attention. The motley company of battle-scarred veterans stopped tending to their weapons and horses to listen. 'We've done passing well these last few months, but time is running short as you all know.' The grim faces of the knights showed the truth of those words. 'It won't be long before Hengist's freeswords catch up to us, we can't hide in ricks forever and keep putting our peasantry in danger.'

There were disgruntled mutterings at that. Urist didn't like to think how many yeomen had been hanged for harbouring them after dark; he had decided to put a stop to the tactic. Some of the others had disagreed, but the way he saw it, there wasn't much point in defending Dulsinor if you were only going to get its subjects killed. Sir Hangrit Foolhardy had launched the cruellest campaign of retribution, strafing the countryside with iron and fire. Hanged? Those were the lucky ones. Half the poor churls executed on his orders had been disembowelled or buried alive.

'I know how vital it's been to our efforts that they feed and shelter us,' the marshal went on. 'But I aim to strike at the heart of our enemy, before they run us down.'

The voices of the men were distinctly more approving now.

'Let's beard Hengist in his lair and skewer the recreant like the swine he is!' cried one of the younger knights.

'Hengist is but a puppet,' said another, 'for his one-armed seneschal, Albercelsus. I say it's him we should seek to slay!'

'Nay, it's his marshal Sir Adso Bastardson we want,' put in another, 'he's the one masterminding this whole invasion. Cut off the viper's head, I say!'

'Peace!' cried Ruttgur. 'Your marshal is addressing you.' The angry chorus subsided.

'All three are in the midst of the siege camp investing Graukolos, too closely guarded,' Urist went on. 'We've next to no chance of getting to any of them.' He sighed, meeting the eyes of the knights closest to him. 'We've done fine service to our land, and repaid the Lanraks for their treachery as much as we could. But it's time to admit that we can't keep this up forever. The ultimate sacrifice must be made - in Wilhelm's name, Reus rest his soul.'

The knights repeated his last words, some of the more devout making the sign. It saddened Urist to say what he had to next, but he'd known from the outset how this would end. Frankly he was amazed to have made it this far, what with his gammy thighbone and all. His own death in battle held no horrors for him – he couldn't think of a better end after all – but the prospect of leading some of the younger knights to the grave did little to please him. That bard's song had better be good.

'We will attack the camp,' he said. 'Or at least, most of us will. Make it look like a heroic last stand, one more desperate attempt to draw some blood before winter kills us anyway. It'll be a feint – I want to convince Adso that our threat has been extinguished. That should provide enough cover for a select party to head south and petition for help.'

Agravine spoke up. 'With all respect commander, but I don't see how that will avail us anything – the Kaarls and the Alt-Ürls have never been friends of ours.'

'No, they haven't,' agreed Urist. 'But it's not them whose help you'll be seeking. You're to travel farther south, to Westenlund. Only Prince Leopold is powerful enough to send an expedition force to relieve Graukolos.'

'Leopold? But what interest is it of his to help us? He's never been a friend of ours either.'

'Nor has he been an enemy,' Urist pointed out. 'And as

for his interest, we're going to make it well worth his while, when we offer him the entirety of Dulsinor in vassalage.'

A shocked silence followed his words. Ruttgur quelled the following clamour, though he looked just as perplexed himself.

'You'd bind us to the Prince of Westenlund?' gaped Agravine.

'Aye, I would,' went on Urist implacably, anger stirring his breast. 'For that would seem better to me than watching as the Stornelendings rape our country into submission. Our forces are scattered and divided – for all we know, we might be the last free company of knights left in Dulsinor. Brigmore is relying on the walls of Graukolos to save him, but they won't protect him forever... it's only a matter of time before the Lanraks discover the tunnel in the Glimmerholt.'

The men shifted uneasily at mention of that. They had come upon the eldritch hole and used it to reconnoitre with Brigmore. Until it had started to turn the men into babbling lunatics, and they'd refused flatly to use it any more. But once he learned of it, Adso would only have to send a party of soldiers through once to take the castle. There was also rumoured to be a secret passage out of Graukolos, but that was said to be inaccessible from the outside. The most impregnable castle in Vorstlund had been rendered vulnerable by a demon's claw.

'He's right,' said Ruttgur. 'We stopped it up with boulders as best we could, but that won't stop the Lanraks once they find it. Even a half-mad sortie of soldiers would be enough to take the castle, Brigmore's only got a few hundred men at best.'

'And even if they don't find it, Graukolos will run out of food eventually,' added Urist. 'We need a relief army, or Dulsinor is finished.'

'But how can you offer such a thing as vassalage in any case?' asked Agravine. 'You don't have the authority.'

Urist flung his arms in the air. 'House Markward is at an end,' he cried. 'Wilhelm dead and his only surviving child missing. His remaining cousins have probably drunk and whored themselves to death by now, I doubt they're aware of the war even if they are still alive! No, we must honour the Stonefist's memory by preserving his inheritance from fouler hands. Prince Leopold is by reputation a just sovereign. It's to him we must turn now, he has plenty of kith who could rule as suzerain here in his name.'

'That'll disrupt the balance of power in Vorstlund,' pointed out Sir Anselm. The oldest knight in their company, he felt the most entitled to gainsay his commander. 'The Treaty of Lorvost states-'

'One prince, two dukes and six earls,' Urist finished for him. 'I know the law as well as you do, Sir Anselm. But that treaty lost its cogency a long time ago – it was supposed to guarantee that every lord was content with his holding, and make wars a thing of the past. You all know how that turned out. And if you really know the law, Sir Anselm, you'll know that I am entitled as commander-in-chief of Dulsinor's forces to sanction such a proposal in time of war. This is my decision, and believe me I have thought long and hard on it these past months.' He raked the company with his gaze. 'I will send a small party south to pursue this suit, the rest shall go with me into battle one last time. If any man holds not with this course, let him speak now or forever hold his peace.'

Anselm's eyes found the sedge of the clearing. A few other knights muttered, but no one spoke up.

Urist drew his sword. Normally he hated histrionics, but he felt the occasion warranted it.

'Then let's saddle up and ride for Graukolos, and give those dirty Lanraks one last visit from hell!'

A chorus of ayes mingled pleasingly with the sussurance of multiple blades being drawn from scabbards. Urist felt relief wash over him. His plan was working.

'We'll make an ending the troubadours will sing of forever,' said Sir Agravine, his face flushing.

'You won't,' said Urist. 'Nor you, Sir Ruttgur. I'll not throw away Dulsinor's two greatest knights on a feint.'

Both knights made to protest, but the marshal silenced them with a wave of the hand. 'My decision is final. You're to take Sir Borwine and Sir Rufius with you – the youngest shall accompany the best, and Stygnos willing live to fight another day. The rest of us had best say our prayers.'

'That's a small expedition party for such an important mission,' put in Anselm.

'Any more than that and it'll draw too much attention,' said Urist. 'They'll need to cross the two Thulias as well as avoid Hengist's freeswords if their mission is to succeed. I'm counting on the Herzog disbanding the mercenaries and sending them home once he's convinced we're all dead. Hired swords are costly.'

'It's a good enough plan, I suppose,' said Anselm as the company began preparing to strike camp. They had been hiding out in the wildlands of Dulsinor north of the castle: a couple of days' riding would bring them to their final fate.

'It's a desperate plan,' Urist corrected as he saddled up his horse, adjusting the stirrup to accommodate his injured leg. That put him in mind of the man who had broken it long ago. What did Balthor make of this sorry day from the Heavenly Halls, he wondered? A strong sword-arm like his would have been a blessing.

'So desperate it might actually succeed,' said Anselm.

Urist put his good foot in the stirrup and mounted his charger. 'Let's hope so,' he answered grimly.

He knew one thing for sure – he'd be seeing Balthor again soon enough.

CHAPTER 18
A MISSION BRIEFED

'Here, pass it along, Adelko!' Hargus beamed as he called for the wineskin, his eyes shining replicas of the stars above. It looked as though he'd had plenty enough already, but Adelko complied with his request. Up and down the cloistered walkway other novices chattered away, loitering against pillars or slouched in sieges, enjoying the rare respite from the monastery's stern regime. It was the last week of Kaldemonath, before fasting and prayers for the Year's End Festival began in earnest; the journeymen allowed the novices some time to blow off steam.

To Adelko it seemed passing strange. Nigh three months he'd been at the monastery, and still he couldn't get used to the normality. Not that his sixth sense ever left off: even here, at the heart of civilisation, he knew things weren't right. Rumours of black magic being practised in the hills abounded; Adelko knew all too well what business they hinted at.

Even if Master Horskram didn't let him in on anything

these days. That hurt him, but he supposed it was inevitable. He had barely seen his old mentor, who seemed to spend much of his time in his quarters, shut up in solitary contemplation. Perhaps the adept's sins weighed on him more heavily when he wasn't busy on missions.

'Adelko's miles away! Don't think he handles Armandy red any better than old Sholto's scrumpy!' Hargus again, reminiscing about the past. That only made Adelko feel gloomier. It also made him more uneasy. One spilled gourd of cider. That, and a candelabrum knocked to the ground, had set him on the path that led him here.

Clumsiness – it seemed a curious tool for the Almighty to use. But perhaps it wasn't strange to Him: just one more thread in the skein of mortal destiny that made up fate's rich tapestry. Assuming Reus really did take a keen interest in His creation, which Adelko was beginning to wonder about.

Question everything. Words of a woods witch, spoken in an ensorcelled bower to torment him.

'Well whatever you say, I'm not nearly drunk enough, Hargus,' he retorted. 'So pass it back here when you're done!'

Hargus exchanged knowing smirks with the other novice they were sharing a cell with, and handed the skin to Adelko. He envied his old friend. Hargus made friends so easily, but Adelko felt more detached by the day. Arik was sat a few cells up from them, talking quietly with a Pangonian noble's son indentured to the Order. The two of them hadn't spoken since their impromptu duel a fortnight ago. That just made Adelko feel more alienated from his surroundings; Hargus was the only novice he was really friendly with. Thank Reus his friend's own mentor had decided to winter at the monastery, extending his stay at Rima.

Taking a grateful slug on the delicious dark wine, Adelko let his mind drift back to his morning's study at the library. Even with the noxious fumes of strong drink in him, he could recall any text he'd read simply by focusing his elan. Gazing up at the star-spattered canopy of sky, he drew his habit in further against the cold, as he contemplated the words he had read. They had been another passage from Arnulf's treatise:

Brothers, we must decide what our founder truly wanted of us! Was it St Argo's intention to erase magic from the earth altogether, or simply to contain it whilst doing away with the viler Left Hand Way? Alas, our great founder's own writings on the subject are frustratingly vague. And yet, we must needs decide — for in allowing the flame of the Right Hand Way to remain alive, are we not constantly opening the back door to the followers of Abaddon's darker path? How many Left Hand mages have we captured and executed who began life as Right Hand practitioners, as Ma'amun, the very Demonfather of Black Magic did himself? How long have we tolerated Druidsbourne, the Earth Witch's Girdle, the Sorcerer's Guild in the Empire, the Warlock Princes of Halepo, knowing full well that from their ranks some of our most odious opponents have emerged?

That our Order has stopped short of declaring outright war on wizards of all kinds is undoubtedly also due to circumstances: the Argolian craft is an abstruse one, requiring long years of study, and few are capable of attaining even journeyman status.

We simply do not have the resources to stage such a conflict, even if we wanted to. And so we have settled for doing what we could over the centuries: burning or hanging black magicians wherever we detected them; shackling, branding and banishing white witches wherever we could.

Yet for all our travails, our efforts over the centuries have been piecemeal: we are simply a response to a call for help, not a pre-emptive force with which to strike at the heart of evil. Though our powers are legendary, we have ever lacked a cohesive vision. Some would say this is a feature of our open-mindedness; but I fear it will be used against us by our enemies within the wider Temple, ere long.

Had Arnulf suspected that his very own words would also be used by the Temple, Adelko wondered? But Abelard of Montrevellyn had been a demonolator himself, an apprentice to an older, darker master... Other texts he had looked at suggested this had been Xamiel, something the texts referred to as a 'sub-avatar' – a manifestation of the greater demon Azathol clothed in mortal flesh – who had taught Abelard in secret. Some loremasters claimed this Xamiel had posed as a preacher and helped to provoke the First Pilgrim War, more than a century ago...

Now here he was, studying in a nation that planned to launch yet another crusade, doing Abaddon's work in the name of the Almighty.

That thought sickened Adelko, but he couldn't say it was altogether incomprehensible. He remembered what it had felt like, to press the staff against Arik's throat, to feel the righteous rage bubbling up inside him... Was that what pious knights felt when they went off to slaughter heathens? Or even how Sir Torgun felt when he slew enemies of his beloved King?

Adelko hated to admit it, but Horskram's admonishments about keeping dangerous company made a lot more sense to him nowadays.

Hargus was frowning at him now. His sixth sense wasn't as keen as Adelko's, but he'd probably picked something up.

'All right, looks as though Adelko has something to talk about,' he said. The other novice stumbled off to relieve himself, making for a perfect opportunity. 'You've barely said a word about anything but studying since we met you here,' he went on. 'You fight like a demon, and you barely knew how to swing a staff earlier this year! You were always good at the lectern, but nowadays you've got lore a journeyman would envy! And your *elan*... Adelko, sometimes I can feel it pouring out of you! The other novices are practically scared of you, no wonder you haven't made any friends here.'

'Thanks for that,' muttered Adelko glumly, not wanting to meet his eye. Hargus was rarely serious about anything, which made the conversation all the more uncomfortable.

'Oh, I'm not trying to make you feel bad,' insisted Hargus. 'I'm trying to be a friend. In heaven's name, Adelko, if you can't talk to me, who can you talk to? What happened to you, on the road? You've told us almost nothing of your adventures.'

'I... can't,' faltered Adelko. 'I've been sworn to secrecy, you see.'

Hargus rolled his eyes. 'Since when did that ever stop you? Is this about your father? If so, you should talk it through.'

Adelko favoured him with a wry grin. 'That doesn't sound like a typical stoical Northlending,' he said. 'I think southern manners are rubbing off on you.'

He was stalling. He could sense Hargus probing him. His friend was an able novice and would probably make journeyman in a couple of years, but his psychic forays felt clumsy and groping to Adelko.

But perhaps where his powers failed him, old friendship might pay off.

Adelko took a deep breath and flicked his eyes to the night skies. The need to unburden was pressing on him like a tombstone.

'Alright Hargus, I'll tell you a few things,' he said in a low voice. 'But you have to swear-'

He felt another presence at his side. Turning he looked up into the stern face of Horskram, granite-like under moon and stars.

'Adelko,' said the adept, completely ignoring Hargus. 'I thought I might find you here. Put that cow's bladder down and come with me.'

Without a second thought, Adelko handed the wineskin back to Hargus. Sparing him a helpless glance, he got up and followed Horskram as he strode past the colonnades towards the inner courtyard. The other novices gawped at them, some making ridiculous attempts to hide their drinks. Adelko felt Arik's dark eyes on him as he passed by. He sensed a darker mood behind them.

'Well it looks as though I arrived just in time,' said Horskram as they approach the gabled archway leading into the courtyard. 'For unless my sixth sense fails me, you were just about to empty the contents of your mind like yon wineskin.'

Adelko flushed furiously. The archway's lintel was crowned with a pediment depicting the archangel Siona, avatar of grace and dignity; Adelko felt neither graceful nor dignified as he followed the adept through it.

Then it struck him. The inner courtyard was out of bounds to novices. What was his old mentor playing at?

'Um, Master Horskram-'

'Have no fear, Adelko,' replied the adept, taking them up a flight of stairs that hugged the inner wall. 'On this occasion, you have full permission to access the sanctum. Special dispensation.'

He steered them around the parapet and into one the covered walkways that allowed the adepthood swifter access to and from their private quarters; Adelko had occasionally spotted Horskram and Hannequin using it to spy on him during combat practice. Up here the air was raw and chilly. The sound of novices chattering drifted up from the cloisters, their voices seeming lost and distant beneath a blanket of night. At this time of year the walkway was dank, the smoking torches offering little in the way of cheer. Adelko felt a chill that went beyond the mere physical... His sixth sense was jangling again. Life-size statues of saints peered at him in the half dark, their graven forms sombre in the torchlight.

They emerged onto a gallery overlooking the ground

floor. Off it were a myriad of doors, the adepts' quarters. Striding the length of this, Horskram took them through one which led into another corridor lined with more doors. He stopped at the last one.

'I have a window overlooking the inner courtyard,' he said dryly, reaching into his habit for a key. 'By virtue of my long-standing service to the Order.'

That was about the extent of the luxury. The spartan cell Horskram let them into was barely larger than the one Adelko had been carousing in; tepid moonlight spilled in through the single window, illuminating a cot and tiny table and stool.

'Sit,' said the adept, motioning to the bed and taking the stool for himself. Adelko did as he was bidden, and Horskram fumbled around for flint and tinder before lighting a mean-looking tallow candle.

'Now,' said Horskram, the wrinkles on his face etched in shadow. 'What I am about to tell you-'

'-is to be kept secret,' Adelko finished for him.

The two exchanged wry glances. Already the novice felt better. More normal. He sensed another mission in the offing, and that pleased him. A lot.

'Prior Johann was recalled from Heilag a fortnight ago,' said Horskram. 'We suspect he is a traitor to the Order.'

Adelko nodded slowly. His old mentor had said as much during their journey through Vorstlund. Presumably Horskram had persuaded the Grand Master that his suspicions weren't motivated by a long-standing rivalry.

'Hannequin has recalled him under pretext of helping us divine the witcheries we have been sensing in the area,' the adept went on. 'You will doubtless have noticed the absence of two of our archmasters at mealtimes.'

That piece of gossip had long done the rounds. 'It's being said that Wolaf has taken ill and Cathbad is on sabbatical.' Even when he'd first heard that, Adelko had had his doubts.

'That is the official story,' said Horskram. 'The true one is that Wolaf is dead and Cathbad is being held on suspicion of demonolatry.'

Adelko gawped. An *archmaster*?

'Cathbad did dabble in the Right Hand Way before joining the Order, but I for one think him innocent,' Horskram added.

Adelko thought about Arnulf's treatise. Were any of them much different from Right Hand warlocks?

'I suspect Johann is involved somehow, as does Hannequin, but without proof we cannot do much,' the adept continued. 'Someone is obfuscating the psychic field, and our sixth sense has become muddied.'

That's what the Earth Witch said about her scrying, thought Adelko. *Another similarity between their powers and ours.*

'So what do you want me to do?' His former mentor clearly hadn't dragged him up here just to tell stories.

Horskram peered at him keenly in the candlelight. 'Hannequin is assigning Johann to give you private tuition. This will be part of your special training, which is known to the adepthood, so that won't arouse his suspicions. You're to spy on him and glean whatever you can. As he trains you, your sixth senses will become attuned, just as yours and mine are. If I was able to sense your loose tongue with young

Hargus just now, perhaps you might divine something about Johann before we leave in spring.'

Adelko was so caught up in the details of his new assignment that he almost missed Horskram's last words.

'Leave? Where are we going?'

But he knew the answer no sooner had the words come out of his mouth. 'The Pilgrim Kingdoms? We're actually going?' He felt his heart strike up a fervid rhythm no wine could induce.

'Should you continue to make headway in your studies, yes,' replied Horskram. 'We're to find out what we can about the fourth fragment. Sir Torgun and the others have already been sent north to try and secure the third.'

'You really think the druids will part with it?'

'Leave them to worry about that,' replied Horskram, 'and focus on your own duties. In any case, they've a war to win in Thraxia before they even get to the Westerling Isles.'

Another war. Adelko thought briefly of his friends, caught up in yet more danger. By comparison, his own task seemed light.

'And don't think your mission will be easy!' said Horskram, divining his thoughts. 'Whether he's guilty or not, Prior Johann is a formidable adept. And from what I've heard, a very hard taskmaster, too. You're to report back to me every Rest-day, until further notice.'

Horskram rose to usher him out; the briefing was at an end. Adelko's head was awhirl as his mentor (or should that be his spymaster?) escorted him back across the walkway and down into the courtyard. Without bidding him good night, the adept closed and barred the gate behind him as he stepped into the cloister. Retracing his steps, Adelko found it deserted; the journeymen had called curfew and packed the novices off to their dormitories. As he trudged back toward his own, Adelko felt his spirits reviving.

Two missions. The second would take him to the Redeemer's birthplace, the holy city of Ushalayim. This was the best he had felt in weeks. As ever, his sense of adventure blinded him to the mortal danger towards which he stepped so lightly.

CHAPTER 19
A TRIAL OF CHAMPIONS

Rowena watched the new arrivals suspiciously as Joram led them into the middle of the camp. As if she didn't have enough to worry about. Lord Penric had been leading the charge against her, gathering 'evidence' of foul play wherever he could buy it. The folly of it! The enemy were nigh upon them, already they had used the imbroglio to regroup. They now fielded an army several thousand strong, if the outriders told it true. At least they hadn't fallen for the enemy's feint and marched north into Abrexta's trap. *Of course we haven't,* she reflected with bitterness and irony in equal measures, *we've been far too busy squabbling amongst ourselves to fight a war badly.*

The First Woman of Clan McCullogh fought to master her temper as she surveyed her guests. Three knights and a squire, with a right strange-looking fellow in iron shackles. Her lip curled in distaste: he had the look of a witch. What was Joram playing at? It was his job to execute such curs.

She paced the boards of the podium impatiently as they

drew nearer. Erected a few days ago, it was where her trial would be conducted.

More like a scaffold to hang me on, she thought disconsolately. Cathsach and her bannermen had rallied around her, but the lords of Garro had remained steadfastly neutral. Penric had insisted on his trial, despite the spurious witnesses he'd bribed being called into question. By the laws of the kingdom, that meant a trial by combat to decide her innocence.

And she knew all too well whom Penric would field as his champion.

Cathsach stepped up beside her. 'Perhaps providence has come to our aid,' he said. 'For it looks to be some right strong knights Master Joram brings with him.' The marshal was devout, like most scions of McCullogh – her ancestor Corradhmor had embraced the Creed and been rewarded with lands for his piety. Or his willingness to slaughter his pagan predecessor, depending on how you looked at it.

'Strong foreign-looking knights,' replied Rowena tersely. 'I like this not, Sir Cathsach.'

Off on the horizon, the wraith-tainted ruins of Anarlion seemed to shriek with an unlife of their own. The spectral warriors who had fought and died for the Old Kingdom of Tul Aerant would relinquish the grave for their nocturnal haunt in a few hours. Rowena hoped she wouldn't be joining them.

'Well, Master Joram,' she said as the adept drew level. 'Your timing is impeccable as always, for you are just in time for the trial.'

Joram's brow darkened. 'I heard the news, while I was

about my business in Craek. So Lord Penric will not be dissuaded by the common good.'

'The common good demands that justice be done!' Lord Penric swept into the clearing, his retinue in tow. 'For we'll not follow a blackguard into battle, not if the very kingdom depended on it!'

As if to announce his arrival, a blustery wind ruffled the pavilions. It carried a bitter chill, and a few snowflakes too – the Thirteenth Cycle was nearly upon them, bringing a hint of the iron-hard winter to come. Time was running out for a successful campaign before the weather brought things to a halt.

'You were ever a schemer, Lord Penric, sick with self-seeking and wont to put your own contumely above any kind of good,' she declaimed, her voice dripping scorn. 'Why can't you set this absurd suit aside, so we can fight the real enemy?'

'My lady speaks the truth and you know it, Lord Penric,' put in Cathsach. 'In Palom's name, rescind your accusation!'

Penric drew himself up, trying to look the tall warrior he wasn't. 'In Virtus' name, I shall not! I hereby declare in sight of all that Rowena, First Lady of Clan McCullogh, owns not that title rightfully, and came by it through foul means! I call for her impeachment forthwith!'

The assembled bannermen and knights looked at one another and muttered. All the nobles had gathered to watch the trial, but many had hoped Penric would recant at the last minute. Looking at his quivering frame, she saw there was no reason to be had in the man.

Palom's wounds, but what had got into him? Even for the Lord of Penllyn this was... excessive.

'And who are these?' asked Penric's marshal, Irvine. A rangy-looking knight with balding grey hair swept back off his shoulders, at least he was handy in the field, unlike his liege. 'Joram, what mean you bringing outlanders upon us at this time?'

One of the knights stepped forwards before Joram could reply. 'I am no outlander, but the rightful Lord of Gaellen,' said the auburn-haired knight. 'Braxus ap Braun salutes thee!'

The handsome lordling bowed with a flourish. Rowena hadn't met Braxus before, but his reputation preceded him. She felt a brief flickering of hope.

'Sir Braxus?' snorted Irvine. 'Last we heard, you'd gone off gallivanting on some fool's errand to the King of the Northlendings. Your father lost his lands while you were away – and his head, too.'

If Braxus was angered by that, he hid it well. 'I am well aware of that tragedy,' he replied. 'Why do you think I'm here? But more to the point, what in the Known World are you playing at? Didn't you hear the lady, we've a war to fight!'

'Aye, that we do,' put in Lord Penric. 'But we'll not be fighting it under the leadership of a woman who killed her father and husband to inherit her title.'

'That is a thrice-damned lie!' blazed Rowena. 'The only reason we're here even debating its veracity is because it's a woman that leads you! Tul Aeren has ever been foremost among the southern wards, ruling the Crimson League is my right! And I've proved thus far I'm more than able to do it, woman or no!'

That silenced her critics. For a few seconds. Then the camp erupted into shouting. Rowena exchanged a despairing look with Cathsach. Men and their pride. The world would ever be ruined by it, as the Redeemer had once said.

Cathsach stepped forwards and called for silence. Only with some difficulty did he get it.

'All right, if it's a trial you want, then it's a trial you'll get,' he said, a resigned look on his ruddy moustachioed face. 'But first we should finish receiving our visitors.' He flicked a glance sidelong at Rowena. The tall blond knight had caught her eye: a more well-made warrior one could not ask for. She flicked her gaze next to the bushy-bearded fellow at his side. By contrast he was stocky and rotund, yet his thews looked to be made of knotted iron – another handy-looking fighter.

Surely one of these three would be her champion?

'Aye, I'd see our guests welcome,' said Penric, answering Cathsach, 'but not without invoking Palom's Peace first!'

Rowena's heart descended to the dank earth beneath the husting boards. Penric mightn't be the best of fighters himself, but he was a wily politicker. He had anticipated their stratagem: the right to request an oath of peace from visitors was an old custom, but all adhered to it.

Speaking in Decorlangue so the outlanders could understand, the lord went on: 'You three are welcome to attend this trial and join our army afterwards, but only on condition you forswear your swords whilst you are in our camp. They'll be returned to you before we march, as custom dictates.'

The tall blond knight shrugged. 'My business here is with the northern army, and I come as an ally of the Crimson League. I, Sir Torgun of Vandheim, do so swear.' Drawing his bastard blade, he laid it at his feet.

The bearded knight was next. 'Sir Wrackwulf of Bringenheim likewise swears only to split the skulls of your enemies. Lacking a blade, may I proffer you this instead?' With a flourish he unsheathed an ugly-looking warhammer and stood it head first on the soil.

'That's enough!' cried Rowena. 'Surely you don't plan to hold a Thraxian to the peace?'

Braxus looked puzzled. If only he knew what she was setting him up for.

But the First Man of Clan Pellyw was implacable. 'Aye, and I will!' said Penric. 'For he's a northerner, and no kinsman of ours!' Mutterings from all factions approved his words. Rowena cursed her countrymen's parochialism – would they ever look beyond the borders of their own fiefdoms?

Braxus still looked confused. 'I don't see any need for this, but have it as you will,' he said, drawing his own blade. 'I've no quarrel with anyone in the League.'

As he skewered his sword into the ground and swore his oath, Rowena felt her last hope dwindle to nothing, carried away on the chill North Wind.

'Excellent!' smirked Lord Penric. 'Now, and it please you, we can get down to business! I accuse Lady Rowena, so-called First Woman of Clan McCullogh and First Lady of Tul Aeren, of low treason by means of treachery. Witnesses have been called and heard, their testimonies disputed. As such, the law permits only one recourse. I call for trial by combat to determine the matter – let the Almighty judge who has the right of this!'

The bannermen and knights of Penllyn began catcalling. Sir Cathsach looked at Rowena with forlorn eyes. She felt her gut tighten.

Lord Fannoch of Garro, acting as arbiter, stepped up to the podium and mounted it. 'Let it be duly noted,' he told the assembly. 'And whom do you nominate to fight as your champion, Lord Penric?'

The weather seemed to grow frostier for Penric's smile, as he uttered the name all had been expecting. 'I call Sir Leathan of Fern Falls.'

A hubbub went up as Penric's command was relayed to a messenger.

How like the man, thought Rowena disgustedly. *He keeps Sir Leathan on the other side of the camp, just for dramatic effect. But every man here has seen him in battle and knows what he can do.*

And therein lay the problem.

'Lady Rowena, you stand accused of low treason,' intoned Lord Fannoch. 'Whom do you nominate to be your champion?'

She looked helplessly at the fearful faces of her household knights. None spoke a word.

'In heaven's name, four-score sworn swords, is there not one among you?' demanded Cathsach.

Silence.

'And vassals gifted with land,' he went on, raking the wealthier knights with his gaze, 'in return for service in the field. Surely one of you will stand?'

Service in the field, but not in a trial – the law was firm on that point. A champion had to step forward of his own free will. As Penric had known all along.

She caught Braxus and Torgun exchanging helpless glances, Wrackwulf shaking his head and frowning at Joram. The weaselly looking mage stared impassively at the scene.

'If no one will stand, then let the Almighty's judgment be duly recorded!' said Penric. 'Lady Rowena is guilty. Let her stand down and be taken in chains. I shall take her place at the head of our army!'

And it won't be an army for much longer, she thought despairingly. *For you lead only half as well as you intrigue.*

The Lord of Garro stepped up to make the announcement.

Just then a voice rang out across the clearing. It spoke Decorlangue haltingly, in a foreign accent, but the words were clear enough.

'I will fight for the lady.'

All eyes turned to the speaker: a dishevelled-looking squire with a scarred face, his chestnut hair billowing in the wind.

∿

Vaskrian scarcely knew what he had done. He'd barely even been able to follow the exchange; despite Hettie's best efforts, his knowledge of the High Tongue was still patchy. On the journey inland from Port Craek, the monk Joram had told his guvnor something about a dissension in the rebellion, but the squire had only caught the gist of it. Strangers never addressed him directly, he was a person of no import.

Now he was volunteering to get himself killed in a duel for another high-born stranger. All the knights present were clearly afraid of the other lord's champion – all except Braxus, Torgun and Wrackwulf that was, but this Penric had evidently taken pains to exclude them from contending. Once again, he'd been overlooked as a common squire. Well, he'd show them. After all, how tough could this champion of Penric's possibly be?

No need to worry in any case, he thought bitterly: the laughter that greeted his acceptance of the challenge made it clear there'd be no duel of justice for him today. *Serves me right for a fool notion. Now Braxus will have to intervene, and I'll probably get another bollocking.*

'Who is this low fellow?' cried Penric, speaking in Decorlangue slowly so Vaskrian could understand the insult. 'He barely speaks the High Tongue, this is no knight!'

'He's my squire and a rash one,' said Braxus, quickly stepping up and grabbing Vaskrian's arm. 'Step back and that's an order!' he hissed in Northlending. 'This isn't your fight.'

Something changed in Vaskrian then, and he suddenly

felt very calm. Turning to look his master in the eye, he smiled. 'It never is though, is it? That's my destiny, to do great deeds and not be honoured for them.'

Braxus stared at him. 'In Reus' name, lad, what are you babbling about?'

"He shall be born low but rise high, yet no man shall honour him with title for his deeds',' said Vaskrian, quoting the words that had tortured him for months. 'That's what she said, the Earth Witch... but really, it's all right, Sir Braxus.'

'Ah, that woods witch has addled your wits with her sorcery, come away now!' Braxus tried to pull Vaskrian back, but he dragged his arm free and walked steadily towards the podium. The high-born lady and her marshal were staring at him too, as if unsure what to do next.

He reached the podium. 'I will fight for you,' he repeated.

More laughter. Clearly the nobles found him very amusing.

'Seeing as no *knight* steps forwards to defend the First Lady's innocence, I pronounce her guilty!' cried Penric. Did his triumphant tone carry just a hint of shrillness?

Rowena exchanged a look with Cathsach, and seemed to make up her mind about something.

'You would fight for my name?' she asked Vaskrian, looking him square in the eye.

'Aye, I would.'

'Very well,' she said. 'Mount the podium, and take a knee.'

As if in a dream, Vaskrian did as she bade him. He was aware of Penric shouting, and Braxus calling out to him, but it all seemed to come from far away. Blood thumped in his temples.

Rowena turned to her marshal. 'Sir Cathsach, your sword,' she commanded. He complied and handed her his blade.

Stepping up to where Vaskrian knelt, she addressed him in Decorlangue. These words he knew by heart, and had done since his early youth, for he had memorised them long ago in Hroghar, when he had daily dreamed impossible dreams.

'Vaskrian of Gaellen, do you solemnly swear to honour me as your liege, to love me and do service in sight of the Almighty?'

Vaskrian's heart skipped a beat as what was happening to him sank in.

'I do solemnly swear,' he managed to stammer.

'Do you swear to defend the weak, the orphan and the widow, and relieve the distress of the world, wherever it is in your power to do so?'

'I do solemnly swear,' he repeated.

'Very good,' said Rowena. 'Let this be the last blow you receive without just reprisal.' The lady nodded at Cathsach, who stepped forward and struck Vaskrian hard across the face.

His iron gauntlet drew a trickle of blood from Vaskrian's mouth. It was, without a doubt, the most delicious wound he had ever received.

Rowena tapped his shoulders with the sword. 'In the

name of Virtus, and of Stygnos, and of Ezekiel, I dub thee knight of the realm. Arise, Sir Vaskrian.'

The young knight rose on legs that were suddenly shaky.

Steady now, he told himself. *You've kept that hot head of yours cool so far.*

Taking a deep breath and letting it out slowly, he felt calm return to him. He suddenly had a vision of Adelko, bidding him farewell at the Graufluss Bridge Tourney.

Don't set too much by the words of a sorceress – prophecies can be misleading.

Sir Vaskrian allowed himself a slight smile. Adelko's parting words. Trust his clever friend to get it right.

'Sir Vaskrian of Liathnoc accepts the challenge on behalf of his lady liege – Rowena, First Woman of Clan McCullogh!' boomed Cathsach. 'Ready the lists!'

The angry shouting and laughter had given way to baying. The nobles smelled blood. His own. Sir Vaskrian spared a glance towards his companions and caught the hopeless look in his old guvnor's eyes.

Why so little faith? he thought disparagingly. *After all we've been through together, surely-*

He suddenly realised Braxus wasn't looking at him.

Vaskrian's jaw dropped as he registered his antagonist's arrival. A hulking figure was making its way slowly through a gaggle of knights and soldiers towards the podium.

Taking him in, Vaskrian swallowed hard. Now he understood.

Sir Leathan was a formidable sight. Taller than Torgun and broader than Wrackwulf, he stalked across the lists to stand before his liege. A surly grin cracked his ogrish features, his hair hanging in matted clumps about his broad round shoulders. He wore a gargantuan hauberk and carried a kite shield that looked like a heater on his arm. He clutched a giant spiked mace, its prongs alone half the length of a man's forearm, and serrated to boot.

The young knight's next breath trembled as he took him in. He couldn't succumb to fear now. With some effort he forced himself to think calmly.

Well, he's no bigger than a Wadwo – and a lot smaller than a Golem. I've faced worse trials. Bigger doesn't always mean better.

'Sir Braxus, my harness!' he called, leaping lightly off the husting. His insouciance was feigned, but he might as well enjoy being a knight if it was only going to last a few minutes. The Thraxian just stared at him nonplussed. Wrackwulf brought him his things.

'He's big, but he'll be slow,' growled the Vorstlending, as he strapped on his target. 'Try to outfoot him if you can. Remember, the bigger they come-'

'-the harder they fall,' Sir Vaskrian finished for him. 'I've done this before, trust me.' He winked at the freelancer before divesting himself of the shield. There would be no chance of blocking Sir Leathan's mace without breaking his arm anyway: this wasn't a duel he could win in a straight fight.

He belted his sword on before drawing it. It was the same fine blade Aronn had given him after the fight with the Golem. He'd kept it honed to a razor-sharp edge. Torgun had taught him some two-handed techniques in Rima, he'd try to make use of those.

Sir Leathan was pacing about as squires finished setting up the lists, roaring at the crowds and lathering them up for a spectacle. Soldiers were crowding behind the knights to get a view: a trial might not interest them, but a duel certainly did. Vaskrian caught the size of the spiked mace-head as Leathan twirled it around, and mastered his rising fear. The thing was the size of a man's head.

One stroke and I'm done for. He'd best be slow, all right.

Presently the lists were ready. Lord Fannoch raised his hands for silence, and a deathly hush fell over the camp.

'By the power vested in me, I hereby witness that these two brave knights shall fight unto the death, to determine the First Lady of Clan McCullogh's guilt or innocence! Sir Leathan, step forwards!'

The huge knight stepped into the lists and leered. Behind him the ruins of a city ghosted the grey skies. Braxus had said it was haunted: that brought Vaskrian a strange comfort as he recalled his adventures.

Don't be so sure of yourself, sir knight, you look puny next to a Gygant, he thought as he recalled the monstrous creature they had freed in the Warlock's Crown.

'Sir Vaskrian of Liathnoc, step forwards!'

Strange, to be named after a place you'd never visited. *Still, I've been in stranger situations.*

The young knight entered the lists and cracked a rakish grin at his opponent, tilting his blade towards Leathan so he could see its keen edge. A flicker of surprise – doubt even? – crossed his brutish face momentarily.

'Do you both vow to abjure use of any spells, potions or

other magic charms?' Fannoch glared suspiciously at Morcant, who beamed back at him.

'Aye,' grunted Leathan.

'Aye,' said Vaskrian. Good job he'd thought to take off the Earth Witch's talisman, though he couldn't see what use it would have been anyway.

'Then let the Almighty determine who has the right of this quarrel! FIGHT!'

Leathan's speed astonished him. Faster than any Wadwo, he came at Vaskrian, sweeping his mace around in a wide arc. The young knight dodged aside, wincing as one of the spikes grazed his forehead.

First blood to him, and we've barely started fighting. Vaskrian scarcely had time for that thought as he dodged the next flurry of blows, each one churning up the hard soil around him. If he'd had any hope of Leathan tiring quickly, he was soon robbed of it. The gigantic knight only seemed to get more energy with each swipe, roaring fit to wake the dead. From the ruined city, ghosts seemed to call for his blood. He really *was* waking the dead.

Leathan grunted with effort as he carved another furrow across the ground, wrenching his mace free for a follow-up strike in a split second. Vaskrian lurched backwards and around, circling desperately.

So far he hadn't managed to get close enough for a single counter strike. Leathan's teeth looked like tombstones as he cracked a grin of his own.

'Come to me, little one,' he barked. 'Let's end this now.'

'Oh, we'll end it all right,' Vaskrian called back, but the

following curse died on his lips. It was hard to insult someone when you barely spoke their language.

So goading him is out of the question, he thought ruefully as Leathan charged again. *But he's clearly losing patience. Used to quick victories, this one.*

A few more movements and Vaskrian found himself with his back to the husting.

Always use anything you can to win a fight, Braxus had once told him. It wasn't chivalry, but it would have to do. Vaskrian tensed his muscles, planting his feet in the ground, daring his foe to come at him again.

Leathan took the bait. Bearing down on him, he raised the mace for a crushing overhead strike. Vaskrian would have to time his next move perfectly...

At the last moment, he lurched aside. Showers of splintered fragments erupted as the mace shook the podium, knocking the nobles off their feet. Vaskrian darted forwards, bringing himself smartly behind Leathan as he tugged at the mace where it lay firmly embedded in the podium. When a huge ball of solid steel covered with serrated spikes is driven into six inches of hardwood, even a strong man needs some effort to pull it free. Leathan *was* strong – it only took him a second to do it.

But a second was all Vaskrian needed.

He'd never been the strongest of fighters, but he'd always been quick. Months of hard combat and training from two of the best knights in the Free Kingdoms hadn't done him any harm either. Taking his sword in a two-handed reverse grip, he plunged it into the back of Leathan's knee, just below the hauberk. His antagonist roared in agony as

Vaskrian pulled the blade free, a beautiful gout of red telling him he'd found an artery.

Leathan was a man used to giving pain. He was not used to receiving it: his absence of scars had told Vaskrian that much before they'd started fighting. Dropping the mace, he clutched feverishly at his spurting leg, wailing pitifully as he slipped in his own blood and went crashing into the podium.

Each second was robbing him of lifeblood: all Vaskrian had to do now was stand back and let mortal frailty do its work. But this was his first fight as a true knight, and he was damned if nature was going to do his killing for him.

'Vaskrian, don't!' yelled Braxus, as he leaped forwards.

But his old guvnor needn't have feared. Leathan lashed out at him with his kite, but Vaskrian had anticipated the obvious move and brought himself up short, completing the feint. The shield whistled past him, inches from his nose. Vaskrian darted in again, aiming his sword at the knight's face in a savage double-handed thrust. Leathan raised his mace-arm to block, and the point punctured through the gauntlet, transfixing his hand. He screamed as Vaskrian tore the blade free, its razor edge taking off half his palm and fingers. His second thrust found Leathan's eye: the socket was big enough to accommodate the width of his blade as he drove it into his brain and out through the back of his skull.

The huge knight shuddered once, twice, and then lay still, slumped against the podium.

Letting go of the hilt, Vaskrian turned a full circle, taking in the stunned faces. He found Braxus's last.

'That's *Sir* Vaskrian to you,' he said, gasping for breath. He could taste Leathan's blood in his mouth. Better than any Pangonian vintage it was, too.

As the astonished crowd began slowly to applaud, and Fannoch pronounced Rowena innocent, the young knight slumped to his knees and raised his eyes to the heavens. Arms aloft, he gave vent to a triumphant, piercing yell.

PART II

CHAPTER 1
A STUDY IN SPYING

A delko shivered in the pre-dawn light, as blustery winds strafed the stained glass ceiling of the library. It was another cold, cold morning. And his reading wasn't doing much to cheer him up. Sighing, he bent his head to the tome once more:

For though an Argolian may indulge in food and wine to some extent, he must always guard against falling prey to the sins of the flesh. And why is it that this vice in particular must be shunned? It is as though, by abjuring procreation, a monk of the Order weakens his connection to this world, so he may be better attuned to the next. Nor are we the only mystic sect to practise such abstemiousness, for many others in Sassania do likewise. The Order of the Silver Shadow, whose mountain lair lies in the Cerulean ranges in southern Nazharya, are said only to enjoy sexual congress upon completion of a mission; their ability to bend time and thought to their will is near legendary in those parts. Likewise, the Zarumani sect of that region are also said to refrain from intimate relations, to bolster their control of elemental magick; and then of course there are the ascetic Sufielis, adherents of the so-called 'little prophet', who are perhaps the most similar to our Order in their ability to vanquish sorcerers and evil spirits.

The dry text was a treatise written by Atho of Westerburg, an archmaster who had lived a hundred years ago. He wasn't the only Argolian to advocate the benefits of celibacy. Pulling Arnulf's treatise across the table, Adelko located the text he needed to cross-reference. Blinking in the candle-light, he read:

A brief consideration of the vows of celibacy that our Order and the Sufielis take will shed light on the thinking behind this, for it is rightly said that he who disowns the pleasures of the flesh finds his psychic acuity greatly enhanced. Even the druids and priest-esses of the pagan islands must forswear physical love once they advance beyond the level of initiate. And it is for this reason that many sorcerers also choose to abstain from the touch of man and woman, though certainly not all wizards have been successful in bridling their lusts.

Adelko leaned back against the wall of his carrel, not welcoming the stone's cold touch through his habit. The sources he had looked at on the subject were unequivocal:

across all cultures, sexual continence had been found to boost one's elan.

Well, what were you expecting? the novice asked himself ruefully. *Licence from an archmaster to visit the stewes?*

A couple of the wealthier novices had been caught sneaking off to the city to do just that last week. They had been rewarded for their sins with immediate expulsion from the Order, and not all the protestations of their rich noblemen fathers had swayed Hannequin on the matter. It had caused quite the scandal, and judging by what Horskram had been saying, the last thing the Order needed was another one of those. How long before people found out what had really happened to Wolaf and Cathbad?

When word of one possessed archmaster and another held pending charges of witchcraft gets out, venal sins will be the least of our worries.

Adelko supposed that put his own problems into perspective, but they troubled him all the same. His passions had accelerated in the three months he had been at the monastery. Anger, lust, pride... emotions that had rarely troubled him before now had to be contended with daily. Perhaps it was part of growing up – next year he would see his sixteenth summer. But the novice couldn't shake the feeling that it had as much to do with his growing powers as it did with growing pains.

Brother Bertram arrived, looking ill pleased at having to be up so early on a chilly winter's morning. Once again, Adelko was glad of his presence: his chosen reading subject had given him little solace.

'Good! Good!' exclaimed Edemus as Adelko fended off his blows. Their quarterstaves came together with a whining clang as he counter attacked; his footwork was becoming more intuitive by the day now, at times it felt as though his sixth sense were guiding his movements. The training master had taken to closing out their hour with a five-minute sparring session, and on his better days Adelko fancied he was almost a match for him. Almost.

Edemus called a halt.

'Excellent work, Adelko,' he said, nodding approvingly. 'Now drop on the floor and hold the bridge position!'

Adelko groaned (and not inwardly) but did as he was told. Supporting his body weight on his elbows and toes after an hour's hard training was agonising, but he was learning to cope with the pain, to find a kernel of sweetness within it and latch on to that... it was the same technique he used to focus past the desires that had so plagued him of late.

'And relax,' said Edemus. 'All right, stretches and then we're done for today. You're making sterling progress, lad – we'll make a fighter of you yet.'

Adelko dared not allow himself any feelings of pride at the rare compliment, but busied himself stretching out his aching muscles. Edemus must have sensed his internal anguish though; by now they were attuned to one another.

'What is it, lad?' he asked as Adelko finished stretching.

The novice sighed. 'Can't stop thinking about Arik,' he mumbled. Better to talk of that than speak about lust with the stoical journeyman. 'It's been a month since we... fought. We've not said a word to each other since.'

Edemus placed a calloused hand on his shoulder (it was a shoulder that was getting broader by the day, it seemed). 'We discussed this already,' he said. 'You and Arik are coming into the full flower of manhood, discovering powers you never knew you had. High emotions will accompany that. Just remember the scriptures, and meditate upon your choler – you control the anger, Adelko, it does not control you!'

'But when I had him on the ground like that, it felt... good, to have that power over him. Sometimes I just feel like I want to surrender to those passions.'

Edemus tightened his grip. 'Adelko, you cannot surrender,' he said, his face growing even more serious than usual. 'This is a test we all must face on our road to journeyman. You have remarkable potential, lad – don't squander it through weakness like yon fool Pangonians did the other week!'

'I know what the Order believes about indulging passions,' said Adelko. 'Only I've met warlocks who did just that to their heart's content, and it didn't seem to affect their powers.' Thoughts of Andragorix and the poor mountain lad he had kidnapped and abused still brought a shudder of revulsion to Adelko. Not to mention the ghastly remains of the succubus they had found in the warlock's bedchamber.

'You speak of the Left-Hand Way,' said Edemus, divining his thoughts. 'Be wary of entertaining such notions, Adelko. Even the pious can fall into darkness if they follow not the light, as the Redeemer sayeth.'

Edemus' words were eerily prescient. His next lesson was private tuition, with Johann.

'I'll redouble my efforts to stay vigilant, Brother Edemus,' he said, before excusing himself.

Horskram had definitely been right about one thing: Johann was a stern taskmaster. And one none too pleased with his change of circumstances, judging by the alacrity with which he thrashed the lectern every time Adelko made a mistake. The Sassanic tongue was an abstruse one, its intonation and modes altogether alien to the Urovian ear. Adelko had to admire Horskram's deviousness: getting a suspect traitor to teach him a language needed for his next mission, while carrying out his current one of spying on him.

'No!' yelled the balding monk, thwacking the lectern. 'You're pronouncing it all wrong – back of the throat, I said! And you're stressing the wrong syllables, again!'

Adelko sighed and closed his eyes. It wasn't easy learning a difficult language, whilst using your sixth sense to try and fathom if the person teaching it was up to no good. Likewise having to conceal his intent made things more difficult; they had become slightly attuned over the past fortnight, but that worked both ways. And as an adept, Johann's sixth sense should by rights be much more honed than Adelko's... was Horskram really wise to use him for this? He'd insisted Adelko was the last person Johann would suspect of watching him, but Adelko wasn't so sure. A couple of weeks into his spying mission, and he had to admit he was probably doing better at learning Sassanic.

Johann *was* hiding something: that much was evident, he could detect a faint throbbing of guilt and tension behind the surly facade. But what that something was, he could not say. For all he knew, it was merely the unseated prior struggling with his own anger and pride.

Even the pious can fall into darkness if they follow not the light.

Nowadays Adelko found himself wondering if the Redeemer had ever done more than utter obscure aphorisms and recondite half-truths, though he could certainly see the meaning behind the proverb.

'You're miles away,' said Johann, his voice underscored with contempt. 'Edemus is training you too hard for that frail body of yours, else you're spending too much energy in the blasted library. Heaven knows why Hannequin has such faith in you. I can't believe I'm here giving you private tuition, instead of presiding over Heilag.'

'I'd heard you were here to help pick out a successor for Wolaf.' Adelko fancied it was worth hedging his bets. Perhaps he could wheedle something useful out of the haughty monk where his sixth sense was failing him.

'You novices hear far too much,' sneered Johann, looking out of a cloister window. 'Leave me to worry about monastery politics, they're none of your concern!'

Again he felt it, as a flaring light seen far off in the distance on a dark night. Something was troubling the prior. Adelko forced himself to focus, channelling his sense.

Fear. Behind the guilt, behind the tension and injured

pride. Johann was afraid of something. Of being found out? But what did he know? And if he remained this tight-lipped, what evidence could they possibly get against him? Argolians had always believed in a fair trial.

Yet more questions. Ones Horskram would want answers to.

The bell for the morning meal tolled. Adelko felt a sense of relief, despite getting no further in his mission. He was famished. The monks of Rima stinted on the exotic imported foodstuffs that ended up in the markets of the city, but they ate heartily all the same.

'Dismissed,' muttered Johann, waving him away with the stick. 'And make sure you practise your phrasing, I don't want you making the same stupid mistakes tomorrow!'

As Adelko left he caught the prior looking out of the window again, a pensive expression on his face.

He was up to something all right.

'... but I've no idea what.' Horskram sat in silence as Adelko finished his weekly report, the meagre candlelight making him look older and more weary than ever.

Presently the adept spoke. 'It's possible he won't say anything to incriminate himself, even if he is guilty. Just keep your sense on him, and find out what you can. You did well to steer the subject around to Cathbad, try to do it again if you can without looking suspicious.'

'You don't think the archmaster is guilty?'

'Of Wolaf's binding? Certainly not. Cathbad was a hedge

witch at best, and totally divorced from the Left Hand Path. No, he is a distraction. But we have to be seen to be doing something, and so his detention is... political. Hannequin will doubtless pardon him in the new year and replace him as archmaster. But in the meantime, the Grand Master needs to find someone who *is* responsible. Because once the Temple gets word of this, they'll be demanding our dissolution if we don't produce a culprit.'

Adelko's eyes widened. 'They could do that?'

'If they persuade the King, he could close down all the Order's monasteries located on his soil. We'd be expelled from our own headquarters.'

Adelko thought on that. 'They say the Order's been suppressed in Thraxia too, on Abrexta's orders.'

'Indeed. Life is getting very difficult for Argolians again, and I've no doubt that's connected to the plot to reunite the Headstone fragments. Whoever is behind it all is taking pains to rid themselves of the one organisation in the Free Kingdoms that can be counted on to oppose their schemes.'

The winter night suddenly seemed less chilling than the thoughts that crept through Adelko's mind.

'So get what you can on Johann,' added Horskram, his eyes becoming keen. 'Because we are operating on borrowed time. A trial would buy us more of that, and give Hannequin the leverage he needs to keep the Temple at bay. That should allow to get us to the Pilgrim Kingdoms, and give our knightly friends time to get back here with the third fragment, or at least have it safely accounted for. And if you and I can secure the fourth too, then we've checked our mastermind. A lot is riding on this, Adelko.'

'Couldn't we just make a show of putting Cathbad on trial? Not to find him guilty, but just as a delaying tactic?' It surprised Adelko how devious he was becoming himself – clearly his year with Horskram had rubbed off on him.

'You mean a show trial? No, Hannequin would never stoop to such – 'twas show trials that nearly undid the Order a generation ago! Besides, Cyprian would see through that in a second. We need something concrete, Adelko – the Supreme Perfect has far too much influence with the King to be taken lightly. The Order must be seen to be cleaning its own house.'

'I understand, Master Horskram. I'll do everything I can to help.'

The adept nodded and rose to escort him back to the outer sanctum. The old monk pinched the candle as they left his cell, plunging them into a moonlit darkness that did little to allay Adelko's trepidation.

CHAPTER 2
A WAR ON WINTER'S EVE

Abrexta smiled as she watched Lord Penric lead his knights south, footsoldiers and archers following in their wake. For a while she had been worried. When she'd watched the outlander defeat Penric's champion it had been clear her gambit was at an end. Not even the ambitious lord of Penllyn could hope to dispute a trial by combat – the benighted Palomedians believed their one-god-in-two intervened in such matters. Perhaps the Palomedian god *had* intervened: her power of suggestion over Penric had been broken, and she had been unable to retain influence over him.

How welcome then to see the First Man of Clan Pellyw abandoning the Crimson League, taking his army back to Penllyn under rainy skies. Clearly his pride would not stand for following a woman into war, even if she had established her right to rule.

Men and their pride, you could always count on using it

as a weapon against them. Abrexta would sue for peace with Lord Penric – after she had crushed the rebel remnants.

Mouthing a word in the arcane tongue, she shifted her mirror's view, taking them in. Bereft of Penric's contribution they made for a forlorn sight in the drizzle – barely more than five hundred knights, with less than twice that number of infantry and some thousand archers.

Without breaking her concentration, she murmured: 'Gann, remind me of our total troop strength now the muster is complete.'

From where he sat quaffing mead at the bedside, her naked Royal High Constable looked up at her, like a skittish deer alerted to the presence of huntsmen. 'Now that we've sent the Kingsfolders down south to join the lords of Garth, there should be a thousand knights and fifteen hundred foot in the field,' he said, after hesitating. 'Twelve hundred archers, too.'

Abrexta let his words meld with her mindset as she quested closer to home, reaching for the loyalist camp. She could see the banners of the Kingsfolders fluttering alongside those of the lords of Garth atop a ridge of high ground overlooking a wood that separated Rathlain from the northerly provinces of Irisfallen and Colherin. A narrow corridor of land bifurcated the bare branches, leading to the fields of Rathlain where lay the rebel army she had just been spying on.

On such a thin strip of sward would the fate of a kingdom be decided. Abrexta was determined that Rathlain, the southernmost ward of Garth province, would be the last gain the rebels would make. The enchantress mouthed the closing words and let the mirror grow dark. She felt tired, but then she always was nowadays – enthralling half the kingdom's nobility was exhausting work.

'You're to head south to join the army tomorrow,' she said. 'Tell Lord Ongus to attack the rebels without hesitation.'

Gann nearly choked on his mead. 'But it's nigh winter – we can't campaign at this time of year, the rains will-'

'I'm aware of orthodox military thinking,' said the sorceress, helping herself to some wine. 'Unfortunately, so is our antagonist. Lady Rowena cannot be counted on to do the expected, and nor should we.'

Gann blinked.

Abrexta sighed impatiently. 'Clan Pellyw has deserted the league – but give her the winter, and Rowena might be able to convince Lord Penric to rejoin the alliance. He's smarting from wounded pride, but that's not an advantage that will last. We must strike now and risk the weather – at any rate, the rains will affect them just as much as us.'

'My lady, you have thought of everything,' he simpered, as she walked to stand over him. Knocking back the last of the wine, she undid her robe and pushed him back into bed. With the right instruction, he was almost a good lover – she'd decided she might as well enjoy pleasuring the fool while she had to do it.

'Now remember, Lord Gann,' she said, climbing into the King's bed beside him. 'Do it how I told you to, and do it *slowly...*'

∼

Sir Vaskrian watched as Lord Penric's army vanished beyond the rain-smudged hills. At his side, he could feel his liege lady's tension as Rowena watched them go.

His liege lady. He could still scarcely believe it. Outwardly nothing had changed – he still wore the same mail shirt, carried the sword Aronn had gifted him, wore the tatty clothes that had seen him all the way from Hroghar.

But everything had changed. He was no wandering squire now, but a knight, in service to a noblewoman leading an uprising against her King. Suddenly everything the woods witch had predicted made sense. He really was destined to rise high... Adelko had told him prophecies could be misleading, and so it had proved. No man, but a woman, had titled him for his deeds.

The youthful knight fingered the hilt of his finely crafted sword. He'd lived to realise the ambition of a lifetime, but Ushira wasn't done playing games with him yet. He didn't need any kind of Argolian special sense to fathom her blessings wouldn't be unqualified.

'I like this not,' said Cathsach. Lady Rowena's marshal spoke Decorlangue in Vaskrian's presence, a courtesy to his new status he supposed. 'We've little chance against the King's forces without Penric's help.'

'I haven't steered us wrong thus far,' was all Rowena said to that.

The three lords had spent half a morning arguing inside the command tent after Vaskrian's duel. Penric had emerged looking flustered and angry, before announcing his intention to leave the following day. Fannoch and Rowena had stepped out after him: one looking helpless, the other defiant.

Bluebloods. Always making life more complicated. Vaskrian supposed he was one of them now – which was fair enough, he'd proven quite adept at complicating his own life.

Don't suppose it'll go on much longer with these odds we're facing, he thought. *But I'll make an end worthy of witch's prophecy.*

His three fellow knights sauntered up to join them. It felt strange to see Braxus acknowledge him with a curt nod before he addressed Rowena.

'You really mean to fight it out? We could fall back over winter, regroup-'

Rowena shook her head. 'We proceed as planned. Outriders report that the enemy is camped two days' march to the north. If we can defeat them now, we can force them to fall back and concede Colherin and Irisfallen. We'll see out the winter as masters of all Garth and entrench ourselves on the King's very borders.'

Cathsach frowned. '*If* we can defeat them,' he said. 'The Kingsfolders outnumber us two to one without Pellyw's troops.'

'Then the victory will sting all the more,' said Rowena.

'You seem passing confident of this victory,' Braxus observed. Wrackwulf and Torgun exchanged uncertain glances. They didn't seem so sure themselves.

'I haven't steered us wrong yet,' Rowena repeated, before laying a hand on Vaskrian's shoulder. 'Yon knight proved my worthiness to lead, in sight of man and god. What more reassurance do you need, Sir Braxus?'

Sir Vaskrian felt a surge of elation at her words, but Braxus flicked a wry glance his way as he replied: 'Well, you've deprived me of a squire on the eve of battle, of that much I can be sure!'

'You'll be a lord of men in time, if you follow my counsel,' said Rowena. 'Think on that, sir knight.'

'I will,' replied Braxus, 'but you'd better be as good as they say.'

Rowena exchanged smiles with her marshal.

'You can join the vanguard,' she said. 'That should give you the perfect opportunity to learn just how good I am.'

Rowena watched the knights leave as they went to join the army. She didn't feel half as confident as she appeared, but remembered her Alcius: *A third of a battle is won by valour, a third by tactics, and a third by leadership.* She couldn't afford to show any weakness in hers, though showing weakness had its uses, as Alcius himself had pointed out. *Always appear weak, when you are strong.* The words of the legendary Thalamian warlord comforted her a little, giving her hope that her plan might yet succeed.

'I hope you know what you're doing,' said Cathsach, speaking in Thrax so the outlander wouldn't understand. She had appointed Sir Vaskrian to her personal bodyguard. It wasn't a move her marshal approved of, but the young knight had more than proved his worth.

'Just stick to the strategy we discussed,' said Rowena. 'The Almighty will determine the rest.'

Cathsach shook his head and stomped off to oversee the departing forces. Rowena felt her tension rise a notch.

'Your marshal doesn't seem confident,' said Vaskrian.

'He's a conservative tactician,' replied Rowena, before laying her hand on his shoulder again. 'Come ride with me in the vanguard – a general should always be seen to lead her troops! I would know more of my saviour and champion. Besides, it'll be good for you to practise your Decorlangue – you'll need to master the High Speech, now you're a knight.'

He flushed at her words. But then she rarely minced them. *No wonder Lord Penric resents my authority – a strong-minded woman, what an outrage to any self-respecting nobleman!*

'I am honoured,' Vaskrian stuttered. His broken Decorlangue was quite charming – a shame to teach it out of him, but needs must. He was almost handsome too, under those unfortunate scars of his.

They mounted up together and joined Cathsach and the bannermen at the head of the vanguard, squires scurrying in their wake to finish striking camp and bring up the rear. She had the army arranged in the formation it would attack in: vanguard, main battle and rearguard composed of knights and men-at-arms, flanked by archers to either side. Lord Fannoch and his own retinue of bannermen rode to the rear of the vanguard – more a mariner than a soldier, the diminutive lord didn't share her appetite for leading from the front.

We're a sorry excuse for an army, all right. Alcius, this had better work.

Braxus and the two other knights he'd brought with him joined them, along with Joram and the mysterious foreign sorcerer he was holding captive. She'd not had time to wheedle the true story behind that out of the adept, but perhaps her new champion could enlighten her.

'So tell me, Sir Vaskrian, how did such a motley band of sworders come to arrive on my shores?'

He told her his story in his halting Decorlangue, and she corrected him as he went. The pauses in conversation gave her time to mull over his words. It was obvious he wasn't telling her the whole tale, not by half.

'So you're here on Argolian business? Why this trip to the Westerling Isles?'

'I can't tell you, milady,' the young knight stammered. 'We... we were sworn to secrecy.'

Rowena pursed her lips. At least his honesty was refreshing.

'I could compel you as your liege, but have it your way – for now. So your plan is to help us defeat Abrexta, then take advantage of the King's generosity in return and have him sail you across the Tyrnian Straits?'

'Well, you'll have plenty of ships to spare if the reports we heard were true.'

'Aye, Abrexta's madcap plan to conquer the Westerling Isles, from what we can fathom. But something impels you all towards those islands. What do the Marcher Lords have that interests you so, I wonder?'

The knight flushed again, deeply enough to make his

burned face look almost demonic in the greying light. Drizzle began to fall again. A few muttered curses went up from the army as they pressed on between the ragged boughs of densely packed trees. Too dense for mounted knights, but enough for footsoldiers and archers to pass through.

She flicked a nervous glance at the woods as she went on: 'And now on top of it, you seem to have recruited Master Joram to your mission, and a warlock he's keeping alive who should have been executed.'

Vaskrian shrugged. 'You're really asking the wrong person,' he said. 'I wasn't important – until now.' He looked at her gratefully. The youth really did look quite handsome, if it wasn't for his scars. Those, and his downcast manner.

'You don't seem so overjoyed for a man who has just been raised above his station,' she observed.

'No, I am,' he answered quickly. 'You cannot know what this means to me. I'll serve you with my life, this swears Sir Vaskrian of Hroghar!'

As another courtesy, she had allowed him to keep his birthplace as an annex to his title. A courtesy... and a novelty, too. Rowena had to admit, it was refreshing to have a foreigner for a bodyguard. A grateful one that would obey her orders without question was also welcome. She didn't have the heart to point out that serving her meant not going to the Westerling Isles with his comrades after this business was done. Already she was quite fond of him, and on top of that he'd probably saved her life.

She grinned at him, not caring if it showed her gawky

teeth. 'Well, Sir Vaskrian, you certainly haven't let me down yet! You're one of the fastest swordsmen I've seen.'

'I was trained by the best,' he said, nodding towards Braxus and Torgun, 'of course I'm good.'

'Ha! You've yet to cultivate the modesty of a true knight – but that will come in time! How many summers have you seen?'

'Eighteen,' replied the knight, as though scarcely able to believe it himself.

'That's a young age to win your spurs – so mark you distinguish yourself in battle!'

'I will,' he replied, warming to the theme. 'I've seen battle before, you know.' And he told her of the civil war of the Northlendings.

Rowena frowned. 'And now here we are in Thraxia, at war amongst ourselves as well. Whatever this secret business is of yours, it's got something to do with it, I trow.'

Sir Vaskrian said nothing more at that, but the glance he shot towards his erstwhile companions told Rowena all she needed to know.

The night was still. The rain had ceased, leaving a muddy bog for the army to bed down in. Sir Torgun wasn't overly troubled by that: what did bother him was going to war at this time of year. It simply wasn't done.

'No good will come of this,' he said to Sir Wrackwulf, 'this weather is far too treacherous for a cavalry charge to be effective.' The pair were sat eating by a cooking fire. Several others were dotted about the camp, but not many; it had taken the squires an age to get even a handful lit in the damp conditions. Most of the knights had retreated into their pavilions for the night. The ordinary soldiers and archers would have to make do with bedrolls.

The freelancer grunted noncommitally as he munched on the last of his lamb shank. 'On top of that, Cathsach and Rowena have the men making stakes,' he said between mouthfuls, 'to protect the archers from enemy horse. This'll be a fight on foot at close quarters, make no mistake.'

'That doesn't concern me,' replied Torgun, anxious to make clear he wasn't afraid. 'But for the less experienced knights and soldiers... some of them are young, this will be their first battle.'

Silence hung heavy between them, broken only by Wrackwulf slurping on his mead.

'You mean it may well be their last,' he said bluntly. 'Strange indeed that two armies should clash at this time of year, but that's what comes of putting women in charge! Still, look on the bright side – plenty more chances for experienced sworders like us to shine, and this Thraxian mead isn't half bad.'

The rotund knight smacked his lips appreciatively as he drained his cup. Torgun frowned and took a perfunctory sip on his. He wasn't even particularly hungry. All he wanted was to meet the enemy. A battle – even in these conditions – would take his mind off more difficult matters. Drawing his blade, he pulled out a whetstone and began to run it along its keen edge. It was already razor sharp, but it gave him something to do.

'If you keep sharpening that thing, you won't have a sword to fight with come morning,' observed Wrackwulf. 'You are overly restless, methinks.'

'Small wonder if I am,' replied Torgun. 'I'm fighting a foreign war, and right keen to get this business done. I relish battle as a chivalrous knight ought – but in Ezekiel's name, Sir Wrackwulf, I would fain return home where I belong!'

Or into Adhelina's arms, an annoying inner voice added.

'Worry not!' said Wrackwulf, clapping him on his broad shoulder. 'We caught sight of the enemy just before sunset. One way or another, this fight will be done by tomorrow's end.'

'One battle, aye, but the war? And we've to get to the Westerling Isles, too.'

'Well, isn't this what you wanted?' asked Wrackwulf. 'War and quest? I've fought alongside you long enough to know this is meat and drink to you. It's not home you're longing for, is it?'

A knowing glint had entered the freelancer's eye.

'I suppose not entirely,' admitted Sir Torgun. He felt his guts churning at the thought of the beautiful heiress of Dulsinor. No pending battle could ever make him feel so.

'Here,' said the freelancer, picking up his warhammer. 'This is what I'll be taking into the fray tomorrow. No need for whetstones, eh? Swap weapons a minute, it's ages since I hefted a sword.'

Torgun could see what his companion was trying to do – cheer him up and take his mind off Adhelina. He had to admire the freelancer's comradeliness, even if he was a scurrilous rogue at heart.

He forced a smile as they traded weapons.

'I can't say a warhammer is my first choice of weapon,' he said politely. The head was a heavy lump of steel, one end tapering in a vicious spike. Torgun was strong enough to use it one-handed, but even so the balance felt all wrong, counterweight or no.

'That's a bastard blade alright,' said Wrackwulf, admiring his sword in the firelight. 'It's not the weight that bothers me, you see, it's the balance – feels all wrong to me.'

The two knights looked at each other and suddenly started laughing. Torgun felt his spirits lift. This was infinitely more like it – how two warriors should be on the eve of battle!

'Having fun playing with each other's toys?'

Braxus smiled slyly as he joined them at the fire. In one hand he carried a wineskin, in the other he clutched his lyre.

Torgun frowned, then remembered his vow. No more quarrelling with his love rival. Not until their mission was done anyway. Though he did not care for the Thraxian's snide humour.

'Ha! I see you've brought toys of your own to the game,' said Wrackwulf. 'Come on then, pass that skin over and give us a tune!'

Braxus tossed the wineskin and brushed his fingers over the lyre strings. Torgun prayed the Thraxian would play something cheerful.

Fortunately, Wrackwulf was thinking much the same. 'But none of your weepy love ballads,' he said, swapping weapons back with Torgun, 'I mean to split Thraxian skulls come morning with this, I want something to stir up my blood!'

Braxus' face darkened. 'I hope you plan on hitting the right Thraxians at least.'

Wrackwulf grinned as he took a pull on the wineskin. 'I've not had trouble finding the right target so far. Here, Sir Torgun, why don't you sharpen Sir Braxus' sword for him while he plays? The Lady Rowena has pinched his squire, and he's probably forgotten how to use a whetstone.'

Torgun's cold stare told Wrackwulf what he thought of that jibe.

'Well, never mind,' winked the freelancer, 'Seriously though, I think the First Woman of Clan McCullogh has taken a liking to young Sir Vaskrian – I imagine she'll be calling on him to do his duty soon and often!'

Sir Braxus rolled his eyes. Sir Torgun shook his head. He respected Sir Wrackwulf, but his lascivious humour was really unbecoming.

I'll have to teach him the finer points of the Code of Chivalry sometime, he thought. *Braxus too, while I'm at it.* 'Perhaps you might play that song for us now?' he practically begged the Thraxian.

Braxus nodded and complied. He sang in Thrax, so Torgun couldn't follow the words, but at least the song was jaunty and uplifting. By the time Braxus was done, several more knights and a handful of soldiers had joined them at the fire. Along with Joram and his sinister captive. The iron shackles binding Morcant caught the flames with an eerie shimmer. Torgun supposed they were something to be grateful for nonetheless: bad enough that the enemy was in the employ of a sorceress, without magic users tainting their own efforts.

'Looking forward to the battle tomorrow?' asked Wrackwulf cheerfully, addressing Joram. 'You can crack a few heads with that iron stave of yours.'

'No,' said Joram, favouring him with a sour sneer. 'Argolians take no part in the wars of mortal men. I'll be keeping an eye on this dastard.' He stared balefully at Morcant, who flinched before his gaze.

'Ah, pity,' said Wrackwulf, as Braxus broke out another tune for the knights and soldiers. 'You seemed happy to beat yon shackled wretch, I thought perhaps you had more taste for good old-fashioned violence than most of your kind.'

Joram glared at him. 'A sorceress slew most of my kind, as you put it. I'll save my vigour for Abrexta, thank you – this poltroon has already proved most revealing about her weakness.'

That didn't stop you wanting to kill him on the spot, thought Torgun. This monk was one to watch – he had a touch of Sir Wolmar about him. The princeling had never reappeared. Probably come to grief in some clandestine duel. Torgun was sorry for that – though they'd never been friends, Wolmar was a valiant knight – but hardly surprised.

What kind of trouble would this tempestuous monk get them into, he wondered? And he'd thought Horskram hard to deal with.

The upbeat notes of the lyre were a welcome sound to

Rowena's ears. At least they helped to drown out the sound of Sir Celtigus, who'd been droning on about a winter truce. She darted her gaze across the bannermen who'd crowded into her tent for a last confabulation before bedtime. She could tell that most of the men present agreed with Lord Fannoch's marshal. Cathsach was looking more worried and pensive than ever.

'Alright, Sir Celtigus,' she said, silencing the marshal with a wave of the hand. 'I've heard your views, and I say there will be no truce! They're spoiling for a fight as much as we are.'

'But we'll be knee-deep in mud at this rate!' protested Celtigus. It had rained steadily on their two-day march to war.

'Which suits us perfectly,' Rowena explained for the umpteenth time. 'The enemy has twice our number of knights, so we need to nullify that advantage as much as we can. If they have to come at us on foot that gives us more time to use our archers.'

'They'll have archers too,' pointed out Fannoch. 'More than we do.'

Rowena allowed herself a slight smile. 'Yes, well... you let me worry about the archer tally, Lord Fannoch.'

'If only that cur Penric hadn't reneged on this alliance,' said Cathsach. 'We could have used his thousand – hillmen are the best shots this side of the With-y-Pass ranges.'

'No use wishing for what we don't have!' barked Celtigus, his bulbous pate shining in the brazier light. Together with his barrel-shaped torso and ridiculous grey moustachios, it made him look more like a jester than a marshal.

Jesters indeed. That's what Ushira had gifted her, to fight this bloody war of attrition. Entitled men not half as clever as they liked to think they were.

'We'll face them down tomorrow with what we *do* have,' she said. 'If we stick to the strategy, the day will be ours.'

A good general listens to his officers, but trusts his intuition always. That part of Alcius was somewhat vague, she supposed, but Rowena's gut was telling her to stand firm.

'Perhaps you'll be dressing up in armour next, so you can lead the charge,' sneered Celtigus. He drew a warning look from Fannoch, but it was too late.

'Aye, and I would too,' blazed Rowena, rounding on him, 'if only I'd had the chance to learn! I may not know how to wield a sword, Sir Celtigus, but I know how to win battles, and by Ezekiel we'll win this one tomorrow! Now I'll not hear another word on it – understood? Or must I get my new champion to chastise more of you?' She motioned towards where Sir Vaskrian stood a few paces behind her. They were speaking in Thrax so he could not follow the conversation, but his thousand-yard stare was intimidating enough. Since he'd slain Sir Leathan half the bannermen were in awe of him.

'Very well,' said Fannoch, putting a restraining hand on his marshal. 'Lady Rowena has the right of this. She's proved her worth in the eyes of the Almighty, let's give her a chance to keep on proving it.'

And likely I'll have to keep on proving it, again and again – for no other reason than that I'm a woman, she thought bitterly.

'All right, enough chatter,' she said, suddenly feeling

very weary. 'We've a war to get up for tomorrow morn. Get some rest, all of you.'

'You realise you're staking everything yon foreigner won for you on one throw of the dice,' said Cathsach, after the others had left. Only Vaskrian remained besides them, standing to attention. 'They won't follow you again if this doesn't work – assuming we even survive.'

'I do realise that,' replied Rowena. 'Cathsach, will you not trust me this one more time?' She caught his eyes, set deep in his careworn face and made all the gloomier by the uneven light of the braziers.

The marshal took a deep breath and let it out again. 'Aye, my lady, I've known you since ye were a girl. Your methods are unorthodox, but I've never kenned a sharper spirit or a nobler heart. I just hope you're not over-reaching yourself.'

Cathsach kissed her hand before stalking out of the tent.

Rowena exchanged a rueful glance with her bodyguard. 'So do I, Sir Cathsach,' she said, to no one in particular. 'So do I.'

Sir Vaskrian smiled grimly at the ugly sight morning bequeathed him. It had rained again in the night, and the road passing between the wooded slopes had all but merged into the soil. The lowering skies breathed a cruel chill across the gathered armies: cruel enough to sting, but not quite enough to turn rain into snow.

His eye scanned the corridor of land. The ground was

a bit firmer towards the fringes of the forest, but Rowena had anticipated that and had the men set up rows of stakes to cover their flanks. Two groups of archers, each more than four hundred strong, were clustered behind these. They were just high enough to get a decent vantage point.

'That should stop their knights using firmer ground to charge our bowmen,' said Wrackwulf. He sounded cheerful, but then he always was. Like Vaskrian, he would be fighting in the vanguard. To either side of them, the rearguard and main battle were drawn up in the same formations: knights to the front, footsoldiers to the rear.

'Don't see what difference it makes putting us up front,' muttered Vaskrian, 'seeing as how we're all to fight on foot anyway.' The order had come from Rowena first thing that morning. She'd almost had to quell another revolt from her chivalry, but Cathsach and Celtigus had managed to carry the ordinance through.

'Aye, I've no idea what yon woman is playing at,' said Wrackwulf. 'They say she won a lightning victory to secure Rathlain though, so the soldiers trust her.'

'They're not the ones having to give up their chargers,' said Vaskrian. 'My first battle as a knight, and I don't even get to be part of a lance manoeuvre!'

'Ah well, at least we'll still be first into the fray, eh?' said Wrackwulf, nudging him. He was trying to be encouraging, but Vaskrian was scarcely in the mood. The enemy were a few hundred yards up the muddied road, arranged into three battle lines to their one. The odds didn't look good, especially given their knights were still mounted.

'Each of those battle lines is at least five hundred strong,' observed Vaskrian.

'Try eight hundred,' replied Wrackwulf. 'More than our entire centre battalion, and probably double what we've got flanking us. It'll be a brutal melee, alright.'

The freelancer was grinning again. Vaskrian couldn't help but share his bravado. After all, this was what he'd dreamed of his whole life – daring battles against insane odds.

'Enough to run away,' he said.

'Enough to be killed,' added Wrackwulf.

'And enough to be ransomed,' said Braxus, finishing the old soldier's joke as he drew alongside them.

'Good day, Sir Braxus,' said Wrackwulf, 'I see you've been persuaded to part with that fine stallion you won at Graufluss, and join the rest of us common serjeants!'

The Thraxian winced. 'I do wish you wouldn't keep bringing that blasted tourney up.'

'Speaking of which, where's your great rival Sir Torgun?' asked Wrackwulf, insensitive as ever. 'I'd have thought our paladin friend would be first to the front.'

Braxus managed a wry grin. 'I think he has to observe some sacred ritual, before he says goodbye to Hilmir.'

Vaskrian could see the pain behind the smile, though: losing the Farovian destrier had almost hurt Braxus as much as tarnishing his honour. Not that any of that would matter if they all managed to die heroically in battle today.

Clarion calls interrupted their banter. Mounting a hastily constructed stockade at the rear of the army, Rowena addressed her troops. Just then, Sir Torgun came jostling through the scrum to join them. He wore his usual impassive expression.

'I see Sir Torgun has his war-face on,' observed Wrackwulf.

'Hush!' said Braxus. 'I want to hear her battle speech – I've never heard a woman give one before.'

Wrackwulf rolled his eyes at Vaskrian. 'I think your old guvnor's in love again,' he whispered, glancing meaningfully at Lady Rowena. Vaskrian pretended to laugh, surprised at the sudden flare of jealousy that strafed his breast. It was Hettie he'd been thinking about, but then she wasn't in his life any more.

Whatever he thought of his new liege as a woman, she wasn't as good as Freidheim at giving battle speeches. But then she hadn't had as much practice as the King of the Northlendings, he supposed. While Rowena declaimed pending victory in a voice that quavered, Sir Vaskrian spared a glance for the enemy troops. Their knights were laughing and bantering with one another in the saddle.

He hoped his mistress was a better tactician than she was an orator.

Rowena sketched a nervous gaze across the banners flapping in the wind. All bore the crimson eagle motif she'd ordained: that had provoked another rash of protest from the nobles, who'd baulked at laying aside their coats of arms, but once again a thousand-year-dead emperor had spoken to her more cogently than any latter-day lord.

Unify your soldiers behind one symbol. Let its cause cohere in the hearts of your troops; let the sight of it strike terror into your enemies, as word of your victories spreads.

So had Alcius done, marching his legions beneath the Iron Hawk and carving out an empire that straddled lands she had never seen, nor probably ever would.

She had her symbol; now all she needed was her victory.

When two sides meet face to face, the first side to march loses. Valour must be tempered by patience, always.

Rowena bit her lip. This part of her strategy would be the most difficult to execute.

'My lady?' the herald at her side queried. Rowena shook her head.

'We wait. The whole day lies ahead of us. I'll not rush into danger headlong.'

On the enemy side, Lord Ongus was clearly thinking much the same thing. Two hours dragged by agonisingly. The skies lightened a little as they birthed mid-morning. Still neither side moved. From the battle line below, she could see Cathsach and Celtigus and Fannoch looking up at her questioningly.

The men were growing restless; like a slowly hardening tide of discontent, she could hear mutterings up and down the ranks.

She needed to act.

Damn it, why won't you take the bait, Ongus? she demanded silently.

'Shall we try archers?' suggested the herald.

Rowena shook her head. 'Nay, we're not close enough yet.' She flicked a glance towards the woods on either side, the spidery branches of the hazels like a web ensnaring them. Legend had it Morgaena, Queen of Targets, had eaten hazelnuts on the eve of battle for inspiration; Rowena didn't hold with such pagan ways, but she was beginning to wonder if a bit of magical aid wouldn't go amiss right now.

Her herald was looking at her expectantly. So were her bannermen. Shutting her eyes tightly, she took a chance and threw Alcius to the wind.

'BANNERS FORWARD!'

When the command came, it almost seemed underwhelming to Vaskrian. He felt none of the battle lust that had possessed him at Linden, just a wearying sense of drudgery as they began to trudge through deepening mud. The liquefied turf sucked at his boots as they took slurring footsteps towards the enemy, making him glad he wasn't wearing full armour; in these conditions his mail shirt and target shield would do just fine.

'BANNERS DESIST!'

The Crimson League came to a squelching halt. They were almost knee-deep in mud now. Vaskrian flicked a glance skywards. At least there was no further sign of rain: the wintry sun gave the thick blanket of clouds a whitish glimmer.

A perfect canvass to paint red on, he thought grimly.

On the fringes of their battle line, the archers were hurriedly pushing their sharpened stakes back into the ground.

Just then, a clarion call from the other side signalled the enemy charge.

A clarion on their side sounded, too: the army was to stand and receive charge. Vaskrian clutched his sword and shield more tightly as enemy knights bore down on them, churning up a cascade of mud as they came.

The bowmen hurried to finish their task. 'They won't be able to nock and draw in time!' cried Wrackwulf. 'They're too busy with their blasted carpentry!'

He was right. The mud wasn't quite deep enough to completely stall the charging knights. They wouldn't gain enough momentum for a lance charge, but they'd be upon the archers with swords before they could shoot. Upon them, too.

Vaskrian watched as the vanguard of four hundred knights pelted towards them, fanning out forty men across and ten lines deep. The iron monster closing on them sprouted myriad fangs, as they drew swords as one.

Planting his feet as firmly as he could in the mud, Sir Vaskrian prepared for his first – and last – battle as a knight.

I hope the troubadours here are as good as Sir Braxus. This'll be a last stand to remember.

The first wave of arrows took the enemy knights completely by surprise. Some found gaps between mail and helm, but most were aimed at their lightly armoured horses. The formidable line suddenly disintegrated as chargers reared, tossing men into the mire.

Vaskrian glanced over to his right. The archers were still busy planting their stakes, pushing them in deep for purchase in the soft soil. But the volley wasn't coming from their flank.

It was coming from the woods.

Wrackwulf gave voice to his thought. 'Archers in the woods!'

Another volley strafed the attacking knights, bringing down another wave. Horses reared and whinneyed in the mud, which soon became thick with a tangle of human and animal bodies. The archers to their flanks had taken advantage of the broken charge to finish hammering in the stakes. Now protected by bristling walls, they turned their attention to their own bows with impunity.

A clarion call from the enemy. The second battle line surged forwards... straight into two more volleys from the woods on either side. Vaskrian could just make them out beneath the grey eaves now, men dressed in bright tartan colours.

'Penric's hillmen!' cried Braxus. 'Those are Penric's hillmen!'

Rowena felt relief wash over her as she watched Penric's archers pepper the Kingsfolders. The hill-folk did not miss at such close range; she allowed herself a gallows grin as she watched knights and horses tumble beneath a swarm of deadly shafts.

Her plan had worked. Penric had cut it fine, but her plan had worked.

Scry on our position, will you? Only now did she wish that

Abrexta could read minds as well as see from afar. *Too bad you can't see through trees, witch.*

Use your enemy's strengths against him if you can. One of her favourite parts of Alcius.

Turning to the herald she nodded, and he gave the order for the archers at the rear to join their comrades. Two thousand bowmen loosed against the enemy. It wasn't unreciprocated: Ongus had ordered his own archers to shoot, but they hadn't moved, and at distant range in such damp conditions their shower of arrows would lack power.

'SHIELDS ALOFT!' bellowed the herald, bannermen in the fray taking up the command. Rowena watched, heart in mouth, as her battle line presented a hotchpotch awning of iron and hide, knights and soldiers raising targets and heaters to fend off the lethal hail. Some of her flanking archers fell screaming, but the panicked enemy had taken the bait and aimed mainly at her footsoldiers. Under cover of the woods, Penric's hillmen continued to nock and draw, picking off knights at will.

One or two enemy arrows reached her stockade, embedding themselves weakly in its coarse grainy wood. The herald ducked instinctively, but Rowena was too jubilant to notice. Ongus was holding his last battle line in reserve, chary of sending them into another deadly volley.

Now was the time. She nodded at the herald again, and he ordered the clarions to sound the charge. Rowena felt her heart soar higher than any arrow, as she watched her ragtag army surge towards the fractured enemy line.

～

Vaskrian felt his pulse quickening as they slogged through the mud. Up ahead it was already carnage: dozens of enemy knights lay screaming in the mire, others struggling to get up and avoid being trampled by panicked horses. By the time they closed the gap, the second wave had caught up with the decimated first rank, running them down and crushing them against their opponents.

Vaskrian screamed, half war-cry and half in panic, as the melee took him in its giant crushing grip. Mounted knights were careening into men on foot, horses' hooves catching the unwary and bringing them low before the steeds were shot down themselves.

His first battle had been chaotic; this one was sheer pandemonium.

The tightly packed men and animals meant there was barely room to swing a sword: the stench of blood, mud and sweat cloyed in Vaskrian's nostrils as he lashed out left and right, not knowing if he struck friend or foe. A dying knight, his neck spurting blood, toppled from horseback onto him and pushed him back over a thrashing charger, several arrows buried in its flank. The beast's throes were enough to hurl him free of it and the knight, sending him tumbling into the bog. Vaskrian felt its tarry brown thickness envelop him, choking the life from him as he struggled to pull himself free... Something heavy landed on top of him, and something heavier still on top of that. A stubborn impulse made him refuse to let go of his sword, and instead Vaskrian tried to use it to lever himself up out of the mud. Agonisingly slowly, he moved his upper body free of the unseen weight, but he'd barely had time to take a breath and his lungs were on fire. If he could just sit up enough to get his head clear of the blasted mud... His body felt as though it were being racked, as he poked his head free of it and took another gasping breath. Slowly the weight shifted further down his body...

Then another body landed across him, plunging him back in. Again he tried to lever himself free, working the fresh weight down his torso, but he was tiring fast. At last he could bear it no more, his mouth opened and filled with the taste of mud and blood as he began to suffocate...

Someone grabbed him by the armpit and hauled him up out of the mire. Looking up and blinking mud away, he saw Wrackwulf's upside-down face. His grin looked like a grimace from that angle.

'Don't worry lad, I'm right behind you! Can't have you dying in your first real battle!' The freelancer yanked him upright as though he were no heavier than a child.

Vaskrian had no time to marvel at his strength. Shoving Wrackwulf out of the way, he thrust his sword forwards to meet the screaming serjeant charging him from behind. The scream turned into a cry of agony as the soldier impaled himself on Vaskrian's blade, the Staerkvit steel puncturing through his cheap brigandine and transfixing his midriff. The dying serjeant ran up the length of it, clamping Vaskrian's head in a vice-like grip and trying to push gauntleted thumbs through his eyes. He was just about to let go of his sword and grapple with his opponent, when he felt something warm and sticky wash over his face. The pressure lifted off his eyes and he opened them to see the serjeant slumping off his blade, a mangled mass of bone and brains where his head had been.

Behind him stood Wrackwulf, clutching his bloodied warhammer.

'Come, lad!' he grinned. 'Let's not tarry!'

Gazing about him, Vaskrian saw that their part of the melee had given way a little. Enough to breathe and choose a foe, even. A few spears' length away in all directions and the scrum was still at its worst, though; the young knight felt sickened by the sight of flesh and steel and leather being crushed together, as men and horses suffocated and drowned.

This isn't a battlefield, he thought. *It's a slaughterhouse.*

Rowena's lower lip was almost bloody from chewing it. Though not as bloody as the horrific spectacle she had conjured up. The third wave of enemy troops were fodder for her archers as they joined the fray: Ongus had finally seen the futility in deploying horses and ordered his remaining knights to dismount. That would save him a few hundred chargers, but meant his last battle line was an easy target for Penric's hillmen. The flanking archers had taken up the stakes to use as spears against loyalist knights and soldiers who managed to break free of the melee.

'It looks as though we're winning,' commented the herald. 'Your tactic was a success, milady, though I had no idea Penric would be joining us.'

'It had to look good, so we'd fool Abrexta,' said Rowena.

'Penric is an overweening man, but he abides by the law. We agreed the strategy in private, Brother Joram confirmed that witches can see but not hear across distances – we just had to look like we were arguing while we plotted.'

The herald nodded approvingly. 'You must have cut down half their knights before they could engage,' he said. 'A goodly number of serjeants and soldiers, too. You've evened up the odds nicely, ma'am.'

Hopefully enough to carry the day, she thought nervously as she scanned the tangled thickets of human and animal flesh. The worst of the clusters were starting to ebb, as thrashing men and horses became still corpses, though she didn't like to think how many on either side had met a muddy end rather than a bloody one.

War is heroic only in its aftermath. One of Alcius' less popular quotes, but a true one for all that.

The knight's great helm took the brunt of Vaskrian's first pass, but the blow was enough to send him staggering and slipping back into the mud. An awful strength galvanised his limbs, some maniacal battle rage the like of which he'd never yet experienced.

And Reus knew, he'd always been an angry young man.

Vaskrian pulverised his opponent's defence with a follow-up flurry of blows, splintering the fully armoured knight's heater and making ruins of its star-spangled escutcheon.

You won't look upon the stars again in this life, he thought grimly as he struck the knight on the helm again. And again. And again.

Someone crashed into him from behind, putting him off his kill. Half turning, he aimed a furious blow at the serjeant, cutting through his brigandine and felling him in a crimson rain. He didn't bother to see if it was friend or foe (they were all foreigners here anyway), but turning back to his prey, he saw the knight had lurched up out of the mud slick.

He stood back, grinning wolfishly as the knight lunged at him. And... parry, disengage. The same move he'd watched Braxus use, time and again. He had it down perfectly now. The knight barely had time to register his attack had been foiled before Vaskrian's riposting blade found his armpit.

With a screech that sounded almost ladylike, the knight slumped back into the mud, feebly clutching at the blood seeping from under his arm. Even so, Vaskrian could see the blow wasn't lethal. The knight's eyes were wide open with terror beneath his helm, and he was screaming a word over and over again.

Clutching the underside of the helm, Vaskrian wrenched it free, exposing a frightened aristocratic face framed by aventail and coif.

Vaskrian reckoned he just about knew enough Thrax to recognise the word *mercy*.

He could take the knight prisoner. As a knight himself, he was entitled to ransoms now. A vassal's annual earnings could run to hundreds of sovereigns (or whatever the hell they called gold coins here). It would be a nice little earner for him, a fine start to his knighthood.

Vaskrian grasped his fallen foe by the coif, yanking it down and using it to drag him towards the side of the battlefield.

Then a strange thought came upon him. He remembered the night in the clearing, months ago, when he'd thrown the pot of soup in Derrick's face. He remembered finishing the squire off, pushing his steel dirk into the hapless blueblood's throat.

He'd always been ashamed of that deed. But now he could kill with impunity on the battlefield. He need feel ashamed no longer.

And a knight was a tidier kill than a squire.

One cruel deed to drive out another, he thought with a strange coldness. Letting go of the knight, he reversed his grip and plunged his sword down inside the man's collarbone, enjoying the prolonged shriek that exited him as the blade slid all the way down into his bowels.

The knight's eyes fluttered closed, and Vaskrian pulled his blade free with one easy motion. In the eye of a churning storm of steel and blood, he felt oddly calm.

There would be no ransom money for him today. But Derrick never came to visit again.

Abrexta's lip curled in a snarl as she watched the Crimson League decimate her army. Feverishly she tried to find Lord Ongus, touching the mirror and shifting focus. She'd given him an amulet that would allow her to track him, though it didn't work so well at long distances. Or when its wearer was caught up in the middle of a frenetic battle that his side happened to be losing.

She switched tack, zoning in on Gann. She'd sent the young lordling south with strict orders to defer to Ongus in all matters, though he was nominally commander-in-chief. Presently she found him: coughing up the last of his life to the side of the melee, his slender body transfixed by a stake as his limbs twitched feebly in the mud.

Cursing loudly, she switched focus once more, questing for Ongus again. Where was he, gods be damned?

The rebels were gaining the upper hand now, the hillmen in the woods closing on the scrum with hand axes and making light work of her knights and soldiers, bogged down and exhausted by their heavy armour. Her forces were completely surrounded. Only her own archers remained, but they appeared flustered and uncertain. Shoot now, and as like as not they'd hit their own men.

She should never have taken her eye off Lord Penric like that. She had scryed again on him once briefly, but he'd been leading his knights and soldiers back steadily south. She hadn't thought to question the absence of his hillmen, thinking they'd simply been disbanded back to their highland homes in the east.

This Rowena had well and truly played her for a gull.

At last she found Ongus. Channelling her elan, she tried to influence him, commanding him to sound a retreat and order the archers to give covering fire. It was another difficult use of her magick, but with dozens of

Kingsfold bannermen dead she had fewer knights left to enthral.

She felt rivulets of sweat streak her face as she strained her powers of suggestion...

Rowena heard the enemy sound the clarion for retreat. It was a desperate sight, watching fatigued knights and soldiers turn and try to hack their way past Penric's hillmen.

Too bad the lord of Penllyn couldn't bring his knights and soldiers back to the fray, but she'd needed them to complete the feint: doubtless Abrexta would have used her sorcery to scry on Penric as he made show of deserting the rebellion.

No matter, so long as her next move worked. The First Lady of Clan McCullogh gave the herald her final command.

Vaskrian was butchering an enemy squire, thinking it miserable work for a knight, when he heard the trumpet blast.

Pull back? What was his guvness playing at now?

He exchanged a confused look with Wrackwulf, who had just finished turning a serjeant into a quivering pile of pulped flesh and broken bones.

Looking about the melee, he could barely see mud for corpses. As far as he could tell, most of them belonged to the enemy; there seemed to be more men wading through bodies to his rear than there did before him. Assuming he was even facing north any more. A glance towards the King's standard, planted just behind the enemy archers, told him he was. He squinted at them as the hundred-odd remaining loyalist knights and soldiers sloughed through the reddened quagmire, Penric's hillmen parting to let them go.

Vaskrian returned his gaze abruptly to the loyalist archers, now a flurry of activity in front of the King's standard.

They're nocking and drawing, he had time to think, just before the next command from their own herald rang out.

'Knights and soldiers form! SHIELDS ALOFT!'

Vaskrian had to smile. *She's a clever one all right, my lady. If we'd gone after them, we'd have ended up within range and been sitting ducks.*

When the hail came it was weak like ice water, shafts glancing harmlessly off their shields. A few of Penric's archers didn't make cover of the trees in time and got picked off, but by and large they escaped unscathed.

Another clarion gave the order to march. They slogged their way agonisingly through flesh and mud, moving more slowly than a laden sumpter. Ten yards on and the clarions called a halt again.

Once more the command was relayed down the line.

'SHIELDS ALOFT!'

At closer range the storm of shafts had more potency; one man went down screaming not far from Vaskrian. Wrackwulf grinned at him beneath his target. He barely seemed to care as arrows spattered around them.

'She knows what she's doing, your mistress,' he said.

'This is a game of wills and no mistake – see who breaks first!'

Again they repeated the manoeuvre. This time they managed to push past the last of the corpses before halting and presenting shields. The mud was slightly less deep here, but still enough to slow a man down. The surviving loyalist knights and soldiers had yet to draw level with their archers; Vaskrian could still see them straggling towards them liked lamed beasts.

The next command to shoot came from their side. Vaskrian risked a glance from behind his shield. The original two companies of archers had taken up their bows again, having resumed their flanking position. No need to bother with the stakes any more.

He watched as two curtains of arrows arced across the corpse-coloured skies and converged on the loyalist archers...

Rowena yelled triumphantly as she watched the shafts fall among the enemy archers. Her own bowmen had fallen back in a flanking manoeuvre., but were still at closer range than before.

Anticipate your opponent's tactics, and turn them against him if you can.

She clapped the herald on the shoulder in most unladylike fashion, as the royalist archers panicked and broke. Behind them, the surviving knights and soldiers were struggling to catch up: she had to hope Lord Penric's hillmen would act on their own initiative, she couldn't communicate with them now they had fallen back into the woods.

Fortunately they did. Their shafts began to fall upon the last of the knights and soldiers, picking them off at close range. By the time the King's archers had fled from sight, not one remained.

'Crushed and routed,' beamed the herald. 'A marvellous victory, if I may say so, ma'am.'

'You certainly may,' said Rowena, favouring him with a lupine grin. 'We've done old Alcius proud today!'

The herald stared at her, nonplussed.

'Never mind,' she added, still smiling.

Abrexta watched the archers turn tail with hatred bubbling over in her heart. She'd lost contact with Ongus when the hill rabble started shooting again – she could only assume he was dead, too.

She'd staked half her army on driving the rebels back and crushing them. The other half would have to pull back across the Royne – all of Garth was lost to her. At least winter would buy her some time to regroup. But come spring, the Crimson League would be at the borders of the King's Fold, ready to fight her again.

We'll see about that, she thought, touching the mirror and shifting her elan elsewhere.

CHAPTER 3
DREAMS OF HOME

Arun frowned at his youngest son, and sipped on his ale. He looked older than Adelko remembered him, more careworn.

'You've not been doing us proud, Adelko, not at all,' he said, shaking his grizzled head. He seemed more sad than angry.

Adelko opened his mouth to speak, but no words came.

'Travellin' the land and fightin' spirits and demons is one thing,' his father went on. 'But spying? I didn't raise my sons to be sneaks.' He shook his head again and took another pull on his ale.

Once more the novice tried to protest, but again his mouth just moved silently.

They were in his old homestead in Narvik, with its two rooms. He was alone with Arun, though somehow he sensed the others were close by, watching him: his Aunt Madrice, his oldest brother Arik, his older brother Malrok.

'Ye'll end up like Ulam if you carry on like this, so ye

will,' his father went on, staring disconsolately into his flagon. 'And to think I gave Master Horskram my leave to take you on. This is what it comes to... my son, spying and sneaking.'

The sound of the pre-dawn bells woke Adelko. Sitting upright, he looked around him. In the half darkness he could just make out Hargus, his stocky frame rising and falling gently beneath his blanket. He always slept like a log; normally it made Adelko jealous, but this morning he was grateful for being a light sleeper.

How apt that he had not been able to speak in his dream. Today was another Silence Day: the entire monastery would observe them until the Year's End Festival, when they would celebrate the Redeemer's first call from Sha'abat.

Sha'abat. First of the Prophets. Known to Palomedians as the False Prophet, the very reason why crusaders flocked to the Wheel to slaughter the heathen Sassanians in the name of the Almighty. That same prophet who had guided their own. His Sassanic lessons with Johann had brought him closer to an understanding of how the Creed and Faith intertwined. Did the prelates of the True Temple stop to consider the history of their own religion when they were busy preaching holy war, he wondered?

The ways of mortal men made absolutely no sense at all; the longer he pondered on it, the more inescapable he found that conclusion. The Earth Witch had told him to question everything, but the more he did the more elusive answers became.

At least he had the answer to one question: his spying mission would end, today. Gathering up his things, he sloped off to the library to prepare for his lesson with Johann.

The Sassanic script was a beautiful one, and Adelko had lost no time in mastering it as he studied the Nazharyan and Kallandhari dialects of the language. Johann stared out of the window at the light dusting of hoarfrost in the courtyard outside: in the final month of the year, winter had finally come south.

Unlike the straight angular lines of the Thalamian alphabet, the cursive symbols of the Sassanic script flowed one into the other, in a way that was pleasing to the eye. He tried to concentrate on that beauty, and not the content of the words he was scratching out. Johann had given him a passage from the *Holy Book* to translate that morning.

That wasn't what Adelko was working on, however.

The novice cleared his throat to indicate he was done, and pushed the scrap of parchment across the desk toward his tutor. He was still new to writing Sassanic, but one last glance at the undulating symbols told him he had correctly written his question:

Why did you commission the Bethlers to send freeswords to attack us on the road to Regensburg?

Adelko waited tensely as Johann picked up the scrap of

parchment. He had to focus now, try to attune his sixth sense to the prior's as best he could. He had been studying under him for weeks now, but to date the adept had been a closed book. Adelko hoped to shock his way past his guard, if he could.

The prior's face gave nothing away as he read the note. When he had done so, he returned his dark gaze to his pupil. His face remained blank and expressionless, but Adelko paid that no mind as he coolly met his tutor's eyes.

The silence suddenly came into sharp focus as they remained like that interminably, their eyes locked. Adelko resisted the urge to close his: by distracting himself consciously from Johann's physical presence, he would actually be *acknowledging* that presence.

No, far better to look with one sense while he divined with the other.

After what seemed a long time, Johann flicked his hand in a gesture of dismissal. The lesson was over for today. Gathering up his things, Adelko allowed himself a triumphant smile as he left the cloister.

It would be his last lesson with the surly prior.

'But I sensed it in him!' protested Adelko. 'It was like... like a point of heat behind his eyes, his body was calm but his mind... he knew exactly what I was talking about!'

Horskram frowned and pursed his lips, stroking his beard thoughtfully. It was rough and unkempt; monks didn't shave at this time of year, in forswearance of Azathol's vanity. Adelko felt incipient bristles sticking uncomfortably out of his chin as he waited for his mentor to speak.

He didn't need his sixth sense to know Horskram was not pleased with him. But not entirely displeased either.

'I suppose I shouldn't be surprised to find you breaking ranks yet again,' he said at last.

'No, you shouldn't,' Adelko cut in, only a little surprised at his own temerity. 'In fact, Master Horskram, I'd say that's exactly why you commissioned me in the first place. You knew I'd come up with my own way of completing the mission.'

Horskram favoured him with a half smile in the candle-light. 'Aye, I suppose there's little denying it. But we'll have to discuss your findings with the Grand Master. It's still not hard enough evidence for a conviction.'

'Well short of an outright confession of guilt, I don't see that we're going to get any better,' said Adelko. 'And I can't see Johann giving us that.'

Horskram nodded, glancing absently out of the window of his cell. 'Very well,' he said presently, rising. 'Come with me. We're going to consult Hannequin.'

'What, now?' Adelko gaped. Bad enough they were breaking a Silence Day vow to have their clandestine weekly meeting, was he about to get the Grand Master embroiled too?

'This won't wait until the Year's End Festival,' replied the adept. 'Johann could be making plans to flee right now, for all we know. Good thing we keep the gates locked fast at this time of year.' Ushering him out into the corridor, he added in a whisper: 'Well, young Adelko, it looks as though you're about to see another place novices aren't supposed to – only with permission this time.'

Adelko had come much too far to still feel guilty about sneaking into the Inner Sanctum at Ulfang. Palom knew, the Almighty had punished him for it enough these past nine months. He hadn't lost his old sense of adventure though – the familiar feeling of excitement welled up in him, as Horskram took them back to the main gallery and up another flight of stairs towards the Grand Master's quarters.

The next level was slightly smaller than the one below; just nine doors were set along the circumference of this gallery. Adelko guessed this was the archmasters' quarters, and shuddered at the thought of Wolaf being possessed by Belaach. Small ornate silver lamps lit the precinct, two on either side of each door.

Horskram caught Adelko admiring their intricate workmanship.

'Left to us by the Thalamians,' he said. 'Unlike their blasphemous predecessors, the City Kings of old favoured craft and science above the dark arts. Yon lamps will burn all night long using less than half their oil.'

'And what about the monastery itself?' quizzed Adelko. 'I'd heard it was built by them as well.'

'Only this part of it,' said Horskram, leading them towards an archway where a tenth door should have stood. 'The Inner Sanctum was originally a shrine, built in the time of Alcius the Younger to the war god Tyrn, in honour of his father's great victories.'

Adelko suppressed a shudder as they passed through the archway and ascended a spiral staircase. 'Wasn't that the name given by Thalamians to Azazel?' The archdemon of violence had often been worshipped by pagans, who believed he would give extra strength to soldiers in wartime.

'I did not say the Thalamians weren't demonolators,' replied Horskram, 'only that they rarely practised sorcery.'

Silver lamps continued to light their way up the stairs. Adelko felt grateful for them. In the monastery's sanctified precinct, thoughts of demonkind had troubled him little, but now at its heart he had the same feeling as he had back at Ulfang: his Order's spiritual headquarters held many secrets, not all of them benign. His sixth sense growled broodingly.

At the top of the stairs was a semi-circular antechamber, much like the one he'd entered in Ulfang's inner sanctum when his adventure had begun. This one was lined with twelve sculpted panels, each depicting St Argo performing one of his miracles.

No candelabra for me to knock over this time, he thought wryly, registering more of the silver lamps. A pleasant though pungent aroma caught his nostrils, partly offset by the night breeze wafting in through circular windows set into the antechamber's clerestory.

'Sage,' explained Horskram. 'Hannequin burns it in the lamps at night. Primitive exorcists used it to ward off demonkind before our Order was founded. I don't think he has ever been fully comfortable with the sanctum's original purpose either.'

Perhaps that's why he also lives behind a door of reinforced iron, thought Adelko, taking in the nail-studded monstrosity barring their way.

He didn't get further opportunity to study it, for just then it opened. Framed in gentler light coming from behind it stood a man he had until now seen only at a distance.

Hannequin, Grand Master of the Argolian Order. His new benefactor.

'Well, Brother Horskram,' he said, in a voice that was gentle yet firm. 'I trust you have a *very* good reason for disturbing my sanctity on a Silence Day.'

'How did you know we were he-' Adelko could not help but try to ask the question. Horskram silenced him with a sharp dig to the ribs.

'My humble apologies, Grand Master,' said the adept, bowing. 'But this cannot wait. And it concerns an assignment you ordained. I think it high time you met your protégé.'

He indicated Adelko with a sweep of the hand. The novice felt his Grand Master appraising him with eyes that seemed to see through him, yet take in everything at once.

'Adelko of Narvik, novice of Rima, honoured to be in your presence, Grand Master,' he stuttered, managing a flustered half bow as he did his best to sound formal.

Hannequin's face remained a taciturn mask for a couple more seconds. Then he smiled kindly.

'Well, perhaps it is time I met this young man I've been hearing so much about,' he said. 'Come in then, and tell me your news.'

Hannequin tapped his lips thoughtfully as he pondered

Adelko's story. While recounting it, he'd had the sense not so much of being probed by the Grand Master as of having his thoughts gently rifled, as though he could keep nothing from him.

The room they now sat in was part of a suite of chambers, and lined with crammed bookshelves. Candelabras on the walls and tables furnished the room's gentle light. A sense of tranquillity permeated the place; a fresco of the Redeemer gifting sight to Azincor after the rebel legionary was blinded by his Thalamian captors was the only decoration in the otherwise austere room. The chair he sat on was of simple design carved of hardwood, as were those his mentor and Hannequin occupied.

'Adelko's testimony is valid,' said Hannequin. 'It could be enough to hold a trial.'

'But not enough by itself to convict Johann of treachery,' countered Horskram.

'That doesn't matter – so long as the Order is seen to be doing something to root out the evil in its midst.' Hannequin sighed heavily, and for the first time Adelko thought he sensed trepidation behind the calm veneer of self-assurance. 'I'm under a lot of pressure, Horskram,' he said. 'You know what a zealot Cyprian is – given half a chance the Supreme Perfect would love nothing more than to bring about another Purge. One with more final consequences for the Argolians.'

Adelko felt courageous enough to break his silence with a question.

'Why does His Supreme Holiness hate us so much?'

Hannequin sighed again. 'For the same reason as the

Temple have always despised us – jealousy, of our powers, of our prestige. Often it is said by common folk that our Order is the only useful branch of the Temple, and the closest to Palom by virtue of its powers. On top of that, we've always been ambivalent about the Pilgrim Wars. Many of our most learned savants believe they were started by the archdemons Sha'amiel and Azathol, who each took mortal form to stir up strife between the Faith and Creed.'

Adelko frowned. 'But that doesn't make sense – how can First-Tier archdemons cross over to our world? I thought that's the kind of thing Horskram and I had been fighting to prevent.'

Hannequin looked at him intently, while Horskram held his peace for once. 'They can't unaided, and yes that is why preventing the Headstone from being reunited is so important. However, they are able to tap *sub-avatars*, using these lesser third-tier demons as vessels to project some of their evil onto the mortal vale.'

Adelko thought on that. 'Belaach was a third-tier demon, wasn't he?'

Hannequin nodded. 'Just so. I see Horskram has kept you well informed.' Adelko couldn't tell if the Grand Master approved of this or not.

'It is believed by many in our Order that a hundred years ago two sub-avatars crossed over from the Other Side to the mortal vale,' continued Hannequin. 'One took the form of Khartoun, the vizier advising the Sultan of Nazharya. Khartoun told the sultan to raise taxes on pilgrims to Ushalayim to exorbitant levels, and also encouraged him to persecute Palomedians arriving there to visit the Redeemer's birthplace. The other sub-avatar was known as Xamiel of Aval-ongne – the very perfect who preached the First Pilgrim War in retaliation.'

Adelko gawped. He'd known for a long time that not all was right with the crusades and its causes. But he'd never heard anyone suggest that Xamiel, the firebrand preacher who inspired the first crusaders, was a demon in disguise.

'So you're saying that the crusades are the work of demonkind?' Even after everything he'd witnessed, that seemed particularly odious.

Hannequin let a thin smile razor his aristocratic features. 'I am saying that this is one account of them, held to by certain members of our Order. Such a stance has not endeared us to the Mother Temple.'

Adelko recalled Arnulf's treatise. He could well believe the controversial former grand master would espouse such a view.

Another horrid thought occurred to him. 'So... do you think Cyprian could be...'

'A demon?' laughed Hannequin. 'No. We've learnt to be a bit more vigilant since then. But he is a righteous prig and a cruel tyrant, and power-hungry to boot. He was foremost among the inquisitors who tortured many of our brethren-' The Grand Master's voice stalled as he caught Horskram a sidelong glance. Adelko sensed the pain in his old mentor.

'They didn't!' he cried. 'Not you, Master Horskram, they wouldn't!'

Horskram smiled wanly at Adelko, looking his usual weary self. 'Have your travels with me taught you so little of man's iniquity?' he asked wryly.

Adelko felt a sudden rage bubbling up in him, with an intensity to rival what he'd experienced fighting Arik.

'That's disgusting! And he gets to be head of the Temple!? It's him we should be putting on trial!' The novice barely noticed his fists were clenching. Thanks to Edemus, they clenched a lot harder nowadays.

'Aye,' said Hannequin, in a sorrowful voice. 'It is. But the realities of politics dictate that Cyprian is a powerful man, with a private army of his own, and wealth and influence throughout the Free Kingdoms. It is we who are under his scrutiny, not vice versa.'

'So what can we do?' asked Adelko. 'If he's so powerful, what's to stop him doing what he wants?'

'The same politics he thrives on,' replied Hannequin. 'For our Order sits on the King's lands. Carolus needs Cyprian to push through his new crusade, but he doesn't want a controversy to get in the way of that. So if we can show we are acting to purge ourselves, it is very unlikely His Majesty will take the risk of allowing Cyprian to take matters into his own hands. Remember what I said before – our Order is still revered by many, commoner and noble alike. Carolus can't afford to have that kind of showdown distracting from his precious war.'

Horskram cleared his throat. 'So you really plan to go through with this? Put Johann on trial based on the psychic evidence of a novice?'

Adelko supposed that statement was humbling. But then he needed something to bring him back down to size – these rages didn't sit comfortably with him.

Hannequin looked at them both in turn. 'No, you are

right, brother. The testimony of a novice will carry little weight. That's why I intend to move my plans forward.'

Horskram scowled. Adelko's sixth sense had a different vibration to it now. Something exciting was being kept from him.

'You know my objections to this plan already,' said the adept.

'Duly noted,' replied Hannequin crisply, settling his gaze on Adelko.

'Adelko of Narvik,' he said, 'I have heard a full account of your adventures with Horskram, and I must say I am impressed. Likewise your progress under Edemus has been observed, as has your excellence in all other classes you've attended these past three months.'

Adelko strove – somewhat unsuccessfully – to master the warm feeling of pride that surged up in him.

If Hannequin sensed that, he gave no indication as he continued: 'Your abilities far surpass a novice your age, despite the fact that you joined the Order but five summers ago. In truth I was going to sanction this shortly before you left Rima, but in light of recent developments we'll just have to do it sooner.'

'Do what sooner?' Adelko had an inkling of what was coming next, but could scarcely believe it.

'A novice's testimony will be disregarded out of hand, meaning no trial can take place. But a journeyman's, on the other hand... the rules of the Order would permit me to sanction a hearing in that case. Put Johann in the dock, and I can buy us that time we all need.'

'You'd make me a journeyman?' In spite of everything,

the words sounded alien to his ears. He hadn't even seen sixteen summers.

'Officially yes – once the Silence Period is over. Then we can ordain a trial on the basis of your written testimony. After that you'll have another three months to complete your training, before you leave for the Pilgrim Kingdoms with Brother Horskram.'

The Grand Master's face suddenly became stern, his gaze hard. 'Great things are expected of you, Adelko. The Almighty has sent you to us in our darkest hour – your help will be instrumental in preventing the Headstone from being reunited, and bringing the malefactors trying to meddle in its powers to justice.'

Adelko glanced at his mentor, but Horskram's granite face told no tales.

The novice – soon to be that no longer – smiled. He just couldn't help himself.

'In that case, Grand Master Hannequin,' he said, bowing his head so they couldn't see him beaming, 'It will be an honour.'

'Excellent,' said Hannequin. 'Well, that concludes that. Return to your quarters and begin your vigil tomorrow. Horskram, come with me – we're to arraign Johann immediately. Now we have a case to make, I don't want him disappearing on us.'

Horskram nodded and the three of them rose to leave. Hannequin led them back out into the antechamber, where the silver lamps continued to illuminate the ancient sandstone walls and their panelled reliefs. Adelko glimpsed one of them as they headed back toward the stairs. It showed St

Argo performing his last and greatest miracle: banishing the demon Caza'charth on the shores of the Great Inland Sea.

He felt a feeling of foreboding ghost across his sense of triumph. Caza'charth had been a third-tier demon that had taken its true form in the mortal vale, after the demonologist Saranthar conjured it up. If the Headstone were reunited, Caza'charth would be but a lieutenant in the armies of Gehenna unleashed upon the Known World: he could only hope Hannequin's faith in him wasn't misplaced.

Adelko resolved to spend the rest of the month praying. Hard.

CHAPTER 4
A GIFT UNWRAPPED

'... And this one shows Otekar the Usurper slaying Arthurius the Just in an ambush, you can see how unchivalrous the deed was from the vivid brushwork...'

Adhelina smiled politely, feigning interest as Sir Aremis pointed out the next fresco in the dance hall. She knew the young knight was only trying to be civil, but she'd had enough of Pangonian culture to last a lifetime.

Truth to tell, she yearned for the road again. The Year's End Festival was upon them; a tenday of feasting and dancing would bring in the new annum.

Halfway through the longest tenday of my life, and then we've the rest of winter to go, she thought as Aremis moved on to the next painted section.

'Legend has it Arthurias' court sorceress cursed Otekar and all the line of Purplin,' the knight went on. Clearly his country's history enthralled him. 'His son Otekar II lost an eye in the hunt for the three-horned stag, as you can see here... And in the next one, we have his grandson Otekar III drowning in the Lac Dumont, after his barge foundered during a routine crossing.'

'Wait,' said Adhelina, suddenly paying attention. 'You said Arthurias had a witch serving him? But I thought Pangonians had renounced paganism and embraced the Creed by then.'

'They had – but sorcery had been a venerable tradition since the First Dynasty of Rius,' said a silky voice behind them.

She turned to see an elegantly dressed noble, his posture suggesting a dandy rather than a leader of men.

'Lord Ivon, of the House of Laurelin, most delightedly at your service,' he said suavely, favouring her with a florid bow.

'Helene of Dunstenmere, at yours,' replied Adhelina, lifting her skirts and curtseying. She was back in blasted court dress – the King had insisted on having her outfitted in the latest Pangonian fashion while she remained here. She gathered 'Helene' was a very expensive guest (or so Horskram had grumpily suggested), so it would have seemed churlish to refuse the high-waisted gown of embroidered pink silk and golden templer the royal tailors had practically forced upon her, but she missed her simple woollen riding clothes.

Aremis was looking darkly at Ivon, his hare lip curling in disgust and making him look even more grotesque. Adhelina was shamed by that thought, but more than that she didn't like the keen way the margrave was looking at her.

'The Ruling House of Rius had a sorcerer scion of its own,' Ivon went on. 'But you won't see them putting *that* in the hall frescoes.' His pearly teeth flashed a serrated smile, catching the wintry sunlight that bathed the hall in luminescent beams.

'I should scarcely think they would, Lord Ivon,' said Aremis stiffly. 'Such wicked practices ought not to be commemorated.'

Adhelina suppressed a shudder as she recalled her darker adventures. She had to agree with the young knight there.

'Well, of course,' said Ivon. 'Such things would be *most unseemly* decorating a King's hall.'

Just then Sir Odo joined them. As Royal Seneschal, he was in charge of ceremonies, and one of the few noblemen she had seen sober over the past week. It was mid-morning, and the hall was slowly filling up with bibulous nobles and ladies, many of them already indulging themselves from platters of sweetmeats and goblets of pale pink Mercadian wine. They had spent the morning of the first day of the festival in the magnificent High Temple in Rima, praying and listening to Cyprian preach the virtues of the coming crusade. That had been bad enough. Since then, the Pangonian nobility had not even pretended to show devotion to anything other than debauchery.

'Sir Aremis,' growled Odo, completely ignoring everyone else. 'The King and Queen are ready to descend from the royal bedchamber. Stop flirting with damsels and go and do your duty.'

Aremis flushed crimson, but he was nothing if not a stickler for duty. 'At once, Sir Odo,' he said, clicking his spurs and giving a polite half bow to Adhelina before moving off swiftly. Odo didn't bother with any formalities as he left them, muttering irritably to himself.

'Poor thing,' smirked Ivon, 'having to wear full armour at this time of year. Quite ridiculous if you ask me, but then ceremony must be observed, eh?' Beckoning a serving wench, he took two goblets off a matching silver tray and handed one to Adhelina.

'It's a little early for that, don't you think?' she asked pointedly.

Ivon raised an immaculate eyebrow over the rim of his cup. 'Are you quite sure you're Vorstlending? From what I've heard, your bibulousness puts us Pangonians to shame.'

Adhelina had to smile at that. It was true: back home people prayed more fervently at this time of year, but they drank more deeply too.

'Down south, we believe in getting – how shall I put it? – elegantly drunk,' grinned Ivon.

'Yes, I've noticed,' said Adhelina, taking a sip of wine. It was a delicious vintage, with a hint of strawberry to its after-taste. She had to admit, she found this Lord Ivon quite charming.

'I believe you've been pointed out to me,' she said. 'You're the Margrave of Vichy and... something of an adviser to the King.'

Ivon made a gesture as if to shrug off a trifling matter. 'Oh, I see to things for His Majesty now and then – nothing more.'

Adhelina felt a sense of unease. She suspected the margrave saw to – and saw – a lot more than he was letting on.

'They say you're very well informed on matters of state,' she hedged.

His reply caught her off-guard. 'Yes, but not very well informed about *you* – tell me, what is it you're really doing here? This Dunstenmere you speak of... well, it's soon to be a province of Greater Pangonia. Surely that must bother you?'

Adhelina felt her pulse quicken as she took another sip. Dunstenmere was a minor barony sandwiched between Dulsinor and Stornelund. She'd visited it once or twice as a girl. It was an obscure province, making it ideal for a deception.

Or so she'd hoped.

'Dunstenmere lies in the far north of Vorstlund,' she said. 'You've Prince Leopold of Westenlund to reckon with before you even get near us. So, I'll save my worrying for the new year, if it pleases my lord.'

Ivon laughed. 'The lady of Dunstenmere is certainly not one to mince her words! But you have not answered all my questions... what is it that brings you here? In such... motley company?'

'Chance threw us together on the road,' she said, feeling her confidence return as she ran through her well-practised story. 'My lady-in-waiting and I fled after we were invaded by the Herzog of Stornelund' – she didn't have to fake the hatred that entered her voice at that point – 'who is a rapacious robber baron. From what we've heard, Dunstenmere was just his first conquest and he's invaded Dulsinor.' She stopped, fearing her emotions would get the better of her if she went on.

But Ivon's mind seemed to be elsewhere. 'Mm, yes, the war in the north. Convenient business for our own plans. And yet it's really your erstwhile travelling companions that interest me more, begging your pardon. They arrived with an Argolian adept and were packed off not long after by the same monk on some... mission. My King has little concern for sorcerous affairs, whereas I take a keener interest in such things, you see.' He held her eyes over the rim of a cup he had barely touched.

'Oh, and why would that be, pray?' Adhelina returned. They were fencing now. It was obvious the margrave was trying to learn more and this was no social introduction.

Ivon smiled brittlely. 'The defence of the realm demands it.'

Something in the light seemed to harden, growing more crystalline. Courtiers were thronging the hall now, their hubbub permeating its gabled precinct as the merry-making began in earnest. Minstrels struck up the first tune of the day, but the notes sounded harsh and unpleasant in Adhelina's ear.

Suddenly everything seemed to recede, the lavish court room dropping away from her at giddying speed. She saw as though a bird in flight, cresting high hills that overlooked a deep forest. Atop the highest one beside a gushing river she saw an ugly red groove; like a suppurating wound across the face of the land, it seemed to suck her towards it. Though it was night, somehow she could see everything. Descending lower, Adhelina saw a ring of torches encircling the red groove.

No, not a groove: a stone. Atop it the lithe figure of a

young girl lay prostrate. Towering over her was a figure dressed in black robes, clutching a strange-shaped dagger. Its face was not human, but that of a skeletal beast. The figures surrounding it clutching the torches all looked the same. The central figure plunged its knife into the girl on the stone... as she drew inexorably closer, Adhelina saw that another knife was inserted between the girl's legs. Without warning the girl erupted off the stone, her limbs growing long and misshapen and taking on its bloody hues. Now she could see another figure, this one dressed in white, huddled near the stone, ripping out its entrails with a knife of its own... It slumped over and she felt herself lifting again, high above the awful spectacle... Was that a five-pointed silver star she glimpsed, etched just inside the ring of people?

'My lady? My lady? Are you well?' Ivon's voice sounded as though it came at her across an ocean of distorted sound. As normal sight returned to her, Adhelina saw that at her feet lay her upturned goblet, its contents draining into gaps in the varnished parquet flooring.

'Why, but you're white as a banshee!' exclaimed the margrave. 'Some milder wine for the Lady Helene!'

Wine was the last thing Adhelina wanted. 'No, I'm all right,' she said, and reached out to steady herself on the margrave's shoulder... As soon as she touched him, she felt dark visions return to her, these ones too jumbled to make sense of. She only knew that they terrified her.

Abruptly she took her hand off the margrave. The visions receded.

Adhelina inhaled deeply and drew herself upright. 'I need to lie down, is all. Told you it was early for me to be drinking. I'm a herbalist, I've simples in my chamber that will help.'

'Of course,' said Ivon. His tone and face seemed sincere, but Adhelina thought him anything but. Clicking his fingers, the margrave summoned a couple of page boys to escort her back to her rooms.

It was with a sense of profound gratitude that Adhelina left the hall, and the margrave's presence.

Hettie shook her head in disgust as she watched Adhelina bundled out of the hall. Flirting with every nobleman who came her way and drinking before noon – was this what her oldest friend had come to?

Rima's court was poison. Of that she was sure. The pair of them had barely spoken in weeks, even though they shared a room. Headstrong as ever, her mistress had insisted on going her own way. After everything they had been through – after everything Torgun and Braxus had done for her – watching Adhelina let Aremis court her made Hettie feel sick. And as soon as the simpering knight was sent away, there she'd been with that dandy, a womaniser if ever Hettie saw one.

No wonder you've taken ill, she thought. *That'll be your own conscience catching up with you, you shameless slattern.*

She felt a light tap on her elbow. Turning, she saw a liveried squire.

'Begging your pardon, ma'am,' he said, addressing her in Decorlangue, 'but my master wishes to introduce himself.'

Hettie was instantly suspicious. Her misadventures had taught her all too well to be on her guard.

'And who might that be?' she asked, perhaps rather too sharply.

'I have the honour of presenting Lord Kaye, Margrave of Quillon,' declaimed the squire, backing away to reveal a sumptuously dressed noble. He wasn't anywhere near as handsome as the men who approached Adhelina – Sir Aremis aside, of course. But Hettie supposed that a par for the course. What concerned her more than his plainness was the knowing glint in his eye. She didn't like it.

'Etta of Gutenheim, at your service,' she said, curtseying perfunctorily. She'd named herself after her great aunt and a small town in Dunstenmere. That ought to fool the beastly Pangonians – but would it?

'I am at your service,' said Kaye, returning the curtsey with a sweeping bow. 'Having seen you about court with the Lady Helene, I was anxious to learn if you were enjoying your yuletide stay with us at the palace.'

'Yes, thank you,' replied Hettie. *He'd better not be trying anything on; I'm really not in the humour for flirtation.* She decided a little candour wouldn't go amiss. 'I am a maiden, and prize my virtue most highly.'

The inappropriateness of the remark caught him by surprise. All to the good. She didn't care to impress these snobby lecherous southerners.

'Rest assured, I would not dream of trying to... spoil you,' the margrave said after a pause. At least he wasn't making horrid crude jokes about Vorstlending maidens and horseriding, unlike one churl she could think of. 'My intentions, I can assure you, Lady Etta, are quite honourable.'

Yes, I'll bet they are. I'm not half as pretty as these serving wenches who'll lie with a man for a couple of silvers.

That was hardly a reasonable or nice thought to have, but then she wasn't in the mood to be reasonable or nice.

'Well, that's a blessed relief,' she said. 'For frankly, I'm beginning to tire of Pangonians and their double standards – always on display with the best finery, and such tawdry morals underneath!'

Kaye smirked. 'Well, your boldness of speech does you credit – who would have thought our northern cousins could be so... incisive?'

Hettie sneered in his face. 'Yes, that's typical of Pangonians too – always so superior. Well Lord Kaye, you've introduced yourself – now if it's all the same, I'd rather like to be alone-'

'Are you not concerned about your mistress?' Kaye interrupted her. 'She was taken poorly just now. And the two of you have travelled such a long way together.'

The pointed last remark set her alarm bells ringing. 'Yes, and what business is it of yours if we have? Come spring we'll be on our way.'

'Indeed you will,' said Kaye. 'But where to, I wonder?'

Hettie was about to tell him that was none of his business either, when another noble joined them. He was even more extravagantly dressed than Kaye, and a good deal more handsome.

'Lord Aravin, Margrave of Varangia, at your service,' he declared, bowing even more deeply than Kaye had.

Hettie curtseyed back and rattled off the usual formalities. She was quickly tiring of this. What on earth did two high-ranking noblemen want with her, a lowly guest at best?

'The Lady Etta was just about to tell us where she and her beautiful mistress will be headed when the winter thaws,' Kaye said to Aravin. 'Weren't you, my lady?'

'Actually, no, I wasn't,' replied Hettie.

The two men were crowding her uncomfortably now. Aravin was practically leering at her. He was taller and stronger than Kaye, but she knew right off whose wit she feared more.

'Rumour has it the pair of you will be heading overseas,' Kaye supplied. 'Though I find that passing strange... Your country is about to be invaded by ours, it might be that a couple of runaway Vorstlendings could win back a lot of lost favour by warning their compatriots.'

So that was his game.

'Our ties to our homeland ended the moment Lord Storne invaded and no one did anything to stop him,' said Hettie. 'The rumours you've heard are true – Lady Helene and I will seek a new life in the south.' She felt it worth taking this calculated risk to get the nobles off her back – clearly they had been sent by someone, probably the King. A weaselly character if ever Hettie saw one; she wouldn't put it past him.

'Ah yes,' said Aravin. 'The Pilgrim Kingdoms, land of honey and wine! Or is it the mighty Empire whose luxuries you crave? Such decisions to make! Might I make a suggestion?'

'Pray do, and be swift in the making,' replied Hettie.

Though she didn't like him, she hoped the King would arrive with his entourage soon. This was beginning to feel like an interrogation.

'Rima can be a very fair place itself, to those who have the right friends,' Aravin went on. He leaned in closer. 'Your mistress is a very beautiful woman. With proper introductions, she could make a fine match here at court.'

'And I'm sure someone suitable could be found for her stalwart lady-in-waiting,' put in Kaye.

'Why trouble yourselves wandering the world, when you can have everything a lady could ask right here, in the most splendid city of the Free Kingdoms?' pressed Aravin.

Hettie was about to reply when the herald banged down his staff of office for silence.

'All make way for His Majesty King Carolus, Third of His Name, Guardian of the Creed, First Scion of the House of Ambelin, Lord Protector of the Kingdom of Pangonia!'

Relief put soothing fingers to the tightness in Hettie's chest as the assembled courtiers moved back to allow the royal entourage to enter the hall. Taking advantage of the situation, she nipped past knights and ladies, trying to be unobtrusive as she circled towards the exit.

She had to get back to their room and find Adhelina, fast. More fool them ever to have trusted a Pangonian monarch to keep his word.

Adhelina shut the door behind her and leaned against it, breathing heavily as she listened to the page boys leave.

With difficulty she tried to collect her thoughts. What had she just seen? The light streaming past the open shutters told her it was fast approaching noon, but she felt a darkness in her soul no mortal sun could illuminate.

Moving over to a walnut table by her cot, she rummaged through her medicine pouch and set about preparing a distillation of Sharka's Caress. The tough black node tasted foul enough, even in a tea, but it was good for the Worrying Sickness. Good job she'd insisted the servants bring her a small kettle to use over the fireplace.

Before long she had a brew going. She paced her room fretfully while the mixture bubbled away, trying not to think too hard. When the kettle was boiled, she finished the preparation and swallowed the hot bitter liquid almost in one gulp. She sat down on her cot, rubbing her temples gently. After a few minutes, the potion took effect and she felt her jangling nerves subside.

Now she could think.

That her vision was connected to Ivon, she had little doubt. But how? And was what she had seen even real?

She was just pondering that when there came a knock on the door. Most likely Hettie, come to check up on her. The last thing she needed now was one of her shrewish friend's irritating lectures.

Frowning, Adhelina got up and answered the door.

What she saw surprised her. Standing in the tapestried corridor was a young girl, no older than ten summers, accompanied by an elderly lady dressed soberly.

'You're Lady Helene, aren't you?' said the child guilelessly. 'I've seen you at dinner. You're very pretty.'

'Why, thank you,' said Adhelina, smiling despite her surprise. The same could not be said of the girl; even at her age, it was obvious she would grow to be a plain young woman at best, though her long blonde hair sparkled in the light. 'And who might you be?'

'I have the honour of presenting Lady Iveline, daughter of the late Prince Lothaire,' said the old woman, whom Adhelina took to be her governess.

'Then I am indeed honoured,' replied Adhelina, curtseying. 'Won't you please both come in?'

She was too surprised to know what to make of the situation. But when a princess paid you a visit in her own home, you didn't keep her standing outside.

'My father was the King's younger brother,' said Iveline as the pair entered the room. 'He was very good and brave, not like Uncle Carolus. He's mean.'

'Iveline!' said her nanny sharply. 'You should know better!'

'But it's true,' insisted Iveline, pouting. 'He's mean and he's greedy, that's what they call him in the city.'

Adhelina had been at court long enough to know that was probably true. In official circles, Carolus was known as the Canny or the Wily. In others he was more apt to be called the Vain or the Cruel.

'And how would a young princess know such things?' she laughed, relieved to have closed the door behind them.

Iveline fixed her with a precocious look. Wise beyond her years, the princess was the young girl Adhelina had once been herself.

'I see things,' she said.

'Oh you do, do you?' smiled Adhelina.

Iveline's next remark wiped the smile off her face. 'So do you.'

Adhelina glanced at the governess, who still had not given her name. The old woman looked at her with eyes that were sad and wise.

'Iveline has been given a special gift,' she said. 'The Second Sight.'

'That's right,' said Iveline, 'sometimes I see things that are going to happen before they do. And other times, I see things that have happened already, things nobody knows about.'

The two guests were staring at her now. Adhelina suddenly felt faint again.

'How long have you had the sight?' asked the governess.

'I... don't know what you're talking about.'

'Yes, you do,' said Iveline. 'I can see when other people have it, too. I saw you in the dance hall. You saw something, didn't you?'

'And my guess is you've been seeing things for a while now, haven't you?' added the governess.

It all came flooding back to her right then. Her dream of the Wadwos on the eve of her escape from Graukolos, the subsequent visions she'd had on their journey to the Argael; she recalled Braxus and Torgun telling her of the war they'd fought in Northalde, their descriptions of the Battle of Linden had seemed so familiar to her...

Strange that she had never truly realised until now. How could she have been so... blind?

'Try not to feel out of sorts,' said the governess kindly.

'The sight comes upon us sporadically, sometimes in our younger years, as with Her Highness, sometimes later in life as it did with me. It's certainly not a precise craft.'

Adhelina felt her dizziness subside a little. As it did, her wits returned to her.

'You've been very broad in your accounts so far,' she said sharply. 'Everything you've just told me could easily have been learned at court. How do I know you aren't making this up?'

The old woman just smiled at that. 'Did you tell anyone at court about drugging the guards on your bedchamber door in Graukolos the night you escaped from the castle? A nice trick with the bellows, I must say – your resourcefulness does you credit, Adhelina of Dulsinor.'

Adhelina felt the dizziness come back with alacrity.

'I think we'd better sit down and have some tea,' she said tightly.

Adhelina had just prepared a rather tastier kind of brew than Sharka's Kiss when the door swung open. Hadn't she barred it? Too much on her mind.

Hettie swept in. Turning, she shut and barred the door. Well, Hettie was thinking clearly at least.

'We need to talk,' she began, then trailed off as she saw the new arrivals. The old woman and the princess had sat silently while Adhelina prepared the tea. That only made them seem more disconcerting.

'May I present Her Royal Highness, Princess Iveline and.... her governess.'

Hettie looked so flustered that she didn't even bother to

curtsey. Iveline just continued to sit there, the same serene expression gilding her homely face.

'With all due respect, this is no time for social calls,' said Hettie. 'Adhelina, I really must speak with you in private.'

'Hettie!' scolded Adhelina. 'Where are your manners? This is the King's niece.'

'Well, I'm sorry for not standing on ceremony, but this is urgent!' cried Hettie. She looked rattled all right, her face was redder than a beetroot.

'She's right,' said Iveline. 'Kaye and Aravin aren't nice men either. They're Ivon's friends – and he's the worst of them.'

Hettie and Adhelina shared a gawping double take at the placid princess. By Siona, but she really did have the second sight.

'Hettie, why don't you sit down,' said Adhelina. 'There's enough tea for four.'

Still wearing a startled expression, Hettie did as her mistress bade and Adhelina served the tea.

'I think we'd better listen to what our guests have to say,' she said, taking a seat.

The governess cupped the warm tea in her wrinkled hands and inhaled the steam rising from it. She seemed to recede to a faraway place as she spoke. 'The second sight is a gift from the Unseen,' she said. 'Different to the sixth sense of the Argolians. Some say the sight is their gift to women, where the sense is their gift to men. It is not wizardry, though many an unwise man would have you believe that.'

'Men don't like us having it,' added the princess. 'They hate it when girls have powers that they don't.'

Adhelina and Hettie exchanged wry glances. They could both relate to that.

'Which is why we must be very careful about revealing ourselves,' said the governess. 'Sadly, our word will seldom be taken by men of power. Legend has it that when the Almighty bequeathed St Argo with the sixth sense, it was to counter this growing dominion of mankind – by giving men similar powers to those possessed by women with the sight, it was hoped to redress the imbalance of the sexes caused by how men had chosen to interpret the Creed. In pagan times it was not thus – women were respected more, their counsel often heeded.'

'Go on.' Adhelina felt it best to say little at this point.

'And for a time it worked,' sighed the old woman. 'St Argo was truly enlightened, some say perhaps even more enlightened than the Redeemer Himself, in some ways. The Order he founded helped steer men away from darker roads – it was no utopia, but the worst excesses of mankind were averted. For a time.'

She paused to sip her tea, then turned her slow regard on the damsels again. Her eyes were a piercing blue, Adhelina noticed: they reminded her somewhat of Horskram's.

'But things have changed. The Order has become corrupted, from within. Not as badly as the Temple perhaps, but its powers are fading. A great change is coming, and not necessarily for the better. Powers such as we possess shall wither on the vine, and the Left Hand Path shall blacken the good green earth. Even if we prevent that from happening, things will never be the same again.'

'And what does this have to do with Ivon? Is he... what I

think you're saying he is?' Adhelina's vision still remained stark in her mind, though she wasn't even sure the margrave had been in it.

'Ivon is a dangerous man,' said the governess. 'He is meddling in powers far greater than he can ever hope to control. Alas, would that the King would heed women's counsel...' She smiled sadly.

'But if you know he's up to something,' pressed Adhelina, 'then surely...?'

The old woman shook her head. 'I told you already the sight is not a precise craft, and even if we had solid proof, no one would believe a word of it. As like as not, I'd be locked up in a priory for the afflicted, Her Highness here would be sequestered and never see the light of day again.'

'I told you, men don't like it when we have powers they don't,' said Iveline. The serene expression had not left her face.

'But what about the Argolians?' asked Adhelina. 'Surely they'll believe you?'

'As I said, they have become corrupted – by power. They've waxed too proud themselves. And the Purge has only made them more secretive and suspicious than ever.'

'I travelled with Horskram of Vilno for a while,' said Adhelina. 'Reus knows, he is testy and irascible, but he is not corrupted I don't think.'

The governess nodded. 'That I know. Brother Horskram is among the best of his kind, though he still does not respect women enough for my liking.'

Adhelina reflected on that. It was probably true, she decided.

'We've been watching you,' said Iveline. 'We saw some of your adventures. I got really scared, but she said you'd be all right.'

The princess glanced at her governess with a grateful and adoring look.

'Don't you have a name?' asked Hettie.

The old woman smiled at her, but did not answer the question.

'The monk Horskram is getting closer to the truth,' she said instead, 'but he is surrounded by enemies. That is why he will need your help, in the Pilgrim Kingdoms.' She was looking at Adhelina now. The damsel suddenly felt shivery, though the fire was warm.

'You're going to get better at seeing things,' put in Iveline. 'That means you can help Horskram, even when he doesn't know it.'

Hettie was staring at them now in bafflement.

'Well, we had planned on travelling with him to Panya, on the way to the Pilgrim Kingdoms,' said Adhelina. 'But from there we planned to take another ship, to the Empire.'

'Your destiny is bound up with the Empire as well,' said the old woman. 'But not as soon as you think, or in the way that you now perceive. You will just have to come up with an excuse for changing tack, and going with Horskram to the Blessed Realm instead. Once you are in Ushalayim together, it will become clearer to you what you must do. Ivon and those he is working with must be stopped – Horskram's mission is of paramount importance.'

'Well, I've no idea what on earth any of you are talking

about,' said Hettie, 'but right now, chances are we won't even get out of Rima if I'm right about what's going on.'

'All right, Hettie,' said Adhelina, 'I think it's time you gave us your news.'

Hettie told them of her encounter with Aravin and Kaye.

'I told you my uncle was greedy,' said Iveline when she had finished. 'Even though he got the ransom money for you, he wants to keep you for himself.'

'Which would serve Ivon's purposes perfectly,' added the governess. 'He'll get to keep you here under his nose, to make sure you can't go off with Horskram. Already he has begun to fathom your powers, and he will be aware of your connection with the monk and his mission.'

Adhelina paused, then made up her mind. 'It's to do with this Headstone business, isn't it? A fragment of it was taken from my ancestral home.' She silenced Hettie's look of alarm with a wave of the hand. By now she had decided to trust the old woman and the princess, odd as they seemed.

'It does,' she confirmed. 'You are bound up in a Wyrd, or greater destiny. And your part in it is far from done.'

Adhelina listened to crackling logs as they broke the silence that followed.

'So what shall we do?' she asked at length. 'We've at least two months left before we can sail the Sundering Sea. We can't stay here.'

'The warrior woman you arrived with,' said the old woman. 'She is wintering in Rima, in a house of ill repute. It's the only kind of place that will have such a stranger. I suggest you go and stay with her, wait out the winter. Use her to get a message to Horskram in private, and tell him of your whereabouts. He swore to your swains he would look after you in return for their help, I think he'll keep his word if he can.'

Adhelina nodded. She wondered how much the mysterious woman knew about their lives. And how much she didn't know about the threat to them.

'We'd better get a move on,' said Adhelina, rising. 'Probably best to pack our things and leave now, while the palace is busy carousing.'

The two guests rose. 'That would be wise,' said the governess.

'One more thing,' asked Adhelina. 'What do I tell Horskram? About Ivon, I mean? The vision I had was hardly clear.'

The old woman shrugged. 'Tell him what you saw. What he chooses to do with that information is up to him.'

'Who are you?' Adhelina could not resist asking the old woman as she showed them to the door.

The governess's cobalt eyes had the same faraway look as she replied. 'I hail from the Orne ranges, in northern Gorlivere province. Many years ago, my ancestor counselled an exiled prince in his youth. She could not give him her gift of the sight, but she used it to guide him to wiser ways. That boy grew up to be a king, and when he came into his inheritance, he ruled this realm more wisely than any man before or since.'

Adhelina did not need the sight to know the answer to that riddle. The tale was an old one, sung by bards and troubadours across the Free Kingdoms.

'You're descended from Mariela? The mystic woman who raised Vasirius?'

The old woman smiled again. 'Goodbye, Adhelina of Dulsinor. We shall not meet again, I think. May you use your gift wisely.' She stepped out into the corridor, the princess skipping along beside her. Adhelina watched as they moved up it and turned a corner.

Closing the door behind her, she turned around to see Hettie standing hands on hips and staring at her.

'Well, do you mind telling me what on earth all that was about?' she asked.

'No I don't, but we'd best pack as I do,' replied Adhelina. 'We don't want to dawdle if we're to get out of here.'

Hettie frowned. 'What about the gate guards? Surely they won't just let a couple of foreign damsels leave unaccompanied?'

Adhelina fixed her oldest friend with a cheeky grin. She was still angry with her, but that would just have to wait for another day.

'Hettie,' she said, 'after everything we've been through, do you really think a handful of soldiers will be any match for us?'

Hettie grinned back. It was good to feel the tension between them ebb a little.

'No, come to think of it, I suppose you're right,' she said. 'The poor buggers don't stand a chance.'

CHAPTER 5
OF UNANSWERED QUESTIONS

'Someone, somewhere, is foiling us.' Hannequin's face looked drawn in the pale morning light. Outside, the bells could be heard, tolling in the new year. It didn't promise to be a joyous one.

'If we can't get him to confess, there's no telling who that is,' said Adamantus. The hoary old monk yawned and scratched his chest absent-mindedly.

Horskram scarcely felt more energetic himself. They had spent the entire night interrogating Johann in the holding chamber below the inner sanctum. Questions had been posed, psychic spoors tracked, answers challenged... All to no avail. The prior *was* guilty of something, but had steadfastly refused to confess to any wrongdoing.

'He clearly has been up to something,' put in Edelmir. 'We can all agree his elan is tainted, and that he's hiding his real intentions.'

Gabrien scowled. 'So he commissions the Bethlers to cut

Horskram here down to size – what of it? Those two have been at each other's throats for an age!'

'Given you some ideas, has he?' Horskram shot back. There was no love lost between him and the bumptious Pangonian either.

Gabrien glared daggers at him. 'I suppose you want to put me on trial next?'

'Enough!' cried Hannequin, his placid face frosting over with rare anger. 'The Order is in bad enough shape as it is without the two of you bickering.'

'If only Bartho had been able to help us,' mused Adamantus. 'His elan might have helped.'

'Bartho can't even rise from his cot, never mind conduct Argolian business,' spat Gabrien. 'By the looks of him, we'll be needing three new archmasters.'

'Cathbad is clearly not guilty of anything, and should be reinstated,' said Horskram sharply. 'Even if he hasn't cracked yet, it's obvious Johann is our mole, not him.'

'Assuming there is but one,' sighed Hannequin. 'You're forgetting Wolaf, who apparently consented to be subject to a binding of all things. Whoever is behind it, this conspiracy goes far beyond one man. These are dark times for the Order, I fear.'

Horskram felt the tension tighten like a cord through the Grand Master. It matched his own perfectly.

He had already begun to form his own suspicions.

A psychic examination was a fraught thing. Sixth senses overlapped and intertwined; elans merged and became one and yet not one. The focus in this case had been on Johann, but you could also pick up on other traces if your elan was running really quick.

Oh Gabrien, I would indeed love to put you on trial, thought Horskram. *But Hannequin would never hear of it – he'll just think I'm playing politics with another rival.*

The fat archmaster was involved somehow though – of that he was certain. An ugly seam ran through his animus like a sewer. It wasn't an open one – not yet – but he could sense it roiling away under the surface, a foul stench of corruption that assaulted his sixth sense.

Not enough hard evidence, he sighed to himself. The rules of the Order were strict – a psychic detection alone was enough to pronounce a witch guilty, but not a monk. The latter had to be topped and tailed with a testimony and a confession. In other words, the only way to find an ordained Argolian guilty of breaking with his vows was to break his will.

And so far Johann wasn't breaking. Perhaps Gabrien would though.

'Well, it's the new year,' said Hannequin wearily. 'I suppose we'd best get it started by refreshing ourselves. We'll convene again after sunset prayers, decide what to do next.'

The three archmasters filed out of the auditorium but Horskram lingered, gazing up at the ghostly light pouring down through the oculus.

'Horskram, I believe I gave you an order,' said Hannequin. His voice was gentle, but the tension in him had not abated. 'You're to get some rest as well.'

'I'll not rest till this puzzle is completed,' said Horskram, without lowering his gaze. 'And I've little doubt Gabrien is part of it, too.'

'So you spotted that as well,' said Hannequin. 'Our enemies pile up around us, brother – I fear this will be a very large puzzle indeed.'

'Are we putting him on trial next?' asked Horskram, relieved that Hannequin had detected Gabrien too. It would sound a lot better coming from him.

'All in good time,' said Hannequin. 'When you're gone and new archmasters are installed – I can't have Cathbad back in his siege, though I will exonerate him quietly when the time is right. I have to be careful, Horskram – if we're seen to be doing nothing, the Temple pounces. If we're seen to be doing too much, the Temple pounces.'

Horskram nodded. Much as he hated to admit it, Hannequin was right. If half the High Circle was under suspicion of witchcraft and other wrongdoing, public mood would swing against the Order. Then the King would have no choice but to give in to Cyprian's demands for another purge.

'Well, it seems as though you've things under control, Grand Master.'

Hannequin allowed himself a wry smile. 'Just about, for now.'

Hargus puffed himself up, mimicking a sage of great importance as he read the treatise aloud: "But let us consider briefly whether this balance of powers, between faith and magic, is in fact as Reus wills it to be. If it indeed be His will, then it points to a single ineluctable fact: that we Argolians are not meant to destroy magic users, but merely to keep them in check. Like a farmer culling vermin, we must hold back the population without annihilating it altogether."

He paused as Arik snickered beside him. 'Well I must say, he has a lovely turn of phrase this Arnulf. Are you sure he wasn't a troubadour?'

Arik sniggered again. Adelko frowned, trying to keep a level head. He'd mended fences with Arik that morning, after the silence had been broken. A fresh start for a new year. But more than that he needed his friend's help.

What he did not need was Hargus and his stupid jokes.

'All right, Hargus, you've had your fun,' he sighed. 'Give it to Arik, and let him read it out. I didn't risk my neck sneaking an ancient treatise out of the library so you could play high jinx with it.'

Hargus rolled his eyes and passed the scroll over. Arik took it greedily. But then he always had loved to learn. Adelko could still sense his seething jealousy: word had got out that he was getting unfettered access to the library. It hadn't taken his two friends long to work out why – only novices preparing for their journeyman examination were permitted such.

But petty rivalries were the last thing on his mind.

"Yet certainly, despite our limitations, we have given witches and warlocks a good reason to fear us',' Arik read. "Many of the most meddlesome in this, our Silver Age, have seen fit to surround themselves with servitors mortal and immortal, often sending such to chastise Argolians and thus prevent them apprehending them. Why would they do this if they did not rightly fear our power to neutralise their magicks?"

Arik looked up, frowning. 'Where is this going, Adelko? It's fascinating, but I hardly see what your point is.'

'Keep reading, skip the next couple of paragraphs,' said Adelko, glancing out of the cloister window to make sure no one was about. It was well past the Wytching Hour; no journeymen should be on prefect duty at this time of night, but you never knew.

Arik read on: "Our reputation has been enhanced, not diminished, by these long years of struggle, and our prestige is rightly recognised throughout all the lands of the True Temple – aye, even though its foolish prelates despise and envy us! And yet what would they have instead? A return to those dark days, before the coming of St Argo, when their hapless perfects tortured false confessions of witchcraft from innocent victims, while the true witches went about their business unmolested?"

'I really think I should read this part,' said Hargus. 'Arik just doesn't have the right sense of drama for an old firebrand like Arnulf.'

'Oh for heaven's sake!' cried Adelko, snatching the treatise off Arik pettishly. He hated these fits of pique – they didn't suit him – but he was still struggling to master the new intensities of emotion that accompanied his growing powers.

'"The mainstream clerics have ever had a weak elan and poor comprehension of the deeper meaning of Palom's words",' he read, ignoring his friends as they exchanged bemused glances, "'more preoccupied with tithes and temple revenues and policing the venal sins of mortalkind, they are ill-fitted to the task of hunting down witches and countering elementi and demonkind.'"

'Sounds like Yalba has a bright future ahead of him,' quipped Hargus. 'He'll fit in at the Temple nicely by the sounds of it.'

Arik snickered again.

Adelko rolled his eyes. Their boisterous former companion had long gone his own way.

'One more bit to go, Hargus,' he said, handing him the parchment. 'Try it without the silly accents this time, I know you can do it.'

"'And in turn they call us sorcerers,' continued Hargus, in his normal voice. "There was a time when I would have dismissed such baseless accusations as heresy, grounded in naught but jealousy and offended contumely. Yet now I must confess I find pause for thought... Blasphemous though it be to own such a thing, perhaps there is some truth in those words after all. For can it not be said, after a fashion, that we are wizards who specialise in countering wizards?'"

Hargus looked up from the treatise. 'That's it? This is what you dragged us out of dorm in the middle of the night for?'

'Don't you see?' pressed Adelko, 'One of our own grand masters is saying that we're wizards! Put on earth to counter other sorcerers!'

Arik frowned. 'That's blasphemy, Adelko. And Arnulf's

teachings are widely regarded as having provoked the Purge against us.'

'What provoked the Purge was Abelard of Montrevellyn stirring up trouble,' said Adelko. 'And he's said to have learned at the feet of Xamiel, the preacher responsible for the crusades.'

'Well, you've obviously been doing your loremastery,' said Arik. The bitterness in his voice was palpable – by rights, it should be him studying for journeyman. He was a year older than Adelko.

'Look,' said Adelko, 'I didn't ask to be made journeyman ahead of time. And it's precisely because I respect you both that I wanted to share this with you!'

'Why?' asked Arik. 'Now you've the ear of Master Horskram and the Grand Master, what do you need with a couple of novices?' The question was pointed, but reasonable enough.

'Because right now I feel you're the only ones in this place I can really trust,' said Adelko. 'There's something going on within the Order, something bad.'

'Tell us something we don't know,' said Hargus. 'One archmaster dies under mysterious circumstances and another has disappeared from sight. But who knows why?'

'I do,' said Adelko. 'What I'm going to tell you both, you have to keep an absolute secret...'

His two friends were looking at him keenly in the candlelight. Now they were interested.

He left out some of the details, but told them of the fragment thefts and the sum of his adventures. It was Wolaf's binding that horrified them most.

'Right here, in our headquarters?' Arik's eyes bulged, making him look like a bug in the weak light.

'And you're telling us that this Johann is responsible?' said Hargus. The young monk whistled softly.

'Well, he's connected somehow,' said Adelko. 'The rest of the High Circle and Horskram put him on trial after I gave my testimony. I haven't heard anything more since.'

'So why tell us this?' asked Arik. 'And what does it have to do with this treatise?'

'That's what I need your help trying to work out,' said Adelko. 'If what Arnulf says is true, then it means *we're warlocks too*. Our powers are tapping the same source as they do.'

'So?' asked Hargus.

'No wait,' said Arik. 'I see where he's going with this. If there's been a binding, then it could mean one of ours is a... demonologist.' The young monk looked slightly queasy.

'That's the conclusion I've come to,' said Adelko. 'But I needed a second opinion... from someone I can trust who isn't high up in the Order. Right now, I just don't feel comfortable pursuing this with Horskram or Hannequin.'

Now it was Hargus's turn to go all goggle-eyed. 'You don't think either of them-'

Adelko shook his head impatiently. 'No, I don't. But Johann could be a lot more than just a spy who tried to eliminate Horskram and me on the road. And if he's practising black magick, who's to say other Argolians aren't?'

'But the Order destroys all grimoires on sight,' said Arik.

'Not all of them, it doesn't,' said Adelko. 'When I was sneaking around at Ulfang, I saw a lot of books. I'm pretty sure they were grimoires of some sort. Here, read the next part of Arnulf.'

Arik picked up the scroll again, squinting at it in the candlelight.

"But while we have worked hard to expunge all vestiges of Left Hand magic wherever we have found it, yet we have not proved zealous enough with tomes of the Right Hand Way. In this respect, are we Argolians so different from the apprentices of the Imperial Sorcerers' Guild, or the Druidic synods in the Westerling Realms, or the sorcerer scions of Halepo?"

Hargus whistled again. 'I can see why Arnulf got into a lot of trouble,' he said. Adelko waved him to silence and Arik read on.

"Again this makes me question our real purpose as an Order: our reluctance to fully do away with the artefacts of wizardry makes me wonder whether we are in fact intended by Reus to destroy or simply balance out magic users in the Known World. Such a debate is not new to our Order, and its internecine raging about the cloisters of Rima has contributed to much vacillating on our part. Some of us have proved more zealous than others, calling for all grimoires to be burned; but more moderate views have prevailed, advocating the preservation of the more benign books of the Right Hand Way. This weakness on our part can be imputed to the Order's age-old love of learning, for we hold it sacrilege to burn books and the like as a general rule; possibly we have proven misguided in this matter, though I am no longer so sure of anything."

'Well, Abelard's trove of books was burned in full sight

of everyone in the main square in Rima,' said Arik. 'And that's the last time the Order was exposed to a hoard of tomes like that.'

'Yes, but what about the odd books here and there?' put in Hargus. 'Adelko saw plenty himself at our monastery, and that's a remote outpost of the Order. 'Who's to say there aren't more dotted all over our network, collected in secret over time?'

Arik nodded thoughtfully. 'But those would be of the Right Hand Path, at least. Left Hand books would be burnt without exception.'

'Yes, but how difficult would it be to conceal one among the other?' asked Adelko.

'Our sixth senses would pick up on that, surely?' said Arik.

'Just like they picked up on the presence of a demon bound to an archmaster?'

Adelko's words hung heavy in the silence that followed.

'There's something not right about this place,' Adelko went on. 'I've felt it since I got here. Some... oppression, muffling everything.'

Arik nodded again. 'I've sensed that too.' Adelko wasn't sure if he was just saying that to look as though he was keeping up. But he had to hope he'd at least convinced his friends that he was on to something.

'So what do you suggest we do about it?' asked Hargus. 'I presume you didn't just bring us here in the dead of night to get a second opinion.'

'In the spring, I'll be leaving the monastery again with Master Horskram,' said Adelko. 'I won't be able to keep an eye on things here. I'm going to ask you two to do just that. I need people I can trust to be on the lookout for anything... untoward.'

Arik scowled. 'And what in Palom's name are we supposed to do if we find out anything, Adelko? We're hardly influential within the Order.'

Adelko bit his lip. He hadn't considered that part.

'It'll just have to wait until I get back,' he said finally.

'From another of your secret missions?' asked Arik. 'Is this to do with the Headstone fragments?' Adelko had left out details of his journey to the Pilgrim Kingdoms; he didn't want to risk telling them everything.

'Yes,' he admitted. 'But even if it succeeds, it may not help us much. Not if we're bringing anything back to a vipers' nest.'

Adelko's sixth sense suddenly flared. Without hesitation he snuffed out the candle. They sat in darkness. Then they heard footfalls and saw a light. One of the brothers, probably on his way to use the privy.

'Think we've stayed out long enough,' whispered Adelko. 'It's time we were back in bed.' Fumbling for the parchment, he rolled it up and tucked it into his habit.

The three of them snuck back to the dormitory in silence. Only now did Adelko notice the bitter winter's chill. His mind was awhirl. Always so many questions.

Somebody had the answers.

CHAPTER 6
A REUNION IN PARADISE

'My Harijan queen is beautiful today.' Anupe stroked the redhead's tresses, drinking in the delicious lies along with the delicious Armandy wine that matched the colour of her hair. Perhaps being forced to winter in a Riman brothel hadn't been such a bad fate, after all. Thoughts of Kyra had gradually subsided. She had loved the wild woodlander – as close to a kindred spirit as she would ever get in these benighted lands – but she was gone now, disappeared into the Long Silence that awaited all mortals.

'And my whore is very lusty,' replied Anupe, stroking the slender girl's hip with her calloused hand. It was late afternoon, and the festivities were still in full swing; most of the *Scarlet Paradise*'s patrons would be recovering from the Drinking Sickness ahead of yet another night of riotous debauchery. Some of them were doing their recovering in plain sight, slumped over tables, a knotted tangle of swains and whores who'd passed out the night before.

No wonder they called such places fleshpots.

One couple had managed to shrug off the effects of last night's debauch: a wealthy young merchant from Mercadia and an auburn lass were going at it enthusiastically in the corner, their grunts and moans punctuating the snoring.

But Anupe preferred to couple in private – and even the *Paradise* would baulk at watching sapphic lust played out in public. She drained her goblet and shifted the girl on her lap. Alize was one of her favourites; both compliant and inventive, she charged handsomely but was worth every silver. Set back a few winding streets from the waterfront, the *Paradise* was one of few brothels in Rima that was run and owned by women. That made it more costly, but one thing Anupe wasn't short of was coin. And the Harijan was damned if she'd patronise an establishment where the menfolk preyed on women.

'Come on, Anupe, let's go upstairs,' said Alize, leaning in and biting the Harijan's lower lip. Her breath smelled of wine, but that was better than other things a whore's mouth might taste of. The outlander felt a hot flush creep across her loins, as she moved her hand slowly beneath Alize's smock and up the inside of her bare white thigh...

A banging on the door rudely interrupted their amorous loveplay.

Marianne, the burly madame who was built like a man and had knocked a few senseless in her time, got up from her place by the counter and shuffled over to answer it.

'Customers at this time of the day, at Year's End!' she exclaimed. 'Well, wonders will never cease.'

'Let's go to my chamber,' said Anupe, rising and pulling the wench along with her.

All thoughts of afternoon lovemaking vanished when Marianne opened the door.

She recognised the voice immediately, and turned to see Marianne looking askance at her former employer. Next to Adhelina stood Hettie; both were dressed and packed for the road.

Gods knew, those two were always running away from something.

'Wait, I know them,' said Anupe, sending Alize on her way with a florin in the hand and a regretful shake of the head. 'Best to let them in and bolt the door after – these two usually bring trouble not far behind them.'

'Oh?' said Marianne, arching an eyebrow. 'I'll not have trouble in this establishment. I don't mind entertaining sapphics, but we're not to have any trouble!'

Anupe raised a placatory hand. 'I will take care of this, don't worry. Just have a wench bring another pitcher of wine and two more goblets.'

Marianne shook her head and shut the door, muttering to herself as she went to see to the order. Anupe paid very well for services rendered – that should be enough to allay the madame's suspicions for now.

'Well, I see you've lost no time mastering Panglian,' said Adhelina wryly.

'I told you when we met I learn languages quickly,' replied the Harijan, motioning them to sit on stools at her table.

'I see that isn't all you've been studying,' put in Hettie, glancing around the stew distastefully.

Anupe grinned. 'Do you know, ladies, I think I have almost missed you.'

Adhelina returned the smile. 'You might regret saying that, Anupe, because I've a feeling you're going to be seeing a lot more of us.'

'Well,' said the Harijan. 'You had better tell me your latest story in that case. I am, as you say, all ears...'

The pitcher was more than half empty by the time Adhelina was done. They spoke in Vorstlending, so no one would understand (Pangonians, she had learned, were notoriously bad at learning other people's languages). All the same, Anupe could not help but glance about the taproom, slowly coming to life as wenches moved around lighting scented candles and red-tinted lanterns against the encroaching dusk.

'So the heiress of Dulsinor has another string to her bow,' said Anupe. 'And this mystic woman told you to come and find me?'

'Yes,' said Adhelina. 'You're bound up in this business somehow. We're to stay with you here until we can sail for Sassania on the spring tides.'

Hettie was looking increasingly aghast at that prospect, as roisterers gradually came to their senses, calling loudly for wine whilst grabbing girls who slapped and giggled flirtatiously.

'Your friend does not seem overjoyed at this prospect,' observed Anupe.

'I'm not either,' said Adhelina, 'but if it's a choice between hiding out in a bordello for two months and being held prisoner at court... In any case, we've been in worse places.'

Anupe supposed that was true. Their time on the cursed moorlands in Vorstlund had receded to a dark smudge on her memory, but she gathered the damsels recalled it rather more acutely. The Harijan supposed she had the Argolian sorcery to thank for that much at least.

'Well, it isn't me you will have to convince,' said Anupe, gesturing meaningfully at Marianne as she bustled about the common room. The sound of bow teasing fiddle filtered across the room as a female troupe of jongleurs – the resident house musicians – began warming up. Anupe had a fancy for the one with dyed blue hair, but she wasn't involved in that part of the *Paradise*'s trade unfortunately.

Adhelina beckoned Marianne over.

'What can I do for you?' asked the madame. Her icy tone suggested that 'show me to the door' would be the most satisfactory answer.

What she got instead was another question. An unexpected one.

'How much business do you lose every month to the Crotch Rot?' asked Adhelina. 'And unwanted embarrassments? Whores with child aren't so attractive to most of your clients, I'm guessing.'

Marianne arched her eyebrows again, tugging at the bunched-up copper curls that passed for her hair. 'You'd be surprised,' she said. But the flicker of interest that skittered across her keen green eyes wasn't lost on Adhelina. 'How would you like to have the services of a skilled healer for the rest of the season?' she asked. 'I'm a trained herbalist, I can treat all your women if you like, and take care of embarrassments with Abaddon's Root, too.'

Hettie gawped, her look of horror deepening. Adhelina ignored her and went on: 'All I'd ask in return is a room and board for myself and my companion here, until spring, with *absolutely no questions asked.*'

Marianne pursed her lips. 'We've not had a healer here since Ulla passed two winters ago,' she mused. 'But why would a highborn lady like you be wanting to work in a place like this?'

Adhelina waved a finger. 'No questions asked,' she repeated. 'That's my offer, take it or leave it.'

Marianne frowned. The troupe had started up a merry jig. It seemed at odds with the seriousness of the situation. The damsels were in a tight spot: Adhelina was brazening it out as best as she could.

The madame nodded. 'Alright then, I'll give you a try. A couple of the lasses have taken sick lately, they've not been able to work. We get wealthy types coming here, they won't pay to catch the Crotch Rot.'

'Are they upstairs?' asked Adhelina. 'I'll see to them now, if you like. Just show us where to stow our belongings.'

Marianne called for a wench to show the damsels to their room. Anupe leaned against the table and poured herself another stoup of wine as they got up and left. It looked for all the world as though her fate and theirs were intertwined. And the irascible monk Horskram and his curious understudy too... Just what path had the gods set her on?

But pondering that could wait. In the meantime, it was still a holy day, and that meant taking lots of unholy pleasure. Sipping on the ruby Armandy vintage, Anupe looked around the noisy taproom, her eyes searching hungrily for Alize.

CHAPTER 7

VICTORY'S SWEET AFTERMATH

Vaskrian opened one eye. Ye Almighty, but his head *hurt*. How much mead had he downed last night? And where was he? This bed was far too expansive for a household knight (he hadn't moved that far up in the world, not yet). Shifting his naked body under the ermine furs, he felt a pleasant warm sensation gild his loins as he came up against the no-less-naked form of Rowena. She was snoring gently beside him, her small pert breasts rising and falling.

The young knight opened both eyes and took in her freckled form. Perhaps he was moving up in the world, after all.

He furrowed his brow, trying to recall what had happened. It had been Winter's Reaping, the last day of the Year's End Festival... They had all gotten roaring drunk at Liathnoc, the First Lady's ancestral seat in the western foothills of the Hyrkrainians. There had been feasting, and dancing before and afterwards; a far wilder affair than the mannered court dances of his own folk and the Pangonians... His lady liege had drunkenly ordered him to dance with her.

And that was when it had happened.

She'd told him to kiss her. He'd complied (it was his duty after all). Rowena wasn't as pretty as Adisa, his first love, or half as comely as the whore he'd lain with in Rima. She wasn't even as pretty as Hettie (though he hadn't lain with her, so he supposed she didn't count, not that recollection of the Vorstlending didn't pain him enough to want to suppress her memory).

But for all that she wasn't particularly comely, Lady Rowena had something those other women lacked. Blue blood running through her veins – real blue blood too, not the diluted sort Hettie carried. It hadn't taken much effort on his liege's part to coax him upstairs, where they'd had a lusty tumble before passing out.

Luviah's teats, why couldn't he remember it better? His first noblewoman, he ought to remember it better...

She stopped snoring abruptly and her eyes flickered open. Those emerald green irises had something special about them, even if she wasn't the prettiest of ladies. Reaching out a stubby-nailed hand, she grasped him by the back of the neck and pulled him down towards her.

'Come here, swain,' she grinned. Her gawky teeth didn't bother him over much either; he pressed his lips to hers with a lustful alacrity as they joined tongues. Within a few moments he felt himself stiffen, and shifted his body weight to mount her.

'Pull my hair,' she gasped as he entered her. 'Pull it hard.'

He'd damn well remember their coupling second time around.

Vaskrian watched the morning shadows slowly climbing up the wall, as he cradled Rowena in his arms after their bout. He still couldn't get used to the castle's strange brickwork. It had been built hundreds of years ago, Rowena had said, in the time of the Four Old Kingdoms. The style had been learned from their druiding ancestors; the hotchpotch flints piled one atop the other looked bizarre and uneven. They put him in mind somewhat of the much older ruins he'd seen on his travels, the ones built by Them. That thought made him shudder.

'What's on your mind, swain?' Rowena asked, running her hands absently through the downy hairs on his chest.

'Nothing...' he hedged. 'Just this castle is strange.'

'Well the sages tell it was built by druids, so that's no small wonder.' She kissed him affectionately on the brow. It was his scarred side, and that made him feel awkward, though she didn't seem to care. 'You'll get used to it. And we'll be on the march again as soon as the snows melt.'

Vaskrian hoped so. He preferred war over quest any day – it was usually a lot more straightforward. Although the Battle of Rathlain Corridor had been anything but, come to think of it. He'd never forget the stunned look on Braxus's face when he'd hied up to him after the rout, covered head to toe in mud and blood. Something had changed between them then – perhaps it was more an understanding between equals?

Likewise the others treated him differently now. Even mighty Sir Torgun addressed him in a more formal manner. Oddly, it didn't bring him closer to his fellow knights, and truth to tell being one still felt strange.

'Oh, but you're miles away,' said Rowena. Her breath reeked of wine and mead, but somehow that appealed. She reached down and began stroking his loins roughly. 'Think I need to remind you I'm still here...'

Satyrus' cleft, is she never satisfied? Perhaps noblewomen have more potent desires than common girls. But then, he supposed, another tumble would help with the Drinking Sickness.

She turned around, rubbing slender buttocks up against him, fanning the flames of his returning desire. Vaskrian guessed the First Lady of Clan McCullogh hadn't enjoyed many conquests off the battlefield since her husband passed. She raised a leg enticingly as he gripped her firmly by the waist.

All in all, he couldn't complain about his situation.

When it was over they lay huddled together. The warmth of her body felt all the nicer against the afterglow of their coupling. Already his pounding head was a pleasingly distant memory.

There was one thing he had to know, though.

'So... why me?' he asked at last. 'You could have taken any

high-born Thraxian as a lover, but you chose a scarred outlander instead.' His own modesty surprised him. Perhaps he was learning how to behave like a true knight. Then the thought of the half-dozen men he'd butchered mercilessly on the battlefield cast a shadow across his mind. Perhaps he was just learning to act like one.

Rowena was blissfully oblivious to his darkening thoughts as she turned to face him again. 'Not one of those high-born men had the courage to fight for my honour,' she said, her voice hardening. 'You did, scars be damned. I appreciate character in a man, Sir Vaskrian. You're a reckless young fool, anyone can see that, but you've a noble heart to match.'

Vaskrian flushed with a different kind of pleasure at the compliment.

'And besides,' she smiled, stroking the unburnt side of his face. 'You're really quite handsome, underneath all those scars.' She nibbled his ear as she whispered in it: 'And full of energy too, as befits a man of young years.'

He wasn't entirely surprised when she pulled him on top of her again. Keeping this one happy abed promised to be more challenging than fighting Sir Leathan.

Braxus groaned as he came to. The first thing he saw was an upturned flagon on the trestle table in front of him; the first thing he heard was Wrackwulf snoring beside him. Sitting up groggily, he looked about the hall. His hair was wet; that would be the mead he'd spilled. The crooked feasting room was packed with household knights and the odd serving wench, all in stupors of their own.

No wenches for him last night, or the last tenday for that matter. He'd been far too busy getting drunk since the Crimson League retired from campaigning for the winter. Still he couldn't drink Adhelina off his mind. He'd tried wenching her off it twice shortly after arriving at Liathnoc, and twice he'd failed. The excessive drinking didn't help.

Wrackwulf hadn't had such an issue, though he'd got too drunk for whoring last night. Truth to tell, he'd been grateful for the freelancer's company. He didn't feel at all at home with his distant southern compatriots; the sooner they put Abrexta's neck in a rope and he reconquered his ancestral holding, the better.

Staggering to his feet, Braxus scoured the tables for a jug of mead and got... half of what he wanted. It would have to do.

Hair of the hound that bites, he thought ruefully as he poured the stale liquor into a flagon and quaffed it. Lurching over to a window, he gazed upon the crags and ravines outside, blanketed in thick snow; a silvery powder that dusted the grey-green foothills of the With-y-Passes before swallowing up the higher ranges on the horizon.

Braxus scowled into his cup. He'd always hated the mountains. They gave shelter to the accursed highlanders, who'd so blotted his life. Now he had more reason than ever to hate them.

'Peaceful, aren't they?'

Braxus turned with a start, half expecting to see Wrackwulf risen from his slumber. Instead what he saw was

Brother Joram, picking his way through the snoring knights towards him.

'Twas your namesake that made them so,' continued the monk, drawing level with him and gazing out of the window. 'Braxus Pagans-Bane, Seventh Lord of Tul Aeren, cleansed the foothills you look upon of the last highland scum to infest these parts. Reus willing, and we'll do the same up north when you take back your lands.'

Joram's penchant for violence was still unsettling in an Argolian, but that was a sentiment Braxus could drink to.

'Pagan's-Bane, I like that,' he said, finishing off his souring mead. 'The scions of Tul Aeren have ever dealt the highland folk tidy strokes.'

'Until one of them near got the best of us,' said Joram, his lip curling. 'Twas Abrexta's sorcerous interference that provoked that dissent in our ranks, mark my words. She won't be sitting idly over the winter either – we need to formulate a strategy.'

It was obvious the monk had something in mind, though he could have waited a day to let them recover.

'Go on,' said Braxus. 'You've obviously been thinking about it while we've been busy getting drunk.'

'I have interrogated Morcant at length, and I do believe the blackguard has found a way to destroy the witch. But we have to get to her first.'

'First? Need I remind you, we've a war to fight before that can happen?'

Joram shook his head. 'Too risky. We can't afford to wait until spring. It's high time we were on our way. We need to get behind enemy lines, strike when they least expect it.'

Braxus stared at him. 'You're proposing we travel north to Ongist in this?' He gestured at the skies, from which fresh snow had begun to fall. 'And even if we do get that far, how on earth do we break into the city?'

Joram's lip curled in distaste. 'Yon wizard has a way to help us there, too.'

'It's not the first time we've used a witch to help us get to another witch,' sighed Braxus.

'Set a thief to catch a thief,' agreed Joram. 'These are desperate times, Sir Braxus. Sometimes a lesser evil must be done to avert-'

Braxus raised a hand. 'Spare me the quotes from scripture, Master Joram, I had enough of that growing up.' Even now he couldn't bring himself to mention his pious father. By all accounts his head was still decorating the palace walls, along with those of Vertrix, Bryant, Regan and their squires. Another reason to dread this new mission; another reason to want it all the more.

'Well then, we'd best get the lads together,' he said. 'I believe Sir Torgun spent the festival observing vigil, so at least you won't have to worry about him being hungover.'

Just then Wrackwulf awoke from his stupor with a start. He caught his flagon just in time before it fell from his hand. Seeing it still had some mead in it, he took a grateful slurp.

Joram gave Braxus a wry glance. 'Such tools has the Almighty given me to work with.'

'Speak, you cur.' Morcant glanced up nervously at Joram.

For one moment, Torgun thought he was going to start hitting the warlock again, and was ready to intervene.

He was on edge enough as it was, without the monk resorting to unnecessary violence. He hadn't appreciated being dragged from the chapel either; St Argo's Rood felt warm around his neck in that holy part of the castle. He'd never been much of one for prayer, but after everything he'd seen in the past year... well, it changed a man.

All the less did he like the place Joram had brought them to. The lower levels of Liathnoc were the oldest part of the castle, built a thousand years ago he'd been told. Gazing at the lopsided flints that glistened with a silver sheen, Torgun could well believe those curious stones had been laid by druids. Morcant was being held one level above the lower dungeons. The Spirit Keep, locals called them: they were haunted by ghosts of warriors who had died in the same invasion that razed the ancient city of Anarlion. One knight had told him that previous lords of Liathnoc would lock the worst criminals in the Spirit Keep, where they would be driven mad by the spectral forms that cursed it.

He didn't like Thraxia. It was a strange kingdom that had never fully broken with its pagan past. No wonder his countrymen had fought it for decades.

Quelling such thoughts, he gathered around Morcant with Wrackwulf and Braxus as the mage began to speak. 'Abrexta has mastered the art of daubing, a sub-discipline of Alchemy. Using that, she has tattooed a sigil of power on her body, and with her powers of artifice, that's another sub-discipline of Alchemy...'

Torgun raised a hand. 'In Heaven's name, man, give this

to us in layman's terms! How are we supposed to understand your sorcerous talk?'

'Perhaps now you understand why I chastise him,' said Joram.

Torgun frowned and shook his head at that, as Morcant went on in plainer terms: 'Abrexta's immortality is channelled from her Fay ancestors, through a tattoo and a ring of power she has crafted. Think of it like a sword and a whetstone, the one enables you to use the other properly.'

'Clear as spring rain,' said Braxus. 'Now tell us the part we want to know – how do you plan to nullify said magicks?'

'That is simple enough, once we get to her. You see, Abrexta needs the ring to control the sigil's power – once separated from the first, lose grip on the other she will. Enough that should be to reverse the effects of the magic. Her hundred-odd years will catch up with her then, oh yes indeed!'

'Sounds fine, but how do you separate her from the ring?' asked Braxus. 'I suppose we could cut her hands off.' He clearly relished the thought. *Thraxians, such vulgar people,* thought Torgun disapprovingly.

'Ah, she won't let you get close to her that easily, no she won't!' said Morcant. 'Propose I do that we use Thaumaturgy to tap the power of telekinesis.'

The three knights exchanged blank looks.

'The idolator means he can use magic to pull the ring off her finger at a distance,' explained Joram, revulsion spattered across his face. 'But to do that, we'll have to break past her defences.'

'Which means we need to keep her elan preoccupied as

much as possible, by attacking her while you and Morcant work your wonders,' Braxus finished for him. 'We've fought wizards before.'

Was that a glimmer of respect in Joram's eyes? He nodded and said no more.

'Sorely taxed already her elan is, keeping half the kingdom's nobles enthralled,' added Morcant. 'Probably her main means of fighting us that will be – expect plenty of knights guarding her.'

'Knights we can deal with,' said Torgun.

'Well,' said Wrackwulf. 'That's the fight part taken care of – but how do we get to her in the first place? The weather isn't exactly helpful to our cause.'

'No, but it should conceal us well enough,' said Morcant. 'Though we'll have to travel on foot at this time of year, so expect a long haul!'

'We'll have no problems there,' quipped Wrackwulf. 'I just hope you're up to it.'

Morcant grinned his sly grin. 'I have ways of boosting my strength.'

Joram cuffed him, making his plaited hair waggle absurdly. 'Revel not in thy foul potions,' he spat. 'Bad enough we have to use your services on our sacred mission!'

This time Sir Torgun didn't feel moved to intervene. The sorcerer was clearly a repulsive fellow.

'What about getting into the city though?' asked Braxus. 'We can't just march into Ongist.'

'Another area that is where I can be of use to you,' said Morcant, wincing as he rubbed the back of his head. 'A good enchanter myself, so I am... leave me to worry about the gate guards. They'll be commoners, so Abrexta won't have bothered enthralling them. Make our way through the city easily enough we can, for few folk will be on the streets at this time of year. Then find Abrexta is all we need to do – to enter the Palace of Bending Branches my magicks will also help.'

'I visited the palace a couple of times when I was a youth,' said Braxus. 'I think I can remember my way around.'

Morcant nodded. 'Good, good. A plan we have then! Set off right soon, I advise.'

Torgun felt uneasy. He never liked to admit to fear, but this unnerved him. Once again, they were using a warlock to fight fire with fire, only this time they were bringing theirs with them. He didn't like the cunning glint that entered Morcant's eyes whenever he spoke. But then he'd long since learned to abandon any hopes of propriety. Questing was a strange business these days.

The young knight's unease intensified as Morcant raised his shackled hands. 'You'll be wanting to take these off, too...' He grinned obsequiously, though there was nothing submissive about him.

Joram scowled and grabbed the warlock by a fistful of braids. 'Know this, idolator – I will be watching thee every step of the way. If you so much as try a cantrip on us, I'll know, for I'm attuned to thee. And I'll snap your neck like a twig, mission be damned – do you hear?'

Morcant swallowed and nodded as best he could. He heard perfectly well.

'Good,' said the monk, unhanding him roughly. 'I'll bring

a blacksmith presently. The three of you had best get ready – we've an arduous journey ahead of us.'

'What about Sir Vaskrian?' asked Torgun. 'He's a belted knight now, and one of us. Could be useful to have along.'

Wrackwulf grinned and exchanged a sly glance with Braxus. 'You missed all the fun while you were vigiling,' he said. 'If you think you can prise him from the arms of his mistress, then good luck to you. Personally, I'll wait till Gehenna freezes over.'

'Don't blaspheme down here of all places!' barked Joram. As if to emphasise his words, a cacophonous sound filtered up from beneath the floor, a twisted chorus of cracked voices giving vent to an everlasting pain.

Torgun made the sign and fingered the relic about his neck.

Wrackwulf had gone a shade paler. 'I only meant to say that I believe young Vaskrian's duties lie elsewhere,' he stuttered.

'Lady Rowena may have need of him anyway,' said Braxus. 'If our mission fails, she'll need to fight another campaign come spring.'

Torgun frowned. He didn't entertain thoughts of failure, unlike the feckless Thraxian.

Down in the Spirit Keep, the shades shrieked again. This time it sounded like a hundred men burning across a reverberating valley.

Braxus shuddered. 'Let's get gone from this accursed place.'

Torgun needed no further encouragement.

'Something's happening.' Vaskrian looked down into the courtyard. His friends were there, along with the shady monk and his even shadier captive.

'What could possibly be of more interest out there?' asked Rowena, coming and leaning her chin on his naked shoulder. They'd spent the afternoon in bed. That had been fun, but he now felt more exhausted than he had after the Battle of Rathlain Corridor.

'No, look!' he pointed out of the window. The translucent pane of aurochs cartilage allowed only for blurred vision, but he'd recognise that motley crew on a dark night. 'They're off somewhere – on foot, by the looks of it.'

Rowena frowned. 'I didn't give anyone permission to leave my holding. All right, get dressed and go down to them. Tell them I'll be along directly.'

Vaskrian didn't need to be told twice. His friends were off questing again – without him.

We'll bloody well see about that, he thought as he pulled on his hose.

'Wait! The lady of the castle commands it!'

The three knights turned from the gatehouse to see Vaskrian, half-dressed and shivering, lurching through the snow towards them.

And laughed. Even Sir Torgun couldn't resist.

'Well,' grinned Braxus, 'our bold friend has certainly learned how to play his part.'

'It's not a part, I'm a dubbed knight just the same as you!' yelled Vaskrian.

It was nice to see his erstwhile squire hadn't lost that fiery temper of his.

'All right, all right,' said Braxus, raising his hands in a placatory gesture. 'We were just debating whether to leave now, or wait until dawn tomorrow. Joram here is of the opinion that we should set off right away.'

He glanced sidelong at the burly monk. There was only an hour or so of daylight left: clearly Joram was anxious to get away before Rowena could intervene.

'You can't go anywhere yet,' said Vaskrian. 'You know full well you need to ask the lady's permission to leave.'

'We are on Argolian business,' said Joram sternly. 'This goes above and beyond court niceties.'

'Nevertheless, we *are* on her holding,' put in Torgun mildly. 'It would be discourteous to ignore protocol.'

Vaskrian drew himself up pompously. 'My Lady Rowena has seen you and she is coming now.'

'We heard her doing that half the bloody morning,' chuckled Wrackwulf.

Braxus tried to hold back another laugh of his own, but it was no good. The two knights bent over guffawing. Vaskrian's scarred face looked red enough to melt the snow that dusted it. Torgun put a huge hand to his broad lips to hide his own mirth.

'Alright, very funny,' said Vaskrian. 'Had your little jest, have you? And what are you playing at anyway, trying to leave in a blizzard without me?'

'You can't come with us, Sir Vaskrian,' said Braxus, trying to keep a straight face. 'Your duty lies here.'

That set them off again. Even Morcant was laughing now. Only Joram remained looking dour and taciturn. But then Argolians had little sense of humour.

Unfortunately, the same could be said of the First Lady of Clan McCullogh.

'What is the meaning of this?' she blazed, sweeping into the courtyard a few minutes later. She had dressed hastily, though Braxus imagined that wasn't why her hair was tangled. He tried to keep his mirth suppressed as he replied: 'Forgive us milady, we're taking our mission north. Abrexta must be stopped, the sooner the better.'

She placed her hands on her hips, scrutinising them. 'You seriously plan on going to Ongist in this weather? To do what, may I ask – take on her army single-handed?'

With the greatest reluctance, Joram sketched their mission in a brittle voice.

'Well now, that *is* bold,' she said when he was done. 'If it succeeds, you'll save me fighting a war.'

'That's correct,' said Joram. 'Kill the witch, break the spell. Once we slay Abrexta, the King will be restored to his right mind, along with all the other nobles she's enthralled. Then we can call off this awful civil war. Many lives will be saved this way.'

Rowena pursed her lips and nodded as she considered that.

'It sounds like a madcap plan,' she said.

'With due respect, my lady,' put in Torgun, 'but we have done this kind of thing before. We are experienced...' he sighed as if lost for another way to put it, 'witch hunters.'

Joram managed a wry smile at that.

'All right,' Rowena sighed. 'But for heaven's sake, wait it out until tomorrow. I'll have you properly equipped from the kitchens in the meantime. No use you tearing off into the wilderness half-prepared.'

'That's what chivalrous knights do, ma'am,' joked Wrackwulf. But he acknowledged her suggestion with a nod of his own.

'Well, that settles that then,' said Braxus. 'Let's get back indoors and get some meat and mead down us.'

'Wait,' put in Vaskrian. 'Have I understood correctly? You lot are off to kill Abrexta?'

The three knights exchanged awkward glances.

'I'm coming with you,' said Vaskrian.

Rowena shot him a dark glance. 'Need I remind you that you are my sworn sword?'

Even Wrackwulf knew better than to make a stupid joke out of that remark.

'I know,' said Vaskrian, suddenly bowing and kissing her hand. 'And I'm grateful for everything you've done for me. But,' – he gestured at the others – 'we're bound by... what do you call it?' He looked at Braxus.

'A Wyrd,' supplied the Thraxian. 'A larger destiny holds us together. Your story just happens to be a small part of that.'

Rowena glared at him. 'You are most impudent, Sir Braxus.'

'Aye, but there is truth in his words,' put in Joram. 'Perhaps it would be better if the young knight came with us.'

Rowena looked from Joram to Vaskrian, who had an eager puppy dog look in his face.

Perhaps his mistress works him too hard, and he's desperate to escape her clutches, thought Braxus wryly. But he was secretly glad of the prospect of his company.

'I'll come back,' said Vaskrian, taking a knee in the snow. 'I swear it. Think of it as my next mission for you.'

His look was so earnest that Rowena couldn't help but smile. 'Come back to me, Sir Vaskrian,' she said, gently raising him and planting a kiss on his lips. 'But before you do, come sup with me one last time – all of you! Let's away back in – we'll see you off in right fine style!'

'We'll need Sir Vaskrian refreshed come morning,' Wrackwulf couldn't resist throwing in.

'Oh he will be, don't you worry,' grinned Rowena over her shoulder as she led them back towards the keep. 'I know how to invigorate a man.'

'Rather him than me,' muttered Wrackwulf, so only Braxus could hear.

CHAPTER 8
A FLEET FOR RAVENS

Magnhilda surveyed the skeletal flotilla of warships lining the frozen coast, a warm sense of satisfaction offsetting the bitter North Wind. Let the Lord of Skies beat his wings all he liked – come spring, his powers would be harnessed to wreak devastation on the mainlanders.

'We're using straight-grained logs for the planks, masts and crossbeams,' said Olaf Hrolfson. Landarök's master boatbuilder was a tall, wiry man with greying hair and beard. His tattoos and earrings made him look like the free-sail reaver he had once been, but he took even greater pride in his current work. He gestured up towards the pine forests that swathed the hills overlooking the coastline. 'Even now we've men cutting keels from yonder trees, but that won't last I'm afraid. It's going to get even colder, in a week or two we'll have to down tools until the ices thaw.'

Magnhilda could easily see why. She shivered as she drew her woollen shawl and sleeved cloak of otter fur closer about her. The cold didn't normally bother her much, but in the depths of winter the seas had been known to freeze.

'That's fine,' she said, 'as long as you resume work when they do, and we can have the fleet ready by the end of spring. Now tell me, how many men will these longships hold when they're finished?' She had never fought at sea, being too busy consolidating her holdings in the hinterlands for such luxuries as raiding. In any case, there hadn't been any organised raids in the past century, not since the Treaty of Ryøskil had seen her ancestors brought to heel by the mainlanders under King Aelfric – just the odd freesailor like Olaf here and there.

That would soon change.

'These ones will each hold fifty men,' said Olaf, indicating the fifty ribbed ships hugging the gelid sands with a sweep of the arm. 'They're long enough to fit fifteen berserkers lying head to toe, and six paces wide at the beam. Once they're done, we'll caulk the hulls with tarred animal hair, that and the curved keel should help them move more swiftly and endure the crossing with ease.'

'Wide at the beam as I ordered, excellent,' said Magnhilda. 'For come the thawing they'll be holding a hundred men each, not fifty.'

Olaf blinked. 'A hundred? With respect, Your Majesty, but how will four dozen rowers move that kind of weight? Not with the strongest men could you do such a thing.'

'You're forgetting the White Eye,' said Magnhilda. 'The Sea Wizard, they call him on the mainland – and not without reason. He helped Hardrada sail many men across the Valhalla, he'll do the same for us.'

Olaf's brow furrowed. He was a gods-fearing man and didn't hold with using sorcery in war. Magnhilda laid a gloved hand on his knotted arm. 'Have no fear, Olaf,' she smiled at him. 'Ragnar is my brother – he would not do anything to cross me.'

She hid her uncertainty well. From what little news she'd heard from the Skjel Islands, her brother was going his own way more often these days. Ragnar had only ever taught Magnhilda the rudiments of Enchantment, and Scrying was unknown to her: before the winter had put an end to communication, she'd heard rumours of dire rituals being led by him, and human sacrifices being thrown down the Cauldron.

Something in the deeps was said to be stirring, answering the White Eye's call.

'Come,' she added, eager to banish the thought, 'you said you had something else to show me.'

Olaf beamed as they walked the length of the strand. The ships were far back enough so that the waters could not touch them, but within easy distance for portaging when the time came. Gazing beyond their inchoate forms at the iron-grey seas beyond, she could not help but wonder what her brother was really up to. He'd alluded to tapping some primordial power beneath the waves, spoken of bringing the seas up in arms to aid their strike against the mainlanders.

Ragnar had been insistent on the benefits of this plan, without divulging much in the way of details, but Magnhilda had to admit she was beginning to see things from Olaf's point of view. How much should a queen of men rely on the dark arts to win a campaign?

Her troubled thoughts receded as Olaf brought them to a halt before his masterpiece. It was closer to being finished than most of the other boats. It was also twice as big.

'I've taken the liberty of calling her *Valhalla's Serpent*,' said Olaf, fairly swelling with pride. 'The largest warship we've built since Ryøskil. You'll note the fine work that's been done on the prow – that should terrify the mainlanders when they set eyes on it!'

The carved leviathan had yet to be painted, but already she could see the figurehead was a fearsome sight, itself the size of a berserker. Magnhilda had her mind on more practical matters though.

'How many oars will it use?'

'Thirty-five pairs, so that's seventy in total,' supplied Olaf. 'It's a dozen paces wide at the beam, so it'll carry...' he paused to factor in Ragnar's magicks. 'Two hundred men.'

Magnhilda grinned. 'Olaf, I think we've found the Shield Queen's personal ship! You shall be richly rewarded for your services.'

'My reward is serving the New Kingdom,' said Olaf. 'Your reign will be a long and glorious one. My grandfather and father burned with the injustice of Ryøskil – this'll be a setting to rights of all ills.'

Magnhilda's grin softened into a smile. 'That it shall, Olaf,' she said, laying a hand on his arm again. 'That it surely shall.' Thoughts of Ragnar's recondite witcheries had retreated to the back of her mind. 'Come spring, we'll join this fleet with the Skjel Islanders and put ten thousand warriors on the sail road, and weather of axes shall rain down upon our mainland cousins!'

'That will be a sight to see, Your Majesty.'

They remained like that for a few moments more, looking at the gargantuan ship as the waning sun began to turn it into a silhouetted thing of shadow. As if sensing the seaborne carnage to come, the North Wind blew ever more fiercely, sending the tides lashing inwards with renewed vigour. It was a sight she would fain have looked upon until sunset, but the Magna of the Frozen Wastes had other things to attend to.

'I'll away back to the city now, but thank you Olaf – this has been a most satisfactory inspection.'

The boatmaster nodded curtly, and together they climbed the hills away from the flotilla, back towards the coastal road where their horses were waiting for them.

She found the palace in an uproar when she returned. That told Magnhilda her controversial guest had arrived. He was in the hall, with a twenty-strong retainer of seacarls: Walmond, first of her dead husband's made men. Mead was being quaffed, and by the looks of things a *flyting* was in full swing. Her own seacarls were more than happy to oblige their vociferous visitor.

Unseen, she glid into the hall and watched.

'I have swum amidst the floes of the Valhalla in winter-time,' boasted Walmond, to roars of approval from his men, and catcalls from hers. 'From here to the Farov Isles have my sturdy limbs quested!'

'The only tides you've swum are those of the mead

you've drunk and belched up again!' Roars of laughter, and catcalls from the other side. Magnhilda allowed herself a smile. A *flyting* involved an exchange of boasts and insults – one of her seacarls had taken up Walmond's challenge and was making a good fist of it.

'I have wrestled Gygants in the Fenris Mountains,' boomed Walmond. 'And when I dashed Gromlon's head to pieces on the floor of his cave, the only thing I drank was his blood!'

That was a good boast, she had to admit. Unlikely, seeing as Gromlon had been slain by Søren centuries ago, but a good one all the same.

'The only thing Walmond dashed were his father's hopes for a strong-minded son, when he drowned himself in mead and fought the giants of his fancy!'

More roars. More laughter. More catcalls.

Entertaining as this exchange was, Magnhilda was quickly losing patience with it. She knew exactly why Walmond was here.

She scanned the hall for her own lieutenant and soon found her cousin – a gargantuan figure, loitering in a corner beneath a soapstone oil-lamp dangling from an iron hoop in the rough ceiling. She would have need of Canute Mountainside's services right soon.

Clearing her throat loudly, she stepped into the circle of men and pulled her shawl down.

'I see my made men have given you a welcome, as befits your new status as Thegn of Kvenlund,' she said, silencing the hall.

Walmond blinked over the rim of his mead horn. Then he laughed.

'Now that,' he said, pointing at her while addressing his seacarls, 'is what I call unusual leadership! For since when does our sovereign sneak into her own hall unannounced?'

More hoots and catcalls from Walmond's retinue. These ones aimed at her.

She mastered her rising anger.

I knew Walmond would be trouble, even after we killed his liege, she told herself. *Giving him Guldebrand's lands doesn't seem to have brought him to heel either.*

'I shall come and go as I please in my own hall,' she retorted. 'And you shall give a full account of yourself, Walmond Krakison. Rumour abounds that you are refusing to take the sail road with us when the ices thaw.'

'And you know full well why,' said Walmond, the smile dropping from his face. 'You took many swords from me, when you married off Jarl Bjorg to Gunnehilda. I'll not see the rest thrown away on a fool's errand.'

'Jótland was left sorely depleted by your depredations and Hardrada's disastrous war on the mainland – marrying Bjorg to his widow makes sense, Walmond. If I'm to rule as Magna of the Frozen Wastes, I must rule them with an even hand.'

Her seacarls grunted their approval. Putting Hardrada's spouse back into her holding by making Bjorg its new thegn had been a clever move – Gunnehilda had been popular with the locals before Guldebrand usurped Hardrada's position, and it separated one more loyal jarl from Walmond.

Unfortunately, the new Thegn of Kvenlund was all too aware of that.

'You speak of Hardrada's disastrous war,' he sneered. 'Yet this is the very thing you would send my men to. I'll not make the same mistake as he did.'

Magnhilda's voice hardened. 'You will do as your Queen commands.'

'This is madness!' cried Walmond. He was huge even by Northlander standards, his burly frame seeming to fill the darkening hall as he looked around at the assembled seacarls. 'Hardrada threw away his principality on a single throw of the bones – now our new queen would do the same with all five! You speak of a glorious new Age of Reavers, but tell me this – when have we ever won against the Northlendings? Oh, we might ravage their coasts for a while as our ancestors did, but eventually they'll outlast us, just as they've always done! We've no siegecraft – Northalde is dotted with castles and keeps, and their knights will ride us down once the element of surprise is lost!'

'Your words are cowardly and have the stench of Logi about them.' It was Canute who spoke, his voice reverberating about the crooked hall as he entered the ring. He even towered over Walmond. 'Has the Shield Queen let us down yet? Did we not take the Stormrider, with nary a loss of our own?'

'That victory was thanks to Guldebrand,' spat Walmond. 'Who, it must be said, died in very strange circumstances on his wedding night.'

A storm of mutterings brooded at that. Magnhilda felt her pulse quickening like the beating of the Sky Eagle's wings. She hated this skulduggery. Her brother had convinced her of its necessity, but now he wasn't here it seemed a base way to win a kingdom.

'My husband's death was a tragic accident,' she said, doing her best to feign grievance. 'You would dare insinuate otherwise?'

'Ja, I would,' said Walmond. 'What's more, I say that spellslinger is behind it all. And but lately, I've been hearing that he's your kin! A sorcerer's moll we have for a queen, I say!'

The hall erupted into angry yelling. She had more than twice his number of seacarls with her, and many more shieldmaidens slouched about the hall besides, but by the laws of her people she could not harm Walmond on her holding.

Unless he consented to be harmed.

'SILENCE!' yelled Magnhilda.

It took her a while to get it, for now the throng was more than a hundred strong; her female berserkers had drifted across the gloomy hall to join the argument. As a rule, her women warriors held themselves aloof from the doings of men, but this was getting too interesting to ignore over a horn of mead. Even the skalds had silenced their music to witness what would happen next.

'I don't recall you complaining of Ragnar's services when he served Guldebrand,' said Magnhilda. 'But now it's a woman who commands them, you tell a different tale.'

She held his angry gaze as her shieldmaidens shrieked their defiance.

One thing she had learned from Guldebrand – and

Ragnar – was that Logi's guile could be as effective a weapon as the Skybreaker's mattock.

Come on, take the bait you wretch, she thought as they held each other in a mutual stare of hatred.

'I'll be damned if I'll serve a woman who sits the Stone of Thoros through Logi's works,' Walmond sneered.

Magnhilda didn't need to feign her anger. 'You would dare accuse me of treason? In my own hall?'

A deathly hush had filled it. Walmond paused a few seconds. Then he sealed his fate.

'Ja, I would!'

Magnhilda had to suppress a smile. *Flytings* were always accompanied by copious amounts of mead. Walmond had drunk his fill, and it had clouded his judgement.

'The Magna stands accused of high treason, by one of her own thegns!' boomed Canute, stepping forwards. 'A blood trial must take place here and now. Unless, Walmond, you recant your accusation?'

The gargantuan red-haired warrior eyed Walmond as a fox eyes a hen. The Thegn of Kvenlund blinked as what he had done dawned on him. Colour drained from his face.

Now she had him. If Walmond retracted, his leverage would be gone for good. Word of this affair would spread quickly through the kingdom. What happened next would be down to a battle of pride and fear.

To Walmond's credit, his pride won.

'I do not recant!' he snarled. 'A duel of justice it is!'

'So be it,' declaimed Magnhilda. 'As Magna of the Frozen Wastes, I nominate a champion, as is my right. Canute Mountainside, do you accept to fight on my behalf?'

She fancied Canute's jowls almost rumbled as he cracked a broad grin. 'I do, your majesty.'

The ashen looks on the faces of Walmond's retinue said it all, though their liege put his bravest face on, loudly calling for his mail shirt and target and sword. Canute had not divested himself of arms and armour; he always came prepared.

A fighting space was cleared between the firepit and the Stone of Thoros. Magnhilda took the latter and called for a horn of mead. As word of the pending mighty clash filtered out of the hall, men and women crammed into it. By the time she was ready to call for the fight to commence, hundreds of warriors had gathered, quaffing mead and wagering on its outcome. The skies outside had darkened, and the variegated colours of the soapstone lamps washed the hall in a spectrum of blues, greens and browns.

Magnhilda raised a hand as the two warriors squared off against one another. The skalds stood next to her throne, ready to strike up a martial tune at her command.

'When the music commences, fight!' she intoned, before nodding at the lead skald. The quartet broke into a frenetic ditty on drums and lutes.

With a roar, Walmond charged Canute. Her champion was wielding a great two-handed poleaxe; in his huge scarred arms it looked like a twig.

Walmond was a great warrior. His bulging thews were covered with rings taken from men he had gifted with the sleep of the sword. But Canute was more like a tempest than a mortal man in combat. The sail road and the plough road he had drenched with battle sweat, more times than

Aurgelmir had teeth. Walmond was Kvenlund's greatest champion; Canute was the kingdom's.

He didn't even bother to counter attack, instead keeping Walmond at bay with fearsome swipes of his axe. Walmond changed up his manoeuvres, a desperate light entering his eyes as he tried and failed to find a way past Canute's reach. Walmond was a hulking man, who used his strength to overwhelm opponents. That had served him well enough – until now.

Gasps went up from the crowd as he feinted to Canute's left, before coming at him on the right side and slashing him... across the forearm. Another scar to add to the Mountainside's tally; cutting an arm was as close as you got to harming Canute. He grinned then, his eyes like hoarfrost as he circled around his prey. The skalds took the music up a notch. Magnhilda drank deeply, enjoying the spectacle.

Twice more Canute let him come at him, toying with the thegn as a man toys with a child in play. Another gasp went up as Walmond caught him on the forearm again. This cut was deeper than the last, and Canute did not smile this time.

What he did was counter-attack.

Like a long-threatening storm it broke. Did Thoros yell his encouragement from the firmament as Canute rained down mighty blows upon the hapless thegn? Two strokes deprived Walmond of his shield, another of the arm that held it. He slumped to his knees in shock, raising his sword. Down came the axe again, like Hela's scythe... Walmond was left screaming, two bloody stumps where his arms had been, raised in a pathetic gesture of supplication. Down came the axe again, cleaving Walmond's skull in twain, spraying blood and brains to the high rafters.

The skalds stopped playing abruptly. As the notes died off, Canute kicked Walmond's butchered corpse to the dark earthen floor.

'The Queen is innocent!' he bellowed, twirling his blood-spattered axe about his head for good measure. 'In the eyes of Tyrnor, her trueness has been proven!'

No one dared doubt him.

Canute stroked his forked braids nonchalantly as Walmond's seacarls despondently gathered up his remains. If her champion regretted he wouldn't have the chance to add the thegn's fingerbones to ones from other slain warriors he already had woven into them, he hid it well. He completely ignored his injuries, though blood trickled steadily from them.

'It looks like the thegndom of Kvenlund is vacant once again,' mused Magnhilda. 'Perhaps I should install you in his stead, Canute.'

Her right-hand man shook his head. 'Nay, Your Majesty, my place is here by your side, always.'

The Shield Queen beamed at him. 'It is well,' she said. 'Ho there!' she barked at Walmond's retainers. 'Take this news back with you – the Jarl Vilm I summon here. He shall be raised to Thegn of Kvenlund.'

'A wise choice, my queen,' said Canute after the seacarls had left. 'Vilm has nursed a sore of jealousy ever since Bjorg was made Thegn of Jótlund.'

'I shan't be letting either Bjorg or Vilm off the hook so easily,' said Magnhilda. 'New jarls for both principalities must be created, to act as a check on their power. I will leave you to appoint them – from Scandia. And you will choose berserker women.'

Canute raised a monstrous eyebrow. She knew his loyalty was assured, but even so traditions died hard.

'Well, what did you think?' she asked him, indicating the female acolytes of Tyrnor with a sweep of the arm. 'That I'd be made ruler of all the Frozen Wastes, only to surround myself with men? Nay, Canute – I said this would be a new age, and it will be. Jarlas shall rule where men once did.'

Canute bowed his head. Loyal indeed he was. 'It shall be as you say, gifter of rings.'

'Excellent,' she grinned, beckoning for more mead. 'Now let us have feasting, and music! I would celebrate your victory on behalf of the realm.'

As the skalds played and slaves brought out tables for the laying of provender, Magnhilda threw a leg rakishly over the rough-hewn arm of her throne. It felt good to be Queen – perhaps using skulduggery once in a while was worth it, after all.

Then the North Wind made its presence felt, pushing through gaps between flaps of hide and fur covering the windows. The slaves were lighting braziers, but she felt Thoros touch her with his icy fingers. Somewhere across the deep dark seas, her brother was doing what he'd always done since childhood: making demands of the gods no mortal had a right to make. She'd always been fiercely loyal to him, until she'd been forced by expediency to banish him. Even then, he'd assured her, all would work out for the best. And so it had proved. She had not stopped believing in him.

And in return, he had helped put her on the Stone of Thoros.

But Logi's works were being done. Only a fool could deny that Walmond had a point. And, as the farseers and priests told, the Trickster God gave with one hand and took with six others.

As the rising wind battered the palace, Magnhilda drew her cloak about her more tightly.

CHAPTER 9
THE WYTCH'S COTTAGE

The raw wind cut through his woollen clothes. Numb as his skin was, Vaskrian shivered before its bitter sting. Without horses the way had been slow and painful, sloughing knee-deep through snow for the first couple of days as they left Liathnoc behind. The curious hybrid fortress had appeared to grin at them starkly, mocking their slow progress as they picked their way down from the mountain on which it was built. At least cross country the snow wasn't quite as deep, though it still hampered their progress. The Fernwood lay but a dozen leagues from the castle, but it had taken them several more days to reach it. Now it beckoned to them, a raggedy line of silver-barked trees, their spidery boles giving off the same eerie sheen that dusted the jagged stones of Liathnoc.

As much as he longed for shelter, Vaskrian couldn't say he welcomed the sight. Another spooky forest was the last thing he needed.

He glanced at his companions. Torgun never seemed to

tire, and curiously enough neither did Morcant; the pasty-faced mage skipped along lightly as though on a summer jaunt. That doubtless had something to do with the silver hip flask he sipped from every now and again, though Vaskrian wasn't about to ask him for a swig. Wrackwulf and Joram seemed hardy enough against the cold, and only Braxus appeared to share his discomfort.

A bit of errantry to toughen us both up, he thought wryly. It was still strange thinking of them both as knights, although in truth Braxus was a lord now. Or soon would be, if they succeeded in their next mission.

A renewed flurry of snow-spangled wind had him pulling the hood of his cloak down further. Apart from their winter clothes and bedrolls, they were lightly equipped; no shields or heavy armour, just a mail shirt and a single weapon each, they'd agreed, nothing to draw suspicion or encumber them too much. It felt more like an assassin's mission than a knightly quest, but then that's what you got for taking up with Argolians. Adelko aside, Vaskrian couldn't say he'd met one he liked. How was his old friend doing, he wondered? Probably safe and warm back at the monastery, the lucky git.

'You said these trees are magicked?' He felt nervous enough to ask Morcant the question a second time. The mage had once called the Fernwood home. Back when he'd been understudy to the very enchantress they were trying to kill.

'In a manner of speaking,' replied the mage. 'Back during the Middle Time, before the Long Years' Sundering, my ancestors walked among our Thraxian cousins and retaught them the old ways. Blessed by the Moon Goddess were these woods you now see, and many a fair fruit grew from their boughs. All that was lost, with the coming of the Creed.'

'Pay him no mind,' said Joram gruffly. 'He seeks to entrap you with honeyed words of the Four Old Kingdoms, when our ancestors worshipped angels falsely as gods.'

'Yet you still venerate them today, after your own fashion,' Morcant pointed out. 'Gods, archangels, archdemons – what's in a name, I ask you?'

Without breaking his stride, Joram laid his quarterstaff across Morcant's shoulder. 'Make another such remark and I'll crack your clavicle, mission be damned,' he snarled through gritted teeth.

Morcant rolled his eyes, glancing sidelong at Vaskrian. 'Irritable, isn't he?' But he knew well enough to keep his peace after that.

They trudged on across the bleak bleached landscape, the skies tarnishing gradually as the Fernwood beckoned. Fleeting memories of another forest in another land spirited across the back of Vaskrian's mind; his soul felt like a small weak thing, a toy for gods and demons to be tossed lightly around at will.

By the time they entered the Fernwood, the young knight could feel his body tingling all over.

'Dusk is nigh on us,' said Braxus as they paused to rest a while. 'We should think about making camp now we're under cover of the trees.'

'Not yet,' growled Joram. 'We've a place to be tonight.'

The knights looked at him askance.

'Why else do you think he brought you this way?' chuckled Morcant. 'My old homestead he means to take you to! A wizard's cottage is best of all in a magicked woods. But then, any port in a storm as they say...'

He shot a sly glance at the monk. Joram looked at him as though considering whether to break that clavicle after all, but merely grunted instead.

'These woods are the playpen of elementi after dark,' the adept acknowledged. 'At this time of year, Aethi and Lymphi conjoin, to form devils of ice. Sometimes they catch wayfarers and freeze them to death.'

'Thanks for warning us,' commented Braxus. 'Anything else you'd like to tell us about?'

'Well there's the odd fay,' put in Morcant helpfully. 'And the occasional wadwo, too. Then there are the eidolons, shades of the ice fiends' victims, who must stalk these woods till the Hour of All's Ending.'

'We've faced all of those and more,' said Vaskrian, feigning a courage he still didn't quite feel. Would he ever get used to fighting the spirits of the Other Side, he wondered?

'Aye, but 'tis the Boggarts you've to fear most,' replied Morcant. 'Many in number they are, and no less dangerous than fays or elementi. They come from off the Fernly Marshes, to prowl these woods at night.'

'Boggarts?' Those Vaskrian hadn't heard of before.

'Malicious spirits that take the form of stunted, misshapen men,' supplied Joram. 'A grotesque offshoot of Morcant's ancestors and their accursed witcheries. That is what happens when fays and mortals have unholy union.'

He made the sign, a look of disgust making his rough face look even more brutish.

'Never you fear, my old haunt is deeper into the woods,' said Morcant. 'Its witcheries will protect us, don't you worry!'

Reaching beneath his byrnie, Sir Torgun pulled out the relic given to him by the Argolians. The rood caught the fading light with a shimmer. Joram averted his eyes and muttered what Vaskrian supposed was a prayer; pagan though he was, Morcant looked on the thing with a glimmer of respect.

'This was entrusted to me, by the Grand Master of the Argolian order,' said the knight. 'To ward off demonic attacks. Surely it might help us weather such creatures?'

Morcant shook his head. 'The Cloven-Hoofed God and his servants will that talisman abjure, but not other spirits.'

'It's a relic, not a talisman,' barked Joram, but Morcant ignored him. 'Boggarts and elementi will have no pause before it,' the mage clarified.

'In any case, neither relic nor talisman will keep the cold at bay,' said Braxus. 'Even a sorcerer's cottage sounds like a fine resting place after a week in the wilderness, with naught but woollen cloaks and a pallet for comfort.'

'There is another reason I brought us this way instead of via Port Craek,' said Joram. 'If our plan is to work, this poltroon will need... to collect something.' He eyed the mage with revulsion. Morcant smiled his sly smile.

'You seem to know a lot about yon mage's ways,' said Braxus, looking at the monk askance.

'Of course,' replied Joram. 'Twas I that apprehended him, here in the Fernwood. I know all about this wizard and his ways, as you put it. I also know that his accursed lair is probably our best chance of refuge in this accursed forest.'

'Then let's get a move on,' said Wrackwulf. 'Before the bogmen come and get us!'

Vaskrian had a hard time deciding which he hated more – haunted forests, or the wizards who lived in them.

The temperature dropped steadily as they followed Morcant and Joram deeper into the woods, the iron weather making the trees look more like ice statues than living things. The Wytching Hour was upon them by the time they broke into a clearing; Braxus had heard enough curious sounds over the past few hours to believe all the tales he'd heard about the Fernwood.

He spared a sympathetic glance for Vaskrian. Something strange had happened to the lad back in Tintagael that he would never fully get over; his face was as pale as the snow that cloaked the trees, and it wasn't the cold that made him shiver now. He supposed being cursed by Draugbreath would be little different.

I always hated the mountains, on account of the highlanders. I doubt I'll like moorlands much more, from now on.

What they saw in the clearing could scarcely be described as comforting. A cottage – if you could call it that – constructed of what looked like interlocking boar tusks and aurochs horns, its roof thatched with quilted hides and furs of myriad colours.

'Brother Joram here was quite upset when he found he

couldn't put my old home to the torch!' grinned Morcant. 'But then horn doesn't burn so well, alas.'

Joram cuffed him again.

'No more of your insolence!' he barked. 'Bad enough we have to seek refuge in this accursed place without your running commentary.'

'Yon cottage looks warmer than outdoors, even if it is passing strange,' said Braxus. 'Let's get indoors, for Palom's sake.'

Morcant led them up to the door. Only it wasn't a door, or even a flap of hide. Hanging strings of glass beads of a strange luminous violet barred their way. They didn't shift in the wind, but rather seemed to ripple with a life of their own. Looking at their shifting lustre made Braxus feel dizzy.

'Seems as though your prayers wore off,' said the enchanter, glancing at Joram. 'The entryway has reconstituted itself.'

Joram glowered. 'My prayers were enough to neutralise your sorceries long enough to beat you into submission,' he snarled, menacing the warlock with his quarterstaff again. As Morcant cowered the monk nodded brusquely at the rippling barrier. 'Are you going to part it, or do I have to?'

Morcant spoke a single word in the sorcerer's tongue. The beads rolled upwards like an inverted waterfall, disappearing from sight. The four knights made the sign before following him in; even Sir Wrackwulf found a modicum of piety.

Inside, the cottage seemed much bigger. Braxus found that far more disconcerting than the signs of the almighty struggle that had taken place within. Smashed paraphernalia and the charred remains of what Braxus assumed were tomes and scrolls littered the floor, which appeared to be made of tightly interwoven twigs. Broken furniture and torn hangings completed the spectacle of flotsam and jetsam.

'Looks like the rest of the damage I did has endured,' said Joram, a smug tone entering his voice.

Morcant looked close to tears as he surveyed the ruined lair. 'All those years of homemaking, wrecked by your fanaticism,' he sighed.

'Twas never your home, spy,' said Joram. 'But that of the sorceress we seek to kill.'

'Ah, but it *was* home for a while,' insisted Morcant. 'Nigh ten years I stayed here.'

Braxus almost pitied the mage, who wore a wistful expression now.

'Enough reminiscing,' said Joram. 'Show me what I failed to uncover the last time I was here.'

The sly expression returned to Morcant's face as he incanted a few more words. The twigged floor parted at its centre, revealing another chamber below ground.

'Ingenious,' said Joram. 'A wonder I didn't sniff it out before.'

'We've long learned to counter your sixth sense,' said Morcant. Now it was his turn to sound smug. 'Though perhaps a more devout adept might have seen through my illusion...'

This time, Torgun stepped in and grasped Joram's arm before he could hit Morcant. 'Strike him again, and you'll have me to reckon with,' said the knight. 'I don't like yon mage any more than you do, but I'll not have you chastise an ally, pagan or no.'

Braxus knew all too well how dangerously deceptive the Northlending's mild tone was. Fortunately, so did Joram: his sixth sense worked well enough to tell him that much at least.

Scowling, the monk shook his arm free. 'Let's be about it, then,' he snarled. He went to take the torch Wrackwulf was holding, but the wizard held up a pudgy hand.

'No need for that,' he smiled.

Morcant incanted another spell, and the flames from Wrackwulf's torch suddenly grew long and large, distending with an unnatural life and changing hue rapidly. Two bolts of multicoloured flame shot from the taper: one struck the charcoal in the firepit, igniting it instantly; the other condensed into a blue-white ball of light that hovered just below the rafters, which appeared to be made of some kind of warped animal cartilage.

'Blue light too harsh?' inquired Morcant. 'Perhaps something softer... a pale green maybe. Ah, yes, much better!'

Joram made the sign again. Braxus just felt glad of the warmth that suddenly permeated the cottage.

'I think you can put the torch out now,' said Morcant helpfully. Wrackwulf blinked and complied, shaking his head. 'Bloody sorcerers,' he muttered.

The hidden underchamber was reached by a bendy ladder made of vines, crisscrossed with more boars' tusks.

'I'd best go down with them,' said Braxus to the other knights. 'Make sure they don't kill each other.'

The cellar was little more than a cubby hole, crammed

with rickety shelving made of the same curious twig structure as the floor. These were lined with assorted bottles, jars and other curios. Braxus hacked on the dusty air while Morcant rifled through them, humming and pocketing several vials as he went.

Finally he produced the item he was looking for: a talisman fashioned of brass to resemble a closed eye. Kissing it reverentially, Morcant put it about his neck.

'We're done here,' he said. Joram looked as though he had half a mind to start destroying the contents of the underchamber, but instead merely clambered back up the ladder. Braxus came last, only too glad to get out of its cramped earthen precinct.

Back upstairs the others had made themselves as comfortable as they could, squatting around the fire as they broke out the dried fruits, hard biscuit and cured meats Rowena had provided them with.

'So, are you going to tell us what that charm does?' asked Braxus as they rejoined their comrades.

Morcant smiled and stroked the pendant. 'A year and a day this took me to fashion,' he said. 'For the artificer's craft is a slow and painstaking one. As long as I have this, I can block Abrexta's scrying. It allows me to counter-scry on the move, as it were.'

'You mean she's been tracking us all this time?' gaped Vaskrian.

'Not anymore,' said Morcant. 'Now she can't see where we are.'

'Won't she still know we're coming for her?' asked Vaskrian.

'She won't know anything for sure,' said Joram. 'Not from here on in.'

'All the same, she might prepare the guards at Ongist,' put in Wrackwulf. 'Just in case – she already knows we're on the move.'

'A friend who can help us there I believe I have,' said Morcant. Turning towards the door, he spoke the language of magick again. Only this time it didn't sound as though he were reciting a spell. More as if he was... talking.

A few moments later, a fox appeared at the doorway. To their astonishment, the creature padded into the cottage and over to Morcant, before settling in his lap.

'My familiar,' explained the warlock. 'He'll be our eyes and ears. If Abrexta has prepared any nasty surprises for us, we'll know about it.'

'Now I've seen everything,' said Wrackwulf.

'Much as I hate to admit it, you are proving most useful,' said Joram.

Morcant snickered as he stroked the fox. 'You must be very glad you didn't execute me now.'

Joram's face darkened. 'Your fate has yet to be decided, warlock.'

Braxus decided it was time to intervene, before the monk started hitting their useful ally again.

'You say you were raised in the Island Realms,' he said to Morcant. 'We're headed there afterwards... what can you tell us about your homeland?'

The enchanter stretched his hands towards the smouldering charcoal, rubbing them together gently. The magic light above caught his pale skin and eyes, giving both an appropriately preternatural look.

'An old people we are,' he said. 'Four thousand years have passed since the Moon Goddess arrived on our stricken shores, gifting us with the language of magick. For centuries by then, we had languished through the Age of Darkness, in the aftermath of the Breaking of the World.'

'Caused by the very sorcery you now praise,' interjected Joram.

'No, not caused by the sorcery we use!' said the mage, rare heat entering his voice. ''Twas the Left Hand Way that brought down the wrath of the Unseen, not the clean Right Hand Path.'

'There is no clean path of sorcery,' sneered Joram.

'So you say,' replied Morcant, 'but what of your ways, Argolian? Do you not channel the power of the Unseen yourself when you call on the Second Prophet to aid you?'

'Miracles are not magic,' said Joram stubbornly, though he suddenly seemed troubled.

'So you say,' repeated Morcant, the sly smile crossing his face once more.

'Perhaps it would be best if you let the warlock speak without interruption,' said Torgun. 'He has already alluded to events that foreshadowed our mission, and obviously knows the lands we journey to well.'

In other words, shut up and let the man speak, thought Braxus. He didn't often agree with his love rival, but now was one of those times.

'Ruled we are in tandem, by the Marcher Lords and the

Druiding Council,' Morcant went on. 'The latter is taken from nine of our most powerful magic users. Four druids, four priestesses and one hermaphrodite – the Grand High Druid.'

'Hermaphrodite?' Torgun blinked. Vaskrian and Wrackwulf were already looking bored.

'He means a eunuch,' said Joram, looking suddenly queasy as he chewed on the last of his food. 'They castrate promising young disciples at an early age.'

'We have far more respect for the Feminine Principle than do you,' said Morcant. 'For one who embodies both sexes is blessed in the eyes of the gods.'

'There is but one god,' Joram reminded him.

'Whatever you will,' sighed Morcant. 'But tell me this – why do you Argolians abjure the pleasures of the flesh?'

'To rise above them,' said the monk. 'To transcend the body, that we may tap the powers of the Unseen.'

'That is exactly why we castrate our most promising disciples,' explained Morcant. 'To help them attain just such a state of being.'

'It is a barbaric practice,' said Torgun. 'No civilised people would ever embrace such.'

'Oh, and making war for sport and working your peasantry into early graves to feed a bloated nobility is?' asked Morcant.

'The House of Hamlyn has ever treated its yeomanry justly,' spluttered the knight. So far as Braxus could recall, it was the first time he had ever seen the Northlending look indignant. He was liking the sorcerer more and more.

Morcant cast his sly eyes across Torgun.

'Yes, I'm sure that is true – in your eyes,' smirked the enchanter.

If he keeps this up, Torgun will start hitting him too.

'Never mind all that,' said Braxus. 'What I really want to know is this – how capable are your druids of protecting the Headstone fragment from whoever is seeking it?'

'And do you think it would be better if we took it back to Rima?' added Torgun.

Braxus shook his head. *Typical of the man – always so direct.*

'For seven centuries have we kept it safe, so there's an answer for you!' laughed Morcant. 'A job on your hands you'll have, persuading my masters it would be safer in your keeping.' His face suddenly grew serious. 'But powers stirring there are that we haven't felt in a dozen lifetimes. That is why I was sent here to the mainland. Not able to report back could I, for someone is using powerful counter-scrying.' He paused to reflect. 'Tell the Druiding Council what has happened in person I will, but even then I doubt a risky journey back to your lands will be justified in their eyes,' he said at length. 'Better just to warn the Council of the Nine that an alliance of sorcerers is at work, methinks.'

'It hardly seems worth the bother of going there then,' said Braxus. Already he was thinking about taking his lands back from the highlanders, once they were done with Abrexta. Perhaps it would soon be time to put questing aside.

'Master Joram, what say you?' asked Torgun. 'This is surely something an Argolian is best qualified to decide on.'

Joram frowned. 'I must confess to being in two minds,'

he said. 'I like not the idea of such a cursed thing being kept at the heart of our sacred Order, but nor do I relish the prospect of its being retained by a race of sorcerers. We must look to Reus for divine guidance in the matter.'

In other words, you've no idea. 'In any case, we've a mission to complete and a kingdom to rescue before we even think about going there,' said Braxus, keeping his thoughts to himself. 'I suppose we'd best get some sleep.'

It was only when they stopped talking and broke out their bedrolls that Braxus noticed the sound coming from outside. At first it sounded like the noise hailstones make when they patter against wall and roof. But as he lay down, he fancied he could hear something else, embedded in the wash of sound: a malign whispering, as though sleet and slush could talk.

'The ice fiends won't hurt us while we're in here,' said Morcant, noting his troubled look. 'But that won't stop them cavorting around us all night, to remind us of their presence. Sleep well!' Chuckling to himself, the mage turned over and wrapped himself in his cloak.

Doing likewise, Braxus closed his eyes, and tried not to think about the ethereal blizzard enveloping the cottage.

CHAPTER 10
WATCHING THE WATCHMAN

'You're to apply a dose every morning and every night,' said Adhelina, trying not to show her repugnance. She'd been at the *Paradise* for a fortnight now, but still hadn't got used to the sight of diseased crotches. But then, she supposed, treating whores was a lot better than treating knights and soldiers butchered in war.

Women might get themselves into a sorry state; men could always be counted on to do worse.

Alize grinned. 'Thank you Helene,' she said, getting up from the bench and pulling her smock back down. 'I'd have lost a pretty penny if it wasn't for you and your magicks.'

'Linfrick's Node isn't a magic, it's a medicine,' said Adhelina patiently. 'That'll see to your rash – but those are just symptoms, remember? If you want to be cured of the Nether Itch, you have to drink the tea I gave you every night, too.'

'I will, milady,' said Alize, smiling gratefully and kissing Adhelina on the cheek. 'And I promise I'll only lie with your friend Anupe for the next couple of nights,' she whispered. 'No men, just like you said.'

Adhelina, caught off guard by the affectionate gesture, couldn't help but blush. 'Yes, please see you do,' she smiled. 'Otherwise the treatment will take longer to work – a couple of nights off whoring will cost you a lot less than a couple of months.'

'Yes, Helene, thank you,' repeated Alize, before skipping towards the door. Turning back, she fixed Adhelina with a look that could only be described as brazen. 'You know,' she said, wrapping a bare leg coyly around the door jamb, 'when I'm better, if you want a free one... you've only to ask. You're ever so pretty.'

Adhelina turned from Alize's hot-eyed stare, her blush deepening. 'No really, that... won't be necessary,' she said. Though she could not deny part of her was tempted: watching strangers couple night after night hadn't made her enforced celibacy easier to bear.

Twenty-one summers, and not so much as a kiss, she thought ruefully. *The beautiful heiress withers in bloom.*

She shoved the thought away. Self-pity was unbecoming in a noblewoman, even one in exile.

'Go on,' she said, not unkindly. 'Get thee gone – and behave yourself!'

Alize smiled sweetly, and disappeared out the doorway.

'Next,' called Adhelina, looking wearily around the cramped little room she'd been given to treat the doxies. It was late afternoon already, when she was done she'd fix herself some silverleaf tea and have a proper-

'Well now, it seems as though you're moving up in the world.'

She turned, startled at the male voice. One she recognised. Even before he had pulled down his cowl, she recognised Horskram.

'What in the Known World are you doing here?' she gawped.

'I might ask just the same of you,' said the monk. 'You sent me a letter, remember?'

She'd sent it a week ago, detailing her meeting with Princess Iveline and her governess. She'd credited them with her revelations about Ivon; she couldn't have the monk knowing about her gift. Not yet, at any rate.

'I hardly expected you to come here yourself,' she spluttered.

'Sometimes, Ushira moves in mysterious ways,' said the monk, taking a seat on the bench. She couldn't help but wonder if the celibate monk would do that if he knew who'd been lying on it, and why. 'The Order had to expel a couple of novices for attending the stewes recently – my cover story is that I have been sent to the brothels of Rima, with strict instructions for their owners to turn away Argolians and report them immediately.'

Adhelina couldn't resist laughing at that. 'I'm sure this is one of your most trying missions yet, Master Horskram.'

The adept's lip curled. 'The Order does not typically involve itself in venal sins, disgusting as they are.'

Adhelina's smile hardened into a scowl. 'Perhaps before you judge these poor women, you might want to look at the circumstances into which they were born,' she said. Despite her own reservations about the flesh trade, she had grown fiercely loyal to her patients, many of whom had had little choice in their profession.

'Yes well, you can take that up with our glorious Mother Temple,' said Horskram. 'The perfecthood are supposed to address poverty, not us.'

She caught the edge in his voice. 'Things don't bode well, do they?' she said. 'Between you Argolians and the Temple, I mean.' Flashes of the second sight had come to her; those and the gossip she overheard from the *Paradise*'s patrons had been revealing enough. 'There are rumours of corruption within your Order too, and the Supreme Perfect wants to act on it, so I've heard. I almost didn't send Anupe with the letter, but I had no idea how else to reach you.'

'No, you did the right thing,' said Horskram. 'I'm sorry it took me so long to come here, but as you know we've been... preoccupied.'

A pregnant silence followed.

'So... what will you do?' she asked. 'About this Lord Ivon?'

His reply surprised her. 'Nothing.'

Perhaps the old governess was right about no one taking a woman's word. 'Nothing? But I – she was convinced she saw something...'

She felt a point of tension between them. Was that the monk's own sense probing her for the truth? A strange calmness entered her, neutralising the feeling. The adept continued, oblivious to her slip of the tongue.

'We've begun proceedings against a senior member of our Order,' said Horskram. 'That's enough to stay the King's hand for now. But if I start accusing one of his closest advisers of witchcraft, things are going to get very ugly. Ivon is one of the most influential nobles at court. Your mystic friends may well be right about his being involved, but we simply can't afford to stir things up right now.'

Adhelina blinked. 'But he could be the one behind it all!' she protested. 'If we apprehend him, you might not even have to go to the Pilgrim Kingdoms.'

Horskram fixed her with his steely eyes. 'And if he isn't? If he's just another lieutenant like Andragorix, then we've overplayed our hand – an attack on Ivon will be seen as an attack on the King. That makes him more likely to give in to Cyprian's demands for another Purge.'

Adhelina pressed a clammy hand to her forehead. She felt dizzy. Pangonian politics made her sick. 'So once again we have to hold back, because of your precious Order and its reputation,' she said.

'Our precious Order has guarded the Known World from the very calamity we are trying to avert, for half a millennium,' Horskram reminded her. 'And yes, it has become corrupted from within. That's why we need time to put our own house in order! Trust me, Ivon and whoever else may be plotting this thing would love nothing more than to see the Argolians finished.'

Adhelina sat down on a crooked stool next to her table of medicines. *The mystic woman says I'm supposed to help him, even when he doesn't realise it,* she thought. *But how, exactly?*

'So what do you suggest we do?' she asked at length.

'First, I want more details. Your letter was brief. Tell me more about the King's niece and her guardian.'

Cautiously Adhelina went over her story, leaving out the

part about her own gift. She could feel the adept's psyche brushing against hers throughout – but she was somehow able to distract it. Without his even knowing.

'We've long been aware of these mystics,' said Horskram after she was done. 'They abound in the Sassanian realms in particular. And there is perhaps some truth in what they say, about the sight being women's gift as the sense is men's. But neither is an exact science – Reus knows, ours has been scrambled for long enough now!'

'All right then – what's the plan?'

'We'll bide our time for now,' said Horskram. 'I'll inform Hannequin – I've already disclosed the contents of your letter. We'll keep an eye on Lord Ivon and his cronies while Johann's trial plays out. When the time is right, the Grand Master will move against him. In the meantime, our mission continues as planned – Adelko and I will travel to the Pilgrim Kingdoms. You may as well join us as far as Panya, I don't think Rima is safe for you any more. Your original plan to get to the Empire seems as good as any to me.'

Now was the time to put the first part of her plan into action, Adhelina decided.

'We're coming with you all the way to Ushalayim,' she said, praying the sight would keep working for her. 'Before I left the palace, I mentioned that the Empire was my destination. I still don't trust the King – I wouldn't put it past him to have sent orders ahead to the Queen of Mercadia to have me arrested if I show up at Panya.'

Horskram frowned, peering at her intently. Once again she felt their psyches collide... before parting again gently.

'What makes you think he'd go to that length?'

'The tidy ransom he believes I'm worth to the Vorstlend-ings,' said Adhelina, knowing this part of her dissimulation was true enough. 'He knows I'm high-born, and probably regrets letting me slip through his fingers. A city-wide search would take a lot of effort, I'm guessing that's why he hasn't sanctioned it. A single messenger sent south, on the other hand... From what I know of the local geography, Panya is a major stopover on the sea trading routes heading out of Montrevellyn. He'll have anticipated us.'

'Your lore does you credit, but we're heading to Panya ourselves,' Horskram pointed out. But he appeared to believe her story.

'Of course we are, but this way I don't have to set foot in the city. If I stay amidships, there's far less chance of being taken by Queen Edelmira's soldiers at Panya.'

Horskram scratched his beard as he thought about it. He wasn't picking up on her lies; so far her plan was working.

'It seems a roundabout way to avoid a potential rather than an actual risk,' he mused. 'And the Pilgrim Kingdoms aren't safe – they're shortly to be at war. I don't like the idea of it.'

'Oh, we won't stay there over long,' said Adhelina, trying to sound confident. 'I just want to take the roundabout way, as you put it, to throw Carolus off the scent. Once we reach the Pilgrim Kingdoms, we'll take a ship from the Holy City to Khronos in the Empire. My guess is the King will never think to send word of me to the King of Ushalayim.'

Horskram cocked his head. 'Ingenious,' he said at last. 'You are as subtle in your thinking as an Argolian. Would that you had been born a man.'

Adhelina didn't return his half smile. *Iveline's governess was right about him not respecting women enough,* she thought. *Born a man, indeed!*

'Very well,' said Horskram at last. 'I take it your two companions won't object?'

'They are both accustomed to long journeys, and longer detours,' said Adhelina firmly. 'You leave me to worry about them.'

'Fine, but make sure you keep an eye on both of them, especially that wilful Harijan,' said Horskram as he rose to leave. 'Where are they now?'

'I'd imagine Anupe's enjoying the company of my last patient,' said Adhelina. 'As for Hettie, she's probably in the common room, playing cards.'

Horskram arched an eyebrow. '*Cards?*"

Hettie surveyed the woodblock carvings in her hands, then flicked her gaze sidelong at her two opponents. It was a few hours before the jongleurs were due to start playing – that should give her time to fleece them some more.

Cards. What a wonderful invention! Another of those clever things to come out of the Empire: constructed from a more refined version of parchment called *paper*, the intricately decorated things had been something of a revelation. She'd never seen the point in playing dice. All down to random chance, how could you have any control over such a game?

But cards, now that was a different matter.

When it was her turn, she laid down the King of Gauntlets, the Queen of Swords, and the Knave of Souls with a flourish.

'Full run,' she smiled, before clawing the pile of coins in the middle of the table towards her. 'Another round, ladies?'

'Not a chance,' said Tyla, throwing down her hand in frustration. 'I'll have to perform all night just to win back what I've lost.'

'Same here,' muttered Reia, her corn-yellow curls waving as she shook her head. 'I don't know how you do it, Etta.'

'It's all about having an eye for detail and a good memory,' grinned the damsel. 'A touch of mathematics helps, too – I've my mistress Helene to thank for that much at least.'

You also need to know how to lie and bluff like the Fallen Angel, she added silently. *I've had a fair bit of practice at that this past year.*

'I wish I'd never shown you how to play,' said Tyla dolefully, before draining her winecup.

'Yes, I think you ought to cover my losses just for that, Tyla!' said Reia, downing her own.

Hettie sat back contentedly and put the last of the silverweed Adhelina had given her into one of those new-fangled pipe things she'd purchased with her winnings. A lot of the girls smoked something called *shisham*, imported from the hot south, but she didn't like it – too heavy by far. Adhelina had also warned her it was more addictive than silverweed.

The girls were moving about the taproom now, lighting the red lanterns and scented candles as nightfall approached. Much as it amazed her, Hettie had actually come to like this place. The fornicating did take some getting used to – but then the great hall of Graukolos had hardly been much different on feasting days, when the knights got really drunk and paired off with the serving wenches.

And at least in this place, the women were sure of some reward for their services. Though she hardly approved of such licentiousness, Hettie had to admit she felt a lot more comfortable at the *Scarlet Paradise* than she ever had at the Riman court.

Such strange tides Ushira carries us on, she thought as a passing girl refilled her winecup. *If only Adhelina and I could sail them in better spirits.*

Things had remained tense between the pair of them. They shared a room in the garret of the building, but didn't speak much. Her mistress was often tired; Hettie helped out where she could, but there was only so much she could do. And when Adhelina was in one of her irritable moods, she was best avoided altogether.

The gold-painted doors of the *Paradise* yawned open to admit the first lechers of the day. Hettie surveyed the two young merchants distastefully, but her curiosity was piqued: their frock coats and broad-brimmed hats marked them out as citizens of the Empire. Those given rare special dispensation to leave their country, to trade with the outside world.

They must be from Khronos, she thought. *The very place we're trying to get to – unless this blasted Wyrd thing says otherwise.* Adhelina had already hinted that their trip to the Empire might be delayed, but refused to elaborate. That had annoyed Hettie even more: it had been her bloody idea to go there in the first place, now she was on about this sight business and having a higher purpose.

The two merchants sat down and loudly called for girls and drink. Hettie had a mind to challenge them to a game – it was imperial merchants who'd introduced cards to Rima, so they'd certainly know how to play. She'd love to empty their purses before they could pay for any girls – that would wipe the lecherous smiles off their faces.

She was just considering that when she caught sight of a hooded figure dressed in grey making its way swiftly down the steps from the rooms upstairs. At first she thought it must be the silverweed. An Argolian? Enjoying the services of a brothel? Now she'd seen it all – she must have been too engrossed in her game to notice him come in.

'They sometimes come around here,' said Tyla. 'Offering money to the madames to turn away stray novices.'

'That, and turn them in,' sniggered Reia. 'Marianne makes good money off the Order, she does!'

Hettie smiled perfunctorily. The monk was moving swiftly, but she recognised that confident gait anywhere.

So Master Horskram did get our message, she thought.

The adept left just as a gaggle of drunken craftsmen pushed their way in. She spotted Adhelina at the top of the stairwell, and rose to go and meet her.

She was halfway to the stairs when one of the new arrivals mistook her for a whore. It was a mistake he would soon regret making.

'Hey, come 'ere!' the craftsman bellowed, grabbing her by the arm. 'Ow much to take me in yer mouth, sweetheart?'

Hettie favoured him with a coy smile. Delicately, she removed her arm from his grip.

She turned to address a passing serving girl carrying a platter with a jug of wine on it.

'Do you mind if I borrow this?' she asked. Without waiting for an answer, she turned and emptied the contents over the offending craftsman.

The rising laughter faded as he stepped towards her angrily, fists bunched. Taking a step back, Hettie swung the pitcher. With a yowl the craftsman went down, clutching a bleeding forehead. His friend made to intervene, but suddenly found Anupe pressing a dirk to his neck.

'This lady is – how do you put it? – not for sale,' said the warrior woman.

'All right, that's enough!' yelled Marianne, bustling over. 'You bloody craftsmen are all the same, save up your wages so you can come here once a month, and think you own the place! There's rules of decorum to be observed in the *Paradise*, see? You order *before* you touch – got that?'

The fierce madame cowed the craftsmen into quiescence. Her fists were the size of her heaving breasts, and Reus knew those were big enough. No one ever dared ask if Marianne had once been for sale herself, and Hettie didn't care to either.

Turning to Hettie she scowled. 'As for you, missie, can't have you getting in the way o' business – I told you, after dark you have to go upstairs.'

'I was just leaving,' replied Hettie, putting the pitcher down and heading over to the stairs.

'And tell Helene to get down here,' bellowed Marianne

after her. 'She'll have to patch up this idiot, can't have him bleeding all over my girls, now can I?'

Adhelina had seen it all and already come downstairs. She looked irate, as usual.

'For heaven's sake, Hettie!' she said in their native tongue. 'I've just come off shift, and now I have to give first aid to this buffoon. Thanks a lot.'

'My pleasure,' replied Hettie sarcastically, drawing on her pipe insouciantly.

Adhelina shot her a venomous glare, before helping the injured craftsman into a chair. His fellows were leering at her in admiration.

'Don't even think about it,' warned Marianne. 'She's not on offer either.'

'So what did our noble leader have to say?' asked Hettie, still speaking in Vorstlending.

'The plan remains the same. We winter it out here and leave in spring with the monks,' replied Adhelina, while tending the craftsman's wound. 'We're going all the way to Ushalayim with them. I've persuaded him we're detouring to throw the King off our scent, but we'll find our own lodgings once we get there and help him however we can.'

'I still think this thing about you having a higher destiny is nonsense,' said Hettie.

'Oh really?' replied Adhelina, without looking up from her patient. 'I'd have thought you'd welcome a new adventure. After all, you're becoming quite the brawler and gambler of late – that's the second man you've clobbered since we got here.'

'Don't judge me, Adhelina,' said Hettie. 'You're the one

who brought us to this pass in the first place. And I don't spend half my days with my head up a whore's skirt.'

The last jibe was unfair, and she regretted it instantly. But words once spoken couldn't be unsaid. Adhelina tensed momentarily as she bent to dress the craftsman's wound. Her face flushed scarlet beneath her shawl.

'Why don't you go upstairs and amuse yourself?' she said coldly, as she mastered her anger. 'Leave me to clean up the mess you've made.'

'Sounds like an excellent plan,' said Hettie, before turning on her heel and stomping over to the stairway.

From where she sat with Alize on her lap, Anupe watched the two damsels bicker it out. She turned to kiss the doxy full on the lips, and laughed.

'Those two really need to get a room,' said the Harijan.

'But they already have a room,' grinned Alize.

'Not quite what I meant,' said Anupe, leaning in to kiss her again.

CHAPTER 11
A COLD WELCOME

I t was a relief to be released from the smothering grip of the frosted trees. Sir Vaskrian inhaled the icy air, caring little for the renewed cold as the wilderness opened up before them again. Ahead was the River Fern, a silvery streak petrified by winter's touch; beyond that the marsh-lands stretched off into the gloom, covered in a wreathy blanket of sylvan fog.

'Give the Fernlies a wide berth we will,' said Morcant. 'We'll leave them on our right and strike north-west from here.'

Joram nodded. 'That's our way onwards in any case,' he said. 'We've at least two dozen leagues to cover before we reach the Royne. Once we cross that, we'll be in enemy territory.'

Sir Torgun flicked a glance up at the pewter skies. 'We've barely an hour before it gets dark,' he murmured. 'Should we risk crossing now, or wait till tomorrow?'

Morcant smiled. 'Surely the bold knight is not afraid?' he said.

Torgun frowned at him. 'I quail before no danger, but foolhardiness and courage are not the same things, wizard.'

'For once I agree with yon sorcerer,' said Joram. 'If we bed down at the forest fringes, we'll be targets for the Boggarts. You don't want to meet them, trust me!'

Vaskrian suppressed a shudder. It had been two days since they'd left the cottage behind; their second night in the forest had been a bleak one, spent in a shallow cave. At least the ice fiends hadn't returned to torment them, but he'd heard something else... Strange mutterings and laughter. It reminded him of Tintagael, though it was different too somehow. That place had felt like they'd been the intruders; this felt more the other way around, as though the denizens of the Other Side were invading their realm.

'I think I agree,' said Vaskrian. 'Let's just put these bloody woods behind us!'

Another hour brought them to the Fern. Its banks tumbled pell-mell towards the glassy river, its frozen sluices looking like the design of some mad architect in the wakening starlight. The clouds had parted somewhat, Vaskrian supposed that would help them.

'Frozen solid is the river at this time of year,' said Morcant. 'We should be able to cross on foot easily enough.'

The mage activated another one of his fireballs. Vaskrian

did not appreciate the lugubrious mauve tinge he favoured this time. The darkness closed about the fringes of its light, like a living thing that meant them no good.

'Let's not tarry then,' said Wrackwulf. 'The sooner we're across, the better I shall like it!'

The way was slow, for the slippery surface was treacherous. Only Morcant seemed to have no trouble, continuing to skip lightly as though on a pleasure trip to fayre. They were about halfway across, and stars were ghosting a firmament gradually revealed by retreating clouds, when the strange figures appeared. They were feminine, and seemed to move in the blinking of an eye to a different place from where they had previously stood every few seconds; it looked to Vaskrian as though they were fashioned of starlight.

They could even have been called beautiful... but beautiful could mean deadly, too.

'The Handmaidens of Orcus come to make sport,' breathed Morcant, 'as is their wont in dead of winter!'

'Who in the Known World is Orcus?' asked Vaskrian, knowing already that he didn't want to know.

'Tis the name paganers give to Azrael,' said Joram. 'Yon figures you see are ghosts of women bound to the Angel of Death. They were concubines in the time of Thraxingatorix, sent to him as dowry by all the lords of the realm, when he attempted to unify the Four Old Kingdoms a thousand years ago. The ship bearing the maidens foundered, so the legend goes, and with it the High King's attempts to create a single kingdom.'

'Their shades are doomed to linger here as brides of

death, till the Hour of All's Ending,' added Morcant, taking an unwholesome relish in his dramatic turn of phrase.

Peering through the gloom, Vaskrian saw that the shimmering forms of damsels had stopped disappearing and reappearing, and begun to glide gently to and fro across the frozen Fern, ghostly water dripping from their fine apparel. Were they... dancing? Yes, they even had dance partners too, skeletal figures that glimmered with a lucent fire, their mouths agape in a perpetual grin as they cavorted with the captive souls.

Joram began intoning a prayer. Vaskrian wasn't sure, but it sounded like the same one he'd heard Horskram and Adelko use. The words always comforted him when those two uttered them; but somehow in Joram's mouth they sounded harsh and ugly.

He felt his entrails stiffen as they continued to trudge across the river, now passing among the whirling dancers, who were becoming ever more frenetic in their diurnal dance of death. Pair by pair, the ghostly troupe broke off and turned to look at the travellers as they passed by. Sussurant words drifted across the ice to encircle them giddily:

So far have you come, so weary ye are!
   Forsake further steps and rest yourselves here!
   After life's fitful fever, sleep thee well!
   After life's trial and error, rest thee here!

. . .

'Pay them no mind,' said Morcant. 'They seek to entrap you with glamoured words.'

'I've done this before,' hissed Vaskrian. 'You don't need to tell me that!'

Glancing sidelong at the other knights, he saw the struggle written plain on their faces. They hadn't survived Tintagael, perhaps that made them more vulnerable.

'He's right,' said the young knight, suddenly feeling sure of himself. 'They can't force you to do anything unless you surrender your will to them!'

Sir Torgun clutched the Circifix of St Argo. 'The lad is right,' he said, his voice cracking. 'Push on, for Palom's sake!'

A cold sere wind began to strike up from the direction of the marshes, harrowing up the hoarfrost and transforming it into a flurry of lambent dust. Gradually the ghostly dancers began to diminish, their shapes breaking up as if at the rising wind's touch.

The last of them had just disappeared when they began to hear laughter.

'What in the Redeemer's name is that?' asked Braxus, suddenly finding his piety again.

Joram gave no answer, but continued to recite his psalm.

'Taken an interest in us the Boggarts have,' said Morcant, his voice tinged with fear now. 'They're coming to pay us a visit from the marshes.'

'I thought you said we should press on to avoid them!' cried Braxus.

'I didn't say they wouldn't find us anyway,' replied Morcant. 'At least this way, a chance to outmanoeuvre them we have. If not, I can always try talking to them.'

'In other words,' said Wrackwulf, 'we'd better start moving faster.'

As best as they could they marched across the ice, slipping and stumbling as they went. At least they were more used to walking on it by now, but the way was still slower than Vaskrian would have liked. He felt his hackles rise in time to the keening wind; soon its rawness had him feeling like a ghost himself. At last they could see it: the river's edge beckoning to them tantalisingly, beneath an obsidian sky punctuated only by moon and stars. The clouds seemed to have parted unnaturally quickly.

'We're nearly there!' cried Torgun.

But nearly there wasn't nearly good enough. Gradually more shapes began to be discernible; shadowy figures visible only by pale lantern eyes that gleamed malevolently. They were small, about half the size of a man, and shuffled towards them with an ambling gait that seemed unnaturally fast.

In seemingly no time at all, they were surrounded by a ring of the creatures.

Morcant called out something in a strange tongue. Vaskrian wasn't sure if it was the magic language or some other speech. Whatever it was, the Boggarts seemed unimpressed. Malicious snickers cut across the sound of the snapping wind. They appeared to be dressed in hooded cloaks, but walked barefoot across the ice; straggly beards that looked to be made of twisted metal glinted in the baleful light of their eyes.

Taking them in, Vaskrian drew himself up and sneered.

After everything we've been through, that's the best this land can throw at us?

The wizened creatures were still snickering. Exchanging amused glances with the other knights, Vaskrian found himself chuckling too.

Such ridiculous creatures, he thought. *Can Morcant and Joram really be scared of this lot?*

His chuckling deepened into laughter. The three knights joined him, giving vent to belly laughs of their own.

Feeling his mirth intensify, Vaskrian bent over double. He laughed harder and harder.

And found he could not stop.

The four of them were still writhing around on the ice laughing when the ice fiends coalesced around them. Through his painful gut spasms, Vaskrian was dimly aware that the Boggarts had vanished; but thought of the creatures remained imprinted on his mind, and he couldn't stop laughing.

What's so blasted funny? he had presence of mind enough to ask himself. Next to him Wrackwulf was slapping the ice as though he'd just seen the best jester in the land perform; even stoical Torgun roared with mirth, pointing up at the uncaring skies, as though the heavens concealed some great cosmic joke. Braxus just hugged himself, rocking back and forth as he chuckled manically.

Morcant incanted words of power as the ice fiends tore into them, and Joram switched prayers. Through tears,

Vaskrian could make out the swirling forms of blue tornadoes, dark slits for eyes above gaping maws that appeared lined with icicles.

He heard his companions joining their screams to his as an ice fiend enveloped him...

Vaskrian felt it as a point of warmth at the centre of his chest, growing steadily to spread across his entire body. The gelid apparition swirling about him suddenly paused, seeming to undulate in the darkness. Through his painful spasms, the young knight reached for the amulet about his neck, pulling it from beneath his mail shirt. The pendant the Earth Witch had gifted him glowed with a shivery light of its own. He was dimly aware of a figure dashing over towards him. Ripping the talisman from Vaskrian's neck, Morcant shouted more words in the language of magick. The writhing devils swirled about them, breaking off from their depredations.

Vaskrian felt the horrid laughter begin to subside as he watched the ice fiends break up. Cold water splashed about them in cascades, as vortices of air disappeared up into the night. Morcant continued to incant his spell, the words jarring with Joram's prayer. As the last of the laughter ebbed out of his body, the young knight felt himself slipping over the edge of a precipice, tumbling headlong into a yawning chasm that swallowed him up...

He awoke to an aching in his guts. Being punched in the stomach by a gauntleted knight couldn't hurt so much.

Wincing, he sat up. Joram and Morcant were huddled beside a brazier, which appeared to burn with a luminous green light. The pair of them were arguing, though they were speaking too fast in Decorlangue for Vaskrian to follow. At the wizard's skirts, his fox familiar lay, impassively soaking up the ethereal heat.

Glancing about him, Vaskrian saw his companions lying nearby. All three appeared to be out cold. A look upwards told him it was well past the Wytching Hour.

'Ah, awake you are,' said Morcant, breaking off his argument as he noticed Vaskrian. Reaching into the folds of his robes, he produced the periapt he'd taken from him. The light that transfused it had subsided. 'Here, you'd best take this back – a potent talisman that! You must have sorcerous friends in very high places.'

Joram favoured Vaskrian with a dark stare as he sheepishly took the pendant.

'That piece has spirits of air and water bound to it,' Morcant went on, enjoying the monk's ire. 'Able to use it I was, to dispel yon ice fiends.'

'The prayers of my Order would have accomplished the same thing, given time,' said Joram, 'as I was saying.'

'Given time, our four laughing friends would have been turned into statues of ice,' Morcant replied with a shrug.

'What happened to us?' asked Vaskrian. Groans told him the other knights were beginning to stir.

'A Boggart's power lies in its ability to enchant,' explained Joram. 'It made you as helpless children, to be left as prey for the other denizens of this land – had we not intervened.'

'So much for the healing power of laughter,' said Wrack-wulf gloomily. 'Ye Almighty! I feel as though I've been kicked in the ribs by a stallion.'

'Far from the worst thing that could have happened to you,' said Morcant. 'Alive and well, my brave knights? Best press on we had, in that case – while still we can...'

They walked for hours, making hard but steady progress against a rising wintry sun. Only when they had left the river and marshes far behind did Joram call a halt, stopping at a burned-out manor house, its charred beams disguised by a blanket of white.

'This demesne belonged to a loyalist knight in service to Lord Máedóc of Rathlain,' said the monk. 'The cellars should shelter us well enough.'

'Fine lodgings for questing knights,' commented Braxus dryly.

'It's better than anything we've had since the warlock's cottage,' put in Wrackwulf. 'It'll do nicely.'

The band made their way down a flight of rickety wooden steps. The cellar was dusty but warm enough. Braxus grinned as he eyed the wine rack, half-full of bottles.

'Looks like yon knight had a taste for imports,' he grinned, hefting a bottle of ruby red liquid in his hand. 'Perhaps you're right after all, Wrackwulf.'

'Well, don't just stand there beaming at it,' said the free-lancer. 'Uncork the thing and pass it round!'

Braxus complied gladly. But by the time his turn at the

bottle came, Vaskrian was curled up in the corner on his bedroll, fast asleep.

That night he dreamed of strange watery kingdoms, where hybrid fish-men warred against horrid toad-like creatures in the salty deeps of the sea. Spirits of air and water swirled about them, conjoining around him and keeping the ocean's cold embrace at bay.

CHAPTER 12
A REFUGE FOR ROYAL FUGITIVES

'He seduced my Lyra an' got 'er with child, I'll be damned if I'm a givin' 'im back 'is cow!' spluttered Arro the carpenter.

'Ye've no right comin' to my land in dead of night and stealin' er from me!' shot back Ulfrich the husbandman.

'Stealin' yer cow is it? Ye stole me daughter's maiden-hood, ye filthy swyver!'

Sir Manfry sighed and shifted his weight in the creaking pinewood chair. Dealing with the commoners was a tedious business, but part of his duties.

'Enough!' said the vassal, raising a hand for silence. 'As far as I can see, you're jolly well both at fault. Arro, you're to return Ulfrich his property directly. Ulfrich, you're to wed Arro's daughter and make an honest woman of her. I'll send a perfect over to perform the ceremony, as soon as the latest snows stop falling.'

He fixed them both with a stern gaze, though in truth he

was fond of his churls – almost as fond as he was of his horses.

'That should be an end of the matter,' he said, not unkindly. 'Now begone with you – I've other things to attend to.'

The peasants tugged their forelocks and exited the cramped hall, mollified if not exactly pleased.

Princess Hjala stepped from the corner.

'If only my brother ruled the kingdom as wisely as you do your demesne, Sir Manfry,' she said with a wry smile.

'Yes well, good sort, His Royal Highness,' hedged the vassal. 'Just fallen in with a bad crowd, is all. That Lorthar for one – never did like the man, I must say.'

Hjala's lip curled. 'As long as he continues to proclaim my brother a warrior-king foretold in scripture, I think Wolfram will like him well enough.'

Manfry sighed as he got to his feet. Beckoning to his nephew, he ordered the page boy to bring wine. He'd been sheltering the princess and her aunt and brother for weeks now. Prince Wolfram had put a warrant out for their arrest; the trio had taken up refuge in Stromlund, where Princess Walsa's son Wilfred ruled in place of his mad father Willeng. Ordinarily, Wilfred would have turned them in straight away – he held lands in the King's Dominions, and it behoved a baron to be loyal. But kinship ties were strong among Northlendings, even in the heart of the realm, and Wilfred had been unable to do it. Instead he had packed them off to Manfry's demesne, where they could keep a low profile, allowing Wilfred to feign ignorance of their whereabouts. With Northalde still busy consolidating after a war, the crown simply did not have the resources to order a full-scale search of the jarldom to test the truth of his words.

That was what they had gambled on anyway, and so it had proved. All the same, Manfry had been none too pleased about the situation: it simply wasn't proper. He'd even dared to tell his royal guests so, with the greatest respect. Hjala had rewarded him for his candour with a little of her own, and told Manfry about his Uncle Horskram and the dear old fellow's secret mission. Manfry hadn't seen his Argolian relation since they'd celebrated winning the war against Thule months ago, though at the time he'd fathomed his uncle was about some dashed dangerous business. Even with Hjala explaining it to him, Manfry understood little of such matters, but the gravity of the tale had been enough to silence him. For the time being.

'Wolfram is hell-bent on raising an army to attack Thraxia,' Hjala went on. 'When what he should be doing is preparing the coastal defences against a Northland attack.'

'Well, we've not heard a peep out of our barbarian cousins in the last month or two,' said Manfry. 'That's something at least.'

He was normally optimistic about everything, but in this case he found it hard to convince even himself that all would be well. Little news had come out of the north-east since the Valhalla had frozen over, but before then merchantmen docking at Urring and Strongholm had brought rumours of a vast fleet being constructed outside Landarök.

Hjala was shaking her head.

'It's dead of winter and that's why we've heard naught, Sir Manfry,' she said. 'Have you spoken to my cousin of late?'

Manfry bit his lip. Blasted woman, she was deucedly persistent!

'Lord Wilfred is in a precarious position, and has told me not to communicate with him unless it's a dire emergency,' he hedged. 'The way he sees it, the less he knows about your doings, the better.'

He still didn't like the situation. If Prince Wolfram found out they were hiding fugitives from the Regent's justice, he might attaint Wilfred and strip Manfry of his lands. He might even relieve him of his head, too – a lowly vassal conspiring in the great games of high nobles, it was bad form, very bad form indeed. It didn't help matters that Lord Ulnor himself was a scion of Canwolde. Walsa had married into their house, so they didn't share blood ties, but her son Wilfred was another matter – Manfry hated to think of his liege being torn between such influential relatives.

All in all, it was a right bally mess they were in.

'This is most irregular, ma'am, most irregular,' he said, screwing up his courage to protest again. 'To put your cousin Wilfred in this plight, it really is-'

'Dammit man, we've told you already what's at stake,' flared Hjala, losing her composure. 'Threats to the realm – and all other realms of the Free Kingdoms – are multiplying! This Sea Wizard is behind the invasion plan, just as he was behind Thule's uprising. Horskram says Ragnar but serves an even darker master – if your uncle's mission is not to be in vain, we must bring the country to its senses! On top of that, we've heard nothing from Sir Wolmar in months –

you'll recall father sent my cousin as an emissary to Pangonia, to warn the King there of this frightful business. Well it
looks as though he's vanished into thin air. Suspicious, don't
you think?'

Manfry frowned at that, not wanting to meet her eye.
'Meaning no disrespect, Your Highness, but young Sir
Wolmar was forever getting himself into trouble. Who's to
say he didn't simply make some powerful enemies at the
Riman court?' He didn't dare give voice to his final thought
on the matter; even now, it wouldn't do to criticise the blood
royal.

Hjala sighed heavily. 'You may well be right about my
cousin,' she allowed. 'Luviah knows, Sir Wolmar has never
been an easy man to love. But whatever the cause of his
disappearance, it doesn't look as though we can count on
the Pangonians for help in this business any time soon –
King Carolus evidently has his mind bent on his own affairs
of state.' Stepping closer, she grasped his wrist. 'Sir Manfry,
the north *must* hold. If Northalde goes to war against
Thraxia, we'll be divided and weakened. That can only play
to Ragnar's hand – and strengthen the alliance he serves.
Next to that, domestic intrigue and politics are but a trifling
game.'

Manfry was about to reply when there came a banging
on the door. A servant scurried to open it. In strode
Thorsvald, followed by a flurry of snowflakes. He might be
on the wrong side of the law, but he was still a fine man –
perhaps the best Sealord the realm had seen in generations.
Until his brother Wolfram had attainted him, that was.

'Your Royal Highness,' said Manfry, taking a knee dutifully. He might not like his predicament, but protocol was protocol.

'Up, up,' said Thorsvald impatiently. 'I've news for you both. Where's Aunt Walsa?'

'Taking a nap,' said his sister. 'You know how she hates the cold.'

'Well, she can hear it from you later in that case,' said Thorsvald, taking a pewter goblet from Manfry's nephew. It was poor cup for a prince, even an attainted one, but then the splendour of the palace was far away. Perhaps never to be regained.

'Please, sire, take a seat,' said Manfry, motioning towards the crooked feasting table. 'You must be tired after your journey.'

'Kolinde is not so far to travel, even in winter,' said Thorsvald, as the three of them sat down on a bench. Manfry's lands weren't far from the fishing village, making them ideally positioned for Thorsvald's mission.

'More to the point, did you manage to make contact?' asked Hjala. Her pale face was intent in the wan torchlight.

Thorsvald flicked a glance in the direction of the servants and page boy. Manfry dismissed them with a wave of the hand.

'Aye, I did,' said Thorsvald, half emptying his cup in a single draught. 'Vaska and his men managed to sail north as far as the ices without being intercepted. He lost half his men on the walk across the Valhalla, but they got to Landarök. They arrived back in Kolinde a week ago. It's true what the merchants at port were saying – never a vaster fleet was seen in the Frozen Wastes since Ryøskil. The Magna must have had them working deep into winter – they'll resume work in spring, and it won't be long before they're ready to sail.'

'How many?'

'Vaska said they couldn't get too close without being spotted, but he reckons at least a hundred, possibly more. Fifty of those he saw under construction were longships of a great size, too.'

Manfry let a whistle escape his bearded lips. 'Well the blasted buggers really do mean business, don't they?'

'Now I trust you see my point, Sir Manfry,' said Hjala. 'We must make contact with Strongholm.'

'Wolfram will refuse to believe it,' said Thorsvald dolefully. 'He thinks me a traitor, and will never take the word of my men – they've already risked their necks by making contact with me.'

'Your sailors were ever loyal for just reason,' said Hjala. 'But it isn't Wolfram I was thinking of. We must tell Ulnor of Vaska's findings.'

Both men looked at her in surprise.

'Ulnor?' gaped Thorsvald. 'But he's the architect of all this.'

'Not quite,' put in Hjala. 'If the rumours we've heard from the palace are true, this invasion of Thraxia was Wolfram's idea. Ulnor is misguided and loath to relinquish power,' said Hjala. 'But he is loyal to the realm and sensible enough. He wanted to secure the line of succession, and retain his influence at court – I doubt he ever intended to launch a war to the west. That idea has all the hallmarks of our hothead brother.'

'That's probably true enough, but it throws up another problem if it is.'

All three turned to look at the speaker. Lady Walsa came shuffling down the steps from the upper floor of the manor house.

'Thought you were asleep, aunt,' said Hjala with another wry smile.

'You didn't think I'd miss this, did you?' said the old harridan tartly. 'What I've just heard is the best bit of gossip we've had around here for weeks.'

Approaching the table, she cupped Manfry's face. 'Just as handsome as his uncle,' she purred. Manfry flushed deeply. Thank bloody Palom his wife wasn't around. She'd passed of the ague a month ago. He'd barely had time to mourn her, what with all this wretched nonsense.

Hjala cleared her throat pointedly. 'You were saying?'

'If Wolfram really has gone his own way,' said Walsa, taking a seat and helping herself to some wine, 'it means Ulnor can't control his puppet regent as easily as he thought. That will make it harder for the Royal Seneschal to convince Wolfram to change his plans.'

Hjala made a disgusted noise. Manfry guessed it wasn't his vinegary wine, though his provender fell far short of what such illustrious guests were used to. 'I said no good would come of that greybeard's meddling,' said the princess.

'Well, we had our chance to stop him and he outfooted us,' said Walsa. 'Now by the sounds of it, Wolfram has outfooted him.' She surveyed them all over the rim of her winecup. 'The question is, what do we do about it?'

Thorsvald's brow furrowed in consternation. 'My brother

has ever craved glory,' he said at last. 'He sorely regrets missing his part in the last war, and would fain atone for that.'

'Tell us something we don't know,' said Walsa.

'No wait, I think I see his point,' said Hjala. 'If we can convince Wolfram that a Northland invasion is imminent, he'll be quick to change tack. A war of conquest in Thraxia, a war to repel Northland invaders – it's all the same to him. As long as he gets to take credit for it, he won't mind.'

'Except that would mean a war by sea,' put in Manfry. 'Hardly His Highness's strong suit.' He glanced nervously at the erstwhile sealord.

'Sir Manfry is right,' said Hjala gloomily. 'He'd have no choice but to reinstate Thorsvald, and there's not a chance of him doing that.'

'But if we convince him we're about to be attacked by sea, he'll have no choice,' said Walsa. 'Thorsvald is the best admiral this country has had in an age. No ruler in his right mind would leave his kingdom more vulnerable to mass invasion!'

'Except you're assuming Wolfram *is* in his right mind,' Hjala reminded her. 'Last I heard, he still has raving fits, that blasted splinter in his brain from the arrow wound he took at Linden – Reus only knows what goes through that head of his these days. Chances are, he won't listen to any counsel that undermines his pride.'

They all lapsed into moody silence as they pondered what to do. Manfry sipped his wine awkwardly.

A right bally mess they were in, and no mistake.

CHAPTER 13

BEHIND ENEMY LINES

Vaskrian almost wept with relief when they sighted the frozen banks of the Royne. For more than a fortnight, they had ploughed their way across the stricken plains of Garth, bleached by winter's touch. The snow had seemed to mock the weary travellers as it took them deeper into its white embrace; the young knight had almost lost track of days that were unmercifully short, and long arduous nights that came to torment them with an awful constancy, sucking the life out of bones chilled to the marrow. The cold had only intensified as they made their way northwards, becoming even worse under rising winds that made a man feel less than human: after a time, Vaskrian could almost believe the Handmaidens of Orcus had taken them all for husbands, to dance upon the hoarfrost till the Hour of All's Ending. Peasant's hearth and vassal's manor had provided the occasional lonely respite from the fierce weather, but not all had welcomed them with open arms. Garth had only just been pacified before the onset of winter, and twice they'd had to draw swords and threaten their way to shelter. No blood had been spilt, but he knew that would change soon enough.

'So how are we going to get past that bloody castle?' Wrackwulf asked, drawing his fur cloak more tightly about him as they looked upon the sparkling river and the fortress that guarded it. Even the hardy freelancer was openly feeling the cold now; all pretence of knightly fortitude had long been winnowed away by the relentlessly cruel weather. Joram did not reply, but surveyed the turreted keep with flinty eyes. It sat at the confluence of the Royne and its tributary, guarding the pass of land that snaked between their source and the Brillwood to the north-east.

'Surely we can just cross the river further downstream?' said Braxus.

'That's our plan,' nodded Joram. 'We'll need to strike west, and walk across the river between Ingrath castle here and the Royne bridge. With any luck, no one will spot us.'

'Never thought I'd find cause to thank the icy weather,' muttered Braxus.

'Thought you'd be used to the cold, being a northerner,' quipped Wrackwulf.

'Oh I am,' replied Braxus. 'I usually spend winters in a castle, by the fire with a keg of mead, and a wench or two to warm my bed.'

'Spare us your lascivious reminiscences, sir knight,' said Joram sourly.

Don't suppose you have many of your own, thought Vaskrian sullenly. The monk's dourness had done little to make the journey easier. The young knight had conceived a healthy dislike for the Argolian; he made Horskram look cheerful.

'Here's where Scratcher can help us,' said Morcant. Bending down next to his familiar, he whispered something in the fox's ear. It cocked its head and bounded off westwards, casting up little flurries of snow in its wake.

'Scratcher will be our outrider,' beamed the mage. 'He'll let me know directly if there are any dangers up ahead.'

'You called your pet fox *Scratcher*?' Wrackwulf shook his head.

'Enough banter,' growled Joram. 'The sooner we get a move on, the sooner I can bring this odious alliance to an end.'

Morcant spared Vaskrian a wry glance as they moved on. 'So much for gratitude,' said the warlock.

Vaskrian couldn't help but smile at that. At least the sorcerer was cheerful, pagan or no.

The skies were darkening again when they reached a safe point at which to cross the river. Vaskrian half expected to see more ghoulish shades and icy apparitions rise up and attack them, but none did.

That didn't mean they were out of danger, though. They had just crossed the Royne, and were scrambling up its rocky northern bank, when Morcant suddenly stopped.

'Wait!' he hissed. 'Scratcher's seen something. Attune further to him I must, so I can see what he's seeing.'

They waited a few moments while the warlock muttered

words in the eerie language of magick, his eyes rolling up into the back of his head. Presently he came back to them.

'Anticipated we've been,' he said at last. 'A patrol of swordsmen, heading this way.'

Braxus cursed. 'They must have been set to guard this stretch of the Royne. I thought you said Abrexta couldn't scry on us any more thanks to yon amulet of yours?'

Morcant bit his lip. 'She can't – perhaps she set patrols before we reached the Fernwood.'

'She would have been able to scry on us up till then,' said Joram, nodding thoughtfully. 'It's possible she's second-guessed us.'

'I love it when a plan comes together,' muttered Vaskrian sarcastically.

'How many of them are there?' asked Torgun.

'A good fifteen or twenty of them,' replied the mage. 'Too many for us to deal with.'

Wrackwulf snorted. 'You haven't been adventuring with us for long enough, outlander.'

'Yon Vorstlending has the right of it,' said Torgun. 'We've faced worse odds ere now. How well equipped are they?'

'Much the same as you, from what I can tell,' said Morcant. 'Light mail and blades.'

Wrackwulf grunted. 'Chances are they're freeswords. No self-respecting knight would be abroad at this time of year. Except for us, that is.'

'If they're mercenaries, they won't be pushovers,' put in Braxus. 'This won't be easy.'

Torgun shot him a reproachful glance. Braxus scowled

back at him. Cowardice was always a touchy point between the two knights.

Can't have bad blood between comrades, or it'll get spilled before long, thought Vaskrian. 'I'm sure Sir Braxus only means to say we should come at them the best way we can,' he said quickly. 'Maybe Morcant and his... fox can help us ambush them.'

'Avoid them altogether I'd prefer,' said the mage. 'Reattune to Scratcher I will, so I can see with his eyes. I won't be able to see with my own while I do, so one of you will have to carry me.' Catching Joram's granite stare, he added: 'Not him.'

'All right,' sighed Wrackwulf. 'You'd best scramble up on my back, then. But if you infect me with your magicks, I'll cut your hands off, understood?'

'If he tries to magick you, I'll crack his skull open before you get a chance to,' added Joram.

Morcant murmured the words again and returned to his trance-like state. Hoisting him on to his shoulders, Wrackwulf finished the climb up the river bank with some effort. The others followed on, closing around him in formation as they began to move across the frosted plain once more.

'We're in the King's Fold,' breathed Braxus. 'We've managed to get this far at least.'

Overhead the stars had begun lightly to dust the firmament. Vaskrian lit a torch. That would mean getting spotted, but he wasn't too worried about that. *Let them come – I'm prophesied to do great deeds.* These days, he found the Earth Witch's prognostications a lot more encouraging. He felt a tingle of excitement run through his wiry frame as he freed his blade of Staerkvit steel, letting it taste the night.

Ezekiel willing, and it'll taste more blood too before long.

The ground north of the river was rougher, the going slow. Their breath came in crystalline exhalations as they waded knee-deep through the snow. Braxus cursed it, and not for the first time. *The sooner we're inside the palace killing Abrexta the better,* he thought. *I do hope she's had the decency at least to keep the hearths burning.*

Morcant guided them onwards, tapping Wrackwulf on the shoulder and pointing, though the whites of his eyes remained eerily luminescent in the light of Vaskrian's torch. Presently the ground levelled off, before moving down into a shallow valley at a gradual incline. Morcant tapped Wrack-wulf on the shoulder again, his eyes rolling forwards. A movement to the right startled them... but it was just Scratcher, scampering over the ridge to rejoin them.

'Outfooted them we have,' said Morcant, getting down off Wrackwulf's shoulders. 'Now all we need to do is find some shelter for the night.'

The valley floor was strewn with skeletal trees and spidery bushes. Over in the distance to their right, the lights of a lonely homestead burned.

'Better keep your swords drawn,' growled Wrackwulf. 'Looks like we may have to demand some hospitality again.'

The snow had abated and the clouds had dissipated, allowing for a clear night under the stars. They were halfway down the valley, when Scratcher screeched a warning.

'Up there,' breathed Morcant, pointing to the other side of the valley. A tall figure stood silhouetted against the nearly full moon. Swathed in furs, it carried a long spear and a hand axe. It stood like that for a while, seeming to scrutinise them. Then it let out a triumphant yell. Bounding effortlessly down the slopes towards them, it slid the last of the way until it reached the valley floor, landing on its feet agilely. It began making its way towards them with loping, confident strides.

Brandishing his sword, Torgun moved down into the valley to meet it. Braxus and the other knights fell in around him, Morcant and Joram bringing up the rear.

They squared off against the newcomer on the valley floor. In the torchlight he looked a ghastly figure, tall and rangy with wild braiding in his beard. His teeth flashed silver as he favoured them with a leering grin, made all the wider by an old scar that carved a rictus across his cheeks. Around his neck he wore a strange necklace, along with an amulet of white stone that pulsed softly in the dark. His body was covered in outlandish tattoos that seemed to catch the subdued moonlight with a strange glint.

'An unexpected pleasure tae meet ye,' he said in thickly accented Thrax, hefting the spear and axe menacingly.

Braxus clutched his sword more tightly as he nudged past Torgun. He felt the hatred welling up in him, mixed with elation at the good fortune Ushira had put his way.

'Cormic Death's Head,' he spat as he recognised High Chieftain Slánga Mac Bryon's feared and despised lieutenant. Over the years, Cormic Mac Brennan had tortured and killed countless numbers of his countrymen, pulling tongues down through slashed throats and giving rise to the legendary Cormic Cravat. The savage's name had become even more feared than Slánga's amongst lowland communities unlucky enough to live near the Brekken Ranges.

Sir Braxus wet his lips eagerly as he stalked towards Cormic. 'My vengeance starts here,' he murmured, raising his sword.

Though she could not see them in her scrying mirror, Abrexta knew her agent had intercepted them. She had realised Morcant was blocking her magic, but that wouldn't stop her communicating with her latest thrall using the talisman she had given him.

Cormic had taken a while to ensorcel. The highland captain's will was strong, but losing so many thralls at the Battle of Rathlain Corridor had brought an unexpected release to her elan. Even after that, it had taken an extra week to persuade the Death's Head to submit to the arts of daubing, for his superstitious fear of sorcery ran deep. But submit he had. And now he would carry out his mission, and assassinate Rowena for her. After he had slain the assassins coming for her in turn.

Truly the Moon Goddess rewards those who help themselves, she thought. *Now I get to kill two birds with one arrow.*

Focusing her elan, Abrexta pictured a fist tightening around a heart as she urged Cormic onwards.

With a blood-curdling scream, Cormic launched himself at Braxus. The knight was caught off guard by the suddenness of the attack; parrying the spear thrust, he ducked out of the way, feeling the flint head of the axe whistle past his nape. Torgun was on the highlander like lightning, aiming a two-handed thrust at his midriff. Cormic could have dodged it, but instead let the blade pass through him, like steel penetrating a snowdrift. The savage laughed as he turned and caught the knight a blow across the chest. Torgun staggered back, a look of bewilderment scored across his face. His sword came away from Cormic's side bloodless.

Cormic thrust his spear at Braxus again, catching him a glancing blow on the shoulder. His mail took the brunt of it, but he couldn't rely too much on his light armour. Taking a step back, he let Wrackwulf and Vaskrian move in, the two knights flanking him with sword and axe. But a fighter who has no need to defend himself is a deadly foe indeed. Cormic let their blades pass through him again, catching Vaskrian a glancing blow to the head with his axe and slicing open Wrackwulf's thigh with his spear point.

An explosion of light. A green arc of fire spat from Morcant's fingers, terminating in a coagulated ball of heat. The barbarian howled as it struck his shoulder, which sizzled as it exuded steam into the night. The smell of flesh cooking strafed the clean night air.

'He's been daubed!' yelled the mage. 'Channelling the element of snow he is – use fire! Blades and staves will hurt him not!'

Vaskrian took a swipe at Cormic with his flaring torch. The highlander recoiled, bringing up his spear in a swift counter attack and forcing the young knight back out of range. Morcant incanted another spell and shot a second ball of fire at him, but this time Cormic was prepared, and ducked out of the way. Ignoring the knights, he charged straight for the sorcerer, bellowing ferociously. Torgun tried to tackle him, but he slipped through the knight's brawny arms like a rain shower. Suddenly halting, Cormic planted his feet firmly in the snow, casting his spear at the warlock. Morcant hurriedly mouthed another spell, and the snow at his feet erupted upwards, condensing into a hard slab of ice that deflected the spear point inches from his face.

Vaskrian attacked from behind, striking Cormic with the torch. The savage screamed in pain as it found his back, swooping around and lashing out at Vaskrian with his axe. The young knight brought up his blade at the last second, though the force of the blow caused him to lose his footing and tumble over into a snowdrift.

With surprising speed for a man of his bulk, Joram stepped over to Vaskrian and wrenched the torch from his faltering grip. The highlander was almost on him as he turned to face him. The monk was fearless enough, whirling the blazing brand about him in a series of arcs, and the highlander was on the back foot for a while.

'Can't you break the spell protecting him?' yelled Braxus.

'It's a different type of daubing,' said Morcant. 'There's no signature item. Destroy the central glyph we must!'

'How in Gehenna's name do we do that?' screamed Braxus.

'Just strike him with flame!' Morcant screamed back.

With another blood-curdling war cry, Cormic launched himself at Joram, swinging down at his head. The monk stepped in with a speed that belied his burly frame, dodging under the highlander's guard and driving the torch into his chest. Cormic screamed again as it burned through his wolf-skin, scorching the flesh beneath. The Argolian followed it up with a kick to the shin. The highlander yelped and began to grapple with the monk.

'He's found the glyph!' yelled Morcant. 'You can kill him now!'

Four hard-pressed knights didn't need any further encouragement. It took many strokes, but Cormic went down, spurting blood from multiple wounds, thrashing the last of his life away in the incarnadined snow. Braxus delivered the death blow with Cormic's own spear, driving it through his heart and transfixing him to the hard ground beneath.

'That was for my father and my clan,' he said, spitting on the face of the corpse. 'May their souls rest a little easier in the Heavenly Halls.'

He looked up to see Morcant staring at Joram. 'A lucky blow, or an accurate one?' the wizard mused aloud.

Joram sneered at him. 'Think you that an adept of the Argolian Order knows not the ways of pagan sorcery? Did I not already prove that knowledge when I overturned your magicks to bring you to justice?' Before the warlock could reply, he added: 'Come on, let's get inside yon homestead – we've two injured knights to treat.'

'Ah, it's just a scratch,' grinned Wrackwulf, ignoring the blood pouring from his thigh wound.

'One more scar to add to the tally,' chimed Vaskrian, gingerly massaging around his cut forehead.

The terrified peasant family offered them little resistance. Joram and Braxus managed to calm them down, though Torgun felt guilty about it. Scaring churls was hardly in his nature, but at least they'd saved them from the loathsome highland savage. The family gave them a wide berth, huddling in the corner and leaving them to gather around the hearth.

'How did he find us?' asked Braxus as Joram treated the knights. 'I thought you said we were protected from Abrexta's scrying.'

'We are,' insisted Morcant. 'She must have sent Cormic south for another purpose.'

'I've led us across the Royne by the most direct route possible without getting tangled up with a garrison full of soldiers,' commented Joram as he bound up Wrackwulf's thigh. 'She must have anticipated us.'

'That means of course she'll be anticipating us some more in Ongist,' said Braxus.

'Never did I say this mission would be easy,' said Morcant, looking almost apologetic now.

'Will she be able to use her magic to protect the rest of her followers?' asked Torgun. He didn't mind the odds against him, but a fair fight would be nice.

'Unlikely,' said Joram. 'Daubing takes up a lot of elan. She'll be taxed enough as it is.'

Morcant smirked. 'You really have studied our ways, master monk.'

'All my life,' replied the monk, unsmiling.

Abrexta's lip curled in disgust as she let her mirror go dark. Beyond that feeling, she now felt a new emotion. Fear. It had never seriously occurred to her that her antagonists might triumph; but they had proved continually resourceful and endlessly resilient. It was beginning to look as though defeat might just be a real possibility.

She muttered a curse under her breath. What was the Master playing at, leaving her up here, all alone to contend with this unexpected threat?

No, she admonished herself. *This is how the Master operates. He is testing my fortitude in the face of adversity – I must not fail him. The Moon Goddess's will must be done through his agency.* A rare gentler thought came to her then. *Womankind demands that it be so – this accursed primitive patriarchy must be overthrown, at all costs.*

Stretching, she got up and walked into the adjoining bedchamber. Looking down on Cadwy's slumbering form, she felt the old contempt welling up in her again, drowning out any gentleness of thought.

Otherwise, prigs like this bumbling fool will ever determine the fate of realms.

Getting into bed besides the snoring King, she forced

herself to calm down. She had hundreds of strong knights and highland screamers at her beck and call. And older servants too, that she could call on if needed. *Let them come – I will be ready for them when they get here.*

As she closed her eyes, Abrexta felt her full lips curling upwards in a smile. When her antagonists arrived, they would not find her defenceless.

CHAPTER 14
TO KILL A WYTCH

'I hate night shifts.' The sentry's hands were numb beneath his leathern gauntlets. But then winters were never-ending in northern Thraxia. *And so is this bleeding night watch,* he thought disconsolately.

The sentry's comrade grunted as he glanced up at the skies, which were somewhat lighter now. 'Reckon sunrise is a couple of hours away, Rath. Summat to be grateful for at least.'

'What's the need for this watch round the clock anyways?' complained Rath. The order had come more than two weeks ago, from the palace. But then strange orders tended to come from there, now it was ruled by a sorceress.

'The Witchy Woman says there's a need, and that's all there is to it,' growled their serjeant, coming up behind Rath and startling him. The southern gatehouse of Ongist's ramshackle walls was crammed to the rafters with twenty soldiers. Something had her spooked, all right.

'Can't see who'd be mad enough to try and break into

the city at this time o' year,' said Rath. The serjeant shot him a piercing glance, and he decided to shut his drinking hole.

'Here, I can see summat!' said the other sentry. 'Over there!'

The three of them stiffened as they peered into the gloom. It was there, just on the fringes of the lantern light – an animal of some sort. The serjeant was already calling for reinforcements from the soldiers' barracks further back in the gatehouse.

'Ach, it's only a fox,' said Rath, screwing up his eyes and squinting into the pre-dawn gloom.

'Aye, and that's something we've been told to take as warning of intruders,' said the serjeant. 'Spears at the ready!'

Rath shook his head, but did as he was told. Orders were orders.

They waited in silence. A few stray snowflakes drifted across their vision in the chilly breeze. The fox remained where it was at the edge of the circle of light, squatting on its haunches and staring at them impassively.

The serjeant barked the rest of the garrison into activity. Soon there were a dozen of them in formation before the entrance.

A cloaked and hooded figure suddenly appeared next to the fox, and began ambling across the circle of light towards them. He looked to be a wizened fellow, hardly much of a threat to a fully armed garrison.

'Who goes there?' barked the serjeant. 'Come no closer.'

'No need for such fuss, no need, no need!' said the blue-robed stranger as he drew nearer, ignoring the command. Rath couldn't place his accent; it sounded similar to the highland scum who'd taken up residence in the palace over the winter. That was plenty enough reason not to trust him already.

He was tightening his grip on the spear when a strange thing happened. The stranger was walking in a direct line towards them and still speaking. With every step, he sounded more and more affable... perhaps Rath was wrong to mistrust him. He looked harmless enough after all, and was apparently unarmed. The other lads looked similarly nonplussed, clutching their spear shafts less tightly as they exchanged confused looks.

But the serjeant was having none of it. Reaching under his brigandine, he pressed a pomander of strange-smelling herbs to his nose and inhaled deeply.

'Oh aye, I see what ye're about,' he said. 'The Witchy Woman's got the measure of yer alright – you'll not be thralling me today, wizard! Lads, at him! That's a direct order!'

Rath and the rest of the soldiers obeyed the command reluctantly. The stranger seemed unperturbed as they closed gingerly on him. When the first soldier to his left went down with a cry, Rath understood the wizard's lack of fear. Out of the blue, they suddenly found four strong knights flanking them.

How on earth did they get the drop on us like that?

Rath didn't have time to worry about that though, as a huge fellow with blond hair came at him, steel flashing in his hands.

In fact, Rath didn't have much time left on this earth at all.

Sir Torgun felt sick as he cut down the timorous footsoldier. This was poor work for chivalrous knights, but sadly necessary. Killing commoners was bad enough; coming at them under a sorcerous shroud of invisibility made it even worse. But Morcant's plan had been the only sensible one – Abrexta had clearly anticipated them and stiffened the gatehouse garrison.

He cut down two more soldiers in quick succession. Best to get this part of the mission over with as quickly as possible. The others were making light work of the surprised men-at-arms; even Joram was weighing in, clubbing a soldier into unconsciousness with a brutal swipe of his iron-shod quarterstaff.

The serjeant yelled the order to retreat, just before Wrackwulf's axe blade found his larynx. A whining metal screech mingled with his gurgling death cry.

'They're lowering the portcullis!' yelled Braxus, dashing forwards. In an instant Torgun was with him. The two of them rolled under the descending grill; coming up, they found themselves surrounded by another half-a-dozen soldiers. The corridor was cramped, so these drew short swords. The commoners were clearly outclassed, but had the advantage of numbers.

In situations like this it was best to play to one's strengths, and pare back the odds swiftly.

A few ferocious seconds saw four more soldiers bleeding their lives away between the flagstones of the gatehouse corridor. The remaining two backed away before the questing swords of the knights. The clash of arms behind him told Torgun that the others were still fighting the rest of the garrison outside.

'We'd best make sure these wretches don't escape and make a hue and cry!' barked Braxus, bearing down on the cowed soldiers. Reluctantly Torgun followed, and they cut them down in short order.

Then he was ware of a sudden movement behind him. Wheeling around, he saw a soldier charging him with a spear, emerging from one of the guard rooms. It was the last attack of a desperate man, and all the more lethal for it. Torgun's bastard blade wasn't the best fit for such cramped conditions, whilst one needs only a narrow space to gut a man with a spear.

Braxus crashed into Torgun with all his might, pushing the knight to one side and bringing them both low. The soldier hurtled past them, tripping over Braxus and landing heavily, dropping his spear. Lurching to his feet, Torgun yanked the soldier up by his brigandine and pinned him against the wall.

'Tell him we'll spare his life, if he helps me open yon portcullis,' he said to Braxus. The soldier's legs were dangling clear of the ground. The man could have tried a kick, but a steely glare from Torgun told him the time for heroics was over. Clambering to his feet, Braxus translated, menacing the soldier with his blade for emphasis.

Hurriedly, the man-at-arms complied, grasping one of the hanging chains connected to the winch while Braxus kept his sword trained on him. Torgun added his thews to the chain at the other side of the portcullis, and with a shriek it began to open. Outside, the others had finished off the rest of the soldiers, and now moved hastily inside the gatehouse to join them. They bound and gagged the surviving soldier at Torgun's insistence. He'd promised the man mercy, and mercy he would have.

'A wonder they didn't use yon murder holes,' grunted Wrackwulf, glancing up at the machicolations set into the corridor ceiling.

Braxus laughed sardonically. 'Do you have any idea how expensive oil is? We could afford it well enough, until that sorcerous bitch emptied the land of coin.'

'Nice of her to make our job easier then,' quipped the freelancer. 'Remind me to thank her for that when we kill her.'

'All right, enough chatter,' said Joram. 'We've work to do.'

They advanced up the corridor, checking the guard rooms along the way for any more surprise attacks. As they approached the inner gate, Torgun clapped a hand on Braxus' shoulder. There was something he needed to say to his old love rival.

'Yon soldier might have struck me down, had you not intervened, Sir Braxus,' he said. 'I owe you my thanks, perhaps even my life.'

The Thraxian managed a wan half-smile. 'I owed you a debt of honour, Sir Torgun,' he said uneasily. 'Consider it discharged. And it wasn't easy saving your skin – you must weigh more than an aurochs!'

Torgun blinked. He would never understand the Thraxian's strange sense of humour.

The inner door was fashioned of scratched dirty oak and

rusted iron nails. *That hasn't seen any upkeep in decades,* thought Sir Torgun. The city walls were in a shocking state of disrepair as well, crumbling away in parts, and the tower nearest the gatehouse had partially collapsed. He'd never really thought about Thraxians except as an age-old enemy, but after seeing the way they lived, he began to pity them. Had they ever been ruled wisely, he wondered?

They lifted the bar and heaved the gate open. The main thoroughfare meandered downhill, dipping at a steady incline towards the River Rundle. The streets were deserted at this time of year, though Torgun knew that wouldn't last: their fight had been a matter of minutes, but chances are someone had heard them.

Morcant muttered a spell as his fox familiar scurried past him and down the street. The mage had explained how invisibility worked: it confounded the senses of all who beheld those under the spell, an illusion that tricked them into believing they weren't there at all. But as soon as they attacked or made any sudden move, the glamour would be broken.

That was the only way Torgun would have complied with the plan. Hiding under a cloak of invisibility was bad enough, but he was damned if he'd fight unfairly.

They moved off down the street, keeping in close formation around Morcant so as to stay within range of his spell. Scratcher scampered off ahead of them, their eyes and ears.

Torgun frowned after the fox. More magic. The sooner this business was done, the better.

～

Vaskrian kept a tight grip on his sword hilt as they stalked the winding streets of Ongist. Even covered in winter's white shroud, it was obvious the place was a right dump. Not a patch on Strongholm, he reflected with pride... then remembered he still served a Thraxian liege. Oh well, at least he was a knight now. It had gradually sunk in over the long hard month's journey to the capital, and during their journey from the Royne to the city he had felt excitement start to build on the foundations of that realisation. Now they were within sight of their mission's ending, that excitement coursed through his veins like an intoxicating draught.

They followed Scratcher, who scampered through the slush-filled roads. Few of them had cobblestones: this lot couldn't even be bothered to pave their streets properly. Twice they went back on themselves, circling through Ongist's warren of crooked alleys to avoid guard patrols spotted by the familiar. Never mind patrols for danger – half the city's buildings looked fit to topple over onto them at any moment.

The young knight felt his impatience rising. Even he knew they couldn't hope to fight their way through an entire city, but he was growing quickly tired of subterfuge. Their last fight had been all too brief.

At last they reached the Rundle. At least the river was impressive, wide enough though frozen solid at this time of year. This part of it was lined with warehouses, presumably where the merchant lot kept their goodies in safe storage. The other side of the street that shadowed the river was lined with grander stone houses. Some of them almost looked well built. *So they aren't total barbarians then,* Sir Vaskrian thought smugly.

But as they drew into the centre of the city proper, all smugness vanished.

The Palace of Bending Branches loomed above them, dark and forbidding against the night. Sir Braxus had spoken of it a few times, of how it had been built in something called the Middle Time, from trees enchanted by the Fay Folk. Gazing upon it now, Vaskrian could well believe the tales. Cyclopean branches straddled the river as they warped unnaturally to form a large elegant wooden building several stories high, built entirely from bough and bole. This organic design made the walls appear to writhe as they tapered upwards through the palace stories, giving the entire building the appearance of being wrought half of nature, half of mortal craft.

The spectacle set his hackles rising straight away. He knew exactly what that place reminded him of, and he wasn't going back there.

'What is it?' growled Joram, as he suddenly brought up short. The monk could obviously sense his fear.

'That place reminds me of... of somewhere I'd rather not go again,' whispered Vaskrian. He seemed to sense rather than see spectral green figures reaching for him with elongated talons, one-eyed hounds barking noiselessly, while in the background a hideous crone leered at him... Vaskrian blanched, he could positively feel his face going whiter than the snowy rooftops.

The burly monk shook his head impatiently. 'Torgun, present thy rood and touch him on the forehead with it.'

The Northlending complied, somewhat awkwardly. The sacred silver felt oddly pleasant against Vaskrian's skin, though it chilled him to the bone. As if from far away, he heard the monk intoning a blessing. Vaskrian felt the fear receding, the visions in his head shimmering like the surface of a dark mere pushed back by a brisk wind. The feeling was still there, but more bearable.

'Better?' asked the adept gruffly.

Vaskrian nodded, though cold sweat beaded his face. 'I think I can manage,' he muttered. He didn't want to fail his first knightly quest for lack of courage.

Torgun proffered Joram the circifix. 'Perhaps this would be best left in your keeping,' said the blond knight. 'After all, it is a sacred relic of your Order.'

But the monk shook his head. 'Nay, it was entrusted to you. I cannot countermand the orders of the Grand Master without his express leave.'

Torgun shrugged and put the circifix back inside his byrnie. As they moved off again, Vaskrian noticed Morcant looking sidelong at the monk, a quizzical expression on his pasty face.

Braxus surveyed the palace while Joram took care of Vaskrian. It hadn't changed a bit since he'd last seen it in his youth, and nor would it in another decade, if the tales told true. It must be at least a thousand years old, dating back to the fabled Middle Time, before the kingdom had become one and embraced the Creed. Before the coming of the Headstone fragment too, come to think of it.

An appropriate place for a witch queen to lair in, he thought. *Perhaps we should have burned it to the ground years ago.*

But this was no time to reflect on things past. A covered bridge fashioned of the same enchanted boughs approached the palace from their side of the river. Braxus knew from memory that this would be barred by an ordinary gate; not all the craft of the Faerie Kindred had survived. Scratcher scurried off, keeping to the shadows as he scouted ahead.

Morcant's eyes rolled up into the back of his head, as he conjoined with his familiar again. Presently they rolled back again, and the fox could be seen scampering back towards them.

'Curious,' breathed the mage. 'Unguarded, the gate! That I was not expecting.'

Joram had finished with Vaskrian, so they moved off again. Drawing level with the palace entrance, they saw Morcant had spoken true: the gate stood unguarded, framed by a lintel fashioned of gigantic boar tusks, its brass nails glinting in the light of two lamps that burned with the same eerie fire Morcant had used on their travels. The wind seemed to drop slightly, though a light dusting of snow still fell.

All too easy, thought Braxus uncomfortably. At least thanks to the dark and the snow, he wouldn't get a good look at the decayed heads decorating the palace's thorny parapet. Not that there would be much flesh left on the faces of his father or Vertrix and the rest of his murdered friends. Still the thought of it made him sick with grief, and he struggled to master his rage.

Can't let my heart rule my head, not now of all times, he told himself grimly as he fought back incipient tears.

'My sixth sense likes this not,' said Joram. 'Smells like a trap to me.'

'So how else do we get inside the palace?' asked Wrackwulf.

Braxus bit his lip. 'There is no other way, not unless we walk up the river and take the Bridge of Silversmiths across it. Then we'd have to double back through Market Circle and approach the palace from the north side.'

'And who's to say the same bait won't be laid there?' asked Joram. 'The entryways to the palace are identical.'

'Can't keep this glamour up for much longer either,' muttered Morcant. 'Drains my powers, it does! Need to save some energy for *her*.'

'In other words, we don't have a choice,' said Braxus, reaching for the brass door handle.

'Wait!' said Joram sharply. 'The gate might be trapped.'

But Braxus was in no mood for caution. Grasping the hooped handle, he pushed at the gate. It was heavy, and Torgun had to help him. The door creaked open, inviting them into the covered bridge's arboreal depths. Morcant incanted another spell, and a lick of green fire darted from one of the magic lamps, coalescing around his fist. The light wasn't as strong as his earlier spell, but enough for them to see by.

'I've dropped the glamour, so we'd best get inside!' he

hissed. 'Scratcher will stay out here. Alert me he will, if anyone approaches.'

Sir Braxus nodded tersely. It wasn't the best plan in the world, but it would have to do. The covered walkway was large enough for two of them to walk abreast, so he and Sir Torgun advanced, with Morcant and Joram in the middle and Wrackwulf and Vaskrian at the rear. The last two closed the gate behind them, leaving the adventurers bathed in the lucent glow of Morcant's light.

Slowly, they began to make their way up the corridor...

Abrexta sat in the darkened hall, tapping her fingers restlessly on the Seat of High Kings. The heroes sent to try her were more determined than she had dared to believe; her doubts had begun to creep back, and once again she wondered if the day would really be hers. But flight was unthinkable. Her pride would not brook it, and worse still the Master would see her punished for such weakness. Once already the White Eye had failed and fled – another setback would not be well received. And Abrexta had no wish to spend the rest of her long days a fugitive and an outcast.

I've suffered that enough already, Kaia knows.

Tightening her grip until her fingernails pressed into the throne's wooden arms, the sorceress steeled herself. She was damned if a woman would back down, where men like Ragnar had quailed.

The Moon Goddess demands better – my sex deserves better.

Before her, the monarch she had dethroned in all but name grovelled at her feet like the fool he was. In the seat next to her sat the warrior chieftain she would rule Thraxia with, no less restless than she was.

Slánga Mac Bryon was a fearsome sight. Even in the bedimmed hall, his muscular frame was a presence, though he was not a large man. Slánga, the man who had united all the clans of the Brekken Hills for the first time in a generation; Slánga, the man who – together with Cormic Death's Head, and his high chieftain ally Tíerchan mac Thoth – had ravaged the northern wards of Thraxia into near extinction, helping Abrexta to consolidate her grip on the realm. Never in her long life had she seen a general so bold, so wantonly dangerous and ambitious for his people. Yes, let others be fooled by his diminutive stature – Slánga was all man, unlike many of her previous lovers. Some men needed ensorcelling, but all he had required was the promise of concubinage. What he failed to grasp was that he was the concubine, not her.

'Where are they?' he growled. He was keen to avenge the death of his lieutenant. Cormic's defeat had come as a shock to him. To Abrexta, the Death's Head had been no different to any other man, just a pawn to be used and discarded when the time was right; but Slánga had loved his right-hand man with that strange passion that men sometimes conceive for one another in friendship.

'Patience, my love,' whispered the enchantress. 'I have other means of espying them once they enter the palace. For did I not tell thee, the building that the kindred made has a very life of its own?'

That same kindred whose ancestry she had tapped in Liathduil Forest, years ago. The benefits had been more than salutary: besides gaining extended long life, sickness and old age had become unknown to her, a nature-defying power that many a Necromancer and Thaumaturgist would envy. Perhaps best of all, her powers of Enchantment had been amplified beyond all measure. Of the Seven Schools, it had ever been her favourite – now, thanks to her artifice and daubing, she channelled faeriekind whenever she used the Right Hand Way to bend men's minds to her will.

But there were other, more specific, advantages a close union with the Fays conferred when one ruled a palace that had been built by them. Shutting her eyes, Abrexta pictured a giant fist closing around a stick figure, as she communed with the spirits her ancestors had bound to its branches centuries ago.

It began as an ominous creaking sound. Braxus and Torgun pulled up short, exchanging furtive glances.

'What in Reus' name was that?' breathed the Thraxian. The Northlending shrugged, peering ahead into the gloom. The corridor was lined with fur skins, drawn across what passed for windows, and the bilious tinge of Morcant's light spell did little to allay his nerves. The ceiling was criss-crossed with interlocking aurochs' horns, the floor carpeted with what appeared to be horsehair growing out of the floor.

'Let's tarry not,' said Morcant nervously. 'Imbued with faerie magicks this place is! Best to hurry.'

'Some witchery is afoot,' agreed Joram. 'I can smell its vile stench. Never did like this place.'

For once we all agree on something, thought Braxus wryly.

Then he heard it again, the same creaking noise.

'It's coming from somewhere up there,' he said.

'It's coming from behind us, too!' said Vaskrian.

As one, they turned and peered back down the covered bridgeway, but all they saw was a stygian maw yawning at the fringes of Morcant's light. The creaking noise came again, only this time it sounded more like a deep groan. And it appeared to be coming from every direction. Morcant intensified his light spell, pushing back the twin folds of darkness that threatened to engulf them. But all that revealed was more of the same, as the corridor stretched ahead before meeting a wall of night again.

And that was when Braxus felt the floor shift under his feet. The cracking of boughs told him the rest. He felt a sickness rise up from the pit of his gorge, as the corridor began to contract.

Abrexta let a satisfied sigh escape her lips as she felt the palace responding to her command. Not even Morcant's magicks could confound the Fay Folk; she didn't need to scry out her would-be-killers now they were inside.

Taking a deep breath, she intensified the sigils in her mindset, picturing the manlike figure disappearing inside the crushing fist.

Panic welled up inside Vaskrian, a venomous tide that robbed him of strength and wit. The passage was warping and cracking, as it mercilessly began to constrict them. Looking up, he gaped as he saw the aurochs horns were now tapering down towards them, like the teeth of a great Wyrm. He felt the horsehairs writhe upwards, growing horribly as they wrapped themselves around his legs, pinning him fast. Next to him, Wrackwulf was yelling like a man gone wood as he desperately tried to hack at the tightening boughs. Torgun and Braxus tore fur skins from the walls, searching frantically for a window, but none were to be found among the slithering branches.

'We need to neutralise the spell!' cried Joram, grabbing Morcant by the shoulder.

'I don't have enough power!' screamed the wizard. 'I can't control the Fays on my own!'

Joram tightened his grip on the mage, and seethed a single word in his face.

'TRY!'

Struggling to compose himself as the passage floor lurched like the deck of a storm-tossed ship, Morcant shut his eyes and began to murmur an incantation. A few seconds later and his light went out, plunging them all into suffocating blackness.

Vaskrian felt rather than heard the scream that tore from his lungs. It seemed to fill his convulsing mind as his entire body went limp. He suddenly felt very light. His horrible surroundings mercifully faded, as he slipped into uncon-sciousness...

It took all of Torgun's fortitude not to succumb to primaeval terror. Bracing himself, he steadied his mighty limbs against the walls as he tried to delay the inevitable. The corridor was possessed of an awful preternatural strength, and the hero knew not even he could hope to keep it at bay for long. Besides him, he could hear Braxus and Wrackwulf hacking desperately at the slowly descending tusks.

Shutting his eyes, he murmured a prayer. Thoughts of his dead companions ghosted across his mind's eye.

I'll be with you ere long, brave friends, he found time to think.

He heard Morcant begin an incantation, and tried to shut the eerie syllables out of his mind. But then he heard a second chant, hard on its heels, more wholesome than Morcant's spell casting, and he recognised the Argolian prayer immediately. The words of spell and psalm mingled awkwardly, their clashing syllables jarring against each other.

He felt his limbs trembling. Sweat lashed off of him. A terrible fire streaked through his muscles, as his body silently registered its torment. Never in all his years had it been tested like this. The fire felt like molten metal as it seeped into his upper torso. He began to tremble from head to foot with the effort.

And then a strange thing happened. The spell and psalm seemed to conjoin, jarring no more, but rather...

Harmonising?

Torgun knew as little of music as he did of witchcraft and prayer, but he could have sworn that was what it sounded like.

He could feel the aurochs horns pressing down against him, pushing against his mail byrnie as they slowly impaled him, scoring grooves against his scalp. Rivulets of blood mingled with his sweat, but he screwed up his eyes and redoubled his efforts. He could still hear Braxus and Wrack-wulf hacking away in the dark, while the strange cadence continued, growing stronger and stronger...

And then he felt the burden lift slightly, as something gave. The horns ceased to press down against him and receded. He steeled himself, ready in case the unearthly maw should close on them again, but instead he felt the passage begin to drop away and the fire in his limbs to abate.

The groaning sound returned, as monk and mage continued their strange song, only now it sounded pained; the passage continued to creak and crack as it retreated, more quickly now it seemed. Torgun collapsed gratefully on the floor, he could feel the horsehairs that had gripped his thighs releasing him too. Next to him, Braxus was weeping for sheer relief.

The eerie song continued for another minute or so before stopping. A few seconds later, light flared up again as Morcant reactivated his illumination spell. Looking around him, Torgun saw the other knights sprawled across the floor of the passage, which appeared to have returned to its original size.

Only Morcant and Joram remained standing, clasping hands as their eyes gazed up at the ceiling, where the aurochs horns were folding back in on themselves.

Joram was the first to let go, shaking his hand as though it had touched horse dung.

'A foul alliance, but a necessary one,' he said disgustedly.

Morcant only gaped at him, his eyes bulging wide. 'But... how was that possible?' he demanded. 'Never in all my years have I heard of such a thing.'

'I used the Psalm of Gramarye's Quenching in conjunction with whatever foul wizardry you employed, to compel the Fays trapped inside this accursed building,' said Joram. 'Our combined powers were enough to defeat them.'

'But that's impossible!' spluttered the mage. 'If anything, your psalm should have hindered my spell, not bolstered it.'

'The Redeemer works in mysterious ways,' was all Joram had to say to that. 'Now come on, there's no time to waste. It won't be long before those accursed nature spirits regroup.'

Traumatised as they were, they didn't need any further encouragement. But as Joram led the way, Torgun caught the mage's eyes boring holes in the monk's back.

Abrexta jolted back in her chair and shuddered, opening her eyes.

'What is it?' growled Slánga, placing a calloused hand on her wrist.

'Don't touch me,' she snapped irritably, rising from the throne. Gesturing to Cadwy, she spat: 'Out of my way, dolt! Get into yon corner where you belong.' She had long given up any pretence of politesse with the erstwhile liege.

As Cadwy loped away obediently, she spoke a single word of power, picturing a lamp and a sunburst in quick succession. The hall flared up with bright light, revealing seven armoured knights standing to attention against the wall. It had taken a lot of up nearly all of her spare elan to enthral them, but it would be worth it.

She barked a command, and the seven knights stalked into the middle of the hall, taking up a defensive position before her.

Slánga got to his feet and moved up to stand next to her.

'We'll nae be needin' yon plumed knights,' he growled. 'My screamers shall deal with yer would-be-assassins.'

Abrexta bit her lip, and said nothing. She wasn't so sure of that.

Torgun practically beamed when they flung open the gate at the end of the covered bridge and emerged into an antechamber. Here the branches sprouted leaves, twisted to form wiry figures dancing and drinking in sybaritic abandon. He didn't care for the effect.

What appealed far more was the sight of the chamber's occupants. Some twenty highlanders slouched insouciantly about the room, dressed in clashing clan colours, silver rings in braids and beards and ears and noses. No sooner had the heroes entered than they surged upwards as one, spears and axes clutched in their hands.

The Northlending's grin turned feral as he tilted his sword towards them. Now this was a foe he would relish fighting.

The nearest three came at him, their scarred faces contorted in ugly screams. Rather than fall back, Torgun stepped in, pivoting and sketching a zigzag shape with his slashing blade. The first highlander tottered back, his scream turning painful as his nosebone opened up; the second reared like a stricken horse, blood pumping from where his larynx had been; the third could only gape at the sight of his severed hand, still clutching its weapon as it twitched on the gnarled floor.

Torgun barged past the last of these, hungrily seeking more foes. A cold battle rage was in him now; after weeks of trudging through bitter snows and their recent ordeal, he had a thirst for blood greater than any he had ever known. Another screamer lunged at him with a spear; it was a deadly attack and would have felled many a lesser knight, but he ducked under it with the speed of a whirlwind, driving his blade in a two-handed thrust deep into the unarmoured savage's midriff. Wrenching the blade free in a wet tearing motion, he sent his foeman tumbling to the floor in a wash of bloody entrails.

The clash of arms around him told that his friends were engaged as well. He felt someone tugging at his cloak. The unorthodox move caught him by surprise, and he nearly lurched off balance. Recovering, he whirled around before the savage could brain him with an axe, and lopped his head clean from his soldiers.

By Stygnos, did these pagan foreigners fight with no honour at all?

Vaskrian felt his courage return to him as he and Braxus and Wrackwulf formed a tight triangle, baiting the highlanders to come at them. To one side, he could hear Morcant muttering another spell; Joram had slipped back into the shadows and was nowhere to be seen.

A throng of slavering highlanders quickly surrounded them. Steel flashed as they began to paint the antechamber with the silver and red hues of battle. A lancing pain through the shoulder told Vaskrian he'd taken a hit: he repaid his assailant by slicing open his kneecap. Even then his berserk opponent wasn't done, and it took couple more strokes to fell him.

More highlanders surged around them. He almost fancied they were back in the accursed tunnel, being slowly crushed to death. A roaring belt of green fire erupted across his vision, forcing him to shield his eyes. When the young knight looked again, he saw the charred remnants of half a dozen highlanders on the floor. He spared a glance at Morcant, who looked drained and surprised.

The last six closed around the three of them. Torgun stepped over to join his three fellow knights, hewing down another savage with a single fierce stroke as he did. Joram appeared from the shadows suddenly, sweeping another highlander's legs from underneath him. Braxus finished the job, gutting him where he lay. Another highlander made to impale him with a flint spear as he did, but Vaskrian sliced his hand, lopping off a couple of fingers. The savage turned on him with a terrible scream, dropping the spear and clutching at Vaskrian with good hand and bad as he tried to bite him. This close, Vaskrian could see his teeth were sharpened. He struggled to disengage, but the savage was fiercely strong and had him at close quarters now, he could smell his reeking breath. He fought desperately to push him away before those teeth closed about his face...

The savage suddenly arched his back as Torgun's blade pierced his heart, driving through his torso and nearly trans-fixing Vaskrian, too.

'My apologies,' said the blond knight as the last high-lander fell dead.

'None needed,' replied Vaskrian, managing a lop-sided grin.

They paused to catch their breath.

'Suppose we owe your wizardry some thanks,' said Wrack-wulf, gazing at the corpses strewn about the antechamber. 'Though it pains me to admit it, you evened up the odds nicely.'

Morcant was still wearing a surprised look on his face, which was now flushed. 'My spell should not have been so powerful,' he said. 'Trying to conserve my elan I was.'

The freelancer shrugged. 'I've no idea what you're talking about, but thanks again.'

'Let's tarry not,' said Joram. 'Our quarry lies beyond yon double doors – I can sense the witch's presence.'

'All right,' said Morcant. 'Remember the plan! Guarded further she will be – distract her as much as possible you must, to give me a chance to pull the ring off her.'

Braxus frowned. Vaskrian's old guvnor looked as though he was starting to doubt the plan.

Braxus' misgivings stayed with him as they approached the antlered lintel of the throneroom double doors. The bloodied knights exchanged glances and curt nods. Joram gripped his quarterstaff in both hands, while Morcant steeled himself. Suddenly the mage started, his eyes rolling back into his head. A few seconds later, he returned to normal with bad tidings.

'Scratcher says more soldiers are coming up behind us!'

'We'd best bar the rear gates,' growled Wrackwulf. 'Something tells me yon corridor will be a lot more accommodating for them than it was for us.'

This they did, before turning back to face the throneroom doors. Only now they weren't closed.

'She's trying to goad us,' growled Joram. 'My sixth sense likes this not.'

'I don't give a peddler's what your sixth sense likes,' said Braxus, advancing towards the open doorway. He didn't like the plan, but what other choice did they have? Besides, his soul yearned for revenge; it positively keened within him for witch's blood.

Torgun advanced at his side. Was that a respectful

glance the Northlending spared him? He secretly hoped he'd redeemed himself in the valorous knight's eyes.

But inside the throneroom was a sight to test any man's courage. Braxus' heart sank as he recognised the seven knights positioned in a semi-circle in the middle of the hall's sloping floor. They were richly appointed in silvered mail and gilded full helms, and their coats of arms told a straightforward tale.

This was a fight not even they could hope to win.

Sir Dantos stood to the far left, a hulking figure resting twin warhammers across his gargantuan shoulders. Next were the brothers, Sir Curwin and Sir Carlyw, each one armed with a heater shield and the viciously spiked mace that was their trademark; Sir Curufin crouched in the centre, a huge battleaxe clutched in both hands; on the right flank were Sir Gwydion and his sons Arianrod and Diarmuid, broad swords and stout targets in hand.

Braxus chewed his lower lip. 'That's the flower of the kingdom's chivalry, lads,' he said, 'and they outnumber us two to one.' A scarred highlander was stepping forwards to join the knights now. His frame was lithe, but exuded potency. Braxus had seen him once before, at the battle of Culhain Fields on the outskirts of Gaellen, four years ago. The savage had slain more than half a dozen good knights single-handedly that day.

'And that'll be Slánga Mac Bryon,' he cautioned. 'A more treacherous fighter you'll not hope to find this side of the Hyrkrainians.'

'How like you my Wytchguard?' The speaker inspired hatred in the Thraxian immediately. Even at this distance, he could see that repute of Abrexta's beauty was well deserved. Dressed in a rich russet red gown and bedecked with jewellery, she looked every inch the sorcerer-queen she fancied herself to be.

'Why don't you give yourselves up?' she pressed, in soothing tones. 'Not even great heroes such as you can hope to overcome me.'

Joram was already muttering the Psalm of Gramarye's Quenching. Braxus felt a battle being fought for his will.

With measured tread, the Wytchguard advanced down the hall. Morcant stepped back and began incanting a spell. Abrexta seemed to pause in shock, raising a hand. On her middle finger was a ring, set with a gem that glowed with an eldritch light. Then she murmured a counter spell of her own, clenching her fist.

'We'll only stand a chance if we stay in formation,' growled Wrackwulf.

'We needs must protect Joram and Morcant,' added Torgun.

The four knights formed a diamond shape directly before the throneroom entrance, while Joram and Morcant hung back behind them in the doorway.

'This will only work if we stay on the defensive,' said Braxus. 'We need to buy them enough time to neutralise her magicks.'

He could see by the expression on his face what Torgun thought of that. 'These are the best fighters in the land, Sir Torgun,' he remonstrated. 'We can't hope to overcome them by force of arms alone.'

'He's right,' put in Wrackwulf. 'They're fully armoured, too.'

Two apiece, thought Braxus as the brothers Curwin and Carlyw lashed out at him. It took all his dextrous ingenuity just to keep their rashing maces at bay; getting in a riposte was unthinkable. Above the clash of arms, he could hear the conjoined chanting of Morcant and Joram. There seemed to be a curious harmony to them, though now wasn't the time for such reflections.

Whatever you've got planned, it had better work quickly, he thought, ducking under Curwin's next swipe as he parried Carlyw's mace. *We've over much on hand, and no mistake.*

Abrexta shut her eyes as she countered her former understudy's Thaumaturgy. *So he did learn my secret after all,* she thought. *I had a feeling you wouldn't be idle in my absence, apprentice.*

She had never fully trusted the weaselly islander, even though they shared a distant ancestry. He'd been useful enough in his own way, teaching her a few incantations she hadn't known. But she'd always been the more powerful of the two: elan ran quicker in her, they both knew it. Clenching her fist harder, Abrexta pictured an upturned hand palm outwards and a shield, countering Morcant's attempt to pull the ring off her finger. She felt the sigil on her inner thigh pulsing, as though in silent approval of her efforts. The telekinetic force receded.

Parallel to that, she could sense the monk nullifying her

attempt to licensor his comrades. That much she hadn't expected – for an Argolian to make common cause with a wizard was unusual. But beyond that, there was something altogether unusual about the monk himself, though she hardly had time to fathom why.

A cry alerted her to other matters. Sir Diarmuid lurched back, blood spurting from his forearm as he dropped his sword. His brother Arianrod and father Gwydion closed on the tall blond knight who had dealt the injury, leaving the scarred young knight next to him to face Slánga alone.

Can't have them breaking through, she thought desperately. Dropping her attempt to draw the enemy knights into her circle of ensorcellment, she changed tack, mouthing a thaumaturgic litany of her own as she pictured a stylised bolt of forked lightning. The crackling burst of energy shot towards Torgun and Vaskrian, but was met by a silvery grey cloud conjured up by Morcant, which absorbed the strike in an explosion of blue sparks. Then their psychic wills locked, each one trying to overturn the other.

Abrexta felt the sweat lashing off of her. She *was* more powerful than Morcant – but he wasn't keeping dozens of knights and nobles under control. She felt vassals dropping away from her command, as she rebent her energy towards combating the rival wizard...

Slánga lunged at Vaskrian. He was armed with just two long knives and scorned to wear armour, but already the young knight knew he was up against it. He turned aside two strikes in quick succession, daring a riposte, but the high-land chieftain saw it coming and dodged aside easily. Another close shave took off Vaskrian's forelock; the follow-up grazed his hip as he twisted aside to avoid being gutted. Falling back he waited, hoping to goad his opponent into overstepping the mark. But the savage was unpredictable, varying his sequence of strikes, now high, then low, then high again before coming in towards his midriff. The young knight almost collided with Joram as Slánga drove him back another step. The monk cursed as he broke off his litany, moving back out into the antechamber. The sound of many voices beyond its entrance signalled that danger was coming from that way, too. The bolted doors behind them began to shudder, as the soldiers tried to batter their way in...

The space in front of Torgun seemed a myriad of blades, as he lunged and parried and riposted. Sir Gwydion and Sir Arianrod were expert swordsmen; it was all he could do to keep them at bay. Next to him Wrackwulf was also strug-gling, as Sir Dantos and Sir Curufin backed him into a corner of the hall, while Braxus looked like a man on his last legs dealing with the mace-wielding brothers Curwin and Carlyw.

Once again, the faces of his fallen comrades flashed before his mind's eye...

And then a side entrance to the hall burst open. In stepped half a dozen knights. They were lightly armed, and had clearly just risen from the knights' wing of the palace.

Torgun felt his heart slump, until he realised the knights were moving towards Abrexta.

Abrexta cursed inwardly as she caught the new arrivals. Under such pressure, she couldn't be careful about whom she released from her Enchantment. While keeping Morcant at bay, she ordered three of her Wytchguard to break off and intercept them. She knew her champions would make light work of the bachelors – but of course that meant giving her would-be assassins a chance to even up the odds...

Braxus breathed a sigh of relief as Curwin and Carlyw disengaged and moved to attack the new arrivals. *About time some of you Kingsfolders came to your blasted senses,* he thought as he moved in to help Wrackwulf. *Thank Ushira the knight's wing adjoins the main hall.*

Curufin was moving over to engage the bachelors, leaving the freelancer to fend off Sir Dantos' twin hammers. Blood was pouring from a cut in his forehead, and he was huffing and puffing with the effort of staying alive.

Braxus flanked the burly knight, and together they pushed back at Dantos. The Thraxian champion was as quick as he was strong, and for a while he kept them at a distance with great doubled arcing swipes. But when Braxus feinted towards his head, Dantos took the bait and raised a hammer to parry. At the last second Braxus curled his blade down and around, slicing across the back of Dantos' calf below the hauberk. At that moment, Wrackwulf sheared clean through the handle of his other warhammer, finding a gap between the metal studs lining it. The champion lashed out at the freelancer, but that gave Braxus the space he needed to step in and strike again, hitting the knight full in the chest. Sir Dantos lurched back with a roar, and before long the two knights were pressing him back into the centre of the hall.

Abrexta focused, summoning more knights from the palace to serve her. The bachelors were putting up a valiant struggle against her Wytchguard, and she'd had enough of close calls. Morcant must have anticipated this strategy however, because he'd used Thaumaturgy to put a locking spell on the door. She didn't have time to lift it.

She sensed Joram as an insidious presence. He was trying that wretched Argolian spell-song again, the one that neutralised magic. She focused her will on a countering spell, as she felt Morcant direct his Thaumaturgy at her ring again. The two were working in tandem now. But she smiled triumphantly as she felt her apprentice yield again.

Not even with the monk's prayers can you overcome my might, she thought triumphantly.

Dantos went down under a rain of blows. It had taken all their combined might to subdue him, but now the respite afforded Braxus a glance across the hall. The three Wytchguard champions were cutting a bloody swathe through the hapless bachelors, so Braxus and Wrackwulf moved to engage them. Out of the corner of his eye, the Thraxian caught a shadow moving to the left of the throne.

He engaged Sir Curufin, while Wrackwulf attacked the brothers Curwin and Carlyw. Only three of the palace bachelors remained standing, but together they were enough to hold the rest of the Wytchguard at bay. For a while.

Abrexta reintensified her elan, letting a couple more thralls go. This time she was careful to make sure they were vassals far away, picturing an unlocked gate and a bird taking flight. The mage buckled under the renewed pressure, collapsing to the floor.

She laughed inwardly. *Did you really think you could overcome me, apprentice?*

It was only when the blow struck her from behind that she realised Joram's psalm had not been aimed at her.

The shriek of agony cut across the din of arms, momentarily distracting all from the fray. Turning towards its source, Braxus saw Abrexta stagger forwards. A spear point protruded from her belly. It disappeared abruptly, to reappear a second later between her breasts. With a choking cry she toppled forwards. Standing behind her was Cadwy, trembling as he clutched the bloodied spear he had taken down off the wall. A mingled look of rage and bewilderment had torn itself across his haggard face.

The enthralled knights ceased fighting instantly. Braxus could sense rather than see the confusion beneath their great helms. As the sorceress that had commanded them twitched the last of her life away, they looked around at her killer.

Leaning unsteadily on the butt of the spear, Cadwy managed to rasp a single command.

'Desist – your King commands it.'

A blood-curdling scream erupted from Slánga's mouth, just as a crashing sound told of the soldiers' success in breaking down the doors to the antechamber. The highland chieftain fled towards a window overlooking the Rundle, Vaskrian in hot pursuit.

'Kill yon savage!' gasped Cadwy. But his voice was weak, and the palace knights were confused by the sudden turn of events.

Wrackwulf slumped to the ground, his head wound getting the best of him as the battle choler drained out of him. Braxus and Torgun dashed over to join Vaskrian at the window, but it was too late. Slánga had hurled himself out of it, landing like a cat on the frozen river, yards below. Before they could do anything, he was gone, loping off towards a weakly rising sun.

The hall was now swarming with soldiers, who moved to apprehend the heroes. They would have overwhelmed them, but Cadwy managed to gasp out another command, with more authority this time. He had to repeat it several times, but eventually it sank in: their King was ordering them to pursue Slánga, and leave the intruders alone.

The enchanted lights had died with their mistress, leaving the sun's wan wintry hues to stroke the hall with gentle fingers. Against it, Braxus could make out Slánga's silhouetted form receding, as he dashed up the frozen river with an agility that defied belief.

Torgun clapped him on the shoulder.

'Take heart, noble Braxus – we'll bring him to justice ere long.'

'I nearly got a blade on him,' muttered Vaskrian disconsolately. 'Damn, but that heathen is *fast*.'

'But what happened?' asked Braxus, too puzzled to care over much about Slánga. 'How did Cadwy break his enthralment?'

'Twas the ways of the Argolians you have to thank for that,' said Joram, stepping over to the witch's corpse and spitting on it. 'I changed the direction of my psalm, to lift the King's bewitchment when I noticed him skulking in the corner.' He spared an abashed glance at Cadwy. 'Ahem, that is... Your Majesty.' The adept managed a half-bow.

Cadwy was still wearing a bewildered expression, though the rage seemed to have gone out of him.

'I have... such frightful memories,' he said blankly. 'How did I ever let a witch into my court?'

'Witches have grown over powerful of late,' Joram told him grimly. 'But now at least there is one less to trouble the realms of mortal men.'

'We need a chirurgeon here on the double,' said Braxus. 'Dantos and Diarmuid are injured, and Wrackwulf too.'

The King nodded blankly, and gave the order to a soldier who had remained. The sturdy serjeant looked every bit as confused as his liege, but did as he bade.

'You'd best be giving orders to empty the dungeons too,' put in Joram. 'Many a decent subject was incarcerated at Abrexta's behest, Your Majesty.'

'I know,' said Cadwy in a hushed voice. 'I... I remember giving the orders.' His emotions overcame him then, and he sank to the ground, holding his head in his hands and sobbing like a child. 'In Reus' name, what have I done?'

'There now, be of some cheer, sire,' said Joram, laying an awkward hand on the King's shoulder. 'The worst is past.'

Morcant had recovered from his ordeal and joined them, though his face looked even more drawn and pallid than usual.

'A most strange encounter this was,' he muttered to Braxus.

'Encounters with wizards are always strange, as far as I'm concerned,' replied the knight.

'Not quite what I meant,' said Morcant, looking suspiciously at Joram. The monk was too busy helping Cadwy over to the Seat of High Kings to notice.

'Well, we won at any rate,' said Braxus. 'When the snows thaw, we'll be able to pursue Slánga and Tíerchan and take back my lands. This has been a resounding victory!'

But Morcant's face remained drawn and uncertain in the pale dawn light.

'Yes, a victory,' was all he said to that.